THE
NORMANDY
CLUB

Praise for Bill Walker

"Bill Walker is a consummate storyteller. Always inventive and always entertaining. You will have a great time with anything he writes."

—Richard Chizmar
Bestselling author of *Gwendy's Magic Feather*

"Walker is a hell of a writer!"
—Harlan Ellison

THE
NORMANDY
CLUB

BILL WALKER

DeLarge Books

2021

To my father whose idea this was...

1

Jack Dunham banged his head against the tinted, plate-glass window and wondered how long it would be before he killed the son of a bitch. He could see it now, playing in his mind like a lurid, direct-to-video movie: He'd put on his jacket, reach into the bottom drawer of his desk, and pull out the .45—the one he'd kept handy ever since the riots a few years back. Slapping a round into the chamber, he'd shove it into his belt, leave his office, and stroll down the hallway, nodding and smiling to all the secretaries, letting his innocent-looking brown eyes and the "cute" dimples he'd always despised lull them into a false sense of security. He'd even stop a minute and joke with one of the art directors, never letting on, never letting any of them suspect a thing. Then he'd stride into the conference room, smile sweetly, and put a Black Talon hollow-point right through Reece's fat, sweaty head.

It would be so simple, so unexpected, so final...

So much for cherished fantasies.

Jack returned to his desk and switched off the computer, consigning his latest rewrite to oblivion. He couldn't stand to look at that drivel another minute. Squeezing his eyes shut, he leaned back in his chair and blotted out everything but the soft hiss of the air conditioning.

It had been a thankless day, a day of countless meetings with intractable clients who sat and listened to his presentations, eyeing all his hard work with the blank, shining orbs of mannequins. Sometimes he wondered what really went on behind those eyes. Were they thinking about what he'd just told them, or were they thinking about the great sex they had the night before, or the fight with their wives or lovers that morning, or the wonderful turd they just made? Sometimes he wondered if their minds were as blank as their eyes.

And then there was Reece.

Crude, profane, and totally without an ounce of creativity in that corpulent lump he called a body, Bryant Worthington Reece IV lumbered through life in wrinkled, ill- fitting Armani suits, acting as if everyone and everything owed him their obeisance. The man took perverse pleasure in taunting underlings about their inadequacies and toadying up to those who could pave the way to greater glories. Jack cracked a weary grin. "Toad" was the perfect word for Reece— his protruding eyes, fleshy face, and blubbery mouth, the perfect mask.

Jack drove Reece from his mind and returned his gaze to the office window. Out on Biscayne Boulevard the crime lights popped on, their harsh, peach-colored rays making the street look wasted and sallow, like an old man sick with jaundice. Rush hour traffic stood stalled for blocks, brake lights glowing, their horns the howls of angry dogs.

He smiled again. No doubt a few homicides in the making there. What time was it, anyway? All afternoon he'd tried to come up with ideas, ideas the clients would gush over, ideas Reece wouldn't shit on, ideas that didn't sound like a tired rehash of every other notion he'd already presented.

But the well was dry.

He stood up, pulled on his gray wool sport jacket and was about to extinguish the desk light when the phone purred. It was one of those modern phones, the kind the manufacturers hailed as "new and revolutionary," with lots of confusing functions and presets, guaranteed not to jar the thinking executive. He thought the thing sounded like it had a head cold. Sometimes, like now, he felt like pitching it through the plate-glass. He debated whether or not to let the voice mail take it, but something made him pick it up. Maybe it was Leslie with some last-minute disaster.

"Hey, Jack. Is that you?"

The warm, nasally voice made him smile.

"Wiley! You old shithead!"

"How are you, buddy?" he said.

"I'm fine, Killer. How about you? You sound close."

"I'm at the airport. Just got in. It was sort of a last-minute thing. I was hoping we could get together... and talk."

Typical vintage Wiley. No thought of calling from home, no warning at all, just his deep, friendly voice on the phone announcing his arrival. As always, he assumed Jack would be free as a bird and ready for a night on the town. He should have been used to it by now, but he never got used to anything where Wiley Carpenter was concerned.

Jack thought of Leslie. He was torn between his friendship with Wiley and the date he very much wanted to keep. He and Leslie had been going out for two months—they spent nearly every night together—and he'd begun to entertain the notion of asking her to move in with him. Wiley's voice receded to a soft murmur as Jack recalled her soft, voluptuous curves, jet-black hair, and those penetrating emerald-green eyes.

"Jack! Are you there?"

"I'm sorry, Wiley, what did you say?"

"You okay?"

"I'm fine. Tough day. Usual crap."

"I know what you mean," he said, his voice edged with fatigue. "Look, you probably got something going, but I won't be in town long. We need to talk. It's important, Jack."

What the hell, Leslie would understand.

"Sure, Wiley," he said. "I'm free as a bird."

"Let's meet at Mike's. I'll be there by seven."

"Okay," Jack said, "the first round's on you."

Whenever Wiley blew into town, which wasn't as frequent as it used to be, they always ended up at Mike Gordon's. On the bay, nestled at the foot of the 79th Street bridge, Mike's was the *only* place to go for the serious seafood lover. The portions were huge and the atmosphere convivial. And if Mike happened to be around with time to talk, so much the better.

But Wiley was never on time, and Jack was often half in the bag by the time Wiley casually strolled in, acting as if nothing was wrong. By that time, Jack would be ready to wring Wiley's neck. But one "Hey, shithead!" and a slap on the back and all was forgiven.

Jack slid his red Alfa Romeo Spider into the parking lot and pulled up to the front entrance. He nodded to José, the attendant, and tossed him the keys.

"*Buenas noches, Señor* Jack."

"You too, José."

It was a hair before seven. The night air hung like a wet rag, smelling of salt and rotten fish. Pushing through the front door, Jack felt a blast of cool air hit him, making his nose tingle. He passed the gallery of boat-racing pictures and a small trophy case, making sure to duck under the fish netting he always managed to snag. A short line stood waiting for tables, and an elderly couple were leaving their names with the tall blonde at the reservations desk. Jack noted the crowd looked lighter than usual.

"Hello, Mr. Dunham, how are you this evening?"

"Fine, Marge. You're looking great."

Her face lit up as she smiled. "You keep that up and you'll have to take me home."

"And have Mike ban me?" he said, feigning horror.

It was a ritual they performed every time he came. Marge was happily married, had been for twenty years. Still, she was a hell of a good-looking woman, and Jack would have jumped at the chance had she been serious.

"Mr. Carpenter arrived ten minutes ago. He's in the bar."

"Wiley? Wiley is *early*?"

She smiled and shrugged, as if to say, "Ain't it a kick," and took the names of the couple behind him.

Mildly surprised, Jack pushed through the bar crowd and spotted his friend nursing a martini, a far-off look in his eye. The martini was the second surprise. Wiley never could hold his liquor, and he always drank a watery highball or, most times, a seltzer with a lime twist.

When Jack walked toward him, Wiley gulped the drink and signaled the bartender for another. My God, how he'd aged. His hair, a once luxurious black, had turned gray throughout, and had noticeably thinned. And in spite of a healthy-looking tan, Wiley's face had a haunted look around the eyes where crow's feet now spread from the corners, like cracks in a windshield. Seeing this, Jack couldn't help wondering if he looked as old to Wiley.

"Hey, Jack, you're lookin' good" he said, patting him on the back. "Can I get you anything?"

"Sam Adams."

"Scotty! A Sammy for my buddy."

When the bartender returned, Jack waved away the frosted glass and took a long swig from the bottle. Wiley stared at him, his hands drumming on the bar.

"How are Ellen and the kids?" Jack said.

"Oh, fine. Ellen's taken up ceramics. And John's just starting fifth grade. Can you believe it?"

He toyed with his drink, staring into it as though it held some deep, dark secret. He twisted it around, leaving rings that reminded Jack of the Olympic emblem. He got the distinct feeling that Wiley wasn't here to talk about his family. Something was eating at him, and whatever it was wasn't coming easily.

"What is it, Wiley? Is Ellen sick? For God's sake, spit it out. I know you didn't come all this way to catch up on old times."

Wiley looked up at him and, for the first time that evening, made eye contact. There was a drop of sweat that trickled from his right temple and hung poised on his chin, ready to drop. His left eye twitched, as it always did when he was nervous.

"I came down here because I discovered something."

Jack leaned closer.

"I know why the Nine Old Men changed the name of the club," he said.

For the last twenty years Jack and Wiley held memberships in The Anderson Club, an exclusive country club just outside of Ridgefield, Connecticut. Jack thought himself as good a clubman as the average guy, although, as a non-resident member who now lived in Miami, he'd been back only a couple of times. Even after all that time, nothing much had changed about the place. It was still the same comfortable bar with the hunting scenes on the wall, and the immaculate brass rail polished to a high gloss every two hours by old Swithington.

The small, green-shaded lamps that sat on the tables gave a soft glow at night, and even in the blistering sun of an August day, the bar retained a cool aloofness. They served big, reasonably priced drinks and a fair roast beef on Fridays. The golf course was the envy of the county, and the tennis courts remained solidly booked until well after the season. The Anderson Club—now The Normandy Club— differed in an odd sort of way from probably every other club in the country.

There were one hundred members, give or take a couple, most of them in their thirties. It amused Wiley and Jack that all the other members thought of them as the "old men" of the club, except, that is, for *The Nine Old Men*. Everyone called them that, though not to their faces. No one could remember who'd coined the nickname, but it stuck. It made sense because they were nine, they were old—by everyone else's standards, anyway, and because they reminded everyone of the Supreme Court. They kept to themselves most of the time, only mixing with the other members during holidays and the occasional fund-raisers. To everyone they were "The Nine Old Men."

And they ran the club.

There were the usual committees, but they were lightweight affairs that planned the parties and the yearly cotillion. The serious decisions were made by the Nine Old Men. If they felt the club's name should be changed, it was changed. No member vote, no dissension, no objections. But for the most part, that was okay. The average member came to the club to play golf, tennis, and to drink, maybe covet his neighbor's wife in the process.

But the oddest thing about the club was that no one ever had much curiosity about what the Nine Old Men did in "Their Room," up on the top floor of the building. It took up most of the floor and lay behind a heavy, steel door that remained locked at all times. Jack and Wiley always figured they played poker or watched dirty movies, but no one really cared what they did. Someone once had the bright idea of bugging the place, just for fun, but nothing ever came of it. The steel door of the Nine Old Men's room remained inviolate.

"I know why they changed the name of the club," Wiley repeated.

"So do I. They told us."

"They gave us a dumb-ass reason, Jack. Why the hell should a fifty-year-old club change its name because the Nine Old Men found out that Anderson's son was killed at Normandy? That should be all the more reason to keep it The Anderson Club."

"I never thought much about it, but they said something else at the time, about 'how it honored all of the kid's buddies who died along with him, and that's the way he would have wanted it.'"

Wiley leaned forward, his thin face flushed.

"That's a goddamned lie!"

For the first time since walking into Mike's, Jack regretted not going on his date. He'd tried to call Leslie, tried to leave word at the restaurant that he'd be late, but the phone at Luigi's had been busy right up until the moment he'd left the office. Now, the whole evening was going haywire. And this show of temper—if that's what it was—wasn't like Wiley. If anything, he was always a touch too phlegmatic. But when Jack looked into his face, he saw something else there—stark-naked fear.

"For Christ's sake! You came all the way down here to tell me *that*? You could have told me when you called. What the hell difference does it make if they changed the name? Who the hell cares *why* they did it?"

Wiley leaned back and stared at the bar, as if debating whether to go on or not.

"Have you ever heard of Dr. Morris Chessman?"

"No, I don't think so," Jack said, hoping he didn't sound too apathetic.

"Chessman's an expert on parapsychology," Wiley continued. "He taught at Duke for twenty years and researched everything from bending spoons to ghosts. But his real passion is telekinesis—moving objects in space by the power of the mind alone. He's the world's leading authority. Suddenly after twenty years and guaranteed tenure, he up and leaves on June sixth, nineteen ninety-two. Ring a bell, Jack, June the sixth?"

"No. Should it?"

"Chessman left Duke the day the Nine Old Men changed the name of the club."

"Okay," Jack said, "so it was the same day. So what? A million other things happened the same day."

"Granted. And I didn't think much about it, either... until the next week. I was sitting at the bar in the club waiting for Ellen, and who the hell walks in? *Chessman*. And, by God, he walks straight to the elevator, without looking around, almost like he was *trying* not to look around, and he goes right to the top floor. Just like that."

Wiley was beginning to get his interest. A little, anyway. Why would a college professor out of North Carolina show up at the Normandy Club and sneak up to the third floor?

"Maybe he joined the club," Jack said.

"Wrong." Wiley leaned close again. "Dennis Whitney, who puts out the membership list, never heard of him."

"All right, so what's the point?"

"I know *why* he left Duke, and I know *why* he's now living in Greenwich. *That's* the point."

"*What*, for Christ's sake?" Jack said, ready to strangle him.

"The Nine Old Men hired him."

"Oh, come on! Why would a big-shot professor quit a tenured position at Duke and come to work for a run-down club in Connecticut? Doing *what*? It doesn't make any sense."

"He had the best reason in the world—money. The Nine Old Men paid him a million up front."

"What!"

Wiley nodded. "A million up front, plus a quarter million a year for expenses."

"You know this for *sure*?"

"For sure."

"Jesus, Christ. What's he supposed to do for it, shoot the president?"

All the humor was gone from Wiley's expression.

"Worse," he said.

Jack signaled the bartender for another beer.

"All right, go on."

"I'll tell you what I found out. But first I'm going to tell you *how* I found out. That way you'll believe me.

"Don't count on it."

"I hired a safecracker."

"You did *what!*"

"Jack, I had to find out what was in that room upstairs. The club was closed for a week for some minor renovations and cleaning. It was the perfect opportunity."

"So you *burglarized* the place?"

"Yeah, basically."

"Basically? Wiley, are you nuts?"

Wiley's lips compressed into a thin, angry line.

"Shut up and listen, will you?"

"But—"

"Just shut up and listen, Jack," he said.

Jack's beer finally arrived, and he took a large gulp.

Wiley calmed himself, but the impassioned glimmer in his eyes belied his excitement. Jack just wanted to go home, crawl into bed, and blot out the world, forget about that idiot Reece and everything else. But what Wiley said next drove all thoughts of sleep from his mind.

"The guy got us inside in about thirty seconds. All that shit you hear about locks and alarms is true, Jack. It was like nothing to this guy."

"And?"

"It's a goddamn *war room*! I mean maps, aerial photos all over the walls, and one of those big tables like you see in the movies where they plot troop movements. And this'll kill you—a big old Nazi flag on the wall."

"Maybe that's how they get their kicks—playing army."

"Jesus, if you only knew how close you are. Everything in that room, the photos, maps, the table, it all ties into the Normandy Invasion."

"So, they're hooked on D-Day? What's all this got to do with Chessman?"

Jack could see a small vein throbbing in Wiley's forehead and his eye twitched like mad. Wiley took a deep breath.

"They don't want the Normandy Invasion to happen, Jack."

"What are you talking about? It already *happened*," he said, his voice rising.

The man sitting next to Wiley turned and stared at Jack, making him feel like an idiot. He lowered his voice.

"It already *happened*, Wiley."

"They want to change that."

"What do you mean, *change* it? They *can't* change it! Look, you'd better tell me what the hell is going on or I'm going to walk right out of here, so help me."

Wiley reached inside his jacket and pulled out a wrinkled envelope bulging with photos. He spread them out on the bar, his manner becoming more urgent.

"You remember that little Minox camera you gave me a few years back? Well, I thought it would come in handy. Boy, did it."

Jack stared at the photos, trying to take it all in. Wiley began to explain.

"What you're seeing are original German documents detailing the positions of both German and allied forces."

He pointed to another photo that showed a pile of what looked like currency.

"What is this?" Jack asked. "Money?"

Wiley nodded. "A lot of money, enough to choke a horse. And it's German, nineteen forty-four issue."

Wiley flipped to another picture.

"There were files in the safe too. Three of them. Files on Chessman, a guy named Werner Kruger—who also lives in Greenwich, by the way, and *The Plan*. I didn't have time to photograph them, but I looked inside them."

"And..."

And then he told him.

"With Chessman's help they are going to send Kruger back in time."

The beer glass halted halfway to Jack's mouth.

"What? Wiley, tell me you've come all this way to pull a joke on me. Tell me you haven't flipped."

Wiley stared at him.

"You're not kidding, are you?"

"No."

Jack shook his head and decided to humor his friend. Maybe after the joke was over they could get down to some serious drinking.

"Okay, pal o' mine, tell me why the Nine Old Men would *want* to do this?" Jack said, not bothering to hide his sarcasm.

"To stop the invasion, stop it dead in its tracks and let Hitler win."

"What the hell for? What do they have to gain?"

"Power, old buddy... power."

This was all coming too fast and furious. Jack shook his head.

"But wait a minute. The whole reason Hitler lost was because he wouldn't believe his generals. What could Kruger do? Walk up to Adolf and say, 'By the By, the Invasion is coming ashore at Normandy. Be a good chap and move your armies down from Calais?' It's crazy, it'll never work—what am I talking about? This whole thing is nuts. You can't go back in time and you can't change history!"

Wiley looked at his friend, his gaze level and sober.

"They've *already* changed things."

Jack just stared at Wiley, unable to speak. Wiley leaned forward.

"You ever wake up and feel something's not right, that something's different?"

"Yeah, it's called a hangover."

Wiley ignored the crack, his voice hushed.

"What if things *were* different? What if things had changed, only you didn't know it?"

Jack lost his patience. "What are you getting at?"

"Chessman's already sent Kruger back a couple of times. Once to nineteen sixty-three, the other to nineteen fifty-six. It was right there in the files. One of those times he changed something."

"Oh, come on, Wiley, this is getting stale."

"All right, I'll show you."

Wiley got up from the barstool and steadied himself. Jack decided his friend had been drinking far longer than he had. Reaching down to his trouser cuff, Wiley pulled up the left pant leg, revealing a leg crisscrossed with varicose veins and a very ugly knee. Jack was about to make a nasty crack until he saw the lost, frightened look in his friend's eyes.

"What is it?"

"My leg, Jack. It's okay."

"Of course it's okay. It's always been okay."

Wiley slumped onto the barstool, his pant leg sliding back down.

"No, it hasn't. I've had a prosthetic leg since I was fifteen."

"What— Wait a minute—"

"Listen to me. Think about it. Really think about all those years you've known me."

Jack looked at his friend and let the years reel off in his mind: college, those first years at that tiny agency in Detroit, the good times, the bad times, even the times he'd have preferred to forget. After a moment, Jack began to feel hot all over. A sweat broke out and streamed down his face. Suddenly, the world went white as something snapped in his brain, as if a small bomb had exploded. He felt himself reborn, remembering people he never knew existed, moments recaptured, lives relived. He grabbed his head and groaned.

Wiley grabbed his shoulder. "Here, take a drink. You need it."

Jack took the proffered beer and drained it. That quick, knife-like pain he'd felt a moment before subsided into a dull, throbbing ache. He now remembered two Wileys, one with a false leg, one whole. It wasn't that he'd convinced himself. He *really* remembered. It was as if they'd lived two infinitesimally different lives.

"Oh my God," Jack said, his heart pounding in his ears.

Wiley nodded.

"It happened the same way with me. Almost as soon as I read the Nine Old Men's plan. I don't know what Kruger and Chessman did, but somehow, during one of his 'trips,' he set something in motion. One thing led to another, led to another, and so on. Like a ripple on a pond. Somehow the man who hit me ended up coming down that street a fraction later than he was supposed to."

Jack had never believed the old literary cliché about someone's blood running cold. But he did now. Wiley spoke in a low, matter-of-fact voice, but to Jack's heightened senses, Wiley was shouting.

"But how do we know it, Wiley? How *can* we?"

Wiley shook his head. "I don't know. I think something's connecting us. Maybe, and this might sound far-fetched, maybe because we know about Chessman, and Kruger. Maybe the fact that we know they are changing things is enough."

"So, the Nine Old Men figure they can send Kruger back and prevent the invasion? Convince Hitler to move his armies. That right?" Jack said, gripping Wiley's arm.

"Yeah, but that's not the worst of it. It's a two-pronged plan. Convincing Hitler to change his mind is only the *second* part."

Jack's stomach twisted. "What's the first?"

Wiley grabbed his drink and gulped it down, staring at the pictures laid out on the bar until Jack thought he would scream. Suddenly, Wiley turned, his eyes showing the depth of his fear.

"Assassinating Eisenhower."

2

A s Dr. Morris Chessman drove his sputtering Saab through the center of town, he felt his ulcer acting up again. Ever since he'd been awakened at four a.m. by the incessantly ringing phone, his whole digestive tract had been in an uproar. It started the moment he'd heard Armand Bock's gravelly voice on the phone.

"Be at the club by nine."

He sounded even more abrupt than usual.

The car wound its way down Route 7, passing majestic homes set far back from the road. Ancient elms, oaks, and maples hugged the road, their thick, overhanging branches letting the sunlight in through their leaves. The light dappled the windshield, causing an irregular strobe effect that hurt the eyes. None of the natural beauty of the area penetrated Chessman's thoughts this morning.

He stifled a belch and turned through the two stone pillars onto the cobblestone drive. He saw the large, gingerbread-style mansion with its mansard roof, Gothic dormers, and wide, canopied veranda. The whole place struck him as stuffy and arrogant, just like Bock and the rest of his "Waxworks." That's the way he thought of the Nine

THE NORMANDY CLUB

Old Men who ran the place: stiff, unyielding—cold, with beady eyes that revealed nothing.

For a fleeting moment Chessman wondered why he'd ever accepted their offer. But just as quickly, the feeling was gone. He knew exactly why. He desperately needed the cash. A million up front, plus another two hundred and fifty thousand a year for "expenses." This was way too much temptation for a man who felt the call of the gaming tables at Atlantic City. That he was in debt up to his eyeballs was a constant source of worry, but not the cause of his ulcer. His compulsion to gamble had started late in life as a panacea to the pressures of his research. But it became such a colossal problem that his wife of twenty years got fed up and ran off with another of the faculty wives. She was now rumored to be living happily in the Arizona desert on a lesbian commune.

But aside from money, the real reason Chessman had left Duke was that he'd had it with academia. He could no longer stand the never-ending groveling for funding. It didn't matter that his research stood on the brink of revolutionizing life as we know it. All the university wanted was favorable publicity and a published paper every year. Even before Georgina had left with that despicable woman, it was all he could do to keep from puking.

"Fools," he said, his anger overcoming his nervousness.

He swung the car into the circular drive and left the keys with the young attendant. As he stared up at the old house, his stomach twisted, propelling that familiar, sour backwash up his esophagus and into his throat. He swallowed it back down and reached for the roll of Tums.

What is so urgent that they wake me up at four in the morning?

He chewed the chalky antacid, climbed the wide steps, and pushed through the front door. His nose wrinkled at the faint odor of dried flowers when he crossed the small, darkly paneled entryway. *This place smells like a funeral parlor.*

The bar had only one customer at this point, no doubt some golfer tanking up before hitting the links. The only other person aside from the bartender was an old man in tails polishing the brass railing. Shaking his head, Chessman walked quickly over to the small elevator and pushed the button. Even with no one there, Chessman felt nervous, exposed. Bock had specifically told him never to draw attention to himself when he visited. That was a laugh. In such a small club, how could anyone have remained inconspicuous? He stuck out like a sore thumb.

A moment later he heard a small ping, and the mahogany-paneled doors slid open. He hurriedly pushed the button for the third floor and glanced at his watch. Nearly nine. The Nine Old Men did not like to be kept waiting.

The elevator doors opened, and Chessman walked down the corridor to the steel door at the opposite end of the house. Painted a stark, battleship gray, it had no peephole or sliding panel. But there was a camera mounted high up near the ceiling. It eyed him silently, its single, glass orb unblinking. He stood there only a moment before the door clicked open, as if propelled by invisible hands. Chessman swallowed another Tums and walked inside.

The light in the "War Room," as the Nine Old Men called it, remained subdued and indirect twenty-four hours a day, as if the idea of brighter light were anathema to the darkness in their hearts. Chessman crossed the floor, noting the topographical map of the French coastline had been filled with models of ships and soldiers. His eye caught the black, white, and red flag, its swastika making him shudder. His head throbbed, and the air smelled faintly of some pine-scented antiseptic.

In the center of the room sat another large table with ten chairs around it. Nine of them were filled.

The Nine Old Men waited.

"Ah, Doctor Chessman," Armand Bock said. "Do come in."

His voice, harsh and resonant, still bore the imprint of his German birth, though the accent was now very faint. He stood, bowed slightly, and indicated the one empty chair at the foot of the table. Chessman found himself bowing in return and quickly seated himself in the plush chair. It made a hissing sound when it took his weight, and the faint odor of leather wafted into his nostrils.

Armand Bock sat at the opposite end and regarded Chessman with a sly smile. Like all the others, Bock was in his late seventies. He had a full head of frosty-white hair, cut in the severe style of the pre-war German military; black, bushy eyebrows over a pair of shocking blue eyes; and a sharp, aquiline nose. His skin had a healthy bronze color he kept year-round, and he wore his customary, dark blue double-breasted Savile Row suit with highly starched collar and striped tie. His one accommodation to vanity was a small, gold signet ring on his right hand.

"Well, Doctor, I am sure you are wondering why we got you out of bed so early?"

It was not really a question that Bock expected answered.

"We are moving up the timetable. Kruger leaves tomorrow night."

Chessman bolted upright and stared at the group in front of him. To a man they all stared back, their eyes relentlessly boring into his.

"But you can't," he said, groping for words. "Mr. Bock, I'm not ready. Kruger is not ready. There are things yet to be considered…"

Chessman trailed off as Bock's eyes narrowed.

"Someone has been in this room since we last met."

A cold, invisible hand gripped Chessman's heart.

"What?"

"Someone has broken into this room and tried to cover their tracks, but they were not clever enough," Bock said.

The man sprang from his chair, surprising Chessman with his agility, and walked around the table toward him.

"Certain papers were disturbed from the positions I knew them to be in. We have to assume that those inimical to our cause know our plans. We must act accordingly."

"But how could they?" Chessman asked. "No one—"

"Yes. No one knew but the nine of us... Kruger... and you."

Bock's eyes blazed. Chessman felt his bowels loosen.

"Surely you don't think I—"

Bock slammed the table with his fist.

"SILENCE!"

Chessman flinched like he'd been slapped. Bock resumed speaking, his voice even and controlled.

"Do you think we wouldn't know if you had betrayed us? Do you think you would even be sitting here if we even *thought* you had betrayed us?"

Chessman shook his head, deliberately blotting out the image those words conjured up.

Bock began to laugh. It started as a low chuckle and grew into a glorious bellow. The rest of the Nine Old Men smiled faintly, otherwise remaining impassive.

"Have no fear, Doctor. We know you had nothing to do with the burglary, but surely you must see the need for alacrity, *ja?*"

Chessman finally found his voice again.

"Of course, Mr. Bock. I understand completely, but I still feel I must warn you that there are aspects to the experiment that we cannot be sure of."

Bock became attentive.

"Go on, Doctor."

Chessman leaned forward, a rush of confidence flooding his mind. He was on solid ground for the first time since entering the room, and he resisted the urge to smile as he imagined these creaky old men as one of his classes at Duke.

"Both of Kruger's brief forays into the recent past proved successful, yet we cannot be sure of their ramifications. The time-space continuum is very elusive. There are all manner of whirlpools, eddies, and crosscurrents. One small event could have catastrophic effects."

"That is what we are counting on, *Herr Doktor.*"

"But you do not understand. Kruger may change something inadvertently, something we cannot control!"

"Then that is the risk we must take, isn't it? Would you prefer things as they are?"

Chessman frowned and felt his stomach lurch.

"No," he said.

Bock smiled wryly. "You seemed so sure of your theories when we first met, Doctor. Are you doubting yourself now?"

Chessman grew angry again. "No. Absolutely not."

"Then we shall proceed."

"But Kruger is not yet fully conditioned. He isn't ready."

"Why don't we ask him?"

Behind him, Chessman heard the steel door click open again. Without even looking, he knew it was Kruger. Aside from Bock, no one scared him more than Werner Kruger. The man walked into the pool of light surrounding the big, marble table and regarded Chessman with an ironic smile. On Kruger it looked like the grin of a hungry wolf. He stood six feet tall, with the tough, wiry body of one who worked out and ran many miles a day. His ice-blond hair was cut similarly to Bock's, and he had a short scar running from his right temple to a point just a centimeter from his right nostril. It gave him a quick, feral look, a look reflected in his cold, light-gray eyes. He turned to Bock, clicked his heels, and bowed sharply.

"*Guten Tag*, Werner," Bock said, smiling like a proud father. "The good doctor is worried that you may not be ready to make the journey. What do you say?"

Kruger turned to Chessman, his eyes taking on a fierce expression.

"I am ready," he said.

"Excellent," Bock said, clapping his hands together. "All your accoutrements have been assembled. Your documents and money. Is there anything else you require?"

"The Semtex and detonators?"

"Secured and ready."

Suddenly, Bock's eyebrows shot up, as if he'd forgotten something. "*Herr Doktor?*"

"Yes, sir?"

"There is still the one question you have not yet answered to the satisfaction of my colleagues... The most important one of all. If we are to proceed, we *must* have your answer now."

Bock paused a moment, his expression growing grim and determined. "If Kruger succeeds, will we *know* it?"

Chessman remained calm, even though the tension in the room crept up a notch. Bock had brought up the one enigma central to his research, the one single, most important question that could be asked, the one question Chessman dreaded:

If someone were to change history, would any... could any of them be aware of that change and take advantage of it?

The answer to that riddle involved the very nature of time itself.

Up to now, aside from Kruger's two short, and seemingly innocuous, jaunts into the past, everything remained theory and conjecture.

Chessman felt his stomach churn as he scanned the others at the table. The Nine Old Men stared back at him, waiting for his answer, their dead-alive eyes shining like polished obsidian. With his heart pounding and his stomach roiling, Chessman sat up and cleared his throat.

"Gentlemen. As you know, in the course of my research, I have grappled with this one aspect of my theory many times. My calculations have filled hundreds of notebooks and hours of computer time. What I have discovered is that foreknowledge is all-important. If one *knows* that the past will be changed, and then *undergoes* that change, a seed is planted, a seed for what I call the *Paradox Effect*. This effect, when triggered, will have a profound impact on the body in direct proportion to the degree of the paradox. In other words, gentlemen, the greater the change, the more intense the effect will be. Because of this and your advanced ages, I cannot say with certainty that any of you will survive it."

The Nine Old Men nodded, their wizened faces without a trace of emotion.

Chessman continued. "As to your question, the answer is yes. The only ones who will know that history has changed are those in this room. Everyone else will perceive that life has always been thus."

"You are forgetting something, my dear professor," Bock said. "Whoever broke in here will know as well."

Chessman looked stricken.

Bock smiled and waved his arm casually. "No matter. We will proceed as planned. If you are right, Doctor, then we shall triumph, and whoever has trespassed will be swept away on the tides of a glorious new history."

Relieved by Bock's reaction, Chessman interrupted, something he would never normally do.

"There is one final detail," he said. "At first, like everyone else, you may be unaware that history has changed. It will then take some catalyst, some small spark, to trigger the Paradox Effect that will bring back your memories of a *different* past. Until that happens, our lives will be as changed as everyone else's. We will remember nothing."

3

Stamford, Connecticut
5 August 1993

Wiley pulled the rental car to the curb in front of a small, nondescript building in Stamford's deserted downtown. Jack yawned, scratched the stubble on his chin, then glanced at his watch.

Six thirty.

"You sure he's going to be there?"

"Yeah, Curly's an early bird," Wiley said. "He'll be there."

Jack nodded, opened his car door, and stepped out onto the sidewalk. The air, redolent with the smells of garbage and exhaust fumes, hung like a steamy, choking cloud over the town. It made his clothes feel sticky, and the area where his shirt collar rubbed his neck itched like a thousand fire ants crawled there. Another dog day in August.

He unbuttoned the collar, stretched, shook his head, and took a deep breath. It was funny. No matter where you went these days, every downtown looked alike. Stamford was no different. Jack recalled the last hectic hours. Swept up in Wiley's fervor, the two of them had jumped into Wiley's rental car and sped to Miami International Airport, arriving there just after midnight. They'd dashed for the last Delta flight to LaGuardia.

"I've got a friend who can help us," Wiley said, when they pulled into the Hertz lot. "If anyone can put this all into perspective, Curly can."

"Either that or he's going to think we're crazy."

"Not Curly."

When the plane banked over Biscayne Bay, headed northward, Jack remembered something else Wiley had said about his friend.

"Curly will help us. Especially where men like Bock are concerned."

"Why? Because he's into all these far-fetched scenarios?"

Wiley shook his head. "You ever hear of Malmedy?"

Jack frowned. "Isn't that where all those GI prisoners were massacred?"

"Yeah. The Germans just lined 'em up and mowed 'em down."

"What's that got to do with Curly?"

"His father was one of them."

The elevator took them to the top floor and opened onto a colorless hallway lit by cool-white fluorescents. There was no need to look for a specific suite, as Stoddard Consulting occupied the whole floor. A lone security guard checked their IDs and phoned them in on the intercom system. A moment later the door clicked open with a loud buzz. They walked through a sea of empty desks and found Curly Williams waiting for them at his office door with a big smile on his face.

"Wiley!" Curly said, enveloping Wiley in a warm bear hug. "How the hell are you, man?"

Wiley smiled, looking a bit dazed, as if the other man had squeezed the breath out of him.

"I'm fine, Curly. Sorry about the short notice."

"Ah, don't worry about it. What're old pals for, anyway? Come in."

THE NORMANDY CLUB

The office itself was as unassuming as the outside of the building, hardly the citadel of a great thinker. It occupied the corner of the building with windows overlooking the city. The desk was simply a piece of thick plate-glass set on an ultra-modern jet-black wrought-iron frame. The chair behind was an Eames, the only concession to luxury. Everywhere else, every available space lay covered with newspapers and magazines from all over the world. The glass desk lay bare except for an expensive IBM notebook computer. Jack found it strange that there were no family photos.

They sat on the two leather chairs facing the desk while Curly walked over to his coffee machine.

"You want some coffee? You guys look a little peaked."

Wiley nodded. "Yeah, we didn't get much sleep. Took the red-eye."

Curly nodded, as if frantic late-night flights were the norm for him, and poured three cups of steaming coffee.

"So, what brings you two to sunny Stamford?" Curly said, passing Wiley two of the cups.

"Jack and I— Oh, excuse me. Curly, this is Jack."

Jack reached out his hand. "Nice to meet you, Curly. Wiley's told me all about you."

"None of it good, I hope." He chuckled.

When he saw his two friends were not laughing, he dispensed with the small talk, went behind his desk, and sat down.

"What can I do for you?"

"First, you've got to promise me that what we're going to tell you will remain here," Wiley said.

"Give me a dollar."

"What?"

"A dollar, give me one."

33

Wiley shrugged and pulled out his money clip. He peeled off a single and handed it over.

"I'm now your attorney," Curly said. "What you tell me is privileged."

Wiley laughed. "You always did love to dramatize."

"Yeah, well, got to keep everyone on their toes or it all turns to crap, ya know? So, tell me, why'd you and your friend come all this way?"

Wiley took a sip of his coffee then placed the cup gently on the table.

Jack watched Curly as Wiley told him the incredible story he'd heard the night before. Curly's craggy face remained impassive, but Jack could tell the wheels were turning.

Curly Williams was every bit the man Wiley had told him about during their long flight. He clearly dominated whatever room he was in with his big, Irish laugh, unruly shock of red hair, and lively blue eyes. In five minutes he could make you feel like you'd known each other your whole lives. He'd played college ball and had just missed the pros by a wrecked kneecap. But Curly's real talent was not physical. He was, in a word, brilliant. The only jock to make straight A's all four years, he'd majored in Political Science with a minor in Speech. From there, it was three years at Harvard Law School, two years as an underpaid associate in a big firm with a zillion names on its letterhead, and then his big break.

During a brown-bag lunch in the Public Gardens, an elderly gentleman struck up a conversation with him about nuclear Armageddon, and what would happen if the Russians did this or the Israelis did that. It was an interesting and challenging way to spend a lunch hour. As Curly stood up to leave, the old man handed him his card. Curly was floored. The old man was none other than Harmon Stoddard of Stoddard Consulting, an ultra-exclusive think tank operating out of Stamford, Connecticut. The man was a legend, often quoted by Curly's Poli-Sci professors at Harvard. But the kicker came when Stoddard offered him a job. Just like that.

That was twenty years ago and now, with Stoddard dead and buried for ten years, Curly ran the company. Presidents and heads of state called Curly by his first name and valued his opinion above their advisors. Some even thought of him as a friend.

"Now you know as much as we do, Curly," Wiley said, picking up his coffee again. "What do you think? Are we nuts?"

"How long have we known each other, Wiley?"

"Twenty-five years?"

"Have you ever known me to bullshit you?"

"No."

Curly nodded. "And I don't believe you've ever lied to me either."

"So..."

"So, I don't buy it for a second. And if I didn't know you better, I'd say it's all a dumb joke. But something put you guys on that plane in the middle of the night... something convinced you. What's your proof?"

Jack told Curly about Wiley's leg and his own mind-snapping realization. He noted, with some bewilderment, that Curly remained unaffected.

"Well, I guess it takes longer for some people," Curly said, shrugging.

"You think we're crazy," Jack said, feeling foolish.

Curly raised his hands. "I didn't say that. But I don't remember Wiley's leg being a prosthetic. On the other hand, if what you're telling me is true, it's goddamned scary. It means they could do anything."

"Can you help us?" Wiley asked.

Curly nodded. "Give me a little time. Two hours and I'll have something figured for you."

He picked up a pen, wrote something on a small pad, tore it off, and handed it to Wiley.

"That's the address of a small, greasy spoon about three blocks from here. The food's terrific and it's cheap. Go get some breakfast and cool out. I'm going to run some computer simulations. Those take time."

"Can't you do it now?" Wiley asked, pointing to the IBM.

Curly chuckled. "Not on this. We have a Cray that we use for the simulations."

Jack was impressed. The Cray was one of the world's most so-phisticated supercomputers, capable of billions of calculations per second, and costing the equivalent of a small country's gross national product. Curly's company was doing more than all right to have one of those stashed away.

The men stood and shook hands.

"I'll see you guys in two hours, okay?"

❊   ❊   ❊

Out on the street, Jack seemed less sure about what had happened.

"He thought we were nuts, Wiley."

"He wouldn't be telling us to come back if he thought that."

"Your friend's being kind. He didn't want to toss you out of his office. Wait and see. When we come back in two hours, he'll feed us some line and send us home."

The lack of sleep finally caught up with Wiley.

"You know, Jack, I'm really getting sick and tired of your lousy attitude. Why can't you think positively for once in your life?"

Jack looked at Wiley, his eyes open in surprise.

"Oh, and I suppose you'd rather have your wooden leg back?" he said.

Wiley opened his mouth and suddenly realized what his friend was saying. He started to laugh, and Jack joined him. They passed two middle-aged women who hurried by, nervous, disapproving looks on their faces. Jack stuck out his tongue and Wiley blew them kisses. Maybe they *were* nuts.

When they reached the small luncheonette, the tiny bell above the door tinkled their arrival. They each ordered the special, blueberry pancakes and eggs, and seated themselves in a booth near the back. Curly was right. The food was delicious.

"Christ, that was good," Jack said as the buxom waitress cleared the table sometime later. Her voluptuous body and easygoing smile reminded him of someone. "You ever hear from Audrey Black?"

Wiley smiled and leaned back. "Audrey Black... Yeah, I saw her about a year ago. She's divorced, got three kids, a great job, and a great, big ass."

Jack laughed and shook his head. Back in college, both he and Wiley fell head over heels for Audrey, a tall brunette with a drop-dead body. The odd thing was, she never knew how gorgeous she was. Born and bred on a farm in the Midwest, Audrey had none of the conceit the city girls wore with snotty pride. She was intelligent, sweet, utterly guileless, and both men had vied shamelessly for her affections. Wiley had won out in the end and Jack had sulked for a week, then he'd met Janet...

The mood shifted and they spent the next hour and a half talking about Bock and Chessman and the awesome power they wielded. By the end of that hour and a half, each man's resolve had hardened, each determined to carry on no matter what Curly said.

"We better go," Wiley said, looking at his watch.

Jack paid the check and neither one paid attention to the little tinkling bell when they left.

❋   ❋   ❋

Everything in Curly's office looked tossed about, as if a cyclone had come through. The big man sat hunched over his small computer typing furiously, his red hair plastered to his scalp, huge sweat stains under his rumpled, white shirt. He looked shell-shocked. Manic.

"Come on in, guys," he said without looking up. "I'm almost done."

Wiley and Jack crept into the room, sat on their chairs, and tried to keep from fidgeting. Jack watched Curly type, his fingers flying over the keyboard, sounding like the sharp chatter of a machine gun.

Finally, Curly stopped and leaned back. A small printer hummed to life nearby. He looked at Wiley and nodded.

"Bendix Medical, right?"

Wiley's eyes snapped over to Jack.

"He knows!" he said.

"Knows what?" Jack said, confused.

"That's the company that manufactured my prosthesis. He remembers, Jack! He remembers!"

Wiley looked like a kid at a carnival, his eyes shining with glee. Jack didn't know whether to feel relieved or scared all over again. Stranger still was that Curly had known the name of the prosthetics company.

Curly rubbed his eyes and sighed. "It all came back about half an hour after you guys left. Scared me green."

Curly got up and walked over to the printer. He scanned the sheets, ripped them out, and passed them to Jack and Wiley.

"What you're looking at is a summary of what the Cray has spent the last two hours doing. I've got to tell you, even after what happened to me, I was surprised."

Wiley frowned. "What do you mean?"

"I mean, I didn't expect what it told me. I ran the simulations, telling my staff I was helping a writer with research. It's something we do every now and then. Nobody thought twice about it. The basic question I posed, given all the data, is 'what are Kruger's chance for success in accomplishing his two missions?'"

"And..." Wiley said.

"It's not what you think. For the Eisenhower mission: four point seven out of ten."

"In other words," Jack said, "about fifty-fifty."

"Yes."

"What about Hitler moving his armies?" Wiley said, gripping the arms of his chair.

"That's the strange part. The odds on that went up to five point one out of ten."

"What?"

"I know. It surprised the hell out of me, but I would have been surprised if the odds on either of these missions were one in a thousand, a million. Time travel is not your everyday occurrence. The computer should have put the odds at infinity."

"Then how?" Jack said.

"The letter."

"What letter?" Jack said, turning to Wiley.

Wiley shook his head. "I'm sorry, Jack. There was so much to tell you... I forgot."

Curly continued. "The computer was told that your man Chessman has a method for getting Kruger back in time. Given that, the odds are lowered astronomically. Assassinating Eisenhower, believe it or not, is going to be dicier for our man. Ike had constant security, and SHAEF headquarters were, for all practical purposes, unapproachable. Still, Kruger could get lucky. If that happens... well, you can imagine..."

"What about this letter?" Jack asked.

"That's the key factor the Cray latched onto. Without it, the odds go way back up. Anyway, one of the 'Nine Old Men,' as you call them, is Armand Bock. We have a thick file on him, by the way. He was christened Armand-Wilhelm *von* Bock."

"Pretty German," Jack said.

"Yeah... pretty German," Curly repeated. "Even more interesting is that Bock's uncle was none other than Field Marshal Fedor von Bock."

He leaned back and smiled, as if waiting for a compliment.

"What about the letter?"

Curly leaned forward.

"Jack, you're not thinking. Armand Bock has written a letter to his *uncle*, a Field Marshal in the *Wehrmacht*, introducing our friend Kruger and asking that all courtesies be extended, blah, blah, blah. It's true that the Field Marshal was dismissed by Hitler in nineteen forty-two, but retired or not, the old guy still has influence with him and the General Staff. And *that* is what turns the odds from guaranteed failure..." He slammed his fist down onto the desk. "...to five point one out of ten!"

"Shit!" Jack said. "What're we going to do?"

"Hold on a minute," Curly said. "Just bear with me, okay? I've got some ideas. Just sit back and let me talk this through and I'll try to answer any of your questions."

Jack let out a deep sigh and said, "Okay, go ahead."

"All right. For the moment, let's deal with the chain of events the Nine Old Men have put into motion. The first question is: Why Kruger? Besides being German and knowing the language, that sort of thing, Bock will give Kruger a glowing recommendation, telling the general that he is someone who will be 'of great value to the Fatherland,' and that Kruger was a boyhood friend. Remember, our friend Bock was around twenty-seven in nineteen forty-four. Kruger is twenty-seven now."

"What if the Field Marshal checks with the young Bock? He won't know anything?"

"I got that covered," Curly said. "The Cray placed Armand Bock in Yugoslavia at the time. He was totally incommunicado for four months." He stood up and walked over to a small dry bar set into a bookcase. "You guys want a drink?"

Jack glanced at his watch.

"At nine thirty in the morning?"

Curly smiled mischievously. "Hell, the liver doesn't know if it's a.m. or p.m."

"No thanks," Jack said.

"Wiley?"

"Yeah, I could use one. On the rocks."

Curly pulled down a bottle of Bacardi Amber, two tumblers, and a small tray of ice from the tiny refrigerator. He quickly poured two fingers into each, added a cube of ice, then walked back to the desk and handed one to Wiley.

"All right. Now comes the central question. Kruger has the letter and access to von Bock and Hitler. So how does he get his armies moved to Normandy? Now that's a bitch. By the way, according to the Cray, the critical unit was the Fifteenth Army under the command of Field Marshal Erwin Rommel."

"You know, Curly," Jack said, "when you're talking about letters, and all that stuff, it sounds logical as hell, but when you start talking about moving armies, I'm right back where I started out—this whole thing is a fairy tale. I don't know why we're even talking about it."

"Because that's what I do. I spend all day long contemplating the bizarre and the ridiculous, because somewhere, someone believes it's possible, that it just *might* happen. That's why *you're* here, Jack—because deep inside it scares you pea-green. If they can figure a way to go back in time, they can move the army. And if I were the Nine Old Men, I'd direct Kruger to concentrate on two people: the Field Marshal, who would get me access to the General Staff... and Hitler's astrologer."

"Oh, come on, Curly!"

The big man's mouth set into a hard line. "Hear me out."

"Sorry," Jack said, feeling foolish, like he was back in school again.

"Anyway, how does Kruger convince them? It's obvious he has only one choice: he has to convince them he's from the future. And there *are* ways to do that, which I'll get to in a minute. But suppose he does? What do *they* do? No matter how convinced they are personally, there has to be a compelling way—and I mean compelling with a capital 'C'—to get them to stick their necks out."

"So, where do you get your five point one out of ten?" Jack said.

Curly stared at Jack, his expression grim.

"He scares the hell out of them. Out of von Bock, Hitler, *and* the General Staff."

"And how does he do that?" Jack said.

"*Very* carefully," Curly said. "He's got to take it one step at a time. Any slipups and he's dead. Look, he knows the future, that's a huge advantage. If the Nine Old Men are smart—and they are—they will drill him with all the important events over the appropriate span of time. One of them is the death of von Bock's sister sometime in early nineteen forty-four."

THE NORMANDY CLUB

"The Cray tell you that?" Jack said.

Curly nodded. "And a lot of other things. Details about the Russian front, Roosevelt's death, Rommel's injury. On and on. The big problem will be to avoid the 'Salem witch-hunt reaction.'"

"What's that?" Wiley said, opening his mouth for nearly the first time in over half an hour.

"Kruger will be walking a very fine line. He has to break through Hitler's absolute convictions about the invasion coming to Calais. Remember, we're dealing with a megalomaniac here, a nutcase. Hitler, I mean. This is the guy that listened to his astrologer rather than his generals. But if Kruger handles it right and can convince guys like von Rundstedt and Keitel that he for damn sure knows the future, he has the most beautiful trump card in the world!"

"What?" Jack said.

"Nuremberg, goddamn it!" he shouted. "The War Crimes Trials! He'll give them all the gory details. When Keitel realizes that he faces a hangman's noose in nineteen forty-six, believe me... the Fifteenth Army will be moved!"

Curly had a wild-eyed look that made Jack nervous. It sounded logical, but something still didn't add up.

"But why should Nuremberg carry any more weight than any other of the stuff Kruger's going to tell them? They could disbelieve that just as easy as the rest."

Curly leaned forward.

"Because Kruger's going to do exactly what *I* would do. *He's going to bring the newsreel films.*"

4

Everyone sat quietly, the last statement hanging in the air like a malignant vapor. Jack's head throbbed, and a part of him still wanted to get up and walk out—forget the whole nasty business. The other part wanted to hunker down and get the job done. And God only knew what that would be.

It was Curly who broke the long, uncomfortable silence.

"Ready for that drink now, Jack? It's almost noon in Bermuda."

"God bless Bermuda," he said. "Same as Wiley's—make it a double."

Curly brought out a third glass, plunked in the ice, and filled it halfway with the golden rum. Then he freshened up his own and Wiley's.

"Well," Curly said, "that pretty much covers the whole scenario, for the moment. There are a mess of other details we can talk about later. Right now, all I want to know is... how do we stop them?"

"How do we?" Jack said.

Curly knocked back his drink. Jack could hear the leather squeaking as the big man shifted his weight in the chair.

"There are only *five* possibilities worth considering. And none of them are without risk. Before we get into that, I want to ask you guys something. Do you *want* to stop him?"

"Jesus Christ, Curly!" Jack said. "What kind of a question is that? What do you *think*?"

"No. I mean, are you prepared to do whatever it takes?"

"Yeah, sure, why not?"

"You don't sound too sure, Jack."

"For crying out loud! I've been up all night, half of it on a plane. I've just spent all morning analyzing a crazy scheme by a bunch of over-the-hill Hitler Youths who want to change history, and you want to know if I'm sure? Shit, yes!"

"Wiley?"

"I'm in."

"All right," Curly said, "let's get on with it. I said there are five possibilities. Four of them offer a slim chance of success. The fifth one is your best shot."

"Right."

"Don't be sarcastic. This is the only one with a hundred percent chance of success. And it is simplicity itself."

He paused again.

"Kill Chessman and Kruger."

"My God," Wiley said, turning white.

Somehow, this did not surprise Jack. Wiley had told him Curly would not pull punches, and he certainly hadn't. But it gave him the creeps to hear this come out of the man's mouth in such a matter-of-fact tone, like someone reading a shopping list.

"What the hell kind of an idea is that!" Wiley said.

Curly bounded to his feet. "It's a practical idea, goddamn it! You brought me a problem to solve. I solved it!

"But *murder*..." Wiley said.

Curly waited while everyone calmed down.

"I'm trained to get at the heart of a problem, not make moral judgments. I didn't *tell* you to kill them. It's an option, not the *only* option. What you do with it is your business."

Curly plopped down, his face beet red.

"But..." Wiley began.

"Shut up, Wiley," Jack said. He turned to Curly, who fiddled with his tie, his eyes everywhere but on him and Wiley. "Curly, let me ask *you* something. Do *you* want to stop them?"

Curly took a deep breath and put his hands on his desk. He looked about ten years older.

"I'm sorry I blew up at you. Anyway, like Bock, we've got files on Chessman. I read those while the Cray was crunching numbers. That's when it all hit me. It felt like my head was exploding."

Jack nodded in silent empathy. Curly continued.

"We have to assume that since Kruger has made two trips, that they are ready to go at any time. I want to help. However I can."

Jack nodded. "Okay, what are the other four options?"

Curly instantly snapped out of his dark mood, almost as if someone had thrown some kind of internal power switch.

"The second obvious option is to just call in the Feds. The FBI, CIA, Defense Intelligence. Take your pick."

"They'd think we'd flipped our lids, Curly," Wiley said. "They'd probably lock us up and throw away the keys."

Curly laughed. "No more than likely they'd start a file on you and keep you under surveillance for a while. Me, I'd lose my job for sure."

"Then why are we even talking about this? It's dumb."

Curly bristled a moment, then let it go with a nonchalant shrug.

"Like I said. It's my business to explore *all* the options. Doesn't mean they're all good."

"What's the rest?" Jack said, motioning for him to continue.

"Kill Kruger, either here or in nineteen forty-four. The past is the best of the two because here, the Nine Old Men would just find a replacement. Back there it will take them longer to find out. At any rate, it's all a delaying tactic. Sooner or later the Nine Old Men will try again. In fact, all the options are canceled out simply by finding another Kruger—that is, except killing Chessman along with him."

"Shit," Jack said, standing and moving to the window.

"Wait a minute! Let's hear the rest of it," Wiley said. He sounded tired and desperate, something they all felt. Curly poured more Bacardi into his glass and continued.

"There are two distinct groups of feasible solutions: those *we* can put into motion and those already in motion back in nineteen forty-four, ones we can exploit. The best known is the July twentieth plot to kill Hitler. It was led by a Colonel von Stauffenberg. Besides the bomb attempt, they tried posting riflemen along the route of an inspection tour but failed because Hitler changed the route at the last moment. His astrologer again.

"Anyway, the bomb blew up but failed to kill Hitler because another officer in the room moved it seconds before it went off. All Hitler suffered was an arm injury and partial hearing loss. If either of those events could be altered so they would occur differently, you'd have one dead Führer."

"And the end of the war," Jack said.

"Precisely," Curly said. "The generals knew that the war was lost by then, and that leads to our final option. There was an ongoing conspiracy known as the *Schwartz Kappel*, or Black Orchestra, comprised of men very high up in the General Staff. They had a plot to issue battle orders that, on the surface, looked like a smart move, but would actually succeed in splitting the German forces, allowing the Allies to pour through the gap and bingo, the war is over!"

"That actually happened?" Jack said. "I mean, the plot?"

"Yes, it's well documented."

"What screwed it up? Hitler found out?"

"No. Believe it or not, the Allies messed this one up. They just didn't believe the German generals, thought it was a trap. There was actually a meeting in Switzerland, but the plan was rejected. As for exploiting that opportunity, forget it. Too far-fetched. Remember we'd be dealing with the military mind-set at that time. Too many people to convince."

He leaned back in his chair.

"Those are the four choices."

"There's one more," Jack said. "We talk Chessman out of doing it."

Curly shook his head.

"It's too late for that. Kruger's trained and ready. My guess is that despite their promises to the good professor, he may soon become a liability to them."

Wiley sat up. "You mean—"

"Yeah."

"Maybe we can recruit him," Jack said. "Maybe they haven't told Chessman the whole story; maybe they fed him a line of bullshit. Hell, we already know he's not allergic to money."

"Go on," Curly said.

Jack glanced at Wiley. He could tell his friend liked the idea by the thoughtful way he stroked his chin.

"We tell him exactly what is going on and he bails out, comes over and trains one of us."

"Why?" Curly said.

"Because if the Germans win and they put a concentration camp in New Jersey, Chessman's going to be first in line. *He's a Jew!*"

"Holy shit!" Wiley said. "Of course!"

Curly eyed them, unimpressed.

"You through?"

"Yes."

"I congratulate you, but there's one small hitch... Chessman's not a Jew."

"Are you *sure*?" Wiley asked.

"Positive. He's Russian. The family name was Chesmanov until his father changed it after they emigrated to the US. As White Russians, they lost everything when the Bolsheviks took over. Chessman hates the commies as much as the Nazis did, and stands to gain as much as Bock if the Germans win."

"Damn," Jack said.

"Also, part of Chessman's methods for achieving his results depends on the subject being psychically adept *before* training. Obviously, Kruger has that ability. Do you? I sure as hell know *I* don't. And there's another thing you're forgetting."

"What?" Wiley asked.

"Once Kruger leaves, if he's successful..."

"Christ."

"You got it," Curly replied.

Jack pinched the bridge of his nose; the dull ache behind his eyes had worsened. "So, where does that leave us?"

"In a world of trouble, Jack," Curly said, "a world of trouble."

5

While the Delta Airlines Boeing 767 sat on the runway waiting for clearance, Jack stared out the window, trying to remember everything Curly, Wiley, and he had talked about earlier that day. It was thirty-six hours since he'd last slept, and it felt like a lifetime ago. All he wanted to do was lie back and pass out, but he knew he wouldn't.

His mind and body hummed like a transformer surging with power, thoughts roiling around his brain in a tempest of confusion: Bock, Chessman, Kruger, Eisenhower, Normandy, the whole mess.

What were they going to do? It all came down to two things: either recruit Chessman, an unlikely possibility given the facts, or go back and stop Kruger. And how was he supposed to do that? Curly had talked about being "psychically adept," as he put it. As far as Jack knew, he was about as psychic as a potato. Still, he and Wiley had to do something.

A ping sounded and Jack glanced above him. The seatbelt light was on.

A voice came over the speakers. "We have been cleared for take-off by LaGuardia tower. All flight attendants please take their seats and cross-check."

The plane picked up speed and Jack felt himself pushed gently back into his seat. The plane rose quickly and banked over Manhattan, turning south. In a little under four hours, he'd be back in Miami. Wiley had begged him to stay, but he had a meeting the next day he couldn't avoid. He'd promised his friend he'd fly back to New York the day after tomorrow. That should be plenty of time.

The ping sounded again and, without looking, Jack knew the seatbelt sign was off. In the old days, it would have meant that the pilot was a smoker. Now that the FAA banned it on all domestic flights, it was more than likely old habit. Jack had given up smoking ten years before and was happy he didn't have to breathe the crap anymore.

"Excuse me, sir, would you care for a cocktail?"

Jack looked up and saw the stewardess smiling at him. She couldn't have been more than twenty.

"Yeah, give me a light beer."

She reached into an ice bucket and pulled out some horse-piss beer and put it on his tray with a plastic cup.

"That'll be three dollars, sir," she said, without losing a watt of her dazzling smile.

He handed her three singles and she continued down the aisle. It wasn't a full flight; the business fliers wouldn't be on until Friday. Jack popped the can and poured the nearly frozen beverage down his throat directly from the can. He didn't really like these bland beers made by the big companies like Miller or Anheuser-Busch, but he'd found they tasted a lot better out of the can. One of those weird things. Like time travel.

"Shit," he said.

"Sir?"

Surprised, Jack turned and saw the pretty stewardess standing next to him again.

"Is everything all right?"

Jack hoped his embarrassment didn't show. He looked at her closely and decided she was probably around twenty-five. She had those apple-pie features that stole hearts but would never sell magazines: long, blonde hair that fell in big loose, natural curls halfway down her back, electric-blue eyes that positively vibrated, and that winning smile that no doubt cost her parents a small fortune.

Maybe twenty-four...

"Everything is just fine," he said, returning her smile.

"Are you going to Miami on business, sir?"

"Yes and no. I am going on business, but I live there too. And please, don't call me sir."

Her laugh was girlish—totally captivating.

Twenty-three...

"What *should* I call you?" she said, sitting on the arm of the seat across the aisle.

"Jack."

"Hi, Jack, I'm Terry."

"Hi, Terry. Do you always flirt so shamelessly with your passengers?"

She actually blushed, and for a moment Jack felt like a dirty old man. Hell, he was only forty-two, he wasn't that old. And if some nubile young thing thought him handsome and virile, who was he to discourage it?

"Only the cute ones," she replied, her eager eyes appraising his body.

Twenty-two...

Now it was Jack's turn to blush. No matter how "liberated" he thought of himself, he was always surprised when women came on to him. Unlike some of the men he knew, he actually found it a turn-on.

"Well, thank you. You've made my day. And believe me, it's been a doozy."

Terry took a pen and a card from her apron and began to write. "My home base is Miami, and I have got two days off before I fly out again. How about we get together for a drink... or something?"

She finished writing and handed Jack the card. It was some other guy's business card, and on the back she'd written: Terry Blaine (305) 555-1506 in a perfect, cursive handwriting.

"I'd love to, Terry," he said, "except I'm going with someone."

She shrugged, her smile dimming a few degrees.

"Well, why don't you keep the number for a rainy day."

Jack watched her walk back up the aisle, her cute, pear-shaped ass twitching provocatively in her blue polyester slacks.

Twenty... tops...

Jack breathed harder when he imagined her sitting by the pool at her apartment building in a red T-back bikini.

You really are a dirty old man.

He took another swig of his beer and switched on the overhead light. He had copies of the printouts, and for the umpteenth time that day he pulled them out and stared at them. His eyes found the name on the page: Eisenhower.

I Like Ike!

He remembered his parents sporting those buttons. He'd barely been five years old when Eisenhower ran for reelection. That was another world, a world of malt shops, Chevy Bel-Airs, hula hoops, and hydrogen bombs. It was a world he barely remembered, a world everyone called the golden age. And Ike had been a benevolent father. No one then could have imagined the horror of Vietnam, Dallas in '63, the eventual erosion of trust in the government by a people tired of being lied to.

He wondered if Ike ever had a twenty-year-old stewardess. Boy, was he tired!

Jack turned his thoughts to the Nine Old Men and tried to imagine what would happen if Kruger succeeded. If Eisenhower were dead at the critical juncture before D-Day, would those under him order a delay? Or would they, angered and determined, pour across the channel, sweeping away everything in their path?

Perhaps that was why the Nine Old Men had a contingency, that no matter what happened, Kruger would travel to Berlin and meet with Hitler and the General Staff. Armed with those telling newsreels of Nuremberg, Jack knew Kruger would succeed. He shuddered and put away the printouts again, took a last swig of the beer, and turned off the overhead light.

Now that the sun had set, the cabin lay in semi-darkness. He yawned. The beer had finally relaxed him to the point where sleep felt possible. He leaned back and looked toward the front of the cabin, where he could see Terry sitting on one of those retractable seats, absorbed in a paperback novel. He smiled as he saw her lips purse and her eyes widen and was captivated all over again. Too bad. But then again, he had Leslie. He closed his eyes and imagined his girlfriend's passionate cries, her soft lips and gimlet eyes. A feeling of well-being stole over him.

He bolted awake. Leslie! Shit! In the rush of flying to Stamford, and the meeting with Curly, he'd forgotten they'd made plans for dinner—tonight. It was bad enough he'd blown her off the night before. Now, he'd done it twice. And the worst part of it was he could have taken an earlier flight, made their date in plenty of time.

THE NORMANDY CLUB

Christ, she was probably waiting for him at their favorite little trattoria down in Coconut Grove right this minute. Damn it, damn it, damn it! He should have called her.

Too upset to sleep, he signaled for another drink and stared out the window, wondering just what it was he would say to her. If he lied, he deserved whatever he'd get. On the other hand, if he told the truth, she would think he was nuts. Hell, some small part of him still thought the whole thing sounded crazy. The plane banked, vectoring toward Miami, and his stomach churned, the acid biting at the back of his throat.

All things considered, this was turning out to be one shitty day.

※　※　※

The cab turned off Brickell Avenue and sped up the concrete drive, slowing as it slid under the overhang of 444 Brickell Avenue. The cabbie, a smiling Cuban with a mouthful of gold teeth, handed Jack his bag and sped away in a cloud of oily smoke, raucous salsa music blasting from blown speakers. A trickle of sweat slid down his spine as he loosened his tie and gazed out over the bay. The moon, plump and jaundiced, hung there, mocking him with its pockmarked smile. He could hear tiny waves lapping against the rotted seawall and the smell of dead fish assaulted his nose, making him queasy. Picking up his bag, he walked into the lobby and opened his mailbox. Empty. Jack winced. Leslie had already come here, probably hopping mad.

The elevator, as usual, seemed to take forever to climb the fifteen floors. He found the wait agonizing. Staring at the walls, he noticed a bit of obscene graffiti some delinquent had carved into the wood-grained Formica laminate: *For a great buttfuck call Consuela. 555-5150.* How long did it take someone using a knife to carve that timeless message? And wouldn't someone have seen him do it? Then again, maybe it was Consuela. Maybe it was her way of advertising her "specialty." Jack laughed in spite of his mood, imagining some fat Cuban hooker with knife in hand. God, what was the world coming to?

The elevator slowed and the doors slid open with a happy ping. Jack grabbed his bag, gave Consuela's advert a parting glance, and trudged down the hallway toward his apartment. Inside, he saw the mail sitting on the dining nook table, a further indictment of his thoughtlessness. He sighed, threw down his bag, and reached for the stack of bills.

"Jack."

Her voice was a whisper, a soft call from his guilty heart. His eyes snapped toward the sound and saw her standing in the sliding glass doorway leading to the tiny balcony. Her green eyes flashed in the faint light, and Jack smelled her Coco perfume blown by the warm breeze from the bay.

"Leslie, I—"

She came to him then, her strapless dress swishing against her sleek thighs, her step determined. Her lips burned against his and Jack dropped the mail, enveloping her in his arms. Her breasts pressed against him and he felt the inevitable stirring in his groin. God, was she soft.

Leslie broke the embrace, peered deep into his eyes, and nearly tore his head off with a slap that brought tears to his eyes.

"That's for leaving town without calling me," she said, her voice tight with fury. "We had a date. Remember? I sat in that restaurant for hours, feeling like a total fool!"

Jack rubbed his face, blinking back the tears.

"Leslie, I'm sorry—"

"Sorry's no good anymore, Jack. If it's not some client coming between us, it's Wiley. It was Wiley, wasn't it?" She stalked to the bar, tried to pour herself a drink, then threw the glass against the wall. It smashed into a trillion sparkling pieces and left a half-moon dent in the plaster. "Damn you!"

"I can explain, if you'll let me," he said, reaching for her. She drew back as if his hand were a poisonous snake.

"Explain then. What was it this time? His wife leave him again? That stupid club? Tell me! I have a damn right to know!"

Jack eased shut the door and came to her. She stiffened and looked away from him when he tried to touch her. "Listen, sweetheart, I'm sorry I didn't call you. I know that doesn't cut it with you at the moment, but something came up, something bad... something really bad. I had to go."

She wrenched from his grasp and went to the dining nook table. Reaching into her purse, she pulled out a key and held it up. "You can have this back. Maybe some bimbo will put up with you. I won't."

She slammed it down onto the table, tore open the door, and stormed out.

"Shit," Jack said.

He caught the elevator doors just as they began sliding shut. "Let me explain. I have to talk to someone, or I'll go crazy. Please don't leave... I love you."

Leslie stared back at him and for one split second, her features softened, her emerald eyes aching. Then, just as quickly, her face hardened into a mask of resolve. She grabbed his hand and pried it off the door, a single tear coursing down her face.

"Good-bye, Jack."

And then she was gone.

He returned to the apartment and, for the first time, noticed how shabby it looked. The furniture, strictly utilitarian, had a sad, neglected appearance that perfectly mirrored how he felt. Like a zombie, he shuffled to the bar and grabbed the half-empty bottle of Jack Daniels, twisted off the cap, and threw it across the room. He tilted the bottle and let the amber liquid burn its way down his throat, coughed, and nearly puked.

His pulse pounded in his temples, and a small throb at the base of his neck promised to turn into a monster of a headache. He took another gulp of whiskey, tasting its smoky, oak-barrel flavor, and found that he liked it.

To hell with Kruger, to hell with Bock, to hell with The Normandy Club and everyone else. Hot tears splashed down his face, but he made no move to wipe them.

"Damn you, Wiley... damn you."

6

Greenwich, Connecticut
5 August 1993

Werner Kruger awoke, and for a moment, knew a tiny stab of fear. Where was he? He sat up on his elbows and looked about the darkened room. It took a moment for his eyes to adjust. The room looked no more than ten by ten and smelled of stale cigarettes and staler beer. The furniture, what there was of it, barely fit the tiny space. There was a double bed, a beaten-up chest of drawers, and a table with two chairs, one with part of a leg missing. It stood skewed to one side, a testament to its tawdry surroundings. Kruger looked out the window and saw the hotel sign flashing alternately red and blue. The Red Robin Hot l, n- Vaca-cy. The light shone through the dingy chintz curtains, making the room appear nightmarish, like some scene from a bad American detective movie. *Mein Gott*, what was he doing here? And then he remembered.

The girl.

He glanced over at her inert form and leered. Her long, red hair hung over her face and she moaned in her sleep faintly, as if replaying the night's carnal delights. After a final run through with Chessman in his small laboratory, Kruger had hit the strip joints, ending up at the Crystal Slipper, a dive that had seen better days. The surprise had been the women. Usually they looked used and worn, but the management at the Slipper must have spent their money wisely, for the women were quite a few cuts above the competition. The evidence bore out in the first few minutes after Kimber hit the stage.

Kimber—*did parents actually name their children that*—had mesmerized him.

She stood over six feet tall, and her fiery auburn locks fell to below her waist. Her body was what Americans called voluptuous, and he called *zaftig*. The breasts, huge mountains of smooth, milk-white flesh, stood straight out, with large pink areolas, and nipples that pushed out the fabric of her skimpy halter top. Kruger suspected they had seen a surgeon's knife. It didn't matter. They'd responded to his touch like any. He'd also been delighted to see, when the G-string finally came off, that she was a pure redhead. She met his complete approval.

Ever since childhood, when the sixteen-year-old girl from the flat upstairs seduced him at the not-so-tender age of twelve, he'd been enamored of redheads. He thought of her now, her smile, wet and inviting. The perfect babysitter, the perfect teacher. Yes, Kruger had been madly in love with Helga Meiner from that moment on and every redhead he saw thereafter. There was something uninhibited about them, something wild. Kimber had screamed and bucked just like Helga had so many years before, and he came inside her four times. Now she lay there like some elephantine lump, and Kruger's mouth tasted like old socks.

He quietly crawled from the bed, careful not to wake her. She groaned again and turned over, her titanic breasts undulating as she moved. Kruger felt his groin stirring and put the thought from his mind. No time for frivolity. Today was the day.

THE NORMANDY CLUB

Kruger threw on his clothes and glanced quickly at his watch. Five forty-five a.m., nearly dawn. He could see the horizon already lightening to a dull gray. Then he saw the hundred-dollar bill lying on the nightstand where he'd casually tossed it the night before. Looking at Kimber, he smiled. There was a way to screw her again after all. He picked up the money, put it back in his wallet, and left the room.

Walking down the dark hallway, he nearly tripped over an old black man sleeping off the empty bottle of Gallo White Port that lay under his head. Even though it was empty, the grizzled old tramp held on to it, his crooked, old fingers curled around the neck protectively.

Another dead soldier.

Kruger's stomach roiled as the odor of stale urine assaulted his nostrils. Stepping over the man, he took the two flights down, passed the snoring desk clerk, and walked out onto the sidewalk. Here the air smelled better, but not by much. The air smelled of diesel fuel and rotting garbage, and the already toasty temperature foretold of the broiling hot day to follow.

Retracing his route from the night before, Kruger walked toward the lot where he'd left his rental car. The small, enclosed cubicle the attendant manned stood locked and fortified with steel bars, a further testament to the squalid nature of the neighborhood. Kruger pulled at his keys and stopped in his tracks. The door to the Toyota Camry he'd rented lay open. Inside, he could see someone working on the dash. His eyes narrowed and his color turned from its usual pallor to a nasty pink.

Hunching over, he crept toward the car. He could hear whoever it was swearing under his breath. Evidently, the Japanese tape deck was not so easy to remove. Americans stealing from the Japanese. Now there was a switch.

61

Moving with the swiftness of a cheetah, Kruger lunged inside the car and yanked the thief out. The thief squirmed and thrashed like an angry house cat thrown into a swimming pool.

"Get the fuck off me, motherfucker!"

The thief was a small, black boy, no more than ten years old. He somehow looked older, as if life on the streets had aged him beyond his years. He stopped struggling and looked Kruger directly in the eyes. They burned with defiance.

"Come on, honky! You wanna mess with me? Well, fuck you!"

Kruger had to laugh at the boy's nerve.

"What you laughin' at, whitey?" he said, trying to wrestle out of the older man's iron grip.

Kruger held him fast by his jacket, an expensive leather and wool number with LA RAIDERS on the back. Kruger also noted the boy's brand-new Nikes, the kind with the red lights in the heels.

Kruger smiled and shook his head. "Such language, young man. If anyone should be angry, it is I."

The boy's eyes snapped up and down quickly, giving him the once-over. He relaxed. He sensed a mark.

"You lookin' fo' some action, my man?" the boy said, his manner becoming sassy. "Got some primo ice. Get you a woman too. You want some pussy? I got the best they is. She sixteen and she let you fuck her any which way they is. You got the green, she make you scream."

Kruger stared at the boy, his expression impassive.

"That don't do ya? How about dick? You like dick? I'll let you suck me fo' a twenty."

Kruger found the boy's patter growing tiresome.

"*Ja*, this ice you say, how much."

The boy smiled. Gotcha!

"It's the best, my man. Fifteen fo' a pop. You in?"

"*Ist gut.* I am in, as you say."

The boy's smile took on an edge of contempt.

"You talk funny, man. Where you from?"

"A long way from here," Kruger said, his eyes taking on a far-away look. He eased his grip and the boy took a step back. For a moment it looked like the kid would scamper away, now that Kruger's guard was down. Instead, he began to swagger towards a nearby alley, his gait very much like a strutting rooster. He looked back over his shoulders.

"You comin'?"

Kruger followed.

The alley was much darker than the parking lot, the light from the lot's sodium vapor lamps too weak to plumb its depths. The boy beckoned him over to an area next to a large, battered dumpster. It smelled even worse back here. In a pool of light farther up the alley, Kruger could see a couple of rats fighting over the remnants of meat a restaurant had thrown away.

"The money, bro, let's see the green," the boy said impatiently.

Kruger walked over to him, his hand inside the pocket of his jacket.

"How about we see red, *ja?*"

"Huh?"

In a blur, Kruger whipped out a switchblade, and swiped it across the boy's throat. Great gouts of dark, red blood jetted out from the wide slice in his neck. The boy's eyes bugged out as he clamped his hands around his throat. It did nothing to stop the torrent of gore. He struggled to scream, his voice coming out like wet, gurgling croaks. In a moment, he slumped over and lay still.

Looking about to make sure no one had stumbled across their

little dalliance, Kruger picked up the boy's limp body and threw it into the dumpster, covering it with some of the loose trash. With luck, no one would discover it for a couple of days. Of course, if the heat of the last few days persisted, that time would be considerably shortened. Kruger wiped the blade on a piece of newspaper, closed it, and put it back in his pocket.

"No one steals from me," he said, a pitiless smile creasing his brutal face. "*Guten nacht*, my little mongrel."

Kruger walked swiftly back to the Camry, got in, and drove off. Normally, he might've let the little *Schwarze* go, but in light of "future" events, he was doing the little bastard a favor. When the new world order came to pass, all his kind would be rounded up and destroyed, just like the Jews, Gypsies, and mentally deficient. It occurred to him that, with the changes he would make, the boy would never be born to begin with. He laughed out loud at that. The perfect crime. All traces of it ceasing to exist in the blink of an eye. Nothing in this decadent, dying country would ever be the same.

※　※　※

Kruger pulled through the stone gates of the Normandy Club and sped up the cobblestone road to the front entrance. He turned off the Camry's motor and stepped out. No one. Not a sound. The grounds lay swathed in darkness, with only the chirping crickets and the ticking of the Camry's cooling engine breaking the illusion of stillness.

Kruger's pulse quickened as he looked up toward the building's top floor.

The third floor glowed, the warm, yellow light spilling from the dormers and out into the night, looking cozy and inviting. He knew they would all be there. Waiting. Bock, Chessman, and the others. They wanted to watch. Never mind that their presence could affect the experiment—the mission. They had paid good money and wanted to watch Werner Kruger fade into the past.

That was what Chessman had said it would be like, a slow fade into yesteryear, like a ghost disappearing into the ether. Kruger smiled. He was right. But what he hadn't told the old professor was that he was making extracurricular journeys. Aside from the jaunts to Dallas in 1963 and Suez in 1956, he'd followed his own instincts. It took no more energy to put oneself back fifty years than it did one day. And that is what he'd done the day before.

Or was it the day before that? It didn't matter. He'd lived the day twice. With one essential difference. He was now thousands of dollars richer.

He'd sat in his rented room and gone through the drill. It was simple, really, so simple that it boggled the mind. It came down to channeling one's telekinetic ability back on oneself. By using a form of mantra, the subject would direct the energy back on himself and whatever objects he had touching his body. The most important aspect was to keep one thought uppermost in the mind: TIME... DATE... PLACE. In this case it was noon... August 3, 1993... the men's room at Hialeah Racetrack. When it happened, his whole body rippled, like a flag snapping in the breeze. From his point of view, the whole world performed a kind of lap dissolve, much like the kind one saw in the movies. One moment he was in one place and time, the next in another. For one brief moment, the two would overlap, making him feel almost godlike.

Breaking out of his reverie, Kruger walked into the building and into the small, paneled elevator, wrinkling his nose at the odor of pine-scented cleanser that assailed his nose. And although someone had just cleaned it, it still stank of tobacco smoke and the Nine Old Men's greed.

BILL WALKER

On the top floor, the door slid open and Kruger strode toward the steel door. It already lay open, the light spilling into the darkened hallway. Was it inviting—or daring—him to enter? As he walked, he heard the timbers creaking under his feet. No doubt the Nine Old Men wanted it that way. No one approached undetected.

He stepped inside and felt the expectancy, the hush that fell across the room, as if he were a great leader about to receive accolades for an extraordinary act of statesmanship. This pleased rather than disturbed him, for in a sense, this was exactly what he was about to do. He was about to rewrite history, to change all that had come before.

Armand Bock stood and applauded, and the rest of them followed suit. Kruger noted that Chessman remained seated, his hands folded in his lap. He stifled the flash of anger that rose in his heart and smiled, bowing graciously.

"Thank you," he said.

The applause died down quickly and Bock came over to him.

"We are at the crossroads of history, Werner, the crossroads of limitless opportunity. Can you feel it?" he said, grasping Kruger's shoulders.

Kruger nodded, unable to think of anything to say. He looked toward the center of the room. The topographical map table had been moved to the side. Under the large, overhanging light now stood a single chair with clothes neatly folded on the seat. These would be the clothes he would wear: the blue gabardine uniform of an RAF Flight Lieutenant. Near the chair lay a haversack containing changes of uniform, British Military ID, orders posting him to SHAEF headquarters in Bushey Park, and £10,000 in various denominations, all issued prior to 1944. Inside the bag, under a false bottom, lay civilian clothes with German labels, 10,000 Reichsmarks, Bock's letter to his uncle the Field Marshal, and the Semtex plastic explosive and detonator.

At first the Nine Old Men had wanted Eisenhower to die quietly, appearing to succumb to natural causes, but they ruled this out as too undramatic. After two years of careful planning, the Allies would have their day off for a funeral and the invasion would proceed as planned, as if nothing had ever happened. No, to strike terror into the heart of the Allies, to stop them in their tracks, something big would have to occur. A small, poisoned dart fired from a pistol using compressed air had no drama.

But there existed one such opportunity for drama that outweighed everything else. On May 15, 1944, Eisenhower and everyone connected with the planning for Overlord had gathered at a small private school in London's West End for a final briefing. Besides Ike, Bedell-Smith, Montgomery, and the others, King George VI and Winston Churchill also attended. With all of them in one room, it presented an unprecedented moment, a moment that never came again, a moment that begged to be seized.

In one fell swoop, the whole of Overlord and the British government would lie decapitated, the damage incalculable. A masterstroke.

The plan might have appealed to Bock's sense of theatrics, but it made Kruger nervous. The security around the Saint Paul's briefing would be nearly impenetrable. Even with his impeccable credentials and flawless accent, there was no guarantee that the man he was replacing would be authorized to go. And even then, ten pounds of Semtex took up a lot more space than a small air pistol. But Bock and the rest of the Nine Old Men held all the cards. It was their way, or no way.

Still, no plan was foolproof, and a backup plan remained in effect. Regardless of the outcome at St. Paul's, Kruger had orders to proceed to Germany. For Werner, this part of the plan still held the greatest hope. He knew he could convince the *Führer* and his Generals to move the Fifteenth Army. He *had* to, or all was lost.

"Would you like some privacy to change?" Bock said.

Kruger smiled. Modesty was not in his makeup.

"Nein."

"English, *Flight Lieutenant Liddington*, English," Bock chided.

"Right you are, squire, good show," Kruger said, snapping to and giving Bock the British salute.

The accent was perfect.

Kruger had spent months listening to tape recordings, zeroing in on the particular regionalism that would both befit his officer status and match that of the real Flight Lieutenant Captain Liddington, a man born and raised in Surrey, educated at Eton and Oxford. He also took care to read magazines and books of the period, absorbing the contemporary expressions then in use. In class-conscious England, an officer with the wrong accent, speaking the vernacular of a future age, would stand out like a sore thumb. Worse than that, it would jeopardize everything. His accent had to be perfect—for 1944.

Kruger quickly stripped down and put on the uniform, starting with the old-fashioned button-waist briefs. In a few moments the transformation was complete. His own clothes he bundled and placed a few feet from the chair. He then sat on the chair and placed the haversack in his lap.

" I am ready," he said.

Bock nodded and looked to Chessman, who got up and approached.

Chessman's expression looked troubled.

"You do realize, Herr Kruger, that there is a chance you may not be able to return?"

Kruger smiled, his lips curling in contempt.

"Yes. But then I will have the pleasure of being away from you, *doctor.*"

Chessman stiffened, his features hardening into an unreadable mask. He turned to the others.

"The lights," he said.

No one moved, but the lights around them dimmed, all but the one directly above Kruger.

"Begin," Chessman said.

✠ ✠ ✠

Chessman felt the acid in the back of his throat and resisted the temptation to reach for a Tums. He wouldn't give Kruger the satisfaction, the pleasure of seeing him suffer. Oh, God, how he hated the man. After working with him for six months, Chessman now knew what Victor Frankenstein felt like after his creation ran amok. Scared and responsible. Though he'd wanted what Bock and the others wanted with equal passion, now he was not so sure. What world would Kruger create? Would he be better off as he'd hoped? Or would nothing change at all? These very questions now ate him night and day, the antacid he gulped continually often useless.

I will remember, I must remember, he thought.

But for all his genius, for all his research, he still did not know if that was possible. In a moment, theory and fact would meet and one would vanquish the other. His attention riveted on Kruger as the man closed his eyes and began muttering.

"Yitgadal V'yitkadash Sh'mei Rabba..."

The mantra he had taught Kruger came from a surprising source and one Chessman felt provided a touch of irony. It was the opening line to the Mourner's *Kaddish*, the Hebrew prayer for the dead. Though Chessman was Russian Orthodox, he'd learned it from the years of accompanying his wife to synagogue. He watched Kruger repeat the line over and over and realized the joke might be on them all.

Suddenly, objects in the room began to shake, as if caused by a mild earthquake. Chessman felt the skin on his face begin to pull. Kruger muttered faster. A golden glow appeared around him. Chessman struggled to breathe.

It was working.

He stared at Bock. The old man's eyes shone with a queer light. The rest of the Nine Old Men leaned forward as one, their sunken eyes reflecting the amber glow surrounding Kruger.

Chessman turned back to Kruger just as the glow intensified. It was now like looking into a small sun. The room shook violently, objects crashed to the floor. And then, amidst all the other noise, Chessman heard it. Soft and faint, at first, it grew in direct proportion to the glow around Kruger. It sounded like voices merging into an unearthly multi-part harmony, a cosmic oratorio, and it grew louder and louder and louder. Chessman and the others covered their ears. The light and sound built to a terrifying crescendo. And in an instant was gone. The spot where Kruger had sat stood empty. Kruger and the bag were gone, as was the chair. Chessman noted that even a layer of the floor where Kruger's feet had rested had gone with him. He could see faint impressions of the man's shoes.

Bock rocketed to his feet.

"WE HAVE DONE IT!" he screamed.

And then the world went black...

7

Miami, Florida
15 April 1994

Jack opened his eyes just as the small *Blaupunkt* clock radio's alarm went off. Even with the buzzer turned off, he still felt like burying his head in the pillows and forgetting the day, but the cheery announcer from WNZI made that impossible.

"Good morning, Miami, and welcome to another sunny day in the Southern Sector. Temperatures will be in the high eighties for the rest of the week and the skies will remain hazy until late today. Seas will be heavy, but the bay should stay at a moderate chop.

"In local news, State Security reports another arrest of terrorists in the Tamiami District. Though no names have been released, State Security reports that guerrilla leader John Franz was not among them. Authorities say an arrest is imminent.

"The last of the Liberty City Ghetto was razed today to make way for the Keitel Terrace Condominium project. According to developer William Bennett, the project is expected to attract large numbers of retirees from the Fatherland. All SS, Wehrmacht, and Luftwaffe veterans will receive special low-cost loans.

"The *Führer* has announced an official holiday in honor of the

BILL WALKER

National Resettlement Bureau's efficient handling of the resettlement of African-Avalonians to their ancestral homes on the Dark Continent. The last boatload left New York harbor early this morning bound for New Iberia. We at WNZI send our heartfelt congratulations to the men and women of the National Resettlement Bureau.

"In world news, fighting in Mexico intensified yesterday as the Sepp Dietrich Division encircled Acapulco. Fighting is house by house with heavy casualties reported. Field Marshal Wayne Kurtz expects the city to fall within hours.

"Back in the Fatherland, preparations for the May fifteenth 'Heroes Day' celebrations are in full swing. As is the custom, Adolf Hitler's tomb will be opened to the public and a televised speech by our glorious *Führer* will go around the world via satellite at precisely twenty-one hundred hours Berlin time. That's oh-three hundred hours for us Southers. And don't you just know *I'll* be watching..."

That was dangerous, Jack thought, as he sat up in bed and clicked off the radio. He could just imagine State Security bursting into the studio and dragging off the hapless announcer, who would, like all of them, proclaim his innocence loudly.

It wouldn't matter.

If State Security said you were guilty, you were guilty. They had no sense of humor, no sense of fair play, no mercy. Jack shook his head and wiped the hardened mucus from the corners of his eyes.

Climbing from the bed, he went to the window, pulled back the blinds, and stared out through the heavy plate-glass onto Brickell Ave. From his vantage point on the fiftieth floor, the bumper-to-bumper traffic reminded him of the tiny Matchbook/Heinkel cars he'd collected as a kid. He still could not get used to living so high up, but his position in the Ministry of Propaganda rated a class-2 apartment, and one *never* refused perks. Not only did it look bad, but it was also just plain stupid. Perks like these made the job bearable. Jack took one last look at the street below, noting that the drawbridge was up. A large *Dönitz*-class submarine passed through on its way from its berth on the newly widened and deepened Miami River to its patrol point off Miami Beach. The entire crew stood on deck, standing stiffly at attention while it glided silently by.

Letting go of the blinds, Jack trudged into the bathroom, turned on the shower, stripped off his underwear, and stood under the steaming spray, letting the water cascade over his body. He closed his eyes and thought back over the last weekend with Leslie. They'd met at a Party function the previous month and both felt an immediate, almost chemical attraction. She worked as a secretary to some party bigwig and, as a perk, got to attend the monthly soirees. The only reason he'd been there was because Reece had ordered him to go. Funny how things worked out. He and Leslie spent the entire evening dancing and talking, hardly taking their eyes off each other. Before they realized it, the band was packing their instruments and they were the only couple left. Neither one wanted to end the evening.

They didn't.

Back at his apartment, clothes came off and flesh fused together in an explosion of heat and passion that surprised them both. Afterwards, with the sun peeking over Biscayne Bay, Jack watched her sleep, marveling at the way the crimson rays played on the contours of her face. He could hardly believe that in less than a day, he'd met and fallen madly in love with someone. Life was incredible.

Snapping out of his daydream, Jack turned the shower ice-cold and nearly screamed. His manhood shrunk under the frigid spray. Now was not the time to get carried away. After a moment, he turned off the shower and got out.

"Shit," he said, looking at the clock embedded in the bathroom wall. It read 0738 hours.

He was late. There was a meeting that morning, a meeting to help coordinate the Heroes Day celebrations. Instituted at the end of *Das Groß Kampf* (The Great Struggle) in 1944 by Adolf Hitler, the day celebrated all the heroes that helped bring about the New World Order. Thousands were honored worldwide, but the men and women personally chosen by the *Führer* each year received special accolades. This year, on the fiftieth anniversary, there were hints of special honors. This was the purpose of the meeting, to help coordinate the celebrations and make any last-minute changes.

"Shit. Shit. Shit!"

With his hair still dripping, Jack threw on his uniform, careful not to forget to pin on the party badge, a minor offense, but one that could nix a promotion. The clock read 0745 hours. He jammed his feet into his boots and bolted out the door.

Jumping into his VW Blitz, Jack slammed his way through the gears, tore out of the underground parking, and streaked into traffic. In the distance he could see another submarine approaching the bridge.

"No, no. Not today," he said, smashing the accelerator to the floor. The little VW sports car rocketed forward, barely clearing the descending barriers on the bridge. He skidded to a stop inches from the rear bumper of a Mercedes Berliner and let out a huge rush of air. Behind him the bridge rose, and the submarine floated through the channel, at the stately pace of a dowager empress, its crew identical to the last one.

"I wonder who's left inside to drive it?" he said, laughing humorlessly. Damn things practically ran themselves with the new generation of computer chips.

THE NORMANDY CLUB

The light turned green and Jack turned onto Biscayne Boulevard. Luckily, his office lay near the downtown area. With a little luck, he'd only be a moment or two late. Besides, it was not as if his presence was crucial. He was merely a cog in the great political machine. Still, Reece would not be happy.

Jack snorted with contempt. If ever the term "political toady" fit anyone, it fit Bryant Reece to a tee. As an ass-kisser, he was an Olympic champion. Reece got where he was, the *Direktor* of Advertising and Propaganda for South Florida, by kissing every fat, warty butt in sight. Ironically, the man would brook no brown-nosing toward himself, not that Jack would ever stoop that low.

As a creative talent, the man was definitely second-rate. His own ideas tended toward the bland and mediocre, and some were out and out plagiarism, not that stealing ideas from one's subordinates and claiming them as one's own would ever be called plagiarism. No, to Reece, it was all part of playing on *his* team. But what really charred Jack's butt was Reece's habit of blaming the failures on his staff. He was quick enough to take credit for the successes, but for the failures he'd throw someone else to the wolves, and not necessarily the person who'd come up with the idea to begin with.

When Jack pulled up to 20th and Biscayne, he spotted one of the black vans belonging to State Security. They were herding a group of what looked like students into the van, their hands held over their heads. The State Security troops stood holding deadly-looking MP89 machine pistols on them, their faces hid behind darkly tinted face plates attached to their helmets. Jack shuddered and pulled away from the light. The Security troops frightened him, but not nearly as much as the ones he *couldn't* see.

State Security was so pervasive, so all-encompassing, that no one ever really knew who was a member. It was rumored that the

BILL WALKER

organization was deliberately compartmentalized below command level so that individual operatives didn't know each other beyond a small cadre. This fostered blind fear and compliance even by its own staff. The only positive ID was a special transponder implanted under every operative's skin. It not only identified them, but also let the higher-ups track personnel via satellite.

At 25th and Biscayne, Jack turned into the gate and presented his ID to the guard. The old man scrutinized it carefully as he did every morning.

"Morning, Mr. Dunham," he said, saluting. "Have a nice day."

Jack drove toward the large, glass building, noting the sun gleaming off its thousands of mirrored panes. It was both impressive and ugly as hell. Built ten years before in a sort of neo-ziggurat style, The Joseph Goebbels Ministry of Advertising and Propaganda occupied over ten acres. It had ten sublevels below the ground that held offices and parking. The twenty stories above ground hummed day and night, controlling the dissemination of information for the whole Southern Sector of what had once been the United States, now fancifully known as Avalon. Jack could recall the opening ceremonies, the ribbon cut by a doddering eighty-seven-year-old Goebbels. During his very brief speech, the old man had mumbled something about the greater glory of the Party and had been quickly replaced by a younger, more coherent speaker.

Jack pulled into his space and saw that it was the last to be occupied. Suppressing his anxiety, he grabbed his briefcase and bounded for the elevator. It opened and disgorged a gaggle of secretaries chattering about some juicy inter-office gossip.

"Floor, please," an electronic voice intoned.

Jack scowled. Whatever happened to buttons? He cleared his throat.

"Twenty."

"Voice print ID correct. Good morning, Mister Dunham."

He rolled his eyes and resisted making a wise crack. It was, after all, only a microprocessor. The elevator moved swiftly, and within seconds the door slid open. He checked his watch and walked briskly down the hall, nodding at people he knew. The conference room lay in the northeast corner. Through the heavy glass, he could see Reece speaking and gesturing as he always did. The man looked spastic when he talked. Sometimes Jack found it hard to keep a straight face.

He reached the door and pushed it open slowly, hoping to glide in unnoticed. Reece never missed a beat.

"So glad you could join us, Dunham. Please, tell us what kept you?" The man's eyes narrowed, and he stopped speaking. Jack knew everyone was staring at him. Oh, God, how he wanted to pound the man's face in! At the very least he wanted to put the creep in his place. Swallowing the nasty comeback that had sprung to mind, Jack smiled and took his seat.

"Sorry, Reece, the drawbridge was up again."

"Ah, the drawbridge. Well, do try and get here on time from now on, Dunham. You can't know how hard it is for us to have a meeting without you."

Jack knew he was blushing, but kept smiling, feeling like a first-class idiot.

Someday...

"Now," Reece began, "as I was saying. Heroes Day, this year promises to be the most exciting we've ever had. Not only will there be the satellite speech by the *Führer*, but on the reviewing stand will be some very special honorees. I've just received some tape from National that will fill in some background. These tapes will be broadcast in the days ahead to whip up the excitement, as well as to inform the public about the accomplishments of our honorees. Lights?"

The lights immediately dimmed, and from a slot in the ceiling near the front of the room, a large *Blaupunkt* High-Definition Flat Screen descended. A tape began extolling the glorious victory in 1944 in The Great Struggle and how the heroes of that "grand conflict" made it all possible. To Jack, it looked like the same old drivel from every other year. Why the hell couldn't anyone come up with something new? Because they had wonderfully creative people like Bryant Reece. He frowned and looked out through the glass. If this went on much longer, he was going to have a hard time staying awake. But something on the screen caught his eye.

It was old, black and white footage from just after the Allies surrendered in Berlin. Hitler smiled, his face flush with the heady wine of victory. He stood with Göring, Goebbels, Himmler, and the usual flock of party hacks on the reviewing stand at the Brandenburg gates. Troops marched by in synchronized goose step, ten abreast, their eyes locked on their glorious leader, who saluted them as they passed. There was nothing out of the ordinary about the scene. Jack had seen ones like it a million times, but something bothered him. Leaning forward in his seat, he listened to the narration, his eyes riveted to the screen.

"As our glorious troops marched past their proud *Führer*, no one stood prouder than Hero of the Reich, Werner Kruger, the man credited with the liquidation of Dwight Eisenhower, Winston Churchill, and all of the jackals connected with the planned Allied invasion of Normandy. Because of this one hero's daring and his possession of crucial Allied secrets obtained on his daring spy mission deep into Allied territory, we charged onward to glorious victory."

The camera cut close to Kruger and then dissolved to a modern shot in color. This time it showed a much older Kruger smiling in front of one of his massive factories. The narration continued.

"Today, Werner Kruger divides his time between factories in Avalon and the Fatherland. In many ways, he has continued to be a hero with his uncanny ability to invest in technologies that have blossomed into enormous and profitable industries: Computers, Genetic Purification, and Defense. Yes, Werner Kruger is every bit the hero he was fifty years ago. On Heroes Day he will join our glorious *Führer* on the reviewing stand to receive the Heydrich Medal for unswerving loyalty to the Reich."

The lights came up and Reece returned to his spot in front of the table, while the flat screen slid back up into the ceiling.

"As you can see, this year's going to be the hottest yet. National's depending on us to get everyone excited. Simms, I want you and Roberts to handle the stations in Occupied Texas and Oklahoma. Make sure they get the promos and copies of the tapes on Kruger and Mannheim. Both of these guys are 'Old Guard' and are getting the Heydrich Medal. We've got to make sure the 'Great Unwashed' are informed, right?"

Everyone began to chuckle.

"Wiley?"

"What was that, Dunham?" Reece said, his lip curling in displeasure.

Jack stared wide-eyed toward the front of the room, sweat pouring down the sides of his face. He hadn't known why he'd said that. He'd just been sitting there when he got this overwhelming feeling, a feeling that felt as though the world was all twisted up, as if everything was wrong. For some inexplicable reason, this name had popped into his head and out of his mouth before he could stop himself.

"Speak up, Dunham, we don't have all day."

Jack shook his head.

"Sorry, Reece. Just thinking out loud."

Reece scowled and went back to his instructions. Jack was barely aware of anything after that, his mind racing with strange thoughts. Who was Wiley? Why had he said the man's name? Was he going nuts, was the pressure of the job finally catching up with him?

"...and Dunham will coordinate with all of you, got that?" Reece said.

Everyone murmured his assent. Reece nodded and walked toward the door. "All right. Let's get to it."

Jack followed everyone out of the conference room and trudged toward his office. His head throbbed with every step, and the world seemed to tilt on its axis, making him dizzy. Maybe he needed a vacation. He'd been planning a trip to the Caribbean colonies later this year. Maybe he should take it now. Jamaica would be great this time of year and Leslie would love it. But who was he kidding? Reece would throw a fit if he tried to leave now. He was supposed to coordinate something for Heroes Day, and Reece would never allow him the time off. Vacation would just have to wait. Now, if he could only remember what the hell the fat slob had asked him to do.

"Hey, Dunham. You okay?"

Jack turned and saw the familiar wry grin and tight skirt. Malloy.

"Hi, Denise. How are you?"

"I'm fine. But you look like you're gonna blow chunks."

Another wave of dizziness washed over Jack, causing him to collapse against the corridor wall. Alarmed, Denise came to him, took his arm, and held him up. Her perfume, normally an understated sexy affair, now smelled cloying, overpowering. Jack had to swallow back the bile that rose in his throat. Denise grabbed his arm and put it around her neck and walked him around the corner to her office.

"Christ, Jack, you gotta stop those lunches at Mike's," she said, straining under his weight. She helped him to the small leather couch, propping his head with a leather-covered pillow.

"You're all heart, Malloy."

Denise's office reflected her personality—contradictory. On one hand it had been tastefully decorated in a sort of feminine power mode: sturdy modern furniture in glass and steel that bespoke of a woman who knew what she was doing and did it very well. Unfortunately, the effect was undermined by the hundreds of troll dolls that sat on every surface, their big, round eyes and fright-wig hair an unnerving sight to anyone who entered. Jack knew they were staring at him, mocking him with their droll grins.

Denise went over to a tiny refrigerator and opened a *Sprudel-Gut* Cola, poured a small amount into two paper cups. She then pulled out a bottle of vodka and poured a liberal amount into hers.

Jack stared in disbelief. "A little early, don't you think?"

Denise handed the nonalcoholic cola to Jack, her mouth twisted in a wry smirk. "You have Reece for a boss, and you ask me that?"

"No thanks. I can't—"

"Knock it back. It'll settle your stomach."

Jack scowled, grabbed the proffered cup, and took a small sip. It tasted good. He swallowed the rest and held out the cup.

"Not yet. You gotta let your stomach take it in small doses."

"Just like you?" Jack said, smiling. He felt better already.

"Hah, hah, Dunham. You always did play hard to get."

Denise turned one of the chairs in front of her desk and sat down, her legs crossing provocatively. Denise Malloy was one great-looking woman. She and Jack had flirted with each other for years and had finally fallen into bed after the last Christmas party. The sex had been great, but later, though it was tempting, each agreed that to jeopardize their working relationship would be foolish. The truth was they liked each other too much as friends, and for Denise it had been a revenge lay. Her lover, a girl from secretarial, had run off with another woman the week before the party.

"And I thought you were just using me."

"Hell, Jack, you know I like it both ways. And you were one hell of a great way to forget that little *nutte*."

Jack smiled. "Thanks. You ever hear from her?"

It was Denise's turn to smile. It was not a friendly one.

"That bimbo she ran off with dumped her in Acapulco."

"But—"

"Yeah, I know," she said, her smile widening. "It got a little hot down there."

"Remind me to treat you nice from now on."

"You always do," she said, her voice warm and throaty. She grabbed his arm and squeezed gently. "If Leslie ever does you wrong, you come to Momma Malloy and she'll make everything better... I'll rip her heart out. Want some more *Sprudel-Gut?*"

"Please."

She went back to the refrigerator and refilled his cup and dumped another couple of fingers of vodka into her own. "So, what do you think of all this Heroes Day stuff?"

"You mind telling me what Reece is assigning me?"

She chuckled, her eyes slightly glazed.

"You really *were* out of it, weren't you?"

She handed him the cup.

Jack shook his head, clearing the last of the fog.

"I'll tell you. It was the weirdest feeling. You ever feel like you were two places at once?"

Denise tilted her head, her eyebrows furrowed.

"Yeah, I know it sounds nuts, but there I was watching that tape and when I saw Kruger, I suddenly began feeling really strange, like I remembered him from somewhere. Funny thing is, I know I've never met him before. Weird, huh?"

"Not really. He reminded you of someone."

Jack shook his head.

"I don't think so, the guy's too distinctive looking. I'd know if he reminded me of my uncle Fred or someone I knew."

He paused.

"Do you know anyone named Wiley, Denise?"

She shook her head, her frown deepening.

"No, should I?"

"No," Jack said, sighing, "I suppose not. But at the same time I was getting those weird feelings about Kruger, this name popped into my head. Snap. There it was. Just like that."

"You sure as hell tweaked Reece."

Jack smiled again.

"One good thing to come out of it, anyway."

Jack stood up, feeling a hundred percent better.

"Well, looks like Momma Malloy's remedy worked."

"You can't doubt the Irish," she said. "It's against the law."

"Whose law is that?"

"Mine."

Jack laughed and gave her a friendly hug.

"Thanks for the shoulder, Denise. I appreciate it."

"Anytime, gorgeous, anytime."

Jack opened the door and walked into the hallway. He was halfway to his office when he realized he still didn't know what Reece had ordered him to do.

"Shit. What a wonderful day this turned out to be."

He walked into his office, shut the door, and plopped into his cushy, leather swivel chair.

Fuck it, he thought. If he knew Reece at all, the man would be in and out of his office all day, changing his mind about this or that. Jack would find out what his assignment was about ten times over from that obstreperous little *depp*.

He turned and looked out the window and sighed. Everything looked familiar, but nothing felt the same.

"Who are you, Wiley?" he whispered.

Somehow, he knew the answer to that question was terribly important, and if he could find that answer, it would change his life. And Jack was just beginning to realize that change was just what he needed.

8

Miami, Florida
15 April 1994

"*Hey, shithead, how the hell are you?*"
"Jack, are you all right?"
"Huh, what?"
"Are you all right? You look pale."

Jack looked up from his plate of food and into Leslie's vibrant, green eyes. Those eyes, so seductive at other times, were now full of concern.

"I'm fine, sweetheart. I think I'm coming down with something." Jack smiled or tried to. He didn't think he was very convincing. Where had that voice come from? Was he losing his mind?

Her smile, warm and sweet, reassured him.

"You work too hard."

"Well, you know Reece."

She frowned. "I wish I didn't. Did I tell you he made a pass at me?"

This got Jack's attention. "What?"

"Don't worry. I wouldn't dream of taking that toad up on it. Besides, it was before we met."

"When was that?"

"At the Party meeting in February. He was the guest speaker."

"Reece?"

"Don't look so surprised. He's quite well thought of in Party circles. You'd know if you attended the meetings."

Her not-so-subtle disapproval annoyed Jack. It must have showed on his face because she quickly changed the subject, partially anyway.

"So, tell me about this morning. I want to hear all about it."

Jack shrugged.

"Nothing much to tell. We watched a tape on Werner Kruger and then Reece—"

"Werner Kruger!"

"Yeah. You *know* him?"

"He's a dream!"

"Leslie, he's old enough to be your grandfather, for crying out loud. Where the hell do you know him from?"

Leslie chuckled, her soft, husky laugh coming from deep within her throat. Normally, it drove Jack crazy with desire. Now it pissed him off.

"Oh, Jack, relax. My boss introduced us a couple of years back when Herr Kruger came through looking at factory sites. All the *Gauleiters* vied for the chance to wine and dine him. My boss won, and I accompanied them to dinner. He was a charming old man. Very continental."

"He make a pass at you too?"

"As a matter of fact—no. But I have to admit, he *was* tempting."

"Well, I think he's a creep."

Leslie's eyes popped open and she leaned forward, her mouth set hard. "Be quiet, Jack!" she hissed.

Jack suddenly remembered where they were and felt a rush of anxiety. State Security was everywhere. Though he and Leslie came to this small, cozy trattoria every week, and were known to all the waiters and the owner, any one of them could be an SS plant.

"I'm sorry," Jack said. "Today was really weird, and I'm still feeling strange."

"What is it? Tell me," she said, her tone softening.

Jack leaned back in his chair, picked up his glass of Chianti, and drained it. He signaled the waiter, who brought the bottle and refilled both of their glasses. Jack waited until the man walked away.

"You ever feel that everything you know is wrong?"

He told her about seeing Kruger and all the strange feelings that washed over him since that moment. Somehow, by telling her the whole story, he began to feel a sense of relief. It didn't last long.

"I don't think you should be confiding in that Malloy woman."

"Why not? She's a friend."

"Jack, she's not to be trusted."

"*I* trust her."

"None of those people can be trusted."

"Just what the hell does *that* mean?"

"You know what I mean. People of her persuasion are unreliable, fickle. The Party doesn't sanction—"

"You're just jealous because she and I had a one-night stand before you and I met."

"Jack, she's a lesbian."

"Bisexual."

"It doesn't matter."

"It does to her," Jack said, smiling rakishly.

"She's being watched. Stay away from her."

Stunned, Jack lurched forward.

"How do you *know* that?" he asked, his eyes narrowing.

A momentary look of alarm passed over her features.

"My boss got a memo from Party headquarters in Washington last week. Now that the Negro resettlement is winding down, he was cautioned to begin looking into homosexuals on his staff. It's the new policy, Jack. They're *all* being watched."

"Wonderful."

"Just please promise me you won't hang around her."

"I have to work with her, for Christ's sake!"

"If I know Reece, it won't be for long."

"Shit."

"I'm sorry, honey, I know she's a friend, but we have to follow Party policy. It's the right thing to do."

"Is it?"

Leslie gazed at him levelly. "Yes," she said.

Jack felt even worse than he had earlier that day. How could he face Malloy in the office and not tell her? How could he look into her eyes and not say anything? He'd feel like a traitor if he kept quiet. He'd *be* one if he opened his mouth.

"Promise me, Jack."

"What?" he said, snapping out of his reverie.

"Promise me you'll act like nothing is wrong when you're in the office."

"Why should that matter to you?"

"Because I care about you and I don't want to see you get hurt because of that woman. She's not worth it. Christ! The thought of you and her together makes my hair curl."

"four point seven out of ten!"

Jack's breath caught in his throat, his eyes bugged out, and big beads of sweat popped out along his hairline.

Leslie's eyes widened, her anger turning to fright.

"Jack! What's wrong? JACK!" She turned her head, looking desperately for help. "Somebody help us, something's wrong with my friend!"

Jack tried to speak but could only manage a strangled gargle. He looked at her, feeling helpless. He could see a tear running out of her left eye. The other patrons sat in their chairs, silly expressions of horror and distaste frozen on their faces.

None of them moved a muscle.

Suddenly, the room telescoped, making everyone look far away and distorted, as if Jack were looking through a fish-eye lens. His throat loosened and he was finally able to speak.

"Curly," he said, and fainted facedown into his pasta.

※　※　※

He awoke in an ambulance as it sped down Collins Avenue toward Hoffman Memorial Hospital. The oxygen mask on his face smelled faintly of rubbing alcohol, and his head throbbed. The EMT, seated next to the collapsible gurney he lay on, turned from a bank of beeping monitors and gazed at him impassively.

"He's conscious," she said, looking back toward the driver.

Jack felt the ambulance slow and the siren cut off in mid-wail. The red lights remained on, sweeping the buildings on either side of the street. The EMT took a small penlight out of her pocket and flashed it in his eyes.

"Pupils moderately reactive."

She then took his pulse.

"What's your name?"

"Jack Dunham."

"Where do you live?"

"Uhh, four forty-four Brickell Avenue."

BILL WALKER

"Who's the *Führer?*"

"Bill Clinton."

"Huh?"

The EMT frowned and turned back toward the driver.

"Pick it up. He's still out of it. Might be an aneurysm."

Jack felt his heart beating faster. His mouth was dry and cottony, and his head ached even more than it had before. What the hell had happened? How could he have stroked out at his age? He moved his face, feeling that everything seemed to work all right. Nothing felt numb. He then tried to move his body and felt the heavy, webbed straps holding him down. Oh, Christ. What was wrong with him?

The world spun around and he passed out.

✳ ✳ ✳

"Mr. Dunham, can you hear me? Can you hear me, Mr. Dunham?"

Another light flashed in his eyes, causing him to open them.

"Ah, Mr. Dunham, you're awake."

"I am now," he said.

The man he took to be his doctor stood in front of him wearing one of those headbands with the mirrors on them. He smiled benignly, the sarcasm of Jack's remark going right past him. He was about fifty, short and balding; he looked a little like Peter Lorre after he got fat. The man smiled and the resemblance grew stronger. He smelled of garlic. Jack noticed a gold-wreathed Party badge pinned to his smock. One of the original hundred thousand to join the American Nazi Party, which formed immediately after the surrender of the Allies in 1944. Of course, this man was too young, possibly an infant at the time. Probably a gift from his father.

"How are you feeling?"

"Like someone kicked me in the head." Jack said, rubbing his temples. "Did I have a—"

"Stroke? Goodness no. You fainted. We ran every test imaginable while you were unconscious. We'd still like to do an MRI, but we need you awake for that."

"Well, Doctor..."

"Forgive me," he said, clicking his heels together. "I am *Doktor* Johann Manstein."

Jack sat up, prompting the doctor to adjust the tilt of the bed.

"Well, *Doktor* Manstein, If I fainted, why do I have this colossal headache?"

The doctor smiled, as if indulging a not-too-bright child.

"We don't know. We are looking to see if there are any organic reasons for your spell, as it were, but so far"—he shrugged—"nothing."

"If it's all the same to you, I'd prefer to go home."

"As you wish. We'll keep you overnight, and if nothing else has manifested, you may leave in the morning."

Jack thought the little man looked disappointed that he wouldn't get the chance to poke and prod him more.

"Thanks, Doc," Jack said.

The doctor bowed again and left the room. Jack settled back down into the bed and let his mind wander. He looked about the semi-private room, noting that the screen was drawn around the other bed. He could hear the rhythmic pumping of an artificial respirator and the steady beep of a cardiac monitor. *Wonder what that poor dummkopf's in for.* Not overly curious, he picked up the remote for the TV and clicked it on. Just the usual daytime drivel designed to keep housewives happy and sell the requisite amount of *reinigungsmittel*. In a word: boring. He stopped on NNN and watched the headlines. Acapulco had fallen. Reporters blathered about kill ratios, while shell-shocked Mexican refugees filed past the cameras, their

backs bowed under the burdens of their remaining worldly posses-
sions. What they carried amounted to a pitiful few items tied into
meager bundles.

Jack thought of Malloy's ex-lover and wondered if she'd gotten
out. He then thought of Malloy and the previous evening came back
in a rush. Just before he'd fainted, he saw the image of a big, red-
haired man slamming his hand on a table. He could still remember
what the man said.

"four point seven out of ten."

What the hell did it mean? *four point seven* out of ten what?
four point seven out of ten doktors *agree that new* Präparat-H *helped
stop the itching and swelling of* hämorrhoiden. Somehow, Jack didn't
think it was that. Frowning, he remembered what he said before
passing out.

"Curly."

Who the fuck was Curly? Jack started laughing as he remembered watching the Three Stooges on TV as a kid before they were
banned as having an unhealthy influence on children. Jack knew the
real reasons from the underground copies he'd seen in college: Hitler had hated Moe Howard's uncanny imitation of him.

A nurse walked into the room bearing a tray with medication.

"Hello, Mr. Dunham," she said, smiling brightly. "Time for your
medication."

Jack started to put up a stink, then thought better of it. This
nurse looked no older than twenty. With her blonde hair, cute-as-a-
button nose, full lips, and perfect teeth, he couldn't refuse.

"This isn't going to knock me out, will it?" he asked, giving the
cup of pills a dubious look.

"No, sir. We'll wake you at oh-two hundred to give you a pill."

Jack raised his eyebrows in mild surprise. He wasn't going to pursue that one. Hardly anything hospitals did made any sense anyway. He took the pills and swallowed them, draining the small cup of water.

"Goodnight, Mr. Dunham."

The nurse smiled again and twitched her cute butt out the door.

They'd better keep her the hell out of the cardiac ward.

He imagined all the cardiac monitors flatlining as she walked by scores of gasping old men, chuckled, and went back to flipping channels on the TV.

"Hi there, handsome."

Denise Malloy stood in the doorway, holding a big teddy bear.

"I brought you a sleeping companion," she said, crossing the room. She stopped at the foot of his bed and placed the bear at his feet, so it sat staring at him. Its plastic eyes reflected the flickering of one of the fluorescent lights, making it look nearly alive.

"How'd you get in here, Malloy? Visiting hours are over."

She smiled slyly. "That nurse who just left here? I came on to her. Made a date in exchange for after-hours visiting privileges."

She shrugged. "*I* thought it was fair."

He must have looked silly with his mouth hanging open, because she began to laugh.

"Come on, Dunham, you know me by now. I was diplomatic about it. And besides, I always go for these blonde, bimbo types. At least Cecily has some brains too."

"Cecily?"

"Yeah, I know. Nobody's perfect. Anyway, how are you?"

"I'm fine," Jack said, still in shock over what Malloy said. He couldn't get the image of her and this cute nurse out of his mind. To tell the truth, it kind of turned him on.

He cleared his throat.

"How did you know I was in here?" he asked.

"Believe it or not, Leslie told me. I called your house to get those demographics that Reece wants for tomorrow. And she was there. I don't think she likes me too much, Jack. She was real *erkältung*. You tell her about us?"

"Well, uhh..."

Malloy nodded. "That's what I thought. I never could stand to know about my lovers' old flames either. Male or female. I guess she and I have something in common after all."

Jack wondered how Leslie got into his place and what she was doing there. He hadn't asked her to move in yet. Then he realized the hospital must have given her his effects, keys included.

He turned back to Malloy and noted the tender gleam in her eye. It only made him feel guiltier for what he knew. He struggled for a brief moment about whether or not to tell her and decided to hell with it.

"Anybody over there?" he said, nodding toward the other bed.

"Just some old guy hooked up to a million tubes. He's out like a light."

"Come here," he said.

Her eyes narrowed suspiciously. "Jack?"

Jack sighed.

"Get your mind out of the gutter, Malloy, and come over here."

She walked over to the side of the bed and sat on the hard-backed chair next to it. He took one more look toward the other bed and gestured for her to lean closer.

"I don't know why I'm doing this, but I guess I've had a bellyful of everything lately. During dinner, Leslie told me her boss got a memo from Washington detailing a crackdown on homosexuals. She told me you were being watched."

"You through?"

"Yeah," he said, puzzled.

"I know."

"YOU KNOW!"

"Ssssh!" she said, looking around the room.

"You know?" he said, his voice a hoarse whisper.

"Yeah, Jack. It was only a matter of time."

"Well, excuse me if I appear to be an idiot, but doesn't that worry you?"

"You ever hear of The Lambda Army?"

Jack frowned.

"No, I didn't expect you would've." She leaned forward. "The Lambda Army is an organization of gay and bisexual men and women dedicated to freedom of thought and expression."

"Gay?"

"We were tired of being called faggot, dyke, and all those other awful names, so we decided to give one to ourselves. Anyway, we're tied in with the ARM—"

"Shit, Malloy, those guys don't just meet in cellars and print pamphlets, they blow up innocent people with their bombs."

"Propaganda, Jack. You remember in your history classes reading about the Reichstag fire?"

"Yeah, so what?"

"Hitler ordered it set. Proved to be what put him over the top."

"How do you know?"

"Because the people of The American Resistance Movement have been keeping the *true* history. None of the bombs they set were anywhere near where people congregated. Only at factories that made weaponry, like Kruger's, and *only* after-hours."

"But the bombing at Miami High School. The ARM took responsibility for that."

Malloy shook her head, her frizzy locks bouncing chaotically.

BILL WALKER

"The Party did it, Jack. They want to discredit us, keep us from building popular support. It worked with you."

"But—"

"You've known me a long time. Hell, I don't just jump into bed with anybody. Would I lie to you?"

And right then, he knew she was telling the truth. Malloy, with all her bravado and smart remarks, was no dummy. She always cut to the heart of a situation and called it for what it was.

"Shit."

"Listen, if you want, I can get you in touch with our contact with ARM. He's a lawyer up north. He'll be in town a week from Monday. Officially, he's here on Party business, but he's really here to brief us on what the other cells are doing and to give us new orders. How about I set you up?

"What's his name?"

Malloy leaned closer and whispered.

"His name is Fred Williams, but everybody calls him Curly."

It all came back to Jack Dunham in the blink of an eye. In that split second of time, a whole other lifetime of memories ripped into his conscious mind like a torrent, like a tidal wave washing away a village in the South Seas. It came on so fast, it blinded him. Jack gripped his head and screamed. His tortured shrieks brought the whole shift running with every medical device imaginable. He kept screaming while they strapped him down and injected him with a heavy dose of Seconal. Only then did his voice die away into an agonized sobbing and finally, to an eerie silence.

Just before the drug blotted out the conscious world, he saw Denise slip from the room, pale and trembling, and looking as if she'd lost her best friend.

She couldn't have known how close to the truth that really was.

9

Miami, Florida
22 April 1994

" I don't think you should be going to work, Jack. You've had a very rough time. You need rest," Leslie said when they pulled out of the hospital's parking lot.

She was right about that. It had been a week of hell. After his "Awakening," for that was what he called it, an abrupt return to consciousness after forty-three years of ignorant bliss, the doctors put Jack through every flaming hoop imaginable. There were blood tests, neurological tests, cell degeneration tests, tests to test the tests' reliability, x-rays, scans, and enemas every day at 1300 hours. Old Peter Lorre was having the time of his life. Jack hoped he never really got sick. God knows what they'd do then.

After all of that, Dr. Manstein released Jack at 0700 the following Monday with two prescriptions and a big smile on his face. He'd gotten his damn MRI after all.

"Are you listening to me? I don't want you going to work today."

"Leslie, I'm fine. Hell, the doctors had a field day for a week, they didn't find a thing. I need to *do* something."

"No, you don't. You've had a trauma and you're going home."

97

Jack was in no mood to argue. He would just let her drop him off and then do whatever the hell he wanted.

"Fine. Just take me home," he said.

She stared at him, her brows furrowed in concern. He knew he should be grateful she cared, but right now all he wanted was to get away from her. Ever since the night at the restaurant, she'd become different somehow—bossy and meddlesome. Every moment she visited him felt like a subtle inquisition. Besides that, what she'd told him about Malloy still rankled him.

"I called Reece and he said it was all right for you to take some time off."

This really surprised Jack.

"I'll bet that was a Kodak moment," he said.

"Now, Jack, you really don't give him credit. He's a reasonable man—"

"Reece? Reasonable? Are you sure we're talking about the same person? Jesus Christ, Leslie! The other night at dinner you were calling him a toad."

"I know, but I was angry about that Malloy woman, and he did apologize for his behavior at the Party meeting, said he'd had too much to drink."

"Now *that* sounds like the Reece I know."

"Anyway, he said it was okay for you to take off next week. They'd get someone to take up the slack for you."

"Great," Jack said angrily, sliding down into his seat. He actually had no intention of ever going back to the Ministry again. Not now, not ever.

They crossed over the Julia Tuttle Causeway and turned left onto Biscayne. An old man dozed on one of the bus benches and a piece of tattered newspaper blew along the gutter. The streets were just waking up, the traffic still light. Being Monday, the road would be clogged with cars in less than an hour. Hard to believe it could ever be this peaceful.

In the distance, the traffic signals blinked in unison from red to green, like a line of ever-vigilant soldiers marching cadence. He reached over to the dash, turned off the air conditioning and opened the passenger window, letting the warm wind blow in. The air smelled of hibiscus interlaced with the aromas of saltwater and gasoline fumes.

Morning.

Even as a small boy growing up in Connecticut, he'd loved this time of day, a time when the sun was low, and the shadows were long. He would get up early every day, make bread and butter sandwiches and take a walk around the neighborhood. While chewing on his makeshift breakfast, he marveled at the rich smells of new-mown grass, the sparkle of everything under a crystalline coat of morning dew, the cheery sounds of birds singing to each other, and the buzz of countless insects. In the newness of each day, the whole world belonged just to him.

"What're you thinking?" Leslie said.

"Oh, nothing. Just bygone days and lost youth," he said, a wistful smile playing across his face.

He'd expected a smile or a cute remark, but not the blank look he got.

Soon they came to the drawbridge, which marked the transition from Biscayne to Brickell Avenue. Fortunately, the subs were not yet on their way out to sea. The tires made a roaring sound when they drove over the metal bridge, and he thought he saw a flying fish splash in the river. The bridge was deserted.

Thirty years before, middle-aged black men with their bamboo fishing poles stood shoulder to shoulder, laughing and drinking their beer from paper bags, trying to catch their lunch. They'd had all been resettled. And now Jack knew what that meant. He knew the Resettlement was a sham, like everything he'd ever been taught. Names like *Auschwitz, Dauchau,* and *Treblinka* came to mind. What were their names here, he wondered? Where were the death camps here?

Jack still marveled at the two lives he carried in his brain, still half-believed he'd gone insane. But he knew that was not the case. That other life, the one where Hitler had died in 1945 in a bunker in a bombed-out Berlin, where Nazis were only a hated fringe group, where freedom of speech was guaranteed, where no one need fear their government—that other life was *real.* He'd lived it as surely as he was now living this one.

He remembered Wiley and all their times together growing up: scraped knees, first loves, high school and college, their first jobs at the agency, joining the Anderson Club, Armand Bock, the Nine Old Men, Werner Kruger, Chessman, and... Curly Williams.

The meeting was tonight, somewhere in Coconut Grove, and Jack intended to be there come hell or high water. He *had* to know if Curly remembered as well. He *had* to know for sure that all he remembered wasn't really the result of some busted blood vessel in his head that Peter Lorre couldn't find.

Leslie put on her turn signal and steered the car into the driveway of 444 Brickell. Jack nodded at the guard, who smiled and waved back, his arm making a lazy arc in the air. The car slowed under the pillared overhang in front of the glass entrance.

"Would you like me to come up?" she said.

He grasped her arm, leaned over, and kissed her lightly on the lips.

"That's okay. I think I want to take a nap."

She nodded, unable to hide the look of disappointment on her face. He felt guilty.

"I'll see you tonight?"

"Uhh, maybe we should take a rain check on that too," he said.

She nodded again as he climbed out of the Mazda and headed in through the glass doors. Leslie hesitated a moment, watching him, then stepped on the gas and rolled out of view.

The mailbox was jammed so full, he could barely pull anything out without ripping it. Inside were the usual Party circulars exhorting everyone to be vigilant against terrorists and wrong thinkers. *Christ. If they only knew.* There were also telephone and gas bills, the Party magazine *STRUGGLE,* and a get-well card from Denise. He smiled and shook his head. He was lucky to have such a good friend.

Good friend...

Suddenly, Wiley Carpenter's earnest face sprang up in his mind. Jack wondered if Wiley were still blissfully unaware of the past, the real past. He supposed Wiley would have tried to contact him in some way. Then again, maybe not. In the rigidly controlled society of Nazi America, all forms of communication were tightly monitored. No one could ever be sure their phones or faxes weren't tapped. And no one could travel as they had before World War Two. World... War... Two. He liked the sound of that. It sounded so much better than the pompous and ego-inflated "Great Struggle." Before that time, everyone could cross state lines, travel to other countries—do practically whatever they wanted. Now to travel anywhere required a ton of paperwork and a million rubber stamps.

America's institutions remained in name only. The constitution had been revised in 1946 after two years of repressive martial law. Curfews remained in effect for ten years. Only after the sixties did things settle down into this stifling homogeneous quagmire they called society.

God, the Sixties.

Both versions of that remarkable decade contrasted in his mind, like black on white. No Rock and Roll existed in this version of the present. Only state-sponsored drivel. There'd been no Elvis, no Beatles, no Rolling Stones, no Jimi Hendrix. Jack choked back a tear as he imagined that great guitarist dying in some unnamed concentration camp, where all his people had no doubt perished.

Driving those thoughts from his mind, Jack stepped into the high-speed elevator.

"Floor, please."

The sterile, electronic voice sounded especially annoying at this moment.

"Fuck you, please," Jack said.

"That request does not correlate. Please state your—"

"All right, all right," Jack said, feeling foolish. "Fifty."

"Voice print access accepted. Thank you, Mr. Dunham."

The elevator shot up the shaft, making Jack light-headed. He watched the LED readout scrolling through the numbers, so fast the individual digits blurred into each other. Presently, it slowed and stopped, the steel doors sliding open with a hiss.

Pulling out his keys, he walked to his door, stopping halfway there.

It was open.

Jack looked up and down the hallway, afraid the burglar might still be there, then decided to risk it. He walked inside and glanced around. Nothing appeared out of place, but State Security were experts at searching. With their highly specialized Search and Seizure Team, they could go through someone's entire house in an hour and leave virtually no trace of their presence. A sweat broke out on his forehead. If they'd been here, what were they looking for?

"Hi, Jack."

He whirled around and saw Denise standing in the doorway leading to his bedroom, her eyes like round saucers. She had a glass in her hand and even across the room he could see she'd been drinking. His eyes swiveled to the bar, where his previously unopened bottle of Thulian Vodka was now half-empty.

"*Gott*, Malloy. You want to give me a cardiac? What are you doing here?"

She crossed the room and stumbled into his arms. Her hair smelled of lavender and fermented potatoes.

"Whoa, hold on, what is this?"

"Oh, God, Jack. I'm sorry," she sobbed. "State Security came this morning. I barely got out the window. I—I think they got Cecily."

"How, why?"

"I don't know, I don't know what to think or who to believe. I think maybe Cecily ratted me out."

Jack shook his head. He still felt woozy.

"Wait a minute. I thought you said they got her?"

"We had loads of time to get out. She wouldn't go, said something about stalling them. Jack, we both could've gotten clean away."

"Jeez, I'm sorry."

"Me too. She didn't use her head." Denise took a deep breath. "Can I stay here? At least until the meeting?"

"What about after that?"

"You don't need to worry about that."

Jack gripped her shoulders. "I do worry. What are you going to do?"

"It's time for me to get out—go underground. Lambda has a network that will get me to Canada. A lot of us are there now. They'll take care of everything."

"You want some coffee?"

"Please."

Denise sat on the small couch while Jack went into the tiny kitchen. Soon the heavenly odor of coffee laced with vanilla beans filled the apartment. Jack brought out two cups, handing one to Denise. She sipped it and sighed.

"Oh, that tastes good."

Jack sat next to her and put his feet up on the glass coffee table.

"So how did you get up here, Malloy? Make a date with the guard?"

She held up a key.

"Don't you remember Christmas?"

"Except for you, most of it's a blank."

She smiled then, erasing the recently etched worry lines from her face.

"Well, let me refresh you. After the party we came back here, and you pressed this into my hand while professing your undying love."

"You make it sound so silly."

"It was, but it was also very sweet."

"What about the elevator?"

"You used your access card to add my voice code."

Jack shook his head and smiled. Sometimes recklessness paid off.

"Well, I'm glad you had this place to come to. I'm glad you're here."

"Me too," she said, grabbing his hand.

THE NORMANDY CLUB

It was suddenly very hard to breathe. He looked into her eyes and saw both fear and desire there. He also noticed for the first time that there were bright green flecks inside the blue of her irises, and that she had a light smattering of freckles across her nose.

Before he knew it, he was kissing her. Her lips felt warm, soft, urgent pressed against his. He felt her tongue wash over his, probing, almost desperate. She moaned deep in her throat, then pulled away.

"Jack, we don't have to—"

"Ssssh," he said, putting a finger to her lips. "Come on."

He took her into the bedroom and he slowly, deliberately, stripped her of clothes. She trembled at his touch, something that really turned him on. Shedding his own clothes, he came to her, their bodies melting into each other. She was not as tall or as amply endowed as Leslie, but her taut, muscular body—the result of hours of workouts with free-weights—felt perfectly at home against his, like a second skin. He kissed her neck, licked her large, brown nipples, and ran his hand down to her thick, dusky mane of pubic hair. His hand teased the soft lips of her vagina and she moaned again, louder, more insistent. Breaking the embrace, Denise pushed him back onto the bed, straddled him, and guided him into her warm wetness.

She thrust, slowly at first, a look of closed-eyed ecstasy on her face. Licking her lips, she pumped faster. Jack thrust upward to meet her, his hands on her slim, curvaceous hips. They both moaned as the pace increased. Suddenly she threw back her head and screamed, then collapsed onto him, spent and sweating.

Jack turned her over and began to kiss her all over her body. He reveled in the muscular lines of her arms. He ran his tongue down the tautly defined muscles of her stomach, each one standing out like a washboard. Writhing, she parted her legs, allowing him access. He bent down and lost himself within her.

✖ ✖ ✖

"You know, you really know how to wear a guy out," Jack said, smiling lazily.

It was now late afternoon. They'd spent the entire day exploring each other's bodies and now, as the sun sank in the west, he felt a warm glow spread through him that he'd never felt before.

"That's because you're in such lousy shape, Dunham."

"Yeah, but what a way to go."

"Oh, brother."

He kissed her and looked into her eyes.

"Marry me, Malloy."

She sat bolt upright, the sheet falling away, exposing her breasts.

"What!"

"Marry me. We'll live in Montreal, eat wine and cheese, make babies."

"Jack, have you lost your mind? What about Leslie?"

His face clouded over. "She doesn't matter anymore. Maybe she never did."

She stared at him, her mouth hanging open in shock.

"You're serious, aren't you?"

"Dead serious."

"Aw, shit, Jack," she said, tears coming to her eyes.

He sat up and put his arms around her. "What's so wrong with that? I love you. And I'm pretty damn sure you love me."

"Damnit, I *do* love you. But you know what I am."

"I don't care."

She looked at him then, her eyes probing his. Jack suddenly felt more naked than he'd ever been.

"Tell me something," she said. "Could you ever share me?"

"I—uhh."

"No, Jack. Tell me the truth. Could you share me with other women? Because I can't give them up. Loving women is part of me. Could you come home at night expecting to find me and, instead, find that I was out with one of my girlfriends?"

"I could try," he said.

She smiled wistfully, caressed his face, and kissed him lightly on the lips.

"You're a liar," she whispered.

He looked out the window, unable to respond to that, knowing in his heart she was right.

"You're also the most wonderful man I've ever known, Jack Dunham. If I could ever be completely straight, I'd marry you in a heartbeat. But—"

"I know," he said, fighting back his own urge to cry. Why did he have to be such a sentimental idiot?

She squeezed his hand and glanced toward the digital clock radio.

"We'd better get going. The meeting starts in an hour."

10

Coconut Grove, Florida
22 April 1994

"Where'd you say this place is?" Jack said, trying to see through the overhanging trees. They had passed through the main drag of Coconut Grove and were now on a narrow two-lane road that led into Coral Gables, the name of which he'd forgotten. In his other life the Grove had been a lively village, with quaint streets lined with cafes and art galleries, and filled with a decidedly mixed crowd of bohemian artists, ex-hippies, yuppie entrepreneurs, society matrons having lunch, and pretty girls in T-back bikinis.

Here the streets lay deserted, bathed in the sickly-peach glow of crime lights. Garbage lined the streets and every storefront lay in shadow, its glass replaced by rotting plywood bearing the stenciled legend: Gerhard's Board-Ups/305-555-7672. This had been a ghetto for the Blacks, much like the one in Liberty City. And like that other place, it was now a ghost town.

"The meeting's been moved," she said, glancing repeatedly in her rearview.

Presently, they found themselves on a small residential cul-de-sac lined with cars. A house at the end, lining the small turnaround, had all its lights on and music pouring out its windows. The music, Jack noted, was the typical state-sponsored crap that somehow remained popular in spite of its mindlessness. Denise pulled into one of the few empty spots.

"Won't this party attract attention? I'd think your people would be nervous about that."

Denise smiled. "Hell, Jack, the party's our cover. This is the meeting."

"*This* is the meeting?"

"Close your mouth, Dunham, and let's go."

When they approached the house, Jack could hear people engaged in spirited chatter, punctuated here and there by someone's hyena-like laughter. It clearly sounded like everyone was having a great time. Through the window, he saw people dancing and eating. Jack's stomach growled. At least he'd get something in his stomach.

They reached the front door and Denise knocked. Three knocks in rapid succession followed by two slow knocks.

Jack saw the light behind the view port on the door go out, indicating someone was giving them the once-over. A moment later, the door swung open.

"Welcome to Lambda, Jack," Denise said.

If he'd looked shocked earlier, nothing could compare to what he must have looked like now. The living room was empty. In the center of the room stood a complex array of video projectors pointed at all the windows. Jack noted that each window had been taped over with rear screen projection material. He could now see the reverse of the scene he saw while approaching the house. Even in here, the illusion was astounding. Outside, it was perfect.

"Incredible," he said, turning back to Denise. She stood next to a tall, lanky fellow who looked entirely average except for the bright, red lipstick he wore.

"Jack, this is Henry Geddings, head of Lambda's Miami chapter. Henry, this is Jack."

Henry held out his hand in the manner of women expecting it to be kissed. Feeling a tad awkward, Jack took the hand, surprised when the grip turned out to be inordinately firm.

"Glad to meet you, Henry."

"Denise, you never told me he was a charmer. You've been keeping secrets."

"That's right, Henry, and he's my secret. Tell all your friends that it's hands off."

Henry smiled, revealing perfect, capped teeth.

"But of course, my dear, we're all friends here. Especially tonight."

"Uhh, excuse me," Jack said. "But where is everybody?"

"Ahh, we still have you fooled, eh?" Henry said. "Follow thus into our secret garden."

"He's a frustrated actor," Denise whispered. "Humor him."

Jack smiled and waved his hand in a flourish.

"Lead on, MacPoof," he said.

"Ah, a wit! I know we shall get on infamously."

Denise shook her head in mock disgust and Jack shrugged as they followed Henry into a small den lined with bookshelves. This room also had a projector pointed at the window. The image was of a man snoring contentedly as he slept on a small love seat. The sound emanated from a small speaker hidden behind a plant.

Henry smiled. "Guaranteed to make most people die of boredom. Everyone except for those shameless peepers in State Security. They'll watch anything."

As he spoke, he reached for a book and pulled it out. Jack heard a click and saw one of the bookshelves swing inward. Behind it lay a flight of stairs leading to the basement. A lone bulb lit the passageway that plunged steeply into the earth. They could hear the faint murmurings of many voices.

"I'm impressed," Jack said. "I didn't know the houses here had basements."

"Well, you remember that craziness in the sixties when everyone thought the Canadians were going to drop the bomb? Everyone built bomb shelters. The people who owned this one were clever about it. Shall we?"

Henry pointed the way and both Jack and Denise padded down the stairs, turning right at the bottom. Jack looked back up and saw Henry talking to a reed-thin man with acne scars on his face, a lookout no doubt. The other man nodded, then pecked Henry lightly on the lips and disappeared, closing the panel behind him. Henry joined them and they walked into the large, smoky room.

For Jack, this was the second surprise of the night. As soon as they walked in, he felt all eyes on him. Some smiled and some looked at him with open hostility, still others had a blank look. None of them were what State Security would have called normal. During the day, these men and women wore regular clothes, spoke and acted just like everyone else. Here, within the safety of a bomb shelter thirty feet underground, everyone felt free to be themselves. Jack saw two women kissing passionately, oblivious to all others around them. Most of the men wore heavy makeup, while the women preferred little to none. For Jack, the whole scene made him feel like the odd man out.

Henry walked to the front of the room while Jack and Denise took seats toward the back.

"Thank you all for coming. Without further delay, let me introduce to you our guest speaker. He is a renowned attorney by day, but by night he fights alongside his brothers and sisters in the American Resistance Movement. Ladies and gentlemen, Fred Williams."

Applause erupted throughout the room, loud and fervent. A man in the front row stood up, immediately dwarfing Henry. He had bushy, red hair and looked like a former football player.

"Curly," Jack whispered, tears coming to his eyes.

Denise leaned over, concern etched on her face.

"You okay, Jack?"

Jack smiled and joined the applause. "Never better, Malloy, never better."

Curly took his place on the makeshift stage, nodding and acknowledging the applause. He waved to a few he recognized. Soon the noise subsided and Curly cleared his throat.

"I'm sure you all know why I'm here," he said.

The room filled with murmuring.

"Well, let me tell you. It's worse than you can imagine. General Order Four, calling for the forced resettlement of all homosexuals and other undesirables will be in effect and commence on May fifteenth, *Heldentag*."

"Hell no, we won't go!" someone shouted.

For Jack, it was almost nostalgic. He suppressed the urge to smile. Curly continued.

"That's the right attitude, but the wrong way to go about it. We can't win if we go off half-cocked. For one thing, you need to know that Resettlement is a deception. No one has ever been resettled."

One of the women stood up.

"I got a letter from my lover just last week. It was postmarked from New Iberia."

Curly's expression saddened. "I'm sure you did, Rena. But I'm sad to say that is the only one you'll ever get."

The woman's eyes filled with tears. "How do you *know* that!" she screamed. "How can you stand up there and tell me that?"

Another woman came to her and put her arms around her. Jack swallowed, his throat feeling tight and scratchy.

"How many of you have black friends or lovers?" Curly asked. "Please, raise your hands. We're all friends here."

A good half of the room raised their hands.

"Have any of you received letters from Africa?"

About half the hands dropped.

"Any receive more than that one?"

No hands remained aloft. Rena sobbed quietly, her hands covering her face.

Curly continued.

"I have with me slides taken at Andersonville Concentration Camp a little over two weeks ago. I have to warn you, these photos are not pleasant. For any of you who have weak stomachs, I strongly urge you not to watch. We at the ARM have shown these at all our meetings to underscore the urgency of our cause. The time for open rebellion is coming, and if we are to emerge victorious, we must know the truth. Lights?"

The lights snapped off and the beam from the slide projector sliced the darkness. When the first image hit the screen, everyone gasped.

"Oh, God," Denise said.

Though they sickened him, the slides held much less shock value than for the others. Some cried openly, others stared in wide-eyed horror, still others ran from the room clutching their mouths, about to be sick. Jack stared, his expression grim.

It was all too familiar: the barbed wire, the hollow-eyed, living skeletons, the leering guards, the bodies. So many bodies. They lay heaped like cordwood, open-mouthed, eyes cloudy and sunken into their sockets. On a few, the expressions looked stunned, as if being dead were a total surprise. There was only one fundamental difference between these pictures and ones from Dachau or Auschwitz: the faces here were black.

The lights snapped back on and Curly returned to his place on the small stage. He scanned the crowd, his eyes sad but determined.

"I'm sorry you all had to see that," Curly said, "but make no mistake, *you are next*. It's too late for our black brothers and sisters. All but a few are gone."

Rena began to wail, her sobs wracking her small body. Denise gripped Jack's hand like a vise.

Curly continued. "Tonight, we are going to break into our cadres and go over the plan. Weapons are on the way from Canada. We are going to strike on Heroes Day. We will show these Nazi pigs just what real heroes are made of!"

"Yes!" someone stood and shouted. The rest were on their feet in an instant, their voices roaring their assent. Curly stepped down from the stage and melted into the crowd surrounding him, patting him on the back and cheering their approval. The rush of warmth and good feelings washed away the earlier moments of fear and horror. Everyone's eyes shone with hope and fervor reborn.

Denise turned to Jack. "Come on. I'll take you to meet him."

They pushed their way through the throng and Jack found his stomach filled with butterflies. Would Curly know him? In a moment they stood next to the big man who had his back to them as he spoke with two women dressed identically in black. A second later he turned and saw Denise.

"Denise!" he said, taking her into a bear hug. "How's my favorite subversive?"

She smiled, blushing a deep red. This surprised Jack. He didn't think her capable of embarrassment.

"Oh, shut up, you big slob," she said teasingly.

"I want you to meet my boyfriend, Jack Dunham."

Jack's head snapped toward her and she smiled again, her eyes filling with love. He returned the look, then turned to Curly and stuck out his hand.

"Jack," he said, knocking the hand out of the way and enveloping him in a hug. "I knew you'd come."

Jack pulled out of the embrace and gripped Curly's shoulders.

"Curly, you know me? You remember?"

"Like it was yesterday."

"All right!" Jack said, grabbing Curly in a hug of his own. "How did it happen for you? When?"

"I was addressing a group of *Wehrmacht* veterans about insurance benefits and afterwards Wiley came up to me."

"Wiley? You've seen Wiley?" Jack was as excited as a kid with a coveted new toy.

"He's fine, Jack. He's in Toronto—with Chessman."

This rocked Jack.

"Chessman? In Canada? Have they—"

Curly shook his head.

"Wiley doesn't have the right stuff. They've tried for months. You're our only hope."

"Me? What can *I* do? I'm no more telekinetic than Wiley."

"Chessman can test you. If you have any ability, any at all, he can develop it, make it stronger."

"But why not get someone up there who can do it already?"

"Because we need somebody who remembers the way it was, the way it's *supposed* to be."

"What about you?"

Curly shook his head. "I'm too high profile. State Security is always keeping tabs on me."

Denise shook her head, totally confused.

"Hey, I hate to interrupt old home week, but would somebody mind explaining just what the hell is going on and how you two know each other?"

She stood there looking so impatient and frustrated, both men laughed. "Oh, great," she said. "Now I'm an idiot too."

Jack hugged her, still chuckling. "I'm sorry, Malloy, it's just so crazy, you'll think we're nuts."

"Try me," she snarled, putting her hands on her hips.

"Come on, you two lovebirds," Curly said, still laughing. "There's a private room back behind the stage. We can talk there."

Curly led them to the front of the room and to a small door that nearly blended in with the cinder block construction. Inside the ten-by-ten room were shelves containing all manner of canned foods. On the floor stood several oil-drum-sized containers of drinking water. The distinctive yellow and black radiation symbol on them told Jack this was the storage room for the shelter. He wondered if any of this stuff was still edible.

In the center of the room stood a small, battered table and four hardback chairs. Denise and Jack sat down while Curly stood.

"Why don't you start, Jack?"

He sighed. Where to begin? It was all so crazy sounding. He turned to Denise and grabbed her hand.

"Have you ever thought you've been somewhere before or felt you've known somebody that you couldn't possibly know?"

"You mean like *déjà vu?*"

"Sort of."

Jack began to tell her the incredible tale of his other life, of how Armand Bock and the Nine Old Men changed the face of America, of the world. How they found Chessman and Kruger and how frighteningly simple it had been to alter history. When he was finished, Curly took over and related his own part of the story, including the moment everything came flooding back when he laid eyes on Wiley Carpenter.

"My revelation was not as violent as Jack's. I don't know why, but suffice to say, it rocked me to the core."

Denise was outwardly calm, but Jack could tell she was reeling from all they'd told her. It was a lot to ask anyone to take in.

"So, because Kruger killed Eisenhower and everyone else in that explosion, then convinced Hitler to move the Fifteenth Army—"

"Everything was changed," Jack said. "You have no idea what our country is like in that other timeline. For one thing, it's called the United States of America. Not this stupid 'Avalon.' You can actually buy a newspaper that tells you the real news, listen to any kind of music you want, speak your mind anywhere, anytime. There's no State Security, Denise. Police have to have warrants to search your home. And Miami. You wouldn't recognize it. The Cubans and the blacks, they're everywhere... and free."

"What about me, Jack?"

Jack glanced at Curly, who nodded.

"We don't know each other back there."

"Maybe we will," she said. "I mean, you said that because you guys knew about Bock and the Nine Old Men's plan, you were able to remember it now."

"Yes," Jack said.

"Then maybe I'll look you up."

"That's only *if* I go to Canada and *if* I can go back and change all this. I don't even know if I can."

Denise looked at him, her eyes filled with fiery determination. "You've got to try, Jack. If you could change all of this, this nightmare, wouldn't it be worth it? Didn't those slides make you sick?"

Jack nodded. "Come with me, then. You said it was time for you to go underground. We'll both go."

"No, Jack. I can't—not now—not after seeing that. I've got to stay and fight. If you're successful, then you'll save millions of lives. If not, then my people will need all the help they can get."

"Damnit, Denise. I'm not going to argue with you. I want you—"

The explosion ripped through the upper floor of the house, drowning out Jack's voice. The room shook and the air filled with the sounds of screams and falling canned goods.

"*Mein Gott,*" Denise said, "it's State Security!"

In between the screams, Jack could hear the chatter of machine guns and barked orders. They'd sent an *Einsatzgruppe*, a liquidation squad.

Curly grabbed them and shoved them toward the end of the room opposite the door. "Come on. There's another way out of here."

"No! We can't leave them!"

Curly shook her. In his large hands, she appeared like a small doll. "You can't help them! They're already dead!"

"NO!" she screamed.

Curly slapped her, making Jack wince.

"Come on, Jack. Help me!"

The two of them grabbed her by the arms and pulled her. Behind one of the shelves was an auxiliary entrance to the shelter: a steel door barred with a stout, oak beam. Curly threw off the beam and pulled open the door. The hinges creaked loudly, and a wave of damp, musty air wafted over them. The room quaked from another explosion, this one sounding closer.

"Let's move it," Curly said.

The three of them dashed into the dark tunnel. Curly slammed the door behind them, making the tunnel even darker. Lit only by a pair of battery-powered emergency lights, the walls were blanketed by a thick layer of grime and moss, and the floor had about two inches of water covering it. Looking down the dim passage, Jack could see the tunnel extended about fifty yards, ending abruptly at a rusty, iron ladder set into the concrete.

The passage was narrow, necessitating that they run single file. They reached the ladder seconds later. Jack could still hear the screams and the machine guns echoing down the passageway.

Denise stared up the ladder. "Where does this lead?"

"Henry never told me," Curly said.

"I hope the hell it's not smack in the middle of this mess," Jack said.

"It doesn't matter. We've got no other way out. Let's go. Jack, you first, then Denise. I'll bring up the rear."

Jack nodded and headed up the ladder. Layers of rust crumbled under his hands and feet, and he prayed it continue to take their weight. If it broke, they were trapped.

At the top of the ladder, Jack found what appeared to be a manhole cover. He pushed. It wouldn't budge.

"This fucking thing is stuck!"

"Push it, Jack. Put your back into it. It hasn't been opened in over thirty years."

Jack looked up and sneered at the cover then climbed another rung. Hunched over, he used his knees to push his back against the cover. He shoved hard, feeling the muscles in his neck popping through the skin with the strain. Backing off, he took several deep breaths and pushed harder still. Suddenly, it gave, nearly causing him to topple off the ladder. Denise gasped.

"I'm okay," Jack said. "I'm going to take a look out."

Rolling the cover away just enough to allow his head access, Jack peered out of the hole. His eyes widened in fright. They were diagonally across the street, no more than thirty yards from Henry's house. Luckily, the manhole stood near a stand of vegetation and between the pools of illumination cast by the peach-colored crime lights. Smoke and flames poured out of the wreckage of Henry's house. A unit of the Coral Gables Fire Department stood by with hoses ready, waiting for the signal to move in. The front yard was a hive of activity, as black-clad members of the *Einsatzgruppe* herded the survivors into black vans. Jack counted only a handful of prisoners out of what must have been nearly a hundred and fifty people.

Poor fuckers, Jack thought. Jack knew they were as dead as those left inside. The best they could hope for was a quick execution by firing squad. Anything rather than what the three of them witnessed tonight. As the troopers shut the last prisoner into one of the vans, the group's leader, a *Hauptsturmführer*, began shouting orders in both English and German. They were leaving! Jack began to breathe again, realizing that they were safe. All they had to do was wait.

"What are you seeing, Jack?" Curly said.

Jack climbed back down.

"They're taking off. They got a few prisoners—"

"How many?" Denise asked.

Jack just stared at her, not knowing how to say it.

"Oh, God," she said softly.

THE NORMANDY CLUB

"HALT!"

A beam of light stabbed the darkness.

Curly's head snapped around. "Shit! They found the passageway. Up the ladder!"

Jack grabbed Denise and pushed her up the ladder and followed her, with Curly right behind.

When he scrambled out of the hole, he found Denise crouching behind the bushes nearby. He turned and watched for Curly. A moment later, his massive shoulders pushed their way out of the hole. Suddenly, a bright beam snapped on, catching him halfway out of the hole. Instinctively, he froze.

"Halt! By order of State Security, you are to surrender immediately!"

Curly looked to Jack, smiled, and then continued climbing out of the hole.

A burst of machine gun fire caught the big man across the chest. Small red dots appeared in a jagged line that quickly blossomed and ran into each other. Blood poured from Curly's mouth and his eyes glazed over. He flopped over onto the ground, dead. Jack felt Denise dig her fingers into his arm. He winced from the pain.

"You can't help him, Jack!" she whispered. "We've got to go."

But Jack stood rooted to the spot, unable to move, watching as two State Security troopers kicked Curly's body. They laughed as it flopped over on its back, and one of them planted a foot on his chest, posing like a big game hunter.

Jack clenched his hands, impotent rage rushing through him. He wanted to rip the Nazi bastards apart, knowing at the same time that it was a foolish and futile thought.

Denise tugged at his arm, her hot breath in his ear. "Jack, please..."

With one last look at his old friend, he followed Denise into the shadows of the neighbor's yard. They rounded the side of the house and crouched against the stucco wall, alert for any movement in their direction. Jack was out of breath, as if he'd been running for miles. He knew it was a combination of both fear and adrenaline.

"What'll we do now?" he said.

Denise closed her eyes, not answering immediately. Soon her breathing slowed, and she opened her eyes. Jack could see a quiet intensity in them.

"We'll wait till they leave. If they haven't impounded the car, we'll go back to my place. I have some emergency funds and a map of contacts stashed. From there we head north to Canada."

"Christ, Malloy, that's over two thousand miles. We have no travel permits, no passports, and after tonight probably no friends either."

"What do you want to do? Give up?" she said, her voice a harsh whisper. "Then why don't you just walk out there now? Maybe they won't shoot you like they did Curly."

Jack was about to say something when an outside light above their heads snapped on. Both of them plastered themselves against the house, hoping, praying the people inside hadn't heard them.

"Harvey," a woman said sharply. "Turn off that goddamned light! You want them coming here?"

"I just wanted to see, *Liebchen*."

"Forget it. It's all over. Didn't I tell you that queer would get his. Now all of 'em are gonna get it. Good riddance, I say."

Denise's look said it all. Of course they had to try and make it to Canada. They had to find Wiley and Chessman. They had to stop this *madness*.

A moment later, the light clicked off and they heard a window slam shut. They both let out the breaths they'd been holding and eased themselves from the wall of the house. Around the corner, they saw the fire department had begun the mop-up. The men worked quickly, laying out hoses and tapping the nearby hydrant. In a moment they were dousing the flames from two different directions. A movement caught Jack's eye and he turned to look farther up the street. A sleek, black BMW 900 limousine cruised up and pulled in behind the fire truck. Jack noted the black and silver antenna pennant: skull and crossbones with a cluster of oak leaves, indicating someone very high up in State Security.

The door opened and a figure dressed entirely in the black, tight-fitting uniform of an SS-*Brigadeführer* stepped out and marched toward a group of SS Troopers conducting the mop-up. They all snapped to attention as the *Brigadeführer* approached. Jack gasped when the figure passed through a pool of light.

"Oh my God!" he said, his eyes wide with shock.

Denise stared at the figure, equally stunned.

The *Brigadeführer* was none other than Leslie! They watched her bark orders. Ignoring the firemen and their hoses, several SS Troopers ran into the house.

"I want to see their bodies, sergeant," she shouted after them. "I want to see that *lesbisch* bitch's blackened skull!"

Leslie turned toward the house where Jack and Denise hid, causing them to flinch involuntarily. Her hard eyes glinted in the sallow lighting, giving them a predatory look. But Leslie made no move toward them. She couldn't see them because the crime lights blinded her. Jack stared at her face, the face he once loved and trusted, and his shock turned to anger.

"That cunt has been playing me for a goddamned chump the whole time! I must have led her right *to* these people."

Denise pulled him back around the side of the house.

She knew what he was thinking.

"Listen to me and listen good. This is no more your fault than anybody's. It's them!"

Jack sighed and rubbed his eyes. They'd seen too much as of late.

"Look, we have to go, Jack. When they don't find our bodies, they'll come looking for us."

"What about the car?"

"Forget it. We'll get another."

Before Jack could say anything, Denise pulled him away from the house and they plunged into the brush, making their way across several yards and onto another street about half a mile from Henry's cul-de-sac. Keeping to the shadows, Denise tested the doors of the cars parked in the driveways of the modest houses they passed.

"Jack!" she whispered.

He stopped and turned around, seeing her at the door of a VW Blitz, much like his own. He watched, incredulous, as she pulled open the door and got inside. Reaching immediately into the glove compartment, she rooted around a moment and came out with a screwdriver. She then wedged the tool into the gap between the ignition and the steering column housing, slapped it once, and out popped the ignition. She smiled with satisfaction, put the car in neutral and released the parking brake. The car began to roll backward into the street.

"Are you crazy?" he whispered, trotting alongside. "What are you doing?"

"What does it look like? We're stealing the car."

"Why don't we just wait until Leslie and her goons leave?"

"Because she knows everything about us, Jack, including my car.

They've spotted it by now. If it suddenly disappears, they'll know we're not dead. With the fire and all, it'll take time for them to realize we're not in the house. We'll get a head start this way. Now shut up and help me push this thing."

"Why? Just start the damn thing."

"Jack, I love you, but you're an idiot. We've gotta start this thing away from this house or the owners will hear it."

Feeling foolish for asking, Jack helped Denise push the car into the street. Supposedly, they were death traps, but there was no Ralph Nader in this timeline, no one who cared to go against the government's safety experts. Once they were out in the street, Denise jumped behind the wheel.

"Keep pushing," she said.

Jack braced his shoulders against the trunk and pumped his legs as fast as he could. The tiny car picked up speed, the small downgrade adding to the vehicle's momentum. Jack gave one last push and stood back. Denise jammed the screwdriver into the ignition, twisted it then let out the clutch. The small engine caught, sputtered a moment, then began to purr.

Jack ran to the passenger side and jumped in. Denise let the Blitz roll forward while she scanned the area in all directions. Satisfied, she stomped on the accelerator, sending the small car screaming off into the night.

"Check the glove compartment for maps," Denise said, making a hard-right turn.

"Where are we going?"

"Jacksonville."

"Wait a minute. I need clothes, some money, a toothbrush, for Christ's sake!"

She shot him a sidelong glance and shifted into third gear. "We don't have the time. Besides, I'd bet my ass that State Security's got your place staked out by now, just in case." She covered his hand with hers. "Don't worry, I'll get us out of this. I promise. But right now, I need to know how to get us there."

"All right, hold on." Jack flipped open the glove compartment and rummaged through empty *Großer Rauch* cigarette packs and battered cassette tapes, finding both a Miami map and a dog-eared Avalon road atlas. He opened the atlas, squinting in the poor light.

"The Hindenburg Highway goes right through downtown Jacksonville," he said. "And according to this, there's an entrance about a quarter of a mile that way." He pointed and Denise took a sharp left. "Why Jacksonville?" he asked after a moment.

"It's the first station on the railroad."

"The what?"

"The Underground Railroad. It's our way to Canada. They'll get us everything we need: money, clothes, IDs, a new car, and weapons. I hope you know how to use a gun."

Before Jack could answer, Denise spotted the northbound on-ramp to the Hindenburg Highway and headed for it, slowing as she passed a traffic cop handing out a citation, blue lights flashing on his Harley. Jack saw the frightened look in the other driver's eyes when they shot past, remembering his own fear only moments before.

On the highway, Denise brought the car up to the legal speed limit.

"We'll spell each other," she said, clicking on the cruise control. "Two hours on, two hours off. Okay?"

"Yeah, fine..."

She frowned. "You all right?"

Jack let out a sigh and faced her. "That guy back there. When we passed him, I couldn't help thinking 'better you than me, pal.' That's what living in Kruger's world has done to me, Denise. And I don't like it very much... or me, for that matter."

"It's done it to *all* of us in one way or another," she said. "The difference between us and the rest of them is that we're doing something about it. So stop feeling sorry for yourself, it doesn't suit you."

"Momma Malloy knows best, is that it?"

"Damn straight, Dunham, so shut up and get some rest. You're going to need it."

Two hours later, after a short nap, Jack took the wheel while Denise slept beside him, her head resting on his shoulder. He tuned the radio to the news and listened for anything about the raid on Henry's house. There was nothing, and that disturbed him even more.

Did they even have a shot at making it to Canada? And if they did, would he be able to succeed where Wiley and Chessman had failed? What if he *couldn't* go back and stop Kruger? What if he had to live the rest of his life in this nightmare?

Jack stopped himself when he realized he had something even more important to worry about—like whether they'd even survive the night.

11

Hindenburg Highway (I-95), Florida
23 April 1994

The sun peeked over the horizon as Jack stirred and awakened. His neck felt stiff, and he couldn't stop a muscle in his leg from quivering. They'd been driving all night, and even with an hour's nap he felt squeezed dry. His head ached and his mouth tasted like an old shoe dipped in dog shit.

"Where are we?" he asked.

"We passed St. Augustine a little ways back."

Denise looked as tired as he did. She gripped the wheel with a manic intensity and her red-rimmed eyes stared out the windshield, snapping to the rearview every few seconds.

"Want me to spell you?"

She shook her head. "No. If I stop now, I'm gonna collapse. We're almost there. Another forty miles or so."

"Where are we holing up?"

"Grab my jacket."

Jack reached over the back of the seat and picked up her stone-washed denim jacket.

"Now what?"

128

"My address book's in the inside pocket. Check under M."

Jack pulled out the black leatherette Day Planner and turned to the address section, then to M.

"Okay."

"See where it says Mom?"

"Yeah?"

"That's where we're going."

Jack frowned. "Your mother runs a station on the railroad?"

Denise burst out laughing. The hours of driving and junk food were taking their toll.

"No, Dunham. That's a code. All the stations are made to look like relatives. That way if the book were ever to fall into the wrong hands, it would look like an innocent address book. It's the address that's important."

"So who're we seeing when we get there?"

"A kind old man who owes me big. But first we need to cruise the place and make sure it's okay. If no one's been compromised, we make contact."

"Assuming you didn't know the person, how do you recognize each other?"

"A simple coded phrase."

Jack shook his head. "You people watch too many James Bond movies."

"Who?"

"Sorry," Jack said, feeling foolish. "Wrong life."

"Tell me more, Jack. I wanna know what your world was like."

Jack leaned back and closed his eyes, letting the memories play out. He smiled, remembering something.

"What?" she said, smiling eagerly.

"I was just remembering something from when I was a kid."

"Tell me."

"When I was fourteen. I wanted to go see a rock concert."

"Rock?"

"A form of primitive music played on electrified instruments, very loud. To the kids of my generation, it was our battle cry so to speak, our rite of passage. Anyway. I'd never been to one and my parents thought I was too young to go by myself. Of course, they were right. But my dad got us tickets for the New Year's Eve show at a place called Fillmore East. I had no idea who the band was, some group called a 'Band of Gypsies.' I was floored when it turned out to be Jimi Hendrix."

He turned to her, opening his eyes. They burned with a quiet intensity.

"I know that name means nothing to you, but let me try and explain. Jimi was a symbol to us. He was a young black man who couldn't get anywhere with his music. He had to go to England before the world recognized his talent. Man, he played the electric guitar like no one ever did... like no one does now. You see those insipid musicians on State TV, plinking away on those wimpy instruments? Believe me, you have no idea what the instrument is capable of— soaring melodies, chords that sound like thunder, screams, bombs going off. Hendrix once did a version of the National Anthem, the one that's banned. It became a classic.

"Anyway, that night at the Fillmore was transcendent. Hendrix explored new territory with his instrument that left everyone astounded. Even my dad, whose taste ran to Easy Listening, got caught up in it. By the end of the night, he was converted."

"What happened to him?"

"Hendrix?

Denise nodded.

Jack's expression saddened.

"He died the following year. It was a stupid, stupid accident. He took sleeping pills, ones that were not his prescription and, without thinking, drank wine. He passed out and choked on his own vomit."

"Shit," Denise said, staring at the road.

"Supposedly, he was still alive in the ambulance, but the attendant didn't have the brains to position him so he could breathe. I can't even begin to describe how I felt when I heard the news. It was like a member of my own family had died. In a way, my whole generation felt that way. Even into the nineties, the other nineties, his music is regularly played on the radio, sounding as fresh as ever."

Denise put her hand on his thigh and squeezed.

"You'll hear it again. We'll hear it together."

Jack nodded and stared out the window for the next few miles. Soon he saw a sign: Gas, Food, and Lodging: 2 Miles.

"Can we stop? I've got to get some coffee and some food before I pass out," he said.

"Okay, but we gotta make it quick. The fewer people see us, the better."

When the rest stop appeared, Denise pulled into the Burger Meister parking lot. Jack stumbled when he tried to walk, his legs rubbery.

Denise grabbed her wallet and they headed inside. Jack got two egg croissants, two apple strudels and a large coffee, Denise some tea. They took a booth near a window so they could watch the car.

"I'll be back in a moment," Denise said, heading for a group of newspaper vending machines by the door.

Jack nodded and bit into one of his sandwiches. Normally, he hated fast food, but right now it tasted like heaven. A moment later, Denise came back. She looked scared.

"Don't act alarmed. Look on page ten."

As casually as he could, Jack took the paper and opened it, turning the pages slowly and deliberately. When he reached page ten, he stopped and stared. There in the middle of page ten were both their pictures side by side. God only knew where they'd gotten the picture of him. It had been taken at some Ministry function and he looked half in the bag. The picture made him look crazed and desperate. Hell, they probably picked it on purpose. Denise's looked even worse.

Underneath was a two-column story about the raid, and their escape. Of course, nothing was mentioned about the shootings and the fire. Leslie was quoted as saying that no expense would be spared to bring the traitors to justice. There was even a reward of ten thousand *Reichsdollars* for any information leading to their capture.

"So, how does it feel to have a price on your head?" Denise asked, half-jokingly.

But Jack was in no mood for levity.

"Like shit," he whispered. "How can you joke about something like this!"

"Calm down. At least it wasn't on page one. It means we're not high priority and few people have seen it."

"We saw it. Who knows who else has? Some of the people here, maybe."

"Nothing we can do about that now. Grab your food and let's go."

Denise laughed softly as she got up, pretending a reaction to something Jack said. They moved through the restaurant nonchalantly. To Jack, it seemed as if every eye in the place was on him, but no one even looked up from their food as they shoveled it in.

Once in the car, Jack freaked out.

"We have to get another car! Someone spotted us. I know it."

"Jack, cool it, all right! No one recognized us."

Denise reached under the seat and pulled out the screwdriver, jammed it into the ignition hole and twisted it. The engine coughed, sputtered a moment, then caught. It quickly settled down into the familiar purr. Jack shook his head, feeling completely foolish.

"Christ, you're right. I'm really losing it."

"It's okay," she said, squeezing his arm. "So you're not a born terrorist and thief, so what?"

He gave her a quizzical look. "And you are?"

"I stole your heart, didn't I?" she said, smiling again.

Her gorgeous smile was contagious. In a moment, Jack found himself smiling as the small VW pulled back onto the Hindenburg Highway.

✻ ✻ ✻

They reached the city of Jacksonville a little over thirty minutes later and, after getting lost on the interchange in South Jacksonville, crossed the St. Johns River over the Fuller-Warren Toll Bridge. The spires of downtown Jacksonville, what there was of it, loomed ahead. Jack, acting as navigator, double-checked the address book and pulled out a street map of the city.

"If we get off at the next exit, we'll be right in the area."

Denise nodded and took the first exit, downshifting as they headed down the ramp.

"Which way?"

"Right," he said.

Taking Riverside, they passed the *Blaukreuz* building and hung a left onto Edison Street. As they drove, they noticed more than a few boarded-up buildings, a result of the violent riots a year earlier. The blacks of Jacksonville had not gone meekly to their doom. From Edison, they turned onto Park and crossed over the railroad yard. The yard looked busy. Jack could see whole flatcars loaded with tanks on their way to Mexico.

Soon they turned onto Monroe, a street with small, two-story buildings that all had a quaint, Art Deco look about them. It was obvious this was an old neighborhood. Denise pulled up in front of a tailor shop at 1515 Monroe. The sign said:

Art's Custom Tailoring

Uniforms a specialty.

"Oh, great, just what we need, a guy that does business with the Nazis."

"Art's okay. His son is one of us. Their favorite tailor is the last place those *scheisskopfen* would think to look."

"Well, let's get this over with."

Jack started to open the door when Denise grabbed his arm. "Hold it," she said.

He looked toward the shop and spotted a black uniformed SS officer coming out with a suit bag, headed for a waiting staff car. A short, stocky man followed him out, smiling and talking animatedly. As soon as the SS officer drove off, the tailor's smile disappeared. He turned and looked straight at Denise, then shook his head. That was all she needed. She put the car in gear and pulled out onto the street.

"What was that all about?"

"It isn't safe right now. He wants us to come back in a couple of hours."

"And you got all that from one nod of the head?"

"After being with Lambda for a while, you get a sixth sense about things."

"So, what'll we do for two hours?"

"Ditch the car."

Again, they drove off. After searching for another twenty minutes, Denise pulled the car into an underground parking garage and parked between a van and an old Nova.

"With any luck, they won't spot this car for weeks. Let's go."

Back at the shop, they found the shade on the glass door pulled down and a sign reading "Back at One."

"He's in there waiting," she said. "Let's take a walk."

Denise put her arm through Jack's and led him off down the street. It would have thrilled him to feel her close like this, but instead he felt vulnerable—exposed.

That was the worst part. Anyone could spot them and call State Security, anyone. After wandering around for another half an hour, playing the window-shopping lovebirds, they came around to the shop again. Instead of knocking on the front, they went around the back. A small sign saying "Art's Tailoring" was affixed to a grimy wooden door next to an overflowing dumpster filled with rotten meat from the butcher next door. Jack thought he would puke as the smell caught his nostrils. And the flies. There were hundreds of them.

Denise knocked on the door, three quick, two long, just like at Henry's house. *My God*, he thought. Was that only yesterday? It felt like a million years ago and their journey had only begun.

The door opened and Art stood there, smiling broadly.

"Denise, my love. Come in, come in."

Jack followed her into the tiny shop's back room while Art bolted the door. Jack noticed that the flimsy appearance from the outside belied the stout, steel construction. It would take a squad with a battering ram to get through it.

"You come so soon? You miss my strudel, *ja?*"

Denise hugged the man who, in spite of his small stature, lifted her off her feet.

"You must be careful, *liebchen*, the SS in Jacksonville have been put on alert. That man you saw coming out of my shop earlier told me. These idiots think they are so superior, yet they tell a lowly tailor, like me, all their secrets. You see the garbage outside? I throw meat in there every day! It keeps away the curious and smells even worse than they do!"

He laughed and then approached Jack, his expression turning hard.

"You are treating my favorite girl right, *ja*?"

The man looked fierce, but Jack detected warmth in his eyes that no amount of false hostility could hide.

"Absolutely," Jack said. "Although you've got to watch her around other people's cars."

Art's eyebrows shot up and he laughed, a big, brassy sound that filled the room.

"That's my little *strudel-mädchen*," he said. "Come, I have your accommodations ready."

Jack looked to Denise, who smiled and shrugged.

Art went over to a metal cabinet leaning against the wall and pushed it aside. Underneath was a trapdoor. With surprising strength, the older man reached down, grabbed hold of an iron ring recessed into the oaken planks, and yanked it up. Jack saw a flight of steps leading downward into what looked like the Black Hole of Calcutta.

The older man saw Jack's apprehension and smiled. "It is not so bad. Come."

Nodding and smiling, Art descended, flipping a hidden light switch on the way. Suddenly a bright light poured from the hole.

Jack shrugged. "What the hell."

Grabbing Denise's hand, they followed Art down and into one of the most charming dungeons Jack had ever seen.

THE NORMANDY CLUB

The room took up half the twenty-by-forty-foot basement; the other half was occupied by a furnace and storage. The rest looked like something from a Victoria's Secret catalog. The queen-size bed had a fancy brass and white headboard with a frilly coverlet trimmed with lace and covered with hand-embroidered pillows. Flanking the bed were Early American-style nightstands, atop which sat oil-filled hurricane lamps that Jack could swear were antiques from the early 1900s. At the foot of the bed lay a mahogany hope chest covered by a large, frilly lace cloth. Against the wall stood a simple dresser and, next to it, a freestanding oval-shaped full-length mirror. The floor itself was covered by an Oriental throw rug.

Denise was stunned.

"Art! How on earth did you do this so fast? It's wonderful!"

She hugged the older man, who smiled and blushed.

"It was Wilhelm's secret place," he said, the blush deepening. "After what you did for him, I think he would be pleased to know you were here."

Denise smiled and kissed him on the cheek.

"I am sorry about the oil lamps," Art said, "but we cannot risk having you use electricity when I am supposed to be closed."

"It's okay, Art," Jack said. "Thank you."

Art bowed and began walking up. He stopped halfway and turned.

"There is food and water in the hope chest and a small chemical toilet in the storage area. Have a good night. I will see you two at oh-six hundred."

He turned and climbed out of sight. A moment later, the trapdoor slammed shut and they heard the scraping of the metal cabinet being pushed back into place.

Jack turned to Denise. "Did I ever tell you I'm a little claustrophobic?"

"Me too," she said, coming over to him, a lascivious grin on her face. "And I've got the perfect way to cure it."

She grabbed him and kissed him wildly. Jack was taken aback for only a brief moment before he enfolded her in his arms.

✠ ✠ ✠

The light from the flickering hurricane lamps cast a warm glow in the basement room, enhancing the illusion that they were back in some simpler time, a time free from fear. Jack turned, careful not to wake Denise, and picked up his watch from the nightstand. The watch read 2300. They still had a long night and an even longer trip ahead of them. Denise sighed, stretched, and opened her eyes. She smiled contentedly, reminding Jack of the scene in *Gone With The Wind* where Scarlett awakens after a night of passion with Rhett.

"Well, don't we look like the cat with the canary," he said.

"Look who's talking. You're the animal."

Jack blushed in spite of himself.

"You hungry?"

"I could eat another horse," she said, grinning.

"Oh, *please*."

Denise giggled, and taking that as his cue, Jack climbed off the bed, padded over to the hope chest, and lifted the lid.

"Well, I'll be. I think your friend is a romantic."

"What?"

Jack gave her a sly look and pulled out a champagne bucket filled with ice and an expensive bottle of *Kupferburg* Champagne, followed by an old-fashioned picnic basket, the kind one paid hundreds of dollars for at overpriced gourmet shops.

Inside the basket sat a cold chicken dinner with potato salad, string beans, a loaf of pumpernickel, and crisp dill pickles. For dessert there was apple strudel.

They attacked the food as if they'd not eaten in days. It tasted magnificent. When they were finished, they lay back sipping the exquisite champagne, cuddled in each other's arms.

"I've got to ask you something," he said. "I know the rest of the railroad will probably be dusty attics and junk food. Why is he treating us like visiting royalty?"

"You remember when he mentioned Wilhelm?"

Jack nodded.

"Wilhelm is his son. He and his lover, Jeffrey, tried to help out the Blacks during the rioting. Jeffrey was killed and Wilhelm was captured and would have been executed had it not been for Lambda. We helped break him out and sent him to Canada."

"Wait a minute," Jack said, remembering. "That was last year? August?

"Yeah. I was down here on vacation when the shit hit the fan."

"Vacation?" Jack said, staring into her eyes. The unspoken question hung in the air.

"I led the team that helped break him out," she said a moment later.

Jack shook his head in astonishment.

"Malloy, you never cease to amaze me."

"And I hope I never do," she said, hugging him.

"But why all this, and how could he know we would be here? He can't treat everyone this way."

Denise shrugged. "He obviously feels he needs to pay me back. And I think he likes to think of me as the daughter he never had. As to how he knew—" She shrugged again. "The Underground probably got the word out about the massacre. People like Art know to keep their eyes open for refugees."

That satisfied him. They lay silently for a while until another question presented itself, one far more important.

"Where do we go from here?" he said.

Denise reached over and picked up the map of Avalon they'd taken from the glove compartment of the Blitz and spread it over the bed. She pointed to Ohio.

"Cincinnati. From there we take 71, pick up 90 in Cleveland and go straight to Buffalo. That's where things can get dicey. Our contact there is responsible for getting us across the border into Canada."

"You don't sound so sure."

"Nothing's for certain. Anything can happen between now and then. We have to keep our eyes open and not do anything stupid."

"Like stealing people's cars."

Denise punched him in the arm and scowled at him playfully.

"That was an emergency."

"Well, what about now? What do you call sleeping in someone's basement?"

"Safe," she said.

Jack was used to controlling his own life, at least as much as those Nazi bastards allowed. Here he felt as helpless as a baby and didn't like it one bit. He wondered whether he was a chauvinist at heart, unable to accept a woman leading the way. But there was really little choice.

"Listen," she said, "I know this is all kind of crazy, but you've got to trust me."

"I do. It's everyone else I don't. Hell, look at me. I was sleeping with goddamned State Security and didn't even know it. How do you think that makes me feel?"

"Like a fool."

Jack nodded and took a deep breath, letting the tension flow out of his body.

"So how do we get out of here tomorrow?"

"Art will buy us a car. We don't have to worry about that, at least."

"What about the Blitz?"

Denise shook her head. "Art knows a chop shop across town. It's already been broken up for parts."

"And, now..."

"And now we stay put."

"Why?" he said, snapping at her.

"Because Art has to arrange new IDs for us. That'll take another day at least."

Jack shook his head. He knew she was right, but he was still frustrated. As romantic as this little boudoir was, he didn't know if he could stay in it for another thirty-six hours.

※　※　※

Jack awoke when the light snapped on, flooding the basement with light. Its brightness made him squint. Art came down the steps followed by another man carrying camera equipment.

"Good morning, good morning," he said. "Is everyone decent?"

Jack turned to Denise, surprised to find the bed empty. In a moment she appeared from the storage area fully dressed. She looked fresh and amazingly well-put-together. Jack didn't know how she did it. Leslie would take hours to "put on her face." Jack would have loved nothing better than to rip her face off if it would bring back Curly and the others.

"I have brought my friend, Roberto," Art said, indicating the other man, who began setting up his equipment. "He will make you new IDs and travel permits. I am sorry to barge in so early, but there is news."

"What is it, Art?" Denise said, sitting on the bed next to Jack.

"Your pictures are on the TV."

"Damn," Jack said.

He got up and threw on his clothes, unconcerned with appearances or modesty. Art had more to tell.

"They have instituted a state-wide search, all the old state borders in the Southeastern sector—Georgia, Alabama, and Louisiana—have been tightened. Everyone going through is being closely scrutinized. There are orders to detain you. If you resist, you are to be shot."

"That sounds like Leslie," Jack said, fuming.

Art went back into the storage area and returned with a wooden case. He opened it and pulled out bottles of hair dye and bleach.

"We must change your appearance," he said.

"I always did want to be a redhead," Denise said, smiling. But Jack was still angry. Denise sensed his ire and went to him.

"It'll be all right. The important thing is to get to Toronto."

He realized she was right, feeling like a fool for letting Leslie get to him.

"All right, let's do it."

An hour later, Jack looked at himself in the mirror and did a double take. Art had dyed his hair jet black along with his eyebrows. With his naturally blue eyes, it gave him a Black Irish look. Art then showed him how to apply the false mustache. With a minimum of practice, he was able to do it himself.

Denise looked even more striking. With her hair straightened and then dyed a deep, delicious red, it looked completely natural against her pale, lightly freckled complexion. It also looked a lot longer, hanging below her shoulders in a sexy, soft wave. In addition, Art had shown her how to use makeup differently, making her cheekbones stand out and her face look thinner. She looked like something from a fashion magazine. Jack whistled in appreciation, causing her to smile and blush a color nearly as red as her hair.

Roberto had them sit on a stool in front of a light gray background identical to the color used by State Security when they took citizen ID photos. He worked quickly, snapping the pictures with professional alacrity.

He spoke for the first time, his accent placing him squarely in New Jersey. "Your new IDs will be ready tomorrow evening, along with travel permits through to Buffalo."

"Thank you, Roberto," Denise said.

He bowed slightly and set about putting his equipment away.

After Roberto left, Art disappeared into the storage area with the makeup case and returned with the weapons. They were the dreaded MP89. No citizen was allowed to own any firearms. The Second Amendment, and the rest of the United States Constitution, had been an early casualty of the Nazi regime. In Avalon, the penalty for possession of a rifle or pistol was twenty years at hard labor. Possession of a fully automatic weapon like the MP89 was death—no trial—no appeal—no mercy.

Jack noticed that Denise was completely familiar with the weapon. In seconds she field-stripped the gun and inspected its mechanisms. It gave off a faint odor of solvent and oil. Satisfied, she snapped it back together nearly as quickly, repeating the procedure with the second one.

"I wish these weren't necessary," Jack said.

"So do I, Jack," she said. "But we have to be ready for anything.

If they recognize us, chances are excellent they will shoot first and ask questions later. Just like they did with Curly."

Jack's eyes blazed. "Show me what to do."

She handed him the weapon. It was short, stubby, and the pistol grip had a spongy, neoprene feel, to facilitate a tighter grip. He was surprised at how light the gun felt.

Denise held up her own weapon and described the gun's features, sounding very much like a government training film.

"The MP89 is a four point five millimeter, select-fire weapon made from hardened steel and a high-strength, polymer plastic. It uses a caseless ammunition that fires armor-piercing projectiles from a disposable magazine containing fifty rounds at either six hundred or a thousand rounds per minute. Do you see that lever on the side near your thumb? That's the safety and selection lever. All the way up is safe. In that position, the trigger cannot be depressed, and the gun will not fire. From there, the first click is single-round fire, second click is three-round burst, third click is full auto at six hundred rounds per minute, last click is full auto at a thousand. Got it?"

Jack nodded.

"Okay. All you need to remember is to take the weapon off safety, point the thing, and fire. Because of the caseless round and the small calibre, there is almost no recoil. It's like firing a cap gun," she said.

Art interrupted. "Roberto will be back tonight with your papers and a car registered in your new identities. You are now Mr. and Mrs. Harold Manning of Toledo, Ohio. You are on vacation and will be visiting relatives in Toronto. You will leave tonight."

"I thought we were staying another day?" Jack said, alarmed.

Art's expression turned grim. "I regret that you cannot. The SS has begun house-to-house searches. They could be here at any time. As soon as everything is ready, you *must* leave. I am sorry."

"It's okay, Art," Denise said. "We appreciate all you've done."

He smiled and bowed his head. "You will look up Wilhelm when you get there?"

Denise went over and hugged the older man.

"I'll give him a big wet one direct from you," she said.

Art sobbed quietly, holding on to Denise. Jack's own eyes began to tear up. He looked away and fiddled with the MP89, trying to remember exactly how Denise had disassembled it. But the details escaped him. He felt angry and frustrated again, but for a different reason: What the hell kind of world would keep a father and son apart?

A world he had to change.

12

A rt came for them about 1800 hours, looking nervous and worried.

"The SS are at the end of the street," he said. "We must hurry."

"What about Roberto?" Jack said.

Art couldn't hide the fright in his eyes. "He is late."

They climbed up the steps, went to the front of the shop, and peered out the door. Several large vans stood a few hundred feet down the block. In the deepening twilight, Jack could make out a squad of soldiers under the command of a *Hauptsturmführer*. As he watched, they filed out of a drycleaner and marched to the next business, a cheap restaurant. The streetlights snapped on when the black-clad soldiers entered the storefront. They would be here in minutes.

Denise turned to Jack. "We've got to go back down."

Hurrying, Jack and Denise scrambled down the stairs and the trapdoor slammed shut. They could hear Art grunting as he shoved the metal cabinet back into place, the scraping noise echoing loudly.

"The light, Jack!" Denise whispered.

He mounted the stairs in two cat-like leaps and snapped it off, plunging the basement into darkness. It took a moment, but his eyes grew accustomed. A small amount of light seeped through the cracks from the floorboards over their heads, revealing dust motes swirling about in the now oppressive atmosphere.

They waited.

After what felt like an hour, Jack heard the bell on the shop's front door tinkling, followed by the clumping of hobnailed boots. Denise grabbed his arm and placed one of the MP89s in it.

"Whatever happens," she whispered, "just aim and fire. We'll take as many of the bastards as we can."

Cradling the weapon, Jack felt for the safety lever and clicked it until he reached full auto. He had no idea how long the magazine would last. Seconds, probably. He knew it wasn't like the movies where the guns only ran out at convenient moments. Here, it was real guns with real bullets. The prospect that it all might end right here froze his heart. Would he be able to pull the trigger? He saw Curly's face, saw the bullets rip up his body, and he knew that he wouldn't hesitate. He gripped the gun tighter.

And they waited...

Suddenly, the clumping got louder, and they heard shouting from the *Haupsturmführer*, the crash of broken glass, and something large thudding to the floor.

"What's going on up there?" Jack said.

Denise said nothing. Jack was sure she knew all too well that Art was being subjected to what State Security called "field interrogation." Simply put, it meant the one being questioned got the crap beaten out of him. If that didn't work, they brought out the cattle prod. That usually did it. If not, they took them back to headquarters and used the drugs. State Security had long ago perfected a regimen of various psychotropic drugs, reputed to reduce the weak-willed to pliable puppets at an impressive success rate of eighty percent. Regardless, they preferred the cruder methods because they enjoyed them.

Denise flinched as Art screamed. His voice rose in pitch as the pain increased. The scream trailed off into a hacking cough and muttered pleadings.

Someone barked an order and the boots marched across the floor. The bell tinkled again, followed by the slamming of the front door. And then... silence.

"I can't stand this," Jack said, moving toward the stairs. He climbed up and put his ear to the trapdoor, trying to hear anything at all.

Nothing.

Art was an old man. If the SS had killed him either deliberately or through their brutal interrogation, they were sunk. Who knows how long they would sit there trapped under a heavy cabinet they hadn't a prayer of moving? They could easily die of thirst or starvation before someone came.

A match flared, and Denise lit one of the hurricane lamps, adjusting the flame to minimize the flicker.

"Let's see if there's another way out of here," she said.

Carrying the lamp, they explored every inch of the basement, becoming more discouraged and disheartened with every passing moment. What used to be windows were now bricked over. There was no way out except through the trapdoor. Despondent, they dropped onto the bed and lay there, staring at the ceiling. Jack prayed that Art had only passed out or that Roberto would come. After a while, the excitement of the last hours took their toll, and Jack's eyes grew heavy. Soon, in spite of their growing anxiety, both Denise and Jack fell asleep.

※　※　※

Jack awoke with a start, the dream he'd been having receding immediately into the subconscious. He remembered nothing except that it disturbed him. But it was nothing compared to their present situation.

"Malloy," he said, shaking her. "Wake up."

"Mmmmm... What!"

She bolted upright, her eyes wide open.

"Jesus, Dunham, don't scare me like that. What time is it?"

He squinted at his watch, his eyes still unfocused from sleep.

"Either oh-two-thirty or fourteen-thirty."

"Shit," she said.

They heard the bell tinkling. Someone was here. Immediately, Jack leaped off the bed and doused the hurricane lamp, then darted over to the stairs and stood, holding his breath, straining to hear the slightest sound.

Who was it?

He felt Denise press against him. Seconds, minutes, hours, they couldn't tell which, they heard a scraping noise. The cabinet. It was moving!

Denise handed him one of the MP89s and he felt for the safety and clicked it off.

"Come on," she said, pulling him under the stairs. They both crouched down... waiting. Jack felt a small bead of sweat run down his spine and his breathing grew shallow and rapid, as if suddenly they were on top of a very high mountain. He wondered if he was about to faint and gripped the gun tighter when he heard the trapdoor creak open and flop onto the floor.

"Denise? Mr. Dunham?"

"It's Roberto!" Denise said, her voice an explosion of sound in the quiet basement. "Roberto?"

"Please. You must come. There is no time to lose." He sounded both relieved and scared.

Jack and Denise bounded up the steps and into the small shop. Roberto had not turned on the lights, but Jack still found himself shocked by the wanton destruction. Every piece of clothing or equipment had been ripped to pieces, overturned, or smashed. Even Art's prized Singer sewing machine lay twisted and rent, its gears scattered across the floor. His eyes darted to the floor, where a dried pool of blood nearly two feet in diameter glistened in the pale light streaming through the shattered plate-glass window. Art was nowhere to be seen.

Roberto stood, his hands shaking. Jack thought he was scared, but he quickly realized it was repressed fury.

"Where's Art?" Denise asked, her voice betraying her growing dismay.

"They took him," Roberto said.

"Oh God."

Denise began to cry. This alarmed Jack in more ways than one. He'd never seen her like this.

"What about us? Has he talked?" Jack said.

Roberto stared at them, his eyes telling the whole story. Jack knew Art was as good as dead and tried putting the thought out of his mind. He'd liked the old man.

"I do not know," Roberto said. "You know he would never betray you... willingly."

Denise shook her head, fighting back the tears. Roberto's eyes flashed as he cocked his head to one side.

"What?" Jack said.

"Quickly. You must go! It is not safe."

Roberto led them out the back door past the dumpster. In the deepening gloom, they could hear a siren, its pulsating wail growing louder as it approached.

"Is everything ready for us?" Denise asked.

"The car is parked around the corner," Roberto said hurriedly. "It is a blue Chrysler/Heinkel, and the keys are under the front seat. Your new papers are in the glove compartment along with extra magazines for the MP89s."

"Thanks, Roberto. I'm sorry it turned out this way."

He shook his head again.

"You need not apologize. This is the risk we take. Art knew as well as any of us. Just get to Toronto. Then it will all have been worth it."

Denise hugged Roberto. "You take care of yourself, okay?"

"Okay."

Shoving the guns under their jackets, Jack and Denise raced out into the street. The siren sounded much closer now, and both knew they had mere seconds to spare.

They found the car a moment later and climbed inside. Sleek and modern, the Chrysler/Heinkel appealed to the mid-priced sporty market. It had a 300-horsepower engine and was renowned for superb handling. Jack found the keys, pushed them into the ignition, and turned. The engine caught instantly, purring like a large cat. There was power there, ready for anything. He pulled away from the curb and sped off down the street. In his rearview, he spotted a black van cross the intersection, followed by the screeching of brakes. He hoped Roberto had gotten away.

"Check the glove," Jack said, taking a corner with a deft turn of the wheel. The car responded to the slightest touch, like he'd become connected to the road. It was a small measure of comfort in a situation devoid of it.

Denise clicked open the compartment and pulled out six extra magazines for the weapons now stashed under their seats. As they were made from a translucent plastic, he could see the squared-off cartridges lined up inside and marveled that so many could be stuffed inside something barely eight inches in length. He couldn't believe each one held fifty rounds.

Next came the new IDs. From what he could tell, they were flawless. He stared at his picture, wondering if the wide-eyed expression betrayed his anxiety. Probably not. No one ever looked good in their ID pictures. Denise put everything back and closed the compartment. Reaching for her gym bag, she pulled out their map.

"Take Monroe to Adams. We should be able to get on the Hindenburg from there."

Jack nodded and swung the car around. Traffic was nonexistent, and Jack had to resist the urge to test the car's power. That would have to wait. For now, they were two tourists on their way north in no particular hurry. Their next stop on the railroad, Cincinnati, lay nearly 700 miles from Jacksonville. It was a long way and almost anything could happen. At least for now they were safe.

Once on the Hindenburg Highway, they took the interchange and got on 10 going west. From there, they took 75 north. They drove straight, stopping only for meals, gas, and border checks when they crossed state lines. As Art had told them, security had been tightened throughout the Southeastern sector. The traffic near the Georgia border slowed to a crawl. Far up ahead, they could see the flashing purple lights signifying the presence of State Security. Time stretched endlessly as they crept forward. Jack could feel a small bead of sweat trickling down the side of his face in spite of the cool blast of the car's efficient air conditioning. The small of his back was soaked.

Another half an hour passed before they were able to observe the goings-on. The SS were methodically searching a car, its inhabitants standing awkwardly nearby, their expressions fearful.

"I can't stand this," Jack said.

Denise held his hand tightly, her smile warm and reassuring. "I've been through this before, Jack. Just stay cool."

Soon, the car at the checkpoint was allowed through. The troopers then scrutinized the papers of the occupants of two more vehicles, allowing them to pass more quickly. Jack realized they were searching every third car. He also realized that they sat seven cars back from the checkpoint. He'd never been any damn good at math, but it didn't take a genius to figure out they would be searched. And if they were searched, the troopers would find the guns. Their fancy new IDs wouldn't matter a whit.

The next twenty minutes passed like an eternity, bringing them closer and closer. Jack had an irrational urge to pull a U-turn and bolt, knowing it would invite disaster. It was just like those moments, glancing over the edge of a dizzyingly high building and that small voice in your head told you to jump.

The car right before them passed through the checkpoint and the trooper in charge, a stocky balding man with a shock of gray in his jet-black hair, motioned him forward.

"Please step out of the vehicle and submit to search."

The search team, consisting of three *Sturmmann*, stood by. Jack stared straight ahead, his hand shaking when he reached for the door handle. It hovered there, quivering, as if it had a mind of its own and was trying to decide what to do.

"Step out of the vehicle at once!" the trooper said, his voice strident and sharp.

"Hey, Charlie!" someone said.

The black-haired trooper, a *Scharführer*, turned his head as a younger trooper, also a sergeant, stuck his head out the window of a portable checkpoint booth.

"Yeah, what is it?"

"Headquarters got a call that Dunham and Malloy were spotted in Gainesville. Wants us to speed things up."

"Yeah, so what else is new?" the *Scharführer* said. "They want every *verdammten* thing yesterday!"

The young sergeant shook his head. "They want you to start searching every ten cars!"

"*Scheissekopfen*," the *Scharführer* muttered as he walked toward Jack and Denise. He motioned for Jack to roll down the window. "Your papers."

It was not a request. Jack grabbed their new IDs and handed them over. The man scowled, gave the pictures a cursory glance, then fixed Jack and Denise with a penetrating glare. Jack managed a pleasant smile, though it felt exaggerated, as if his face was splitting open.

The *Scharführer* thrust the IDs back at Jack.

"Move on," he said, waving them forward.

Putting the car in gear, Jack glided through the checkpoint past a contingent of idle troopers who stared after them with sullen nonchalance. He was giddy, as if suddenly feeling the effect of an unknown narcotic.

"That was too close," Denise said, bringing her arm up from the space between her seat and the door. Her hand clutched one of the MP89s.

Jack blanched. "You would really have used that?"

"Rather than be caught?"

Jack nodded.

"In a heartbeat."

The farther they got from the checkpoint, the less the SS presence loomed. Stopping for gas and some stale candy bars and soda at a lonely rest stop, they pulled into Cincinnati fifteen hours later, exhausted, hungry, and apprehensive. A scan of the local radio stations told them the search for them had widened and intensified.

They slept overnight with a kindly old couple who fed them homemade blueberry muffins for breakfast and sent them on their way at dawn. Aside from another dicey border crossing from Pennsylvania to New York, their trip was uneventful. They reached downtown Buffalo about four p.m. that afternoon and cruised the waterfront. From their vantage point on the 190, they could look across the Peace Bridge into Fort Erie, Ontario.

Canada.

In Jack's other life, people thought of Canada almost as an extension of the United States, so similar were the cultures and languages. Only French-speaking Quebec, always the rebel, felt like a foreign country. Here and now, it was a very real and coveted haven.

"Is that where we cross?" Jack asked, his eyes on the bridge.

Denise glanced up from the map and studied the view. She nodded and looked at her watch. "The Redsons said we should make the crossing right at oh-six hundred."

Jack smiled. Besides making great blueberry muffins, Tom and Betty Redson were experienced travelers. They knew the border guards changed shifts at 0630. Tired and harried, the guards were eager to go home and would pass anyone through who happened along at the right moment. Timing was everything.

"Let's go get a cup of coffee," Jack said.

They took the first exit they saw, sped down the ramp, and took a right. A Burger Meister came into view, its brightly lit sign like a beacon to the weary. He pulled into the parking lot and turned off the motor. Leaning back in the seat, he closed his eyes and took a deep breath. He could hardly believe they'd made it. But the hardest part remained. Would their passports hold up if scrutinized by the border guards? Tired or not, the guards might be on extra alert, looking for a man and a woman traveling together. Though they looked different and drove a different car, something could still go wrong. Jack opened his eyes and touched the false moustache, making sure the spirit gum was holding.

"Wanna go in?" he asked.

"Yeah. Gotta pee."

The inside of the Burger Meister looked little different than the ones Jack remembered from his other life. The main differences were the statue of a fat, droll-looking man in lederhosen and a waxed mustache—the Burger Meister—and a large, flat-screen TV hanging from the walls. Instead of the insipid background music one always heard in these places, the sound from a sporting event blasted over the PA. Jack watched Denise head for the ladies' room and then got into the long line waiting to order food. Fortunately, it moved quickly, and he soon stood in front of a pretty, teenaged girl with long blonde hair and shiny braces.

"*Guten Tag* and welcome to Burger Meister. May I help you? Sir... may I help you?"

Jack didn't hear her because his gaze was riveted to the flat-screen TV, which now displayed photos of him and Denise.

Jack turned to the girl. "I'm sorry. What did you say?"

A look of annoyance flashed across the girl's features and was immediately gone. "May I help you?" she asked.

"Oh, yes. Two coffees, black."

The girl nodded and left the counter, returning moments later with the coffee.

"Six *Reichdollars*, please."

Jack fished the money out of his pocket, paid her, and took the tray of coffee over to a semi-secluded booth that allowed an unrestricted view of both the screen and the parking lot. Denise joined him moments later. She gasped as her eyes found the TV. Their pictures remained on the screen but were now reduced to a smaller window behind the anchorperson. The anchor, an icy blond with plastic hair, had that mock serious expression they all affected. The picture switched to a bruised and battered man being led through a hallway choked with SS and reporters. Jack felt his throat go dry as he realized the man was Art. The anchorwoman narrated over the scene.

"After twenty-four hours of interrogation, suspected terrorist Arthur Heinz confessed to running a station on what is known as the 'Underground Railroad.' Used for funneling fugitives and enemies of the state to Canada, the Underground Railroad is an arm of the hated American Resistance Movement. Through patient questioning and persuasion, Arthur Heinz revealed that he aided and abetted current fugitives, Jack Dunham and Denise Malloy. Before his execution, Arthur Heinz renounced his actions and declared his undying love for our glorious *Führer*."

The camera cut away to a scene in the courtyard of SS headquarters in Jacksonville. Art stood tied to a post, looking defiant. He stoically refused a blindfold. The firing squad raised its rifles and the officer in command shouted for them to aim. The camera zoomed in for a close-up. Arthur raised his eyes and said, "Long live the *Führer!*" The shots rang out and the screen cut back to the anchorwoman, who began reporting a related story.

Jack turned from the screen and saw a tear rolling out of Denise's eye. "I can't believe he would say that."

"He didn't."

"What do you mean, he didn't?" she said, her face flushed with anger. "I saw it. I *heard* him, damnit!"

"Keep your voice down," he whispered.

Denise blanched, remembering where they were. She leaned forward.

"You heard it, Dunham. They broke him. He told them everything."

Jack shook his head and smiled. "No, he didn't."

His smile only served to anger her more.

"Okay, Mr. Smarty-Pants. Suppose you tell me how you know that."

"I don't have to. They're showing it again."

Denise turned and looked at the screen. Sure enough, the network was running the tape of the execution a second time, no doubt on orders from the government. A frightened populace was a cooperative populace.

When the camera zoomed in on Art again, Jack tapped Denise on the hand. "Watch his mouth."

Denise's eyes narrowed and then widened.

"Oh my God! He said 'Long live—'"

"'The ARM.' That's right. He robbed them even of their propaganda until some network hack got the bright idea of finding someone to imitate his voice. Hell, no one would notice except a few deaf people or someone who'd worked for the Propaganda Ministry like us. Don't you see? He told them nothing, he beat them."

"But how? What about the drugs?"

"He's one of the rare ones the drugs couldn't get to. Probably knew it from the start."

Denise beamed, though her joy was tinged with sadness. "We're still safe."

"For now," Jack said, taking a sip of coffee.

Denise began to laugh, stifling it with her hand.

"What?" Jack said. And suddenly he knew. He felt the moustache slip as the spirit gum gave way. The steam from the coffee had loosened it.

"I think we'd better go," Denise said, chuckling.

Feeling like an idiot, Jack put his hand up to his mouth and pretended to cough as they walked from the restaurant.

Back in the car, he reapplied the moustache and held it in place until the glue dried.

"How do I look?" he asked.

"Like Clark Gable."

Jack gave her a lopsided smile and said, "Frankly, my dear, I don't give a damn. Let's get going."

He started the car and they headed back toward the Peace Bridge. Turning onto Porter Avenue, they saw Prospect Park, the Avalon Customs building, the SS garrison adjoining it, and beyond it, the bridge. True to Tom Redson's word, the traffic stood backed up about half a mile. Jack grabbed Denise's hand.

"This is it," he said.

Denise said nothing, bit her lip and nodded.

The traffic moved in fits and starts, and about thirty minutes later they were four cars from the gate. A Customs agent stood with a clipboard and questioned the driver of the lead car. He smiled and nodded. The gate lifted and the car drove on. The next car, a VW Vanagon, pulled up and the customs agent stepped forward, taking possession of the driver's papers. He frowned, turned to someone inside the building, and said something. A moment later a black uniformed SS-*Sturmbannführer* stepped out flanked by three troopers with MP89s. The Customs agent waved the van over to a nearby holding area. Jack could see the man's wife shaking her head and gesticulating wildly. The next car went through almost immediately. Jack noted the car had Canadian plates. He pulled up to the gate.

"Good evening, sir. Your passport and travel permits?"

Jack smiled at the agent and handed them over. He tried to appear calm and cool, but his stomach was twisted in knots. Resisting the urge to stare at the customs agent, Jack looked over at the van. The man and his wife stood off to one side, looking glum. One of the troopers held an MP89 on them while the other two methodically ripped their vehicle apart. When the troopers pulled out the cache of *Reichsdollars* from under the rear seat, their demeanor became combative. The man hung his head as they cuffed him; the woman screamed obscenities at him. Jack swallowed, remembering the MP89s under their seats. All it would take was a cursory search and they would be dead. All it would take was for Roberto's papers to have one tiny flaw and...

"Excuse me, sir?" the Customs agent said. "Would you please pull the car over and come inside?"

Jack stared at Denise. Her eyes betrayed her fear. She nodded as if to say, I love you no matter what happens. Jack nodded back and turned, half expecting to see a dozen guns trained on them. He edged the car over behind the Vanagon and left the engine running.

"If I'm not out in five minutes, go without me."

"No."

"Don't argue with me, Denise, it's not negotiable. Stay here!"

She glared at him, her eyes revealing a flash of mixed emotions. He resisted the urge to kiss her and climbed out of the car. His knees were like rubber as he strode across the two-lane road in the wake of the Customs agent. The agent held open the door of the office for Jack and then stepped in after him, taking a position near the door.

The room resembled every government office he'd ever been in: puke-green walls hung with a picture of *der Führer* and the current head of the Reich Immigration Service, as well as a bulletin board with the latest fugitives. Jack's eyes riveted onto the photos of himself and Denise, given prominent place among the murderers, counterfeiters, and other undesirables. The rest of the room was occupied by several battered file cabinets and a metal desk with one leg badly bent and propped up with several matchbooks. Behind the desk sat the SS-*Sturmbannführer* he'd glimpsed before. The SS man wore a pleasant smile. An incongruity at best. The cracked nameplate on the desk identified him as SS-*Sturmbannführer* Dieter Kreinhorst.

"Good afternoon, Mr. Manning. Where is your lovely wife?" he asked, his voice soft and high-pitched.

The voice stood in marked contrast to the man's rugged features.

Jack stammered out a reply. "She is not feeling too good, something she ate, I think."

The *Sturmbannführer* nodded. "I can well understand. These roadside *pommesbuden* are atrocious, *ja?* Still, what can we do? Shoot them?"

The SS man laughed heartily at his own joke, prompting Jack to join in.

Prompted by some unknown cue, the Customs agent moved to a position behind Kreinhorst and stared at Jack. The mood shifted abruptly.

"I am sorry to say we have a problem here, Mr. Manning," Kreinhorst said.

Jack's eyes flicked to the window. Outside, he could see the car. It stood empty. He began to sweat again.

"What is it, *Sturmbannführer?*"

Kreinhorst picked up the IDs and travel permits. "We instituted a new stamp yesterday. It is not on your permits. We have two very dangerous fugitives on the run. Did you not read of this?"

The man's stare intensified and the water cooler in the corner gurgled. Jack shrugged, smiled, and started to rise.

"Well, a stamp is easy enough to get. My wife and I'll come back with it tomorrow."

Kreinhorst raised his hand, his Cheshire grin widening. "There is another problem, *Herr* Manning..."

The room suddenly felt hot and closed in.

"Oh?" Jack said, oozing into his seat again.

"Yes, you see, these passports are fake."

Jack wanted to run, almost did, until he heard the trooper behind him pull back the bolt of his MP89. It slammed home with a deafening crack. Kreinhorst started to say something then stopped, his eyes widening as he spied something out the window.

"*Nein!*" he cried.

The window shattered, a burst of machine gun fire ripping into the room. The slugs, some of them glowing tracers, caught both Kreinhorst and the customs agent square in the chest. They appeared to dance as the bullets tore through their bodies and slammed into the walls, making a sharp, popping sound. In the brief silence that followed, Jack heard Denise.

"JACK! Get out here! NOW!"

A siren began to wail. Jack scrambled from his seat and dashed out the door. Denise threw him his MP89 just as a contingent of SS Troopers piled out of their guardhouse fifty yards away. It looked as if providence had smiled on them after all. Denise had begun shooting just as the guards were changing shifts.

Denise whirled and fired off a long burst, cutting down the troopers when they brought their own weapons to bear. Two of the SS Troopers were still alive and returned fire. Crouching low, Jack and Denise dashed for the car, putting the Vanagon between them and the troopers. Denise fired a burst, tore open the driver's side door, jumped inside, and slid over. Jack followed. Bullets thudded into the side of the car, missing them by scant inches. The blood rushed through Jack's head and he fumbled with the gearshift like a clumsy idiot.

"Move it, Jack!" Denise said, firing out the window.

Stomping on the clutch, he ground the gears, trying desperately to get it into first gear. The engine seized and died.

"JACK!"

More bullets whacked into the car doors and starred the driver's-side window. Jack ducked involuntarily and twisted the ignition key, nearly breaking it. The engine caught instantly, and he punched the gas and popped the clutch. The tires squealed, leaving a year's worth of rubber on the road. Fishtailing wildly, they raced across the tarmac, slammed through the wooden barrier, and leapt onto the bridge.

Another contingent of troopers called in from a nearby station sped around a corner in a VW *Kübelwagen*, taking no notice of the carnage at the customs office. The *Kübelwagen* hurtled onto the bridge, closing the gap between them and the fleeing Chrysler/Heinkel almost immediately.

Denise pulled out her spent magazine, rammed in another, then released the bolt.

"Stand on it!" she screamed.

"I am, goddammit!"

Trying to keep one eye on the road, Jack scanned the dashboard until he found the "Valet Switch." He reached forward and stabbed it with his finger. Instantly the car drew on an extra 100 horsepower, spinning the wheels. It shot forward, putting fifty feet between them and the onrushing *Kübelwagen*. The engine sounded like a roaring demon as it streaked toward the Canadian side.

In front of them, halfway across the bridge, lay the actual border with Canada. He could see another small contingent of troopers standing shoulder to shoulder, their MP89s raised and ready.

Denise leaned out the window and fired a burst, hitting the tires of the pursuing *Kübelwagen*. In a puff of dusty air, the right front tire exploded, throwing the vehicle into an uncontrollable spin and propelling it through the guardrail. It hung suspended for a split second then plunged the hundred feet to the slate-gray water below.

The troopers in front of them began firing en masse. Both Jack and Denise ducked as bullets punched through the windshield, peppering it. Jack kept the gas pedal to the floor, praying they wouldn't hit a tire or ignite the fuel with a tracer round. Holding his breath, he peered over the dash just as the car raced across the border. The troopers scattered, trying to fire after the speeding car and missing them entirely.

Up ahead, he could see a banner hanging between two of the bridge's overhead supports. On it were the crossed flags of Canada and Avalon, plus the message: Welcome to the Commonwealth of Canada. Never had words sounded so sweet.

13

Hugging the coast, they took the QEW Highway all the way into Toronto, arriving about 2030 that evening.

"It's beautiful isn't it, Jack?"

He nodded, noting the graceful CN tower, its spire reaching toward the sky. To Jack it was a symbol of their quest, a desire to reach the unreachable.

"Yes, it is," he said.

Breaking from his reverie, he steered the car through downtown and straight to Knox College at the University of Toronto. They left the car in one of the lots, deserted but for their own, and headed into the building. The architecture, with its hexagonal columns and flying buttresses, reminded Jack of pictures of Oxford before the Germans razed it. Although not as old as that venerable institution, the university had a sense of tradition, something all but lost in America. Anything that had outlived its function, or did not glorify those pigs in the government, fell before the wrecking ball in the name of progress.

"Are you sure he'll be here at this hour?" Denise asked.

"I didn't know the man except by reputation. In the other world, Chessman was renowned as a night owl. Claimed he did his best work in the wee hours."

They took a massive stone staircase to the second floor and strode down a dark corridor lined with the pictures of countless graduating classes. Jack scanned the frosted glass panels on the heavy wooden doors, looking for Chessman's name. He shook his head, feeling like an idiot. Of course. It was the one at the end with the light behind it.

He approached the door and knocked. No answer. He knocked again, louder this time. Again, no answer.

"Damn, he's not here."

"We'll come back. He'll be here in the morning."

"No. We came all this way. We're *not* leaving."

This time Jack pounded on the door, rattling it in its frame. A moment later they heard the patter of soft footsteps. A shadow appeared behind the frosted glass.

"Yes, who is it?"

"Dr. Chessman? My name is Jack Dunham. I—"

"I am sorry. I have no time for interviews, I am working."

"Doctor, we've come a long way. We're not reporters, we're—Curly Williams sent us."

Jack heard the doctor gasp and then the sound of a deadbolt being thrown. The door swung open and there stood the infamous Dr. Morris Chessman. He stared at them, his bushy eyebrows arched in surprise. He wore a pair of thick bifocals in a synthetic tortoiseshell frame perched on the very end of his bulbous nose. His eyes were a deep brown, almost black, and the whites were slightly yellowed and bloodshot. His hair, thick, wavy, and shot with gray, stuck out at crazy angles as if he'd just awakened. Oddly, his goatee and mustache were still a deep, glossy black. He smiled, revealing teeth yellowed from years of coffee and pipe tobacco.

"So," he said, his voice sounding thick and phlegmy. "You are the two who have caused the SS such embarrassment?"

Jack smiled sheepishly. "Yes."

"Good," he snorted, "they deserve it. Come in, come in, you're letting all the good ideas out."

He turned and walked back into a laboratory that looked like something out of an old Universal monster movie. Electrical equipment abounded, covering every surface. Some pieces were modern, like the rather sophisticated IBM/Siemens PC on the desk, and some ancient, like the gigantic Tesla coil standing in one corner. Chessman caught Jack admiring it.

"Nikola Tesla. The man was a genius."

"So are you, I'm told," Jack said.

Chessman looked at him, contemptuous.

"Bah. If I were such a genius, would I have permitted this?"

"Well—"

"No, young man, let me finish. Science is a wonderful thing... until greed gets in the way. We spend years learning how our universe works and, in some cases, how to manipulate its forces. But only superficially. Nature always exacts its price. And we are paying for it now."

"But Doctor. You had to know what you were getting into."

He nodded and smiled, but there was no trace of warmth or humor in it.

"Oh, yes, I knew what I was getting into all right. Armand Bock seduced me with visions of glory and unlimited funding, of regaining the wealth those Communist bastards stole from my family in Russia. I was blinded, consumed with my own shortsightedness. I forgot what these Nazi fiends were capable of. Bock had me thrown into Andersonville as soon as his memory came back. He didn't want me having a change of heart and putting things back the way they were."

"You mean—"

"Of course. In training Kruger, I found I had the ability as well."

"Then why the hell didn't you *do* something?" Denise said, speaking for the first time since entering the room.

"Because I'm an old man, young lady. And I have a cancer that is eating me up inside."

Jack looked at the old man and noted the dark circles under the eyes, the sallow complexion and the tremor in his right hand. This was a man who had little time left.

"How did you get out of Andersonville?" Jack said.

"I transported out."

"What?"

Chessman smiled again. "When Bock threw me into that hellhole, my abilities were still raw and unpredictable. I spent the months there perfecting them, strengthening them. I have below-average psi ability, which is why it took so long. But I worked on it—hard. Finally, when the camp doctors discovered I had lung cancer and tagged me for the gas chambers, I had to move, ready or not."

Jack shook his head. "I don't get it. I thought this whole thing was a method of *time* travel."

"It is, my boy, it is. But it is also a method for traveling through *space*."

"Whoa," Denise said.

Chessman continued. "One night I sat up in my bunk and began to chant. I had no idea if it would really work with me, but I had nothing left to lose. It only took five minutes and I appeared here in Toronto. It was the most extraordinary event, to actually experience my life's work first-hand. Unfortunately, it has weakened me considerably. So, you see, my dear girl, I cannot do it again. To travel back fifty years *and* thousands of miles would kill me. But I *can* train others."

The old professor's eyes shone with a queer light that made Jack uncomfortable. Could this man, a man who followed the sick dreams of Armand Bock, be trusted after all? Jack looked at Denise and saw the same concerns etched on her face. They were in Canada, they were free. They could just walk out and continue their lives, never looking back. But Jack knew he could never do that. He could never just sit back and let the Nazis keep the world. Eventually, Canada would be attacked. It could even escalate into a nuclear conflict. Better to trust the devil himself than allow that.

"Curly said Wiley was here with you," Jack said.

"Yes, your friend is staying nearby. He has spoken of you many times. It is unfortunate that he is not trainable."

Jack nodded. "That's why we're here. I want to go back. Can you test me?"

Chessman sat up in his chair and stared at Jack.

"Yes," he said. "Come with me."

Chessman strode toward another part of the lab. This room was considerably smaller but no less impressive. Dominating the space was what looked like a soundproof booth of the kind used by audiologists when giving their patients hearing tests. The door stood open and inside sat a simple wooden chair. About head level and projecting from the walls on telescoping rods were two halves of a highly stylized helmet. Completely transparent, it had embedded in the plastic all manner of complex-looking circuitry. At various points on the helmet, thick groups of tiny, multicolored wires emanating from jacks came together into bundles tied by plastic wire ties. These braids then twisted around the telescoping rods and terminated at an intricate network of jacks embedded in the lead-sheathed walls.

Chessman pointed to the device as a father would his child. "This is my Psionic Wave Detector. It uses a principle similar to an EEG. The difference lies in its sensitivity to the psi waves put out by the subject inside the psionic sensor. This will tell us in minutes whether a person has any latent ESP or telekinetic ability."

"Why the lead?"

"Two reasons. One, it is to keep out all other forms of radiation so as not to gain false readings. Two, the detector uses an infinitesimal amount of plutonium as the power source for certain components."

Knowing this did nothing to calm Jack. He didn't like the idea of sitting in anything nuclear one damn bit.

"What about the window? Won't it get through that?"

Chessman smiled indulgently. "That is lead crystal and is over six inches thick. No, my boy, it is as impervious as the lead. Shall we?"

The old professor gestured for Jack to go inside.

He sighed. "What the hell."

Jack stepped into the booth and heard the massive door slam shut behind him with a muffled thud. Weird! Aside from his own breathing, he could hear no sound... nothing. Even anechoic rooms had a minimal level of sound, but this one sounded dead. Listening again, Jack found he could hear the sound of his own head quite loudly. It made him even more uncomfortable.

"Please sit still as I protract the sensor, Mr. Dunham," Chessman said, his voice coming through a tiny speaker in the wall of the chamber.

Jack heard a soft purring and saw out of the corner of his eye the two halves of the transparent helmet moving toward his head. The two pieces came together with a soft click and Jack began to giggle. For all its impressive technology, the Psionic Wave Detector reminded him of the Cone of Silence from *Get Smart*, an old TV show he hadn't seen in years.

"Is it comfortable, Mr. Dunham?" Chessman said. The man sounded impatient. Could he now be as eager as they to right the wrong of this world?

"Perfect, Doc," Jack said, giving Chessman a thumbs up. He felt like an idiot sitting in this tiny box wearing some stupid thing on his head that resembled an electronic Rube Goldberg.

"All right, Mr. Dunham. I need for you to think about one thing only."

"You mean clear my mind," Jack said, thinking of the old hypnotist's cliché.

"No, no, my boy. Not only is that mentally impossible, but it will also give us a false reading. I need you to concentrate on one thought. It doesn't matter what. It could be something from your past, something yet to be, or something that gives you great comfort. Perhaps the last time you and your pretty lady friend were intimate." Jack saw Denise redden, and he smiled. That certainly would satisfy all of the above.

"Okay, Doc. Whenever you're ready."

Jack closed his eyes and thought of Denise, her hard, muscular body, the way they fit together, the way she smiled. He took mental inventory of her and it pleased him. Through these thoughts Jack heard a low hum pulsing through the booth and a warm, almost wet feeling coursed through his body, making him feel as if he were floating. It was odd, but his mouth tasted of amaretto. A moment later he heard a buzz and the floating feeling receded.

"You may come out now, Mr. Dunham," Chessman said flatly.

Jack saw their troubled expressions as he stepped out of the booth.

"What? What's wrong?"

"I am sorry, young man, but your psi ability is far too low. It would take years to bring out only a minimal facility. You would be able to perform parlor tricks at parties to amuse your friends, at best."

Jack felt as if someone had pulled the floor out from under him.

"But... what will we do? I *have* to go back. Curly said that only someone who remembered the *real* world could go back—"

"No, Mr. Dunham, you misunderstood. What I told your friend was that someone who remembered would be the most *effective* candidate. This way, that person would know what to expect. Anyone with enough latent ability could be trained to go."

"Then why wait for us?"

"Because we needed to exhaust the options. Now we have no choice."

"Let me try," Denise said.

"Forget it, Malloy, you can't go back. You have no idea what to do, and a woman has no place trying to stop a trained killer like Kruger."

Denise's eyes narrowed.

"Listen, Jack, and listen good, because I'm only gonna say this once," she said, her voice shaking with repressed fury. "You are one short-sighted idiot. What do you think Lambda is all about? We get our training from the ARM. I'm as good a person to send as any. Better than you. Who saved your butt back there at the border, anyway?"

She was right, but it didn't make him feel any better about it.

"I don't like it," Jack said. "If something happened to you, I..."

He couldn't, wouldn't finish the thought. He didn't want to spill his guts in front of a stranger. But Denise got the message. Her manner immediately softened.

"Oh, Jack," she said, coming to him.

"Yeah... well," he said.

She hugged him and he encircled her in his arms. It wasn't fair. It just wasn't goddamned fair.

"Both of you could go," Chessman said, breaking into their thoughts.

"What?" Denise said.

"If Miss Malloy's ability is high enough, she can take you *both* back."

"But how?" Jack said, confused as hell.

"One thing I discovered is that a traveler can take anything with him—or her," he said, bowing to Denise, "simply by having it in physical contact with his or her body. In other words—"

"All I have to do is hold hands with Jack and—"

"Exactly. You both will transport. That and anything else you wish to take. Weapons, clothes, money... anything."

Without another word, Denise climbed into the booth and waited. "Let's get to it, Doc. Time's a wastin'."

Jack stood back as Chessman closed the door and walked back to the small instrument panel mounted into what looked like a modified lectern. He began flipping switches and turning dials. He watched as the psionic sensor closed around Denise's head. The inside of the booth began to glow a soft blue and a generator hummed. Something that sounded like a giant centrifuge began to whir. The multicolored lights on the panel flashed on and off, casting a bizarre psychedelic display across Chessman's intense features. The old professor leaned over to the microphone.

"Now, my dear, you must do as Jack did. Think of something singular."

She nodded and closed her eyes, her face a mask of concentration.

Jack looked over at the instrument panel and frowned, trying to figure out what the hell he was looking at.

"What you are seeing, young man," Chessman explained, "are the digital readouts for vital signs and the subject's psionic waveform. And that contraption attached to the panel is a modified EEG graph machine, which will give me a permanent paper record of your lovely friend's reading."

A quick glance at his own graph confirmed for Jack what Chessman had said earlier. The psionic wave portion of the graph was nearly flat. He couldn't help feeling a trifle foolish, as if he'd failed an IQ test of some kind.

"My God!" Chessman said.

Jack looked back at the panel and saw the psionic readout racing through numbers at an astounding rate. The needle on the graph leaped about, making huge hills and valleys on the paper. Chessman smiled like a Cheshire cat as he tweaked the settings. He turned to Jack, laughing with glee.

"Your lady friend's abilities are nearly off my scale. Her latent abilities are positively astounding. She is like a dream come true, my boy, a dream come true."

Jack watched Denise, her face like stone as she made the psionic graph's stylus hop on the paper. He glanced at the vital signs and saw they had hardly moved above normal.

"You're right about that, Professor," he said, smiling in awe. "Right as rain."

In spite of his earlier misgivings, Jack was excited. The impossible was now again within their grasp. Depending on how long it took Denise to perfect her ability, they would soon be going back to 1944. Together. As much as the thought had scared him before, he now realized he didn't want to be left behind. With her training, they stood a better chance of pulling it off. God willing, everything would soon be back the way it should be; God willing, they would both survive to enjoy it.

14

Toronto, Canada
26 April 1994

The door to the motel room swung open and Wiley stared in disbelief.

"Hey, shithead, how are ya?" Jack said, smiling broadly.

"JACK!"

Wiley grabbed him in a bear hug, lifted him off the ground, and carried him into the room, laughing like a lunatic. Denise shook her head, followed them in, and shut the door. No matter how old she got, she would never understand men, how every time they got together, they acted like twelve-year-old boys. Even now, they chatted excitedly, recalling times they remembered that, for her, never existed. That was another thing. After all they'd been through, the concept of a completely different timeline where history had taken a decidedly different turn boggled her mind. Even more startling was that each of these men remembered both.

"...and you remember Leslie?" Jack said.

"The brunette with the big—"

Wiley stopped himself, his eyes flicking over to Denise. Jack turned, saw her level gaze, and realized his lack of manners.

"Jeez, I'm an idiot," he said.

"I'm not even gonna touch that one, Dunham," Denise said, crossing the room. "Hi, I'm Denise Malloy, Jack's girlfriend."

Wiley took her proffered hand and shook it. "Nice to meet you, Denise." He turned to Jack. "You still got good taste, ol' buddy."

"In more ways than one," Jack said. "Denise is with Lambda; she helped me get out."

Wiley looked surprised, then his brows knitted in confusion. Denise saw the unspoken question in his wide, hazel eyes. Apparently, so did Jack.

"It's a long, long story, Wiley, and it's not important. What is is that we love each other."

"Well, Killer, that's all anyone can ask for," he said, patting Jack on the shoulder.

Jack moved over to the bed and plopped down on it, suddenly feeling very tired.

"It's been one hell of a week, Wiley. One day everything is fine and the next I'm remembering two different lives and two different histories. It's driving me nuts."

Wiley nodded, his expression sober. "I know, man. It hit me the same way. I was watching TV about six months ago when a documentary about Armand Bock came on. I started feeling really weird, then it clobbered me like a sledgehammer. I thought I'd had a stroke. All these memories came back, everything. Especially you."

Jack smiled. "The worst part was realizing we knew what those bastards were up to... but not soon enough."

"Chessman says that may be why we remember the old life at all. He said something about the very fact of knowing the plot existed planted the seed."

Jack nodded. "Yeah, I know all that. But why the hell didn't we remember when we were fifteen or something? Why now?" He got up and began pacing, his anger building. "Why now? You want to hear something fucked up? I mentioned Leslie because in our old life she was just a beautiful woman with well-to-do parents and a trust fund. Here, she's a goddamn card-carrying, goose-stepping, head-honcho Nazi, a goddamned SS-*Brigadeführer*, no less. And I didn't even know it. Can you believe it?"

Wiley blanched.

"She was what!"

"A *Brigadeführer*, Wiley. In SS lingo, that's a freaking general. I was sleeping with an SS General and all the time she's playing me for a sucker, telling me she's the lowly secretary of some party hack. Christ!" He kicked at a freestanding lamp, sending it against the wall. He heard the bulb pop.

"Shit," Jack said, feeling foolish. He turned and went to the window and stared out at the Toronto skyline. Denise looked at Wiley.

"What is it?" Denise said. "You know something."

Wiley looked at Denise, his eyes like a scared rabbit caught in the headlights on an oncoming car.

"It means they know," he said.

Jack turned from the window, annoyed. "Know what, for Christ's sake!"

"They know, Jack. Bock, Kruger, the Nine Old Men."

Jack's anger dropped a notch, but he still looked confused. "What are you talking about?"

It was Wiley's turn to get angry. "What? Do I have to spell it out for you? They know that *you* know about what they did! Do you think it's just a coincidence that you and Leslie were together in this timeline too? Shit! They put her on you to keep them informed. Somehow they knew you'd found out."

"How *could* they know?" Jack said.

"Who the hell knows how? What difference does it make? The point is, she was probably waiting for orders to snuff you as soon as you exhibited any signs of remembering."

Jack dropped onto the bed, his face as white as the walls of the room. "Oh God," he said. "Then that's how she knew to follow us to Henry's."

Wiley frowned. "What? Who's Henry?"

Denise told him about the Lambda meeting and the subsequent massacre. Wiley took the news of Curly's death better than the knowledge of Leslie's true allegiance.

"At least those fuckers didn't get him alive," he said.

"But why does any of that matter now?" Jack said. "We're over the border, we're free."

Wiley shook his head. "You may be free, but you're not free of them. Tensions between Canada and Avalon have been heating up lately. Ottawa has just expelled all of the Avalonian diplomats, accusing them of running a spy network. Truth is, they were. There could be a war any time."

"They'd be stupid to open a two-front war. Look what happened the last time. Shit, if it weren't for Bock, it would have gone down the crapper the way it should've. Why would they risk making the same stupid mistake here?"

"Politics, ol' buddy, politics." He got up and went to the dresser where there was a bottle of Canadian Club and glasses wrapped in tissue paper. He poured three drinks, passed two to Jack and Denise, and continued. "You see, as long as there is a free country on their borders, they think it makes them look bad. Never mind 'coexisting peacefully with their brother nations' or any of that crap. They have to keep the population in a constant state of paranoia, or they lose control. And that's the key: *control*. The problem is paranoia is catchy. They begin to believe their own propaganda. That's why they watched you, Jack. You were a wild card, a thorn in their Nazi butts."

"Yeah, so what? I'm outta there. They can't touch me. If there's a war, we'll move to the Republic of Alaska."

"You're missing the point."

"Then get to it, Wiley. I'm getting tired of the rhetoric."

"Bock and the Nine Old Men aren't going to sit still knowing you're out there somewhere."

Jack suddenly caught the drift of Wiley's speech.

"Oh shit."

"You got it, partner. They're going to send their ace hero in to take you out."

"Kruger," Denise said.

Wiley nodded.

"All that means is we have to step up the training with Chessman," she said.

Wiley's mood immediately changed. "How'd it go, Jack? How'd you test out?"

Jack shook his head. "About as psychic as a rock. It's Denise that sent his wave machine into conniptions."

"We're both going," Denise said.

Wiley laughed, held up his hand. "I'm sorry. Don't take it wrong, but the idea of Jack hitching a ride on your lap really amuses me."

"It's not something I like, Wiley, but we have no choice, especially now."

"You got that right, Killer. If you don't go, Kruger will find you and rip your head off, for sure. If you go back, you at least have a shot of nailing the bastard."

"He could kill us back there too."

"Maybe. But wouldn't it be better to meet him on neutral ground, so to speak?" Wiley said.

"Hell yes," Jack said.

Wiley turned to Denise. "When do you start?"

"Tomorrow."

"Soon enough," he said, getting to his feet. "Anyone for another snort?"

"We've got to get something to eat or we're going to pass out," Jack said.

"Say no more, ol' buddy. I know a great place where the steaks are sizzlin' and so are the waitresses." He shook his head and turned to Denise. "Oh... sorry."

She grinned. "That's okay, Wiley. I'm up for some jiggling waitress myself. Last one to pinch her butt pays the check. Come, sweetheart."

She hooked her arm through Jack's, and they walked grandly out of the room, leaving Wiley with his mouth hung open like the proverbial barn door. In a moment, he smiled and shook his head, chuckling softly. He grabbed his wallet and followed them.

"You sure know how to pick 'em, Jack," he said, closing the door behind him.

15

Miami, Florida
1 May 1994

SS-*Brigadeführer* Leslie Parsons stood at the floor-to-ceiling window of her expansive corner office and gazed out at the spectacular view of downtown Miami, past the tall buildings, and out onto the azure blue of Biscayne Bay. She could see the puffy-white sails of myriad boats gliding across the smooth, flat water and wished she were out there. Anywhere but here.

They'd gotten away.

Jack and that lesbian bitch had slipped right through her fingers. It had taken the forensic pathologists two days of picking through the blackened bones and dental records of over forty corpses to determine that they'd escaped the conflagration. But Leslie knew it already. The reports from the officer in charge of the Lambda raid told of firing upon three fleeing suspects. One had been wounded fatally, while a man and woman escaped. After IDing the corpse of Curly Williams, she'd known all she'd needed to know. Unfortunately, she could not reveal why she knew this to be true. Bock would not allow it. To keep his ugly secret, she'd had to play dumb and let Jack and that woman get away.

THE NORMANDY CLUB

Damn.

They were out there... somewhere. With a two-day head start, they'd slipped the gauntlet at the Georgia border and headed north. The biggest problem was in dealing with the rash of sightings called in by concerned, yet anonymous citizens. Leslie suspected they were Lambda agents. They'd wasted so much time chasing down the false alarms that Jack and Denise had crossed into Canada in the wake of a bloody shootout that left a dozen troopers dead, plus a high-ranking officer and customs agent leaking vital fluids from over twenty bullet wounds.

But it didn't matter where they'd gone, because she'd fucked up—big time. All she'd had to do, when he was lying helpless in Hoffman Memorial Hospital, was order him removed and taken to Andersonville or the new camp near Orlando. It was idiotically simple. So why hadn't she done that?

She sighed and fought back a tear. That was simple too. She had fallen in love with Jack Dunham. She'd committed the cardinal sin of an undercover operative: becoming emotionally entangled with her assignment. Normally, persons of her rank did not become involved in such operations, but this one had been special. Jack had been special.

DAMN!

Turning from the window, she sat at her desk and stared at the screen of her notebook computer. The cursor flashed in the middle of a paragraph she'd been trying to finish for the last half hour. But she couldn't. She couldn't bring herself to admit failure, not yet.

Ever since her first meeting with Armand Bock all those months ago, she'd felt herself a part of destiny, as if she herself were shaping events. Not that her own life lacked for anything. On the contrary, her rise in rank was not only spectacular, but highly unusual. Some colleagues, jealous of her success, whispered rumors about her fucking her way to the top. How else could a woman become a *Brigadeführer*? To hell with them. To hell with them all. She'd done it through sheer hard work, and a massive stroke of luck. Only to herself would she admit that her looks had helped. Though the party preached equal opportunity for all, it was still a man's world, and long ago, Leslie had learned that beauty had its place. Used wisely, it had carried her far.

In truth, she'd had only one affair with a superior, an older man who helped her because he'd loved her. Not because of some cheap and tawdry "arrangement." When he'd died suddenly of a heart attack, she was surprised to find herself promoted from *Standartenführer* to fill his post, skipping one whole rank and making a score of enemies. That had been a year ago. Since then, she'd distinguished herself admirably, rooting out cells of ARM traitors all over South Florida. This latest raid would no doubt have earned her a citation signed by the *Führer* himself. Except...

Feeling her anger rise, Leslie snapped off the computer and leaned back in her soft, leather chair and closed her eyes. They were waiting for her report up on the top floor. They could wait some more. The phone buzzed, a soft purring that always annoyed her. Her finger stabbed the speaker button.

"Yes?" she said.

"I am sorry to disturb you, *Brigadeführer*, there is a call for you on line five."

Leslie frowned. This was her private line.

"Who is it?"

"He wouldn't say."

This made her angrier.

"Tell whoever it is that if they want to speak with me, they'd damn well better identify themselves or we'll trace the call and send them to Andersonville."

Leslie could hear the fear in her secretary's voice. "Yes, ma'am."
A moment later the phone buzzed again.

"Shit," she said, pushing the speaker button. "What is it, Ruth?"

"You shouldn't threaten your friends," the gravelly voice said.

Leslie felt her blood run cold when she recognized the voice of Armand Bock. Taking a deep breath, she calmed herself and spoke.

"Well, *Herr* Bock, my friends usually announce themselves and don't play silly games."

"Quite so, my dear."

She fumed. She hated his oily, condescending tone.

"What can I do for you?"

"I am having a quiet dinner party tonight. I would be honored if you would come."

"Thank you, *Herr* Bock, but I have a report to finish and I—"

"I would suggest you come," he interrupted. "This concerns the package you lost."

Leslie's throat went dry.

"What have you heard?"

"All in good time, my dear, all in good time. I will send a car for you at seven."

Before she could say anything, the phone disconnected.

"Damn," she said, hitting her palm on the desk.

This was all she needed. Not only would she be reprimanded, but now Bock wanted to get his licks in. Why she'd ever let herself be sucked into this assignment, she'd never know. Thinking back, she recalled the day she'd walked into *Obergruppenführer* Freitag's office and saw Bock sitting next to her superior, chatting like old friends. Everyone knew Bock's reputation, a man who'd gotten rich making armaments and personally instrumental in winning the Great Struggle. To any loyal party member, the man was an icon.

"Ah, *Brigadeführer* Parsons," Freitag had said, getting to his feet. "May I present *Herr* Armand Bock."

The older man stood, bowed, and clicked his heels together. So old world. Such bullshit.

"I'm very honored to meet you, *Herr* Bock," she'd said.

"The honor is all mine, my dear."

The *Obergruppenführer*, rubbing his hands together like some overeager matchmaker, signaled for them all to sit.

"*Herr* Bock has come a long way—"

Bock held up his hand, silencing the man. This impressed Leslie, since her superior was a man not easily dismissed.

"We have an assignment for you," Bock said.

Leslie perked up. This *was* unusual.

"Do you know a man named Jack Dunham?" Bock continued.

"Should I?" she asked, curious.

"Yes and no," Bock said, not elaborating. "He works for the Ministry of Propaganda and we believe he is harboring certain information that may be detrimental to the security of the state."

Leslie shrugged. "Doesn't every one of us, *Herr* Bock? All of us who work for the Party are privy to its secrets."

The older man shook his head, smiling indulgently. He looked like a regal bird of prey with his full head of white hair and his fierce, hooded eyes.

"This information is something he does not remember."

"I'm sorry, but you're not making much sense," she said.

"Forgive me," he said, "but I cannot go into the details. Suffice it to say, when he does remember, the reaction will likely be violent. Both for him and for the state. We want you there when it happens. We want you to become his paramour."

This shocked her.

"Wait a minute. I haven't done covert operative work in years. I have a division to run, I can't—"

"You can and you will," Bock said, his voice harsh.

Leslie looked to Freitag, who studied his hands. The man looked like a frightened schoolboy. She took a deep breath, calming herself.

"Let me get this straight," she said after a moment. "You want me to meet him, seduce him, and hang around until he remembers some obscure fact—"

"I can assure you, my dear, that what Jack Dunham knows is not obscure.

"Fine. So he remembers this *earth-shattering* piece of information, then what?"

"Kill him."

This shocked her as well, not for what he said, but for the way he said it—calmly and casually.

"Don't you want to know what he knows?" she said, incredulous.

Bock smiled again, his expression like that of a sated lion warming itself in the sun.

"We already know, my dear. We already know."

※　※　※

The long, stretch Mercedes limousine rolled sleekly through the streets of Coral Gables, through neighborhoods of large mansions owned by the Party elite of America. Many were winter homes for functionaries who worked in cities farther north. The houses stood on massive lots, set far back from the street and surrounded by high walls and gun- toting guards. They were a far cry from her townhouse condominium on Biscayne Boulevard. Her rank gave her privileges, but it was always money that made the world go round. And the people who'd gotten the money for these gaudy estates did so in ways that were less than aboveboard. Corruption was something she hated but tolerated. One had to go along to get along, especially in Avalon.

"How much farther is it?" Leslie said to the driver.

The man's beady eyes flicked up to the rearview mirror and lingered on her ample breasts, which in the expensive, black evening gown were more accentuated than usual. Bock had insisted she dress for his little soirée, and she felt awkward and on display, like one of the prostitutes in the SS brothels. Leslie fought the urge to reprimand the man. Though he wore the uniform of a lowly SS-*Scharführer*, he was Bock's personal chauffeur, and therefore, untouchable. He knew it too. The man leered and spoke, barely concealing his contempt.

"Not too much further... Missy."

Fuming, she turned and looked out the window. She decided she *would* put the man on report. Let Bock sort it out with his old pal *Obergruppenführer* Freitag. A moment later, the limo slowed and turned through a massive, wrought-iron gate that slid open silently and then closed behind them. In the distance, she could see an obscenely large mansion. It appeared that every light in the place was lit like a tacky Christmas ad.

The limo swept down the drive and pulled in front of the massive portico. There, a liveried butler opened the door, bowed, and clicked his heels.

"Please follow me, *Brigadeführer*," he said, marching up the wide steps ahead of her. He held open the massive iron and crystal door and Leslie stepped into a world that could only be described as mythical. The entryway could have doubled as a ballroom. It had twenty-foot ceilings with walls and floor lined in black and white marble. There was an immense swastika of inlaid obsidian in the center of the floor, surrounded by a wide band of yellow metal that

THE NORMANDY CLUB

could only be gold. An oil portrait of Adolf Hitler hung on the wall, overlooking priceless tapestries and sculptures any museum would grovel for.

"Come, madam," the butler intoned. He began marching across the marble expanse, his heels clicking cadence. Leslie followed, awed. They walked through an extended hallway leading to several rooms whose doors remained closed. One set of double doors lay open, revealing an opulent dining room and table, the length of which could easily seat thirty. It looked ridiculous set for four.

Passing that room, the butler reached another set of double doors. With great ceremony, he pushed them open and led her into the library. This room impressed her as much as anything she'd seen: fluted columns carved from solid mahogany and floor-to-ceiling shelves containing thousands of volumes. From what she could see of them, they all appeared to be first editions, and no doubt priceless.

"Welcome, *Brigadeführer* Parsons, to my humble abode," Bock said.

He stood in front of a massive window, a glass of champagne in his hands.

"Thank you, *Herr* Bock. I—"

"Please, you must call me Armand."

Another shock.

"Very well... Armand. Thank you for inviting me."

He waved his hand casually and said, "Think nothing of it, my dear. May I get you some champagne?"

She nodded.

Bock reached for a bell cord and pulled. A moment later the same butler appeared bearing a tray with a single flute filled with the sparkling wine.

She smiled. *God, this man's ego is monstrous*, she thought.

"May I introduce you to an associate of mine," he said, turning to two figures just walking into the room through another set of doors. "*Brigadeführer* Leslie Parsons, may I present *Herr* Werner Kruger, Hero of the Reich."

He stepped forward and bowed. Kruger appeared older than in the videos she'd seen, and from what she knew, Kruger was about the same age as Bock. Age had not dimmed his persona; there was something dangerous about him, like a coiled snake about to strike. Leslie held out her hand and Kruger kissed it in the old, formal way.

"I am honored, *Brigadeführer*," he said. "May I present my fiancée, Hannah Raeder."

An Amazon, nearly six feet tall, Hannah Raeder had long, red hair, flawless white skin, and proportions that actually made Leslie feel small for the first time in her life. To call this woman merely voluptuous would have done her a disservice. Equally striking was her aristocratic, exquisitely featured face, like that on a cameo brooch. However, what struck Leslie most about Miss Hannah Raeder was the obvious disparity in ages between her and Werner Kruger. Fifty years give or take a decade. In spite of all of her striking qualities and regal appearance, the illusion instantly shattered as soon as she opened her mouth.

"Pleased ta meetya, I'm shooah."

Leslie flinched inwardly at the sound of the woman's horrendous dialect. She could have been a rocket scientist, for all Leslie knew, but she sounded like a bimbo.

"When are we gonna eat, Wernie?" she whined.

Acts like one too, Leslie thought.

If Kruger felt embarrassed or uncomfortable by her crass and tactless question, he didn't show it.

"Soon, my dear, soon," Bock said, smiling indulgently. "Would you excuse us a moment? Your betrothed and I have some business to discuss with the *Brigadeführer*. Hans will fix you a drink in the anteroom."

Hannah gave Kruger a sexy smile and strutted from the room, her curvaceous behind twitching rhythmically beneath the tight, emerald-green gown she wore. When the door closed, Bock's cordial manner disappeared.

"Sit down, *Brigadeführer*," he said.

Leslie took a seat in a richly upholstered wingback chair while Bock remained standing. Kruger strolled over to one of the bookshelves, pretending to absorb himself in one of the old volumes. Bock glowered at her.

"Do you realize how much grief you have caused us? Do you know how serious the situation is?"

Leslie felt her blood begin to boil. "Excuse me, Armand, but I think I have an idea—"

"YOU HAVE NO IDEA!" he screamed.

This time Leslie did flinch. Bock turned nearly purple with rage, his eyes popped out of his head, and a small bit of spittle sprayed out his mouth. In a second he transformed, calm, as if nothing were amiss.

"Let me tell you a story, Ms. Parsons. And please forgive my lapse of military etiquette, but I find these SS titles so cumbersome."

Leslie said nothing.

"It is a story of glorious proportions—of heroic deeds and monumental stakes. But first, a little visual aid. Werner, the pictures."

Turning from the bookshelves, Kruger crossed the room, a manila envelope in his hands. He stopped in front of Leslie, who took the envelope from his liver-spotted hands. She shuddered involuntarily as she looked into his cold eyes. Looking away, she opened the mailer and found two pictures. One was a group of SS men taken about 1944, the other was a class picture that had been taken in 1988.

"What's the point of—" she began. Her voice trailed off when she saw the bright, shining, *young* face of Werner Kruger staring out from both photos. Her eyes snapped up to Bock, who stared at her, his eyes burning with a queer intensity.

"As I said, the story is of epic scope, involving major figures of our time. Have you ever heard of telekinetic transport through the fourth dimension?"

"No."

Bock chuckled. "I thought not. Anyway, our story begins as all stories do, with a hero and a villain..."

He began pacing casually about the room as he told his incredible story of time travel and brutal assassination. He was right. The scope of what he told her *was* monumental. At first, Leslie found it unbelievable. After a while, she found herself leaning forward, hanging on to every word. When Bock had finished, he smiled triumphantly, his eyes shining with a euphoria usually reserved for the criminally insane.

Leslie's mind reeled. Time travel, a world in which the Nazis no longer existed, a world where they had in fact been roundly defeated? It boggled the mind. It certainly boggled hers. But the most incredible part was that she'd known Jack in that life too. Somewhere in another reality, another dimension where things had progressed differently, she and Jack had been together, perhaps lived their whole lives happy and content, away from all of this.

"What I don't understand is how you knew Jack found out."

Bock shrugged. "A simple matter of reviewing the club's video surveillance tapes. Aside from the camera outside the door, there was another *inside* the room. Only I knew about that camera. After verifying that it was Mr. Carpenter and a local safecracker, we killed the safecracker and began a full-time surveillance of our dear Wiley. When he met with Jack Dunham in Miami, we had a man in the restaurant. Unfortunately, he could not get close enough to hear what was said. In any event, we were reasonably sure that he told Mr. Dunham everything."

"But you weren't absolutely sure."

"That's where you came in, my dear," Bock said. "After Kruger went back and all had changed, I had to be sure. If he remembered like we do, then he had to be stopped."

"Right," she said, feeling angry again. "I suppose you knew about me, too, from that other timeline?"

"Is it not obvious?" he said, gesturing expansively. "We watched you from birth, made sure you had all the right advantages, the right promotions..."

Leslie didn't like where this was going.

"Wait a minute. I got those promotions because I deserved them."

"Of course you did. We just made sure the opportunities for advancement were *favorable*."

Leslie felt her mouth go dry. In that moment she knew Bock *was* mad and totally ruthless. He had engineered her lover's "heart attack," had callously swept away a brilliant officer just to serve his own ends. My God, he'd altered the whole universe to those same ends. How many others had been expendable?

Leslie stood up and gathered her small clutch purse.

"If you will excuse me, *Herr* Bock, I am not feeling well."

"Sit down," he hissed. Leslie stopped in her tracks as Kruger turned and moved toward her. The threat was subtle, but obvious. Gripping her purse until her knuckles turned white, Leslie sat down, perching herself so as to be ready for anything, verbal or physical. Bock smiled, but his eyes remained cold.

"Wouldn't you like to bring Jack to justice? Him *and* that woman?"

"Let me ask you something," she said, regaining her composure. "If you knew about Jack, why didn't you just kill him when he was a baby or something? Why let him live and cause you trouble?"

"Because, my dear, as professor Chessman feared, we did not remember our old lives until a few years ago. By then, he was entrenched in the Ministry and, for all we knew, blissfully ignorant."

"So that's where I came in?"

"Exactly."

"In answer to your other question, yes, I want both of them. Their escape is an embarrassment."

"Quite so," Bock said. "Werner will go along to aid you where he can."

Leslie smiled, trying to hide her annoyance.

"With all due respect to the Hero of the Reich, I prefer to work alone."

"I regret that is not possible."

"Look, I don't mean to be rude, but he's too old. He'll slow me down."

Both men began to laugh, their voices echoing in the large room.

"If anything, it is you who will slow *him* down. Werner! Show the lady!" Bock said, barely containing himself.

Kruger stepped forward and walked toward Leslie. She reached for the small Walther pistol inside her purse. Kruger smiled, as if reading her mind, and halted a few paces away. Reaching up to his neck, Kruger grabbed a flap of skin and pulled. Leslie gasped, the gun forgotten, recoiling as the latex mask dropped at her feet. In front of her stood a young and vibrant Werner Kruger, all of twenty-eight years old.

"You see, my dear *Brigadeführer*," Bock continued, "it was necessary to keep the populace fooled. We can't have people knowing the real truth. Now, where are Dunham and Malloy?"

Until that moment, Leslie hadn't really believed Armand Bock's story—after all, pictures can be faked. But with the living proof in front of her, all her doubts swept away on a wave of conflicting emotions. She wanted to kill Bock for using her, but not as much as she wanted to wrap her hands around the neck of Denise Malloy for stealing the man she loved and turning him against her. For that, the bitch would die. But could she kill Jack? During the raid, she was so mad that he had gone off with that other woman, she'd *wanted* him dead, welcomed it. Now, she was not so sure. There was her duty, and there was her life. For the longest time, one had been the other, both intertwined. Now...

"*Brigadeführer!*"

Leslie snapped out of her reverie. "I'm sorry. I was trying to remember something. As to the traitors, we know they crossed the border into Canada," she said.

Bock's features darkened. "Yes, that debacle in Buffalo."

Leslie ignored the interruption. "From there, they could have gone anywhere."

Bock stood and went to the champagne bucket and refilled his glass. "I thought as much. Both Carpenter and Chessman are in Canada as well."

"Then you know where they are?"

"Approximately," he said. "You two will go there tonight, begin searching for them."

"And when we find them?"

Bock drained his champagne flute and threw it into the nearby fireplace. "Kill them all," he said.

16

Toronto, Canada
5 May 1994

Jack and Wiley watched Chessman prepare Denise for the final run-through. For the last nine days and nights they had worked far into the wee hours, expanding and perfecting Denise's abilities. Everyone was exhausted. Just sitting and watching as she progressed from moving pencils to larger objects fatigued Jack. For Denise, the strain must have been enormous. But she didn't complain, and she wouldn't give up, wouldn't stop a day's training until Chessman called a halt, often not until after a full eighteen hours. Now she sat inside the Psionic Wave Detector once again, linked to the machine through the psionic sensor helmet and dozens of extra electrodes taped to her body. This was the moment of truth. This time she was going to try transporting herself.

Chessman bustled around the control panel, making adjustments, looking even more disheveled than usual. He muttered to himself, oblivious to Jack and Wiley.

"Are you ready, my dear?" he said into the microphone.

"Yeah. Now I know what a lab animal feels like," she said.

She tugged at the electrodes taped to her head in obvious discomfort.

"I am sorry about the sensors, but the data your transport will provide will be invaluable."

"That's okay, Doc. Let's do it."

Jack turned to Wiley and whispered, "Are you as nervous as I am?"

"Worse," he said.

Jack looked back at Denise and caught her smiling at him. God, she was beautiful. She hadn't the classic features of Leslie, but somehow when she smiled like that, it lit up a room. Still, he wished he were in that booth instead of her. He couldn't get used to the idea of her going, even if she was his ticket.

"All right, Miss Malloy," Chessman said, "please begin."

Jack leaned forward in his chair. Wiley began chewing his nails.

Nodding confidently, Denise closed her eyes and began chanting. For her mantra, Denise had chosen an old poem by Poe: "The Raven." According to Chessman, it didn't really matter what one said, the point was to focus the mind. Eventually, one wouldn't even need it, the transport occurring with only the briefest moment of pure, concentrated thought.

Through his accelerated training program, Denise had progressed with frightening ease, much faster than Kruger. With him, it had taken weeks. Jack remembered an old saying that stated that work expands to fit the time. Perhaps an inverse corollary existed: *Results accelerate in direct proportion to need.* And they needed results badly. There was no telling when someone would come looking for them.

Jack snapped out of his thoughts when the lights dimmed in the room, the filaments inside the bulbs glowing a dull orange.

"What's happening?" he said, alarmed.

Chessman beamed like a proud father. "Her mind is draining the power from the Wave Detector and using it!"

Jack watched with a mixture of awe and terror when the small interior of the booth began to glow. Denise herself had a small aura around her that pulsated a deep indigo. A second later he saw a pinpoint of painfully bright light emanate from her head. It expanded, filled the booth, blotting out everything. Jack shielded his eyes, trying to see her. A second later, the light imploded in on itself and the booth stood empty.

"Holy shit," Wiley whispered, his voice a hoarse croak.

Chessman clapped his hands together and shouted with glee. "She has done it!"

"Where did she go, Doc?" Jack asked, worried.

"She would not tell me," he said, straightening his glasses and checking the graph spilling from the machine. "She wants to surprise us."

"I don't know about you, but I think I've been surprised enough for one day," Wiley said.

The lights began to dim again, and they turned as one toward the booth. In a repeat of what they'd just witnessed, the room filled with light and a second later Denise stood before them, the electrodes dangling from her head. She had a silly grin on her face.

"Hi, guys," she said.

All three men rushed up to her, talking at once.

"Whoa, fellas, hold on a minute. Give a girl some space." She laughed at her not-so-subtle joke, obviously high on her newfound abilities. Chessman, however, seemed concerned.

"Why didn't you appear back in the booth?" he asked.

Denise shrugged. "I didn't think it mattered."

Chessman shook his head.

"What's the matter, Doc?" Jack asked.

The old man smiled, still shaking his head.

"Nothing at all, dear boy. It means she has mastered the ability a lot better than I'd hoped. She was able to pinpoint her return co-ordinates precisely. This took Kruger the longest to master. She has done it on the first try."

"Jack?"

Jack turned to Denise, who slipped into his arms.

"You miss me?" she said.

"You were only gone a minute," he said, smiling at her.

"I know, but I can't get you a surprise every time."

Jack held her away from him, giving her a mock suspicious look. "Yeah? What?"

She played coy. "Oh, just something I thought you might miss."

He frowned. What on earth could she be talking about?

"Give up?" she said.

"Come on, Malloy. Cut the cat and mouse."

Smiling mischievously, she reached into her pocket, pulled out a large coin, and dropped it in his outstretched hand. Jack stared at it, unable to breathe.

"Oh my God!" he said.

"What? What is it?" Wiley said.

"My Himmler gold piece."

Jack tossed it to Wiley, who turned it over in his hands. Minted in 1954 the year after Himmler's assassination during a state visit to Mexico, the coin had quickly dropped out of circulation and into the hands of collectors. Originally having a face value of fifty *Reichsdollars*, they were now worth a hundred times that.

"You shouldn't have done this," Jack said.

"It's okay, Jack, I was glad to," Denise said.

"No, I mean you shouldn't have gone there. It was reckless and stupid."

"Well, I'm sorry, but I wanted to see if I could travel that far. Excuse me for being thoughtful!"

She stalked into the adjoining room, her anger leaving a palpable silence behind.

"What was that all about?" Wiley said.

"That coin was sitting in a drawer inside my apartment in Miami."

Jack saw Chessman's eyes widen.

"It was a stupid thing for her to do," he continued. "She could have been captured, or worse."

"Young man," Chessman said.

Jack turned to Chessman.

"What might have happened is unimportant," the professor said. "The point is, she has returned safely from a journey of over two thousand miles. She is ready."

"You're sure?"

"Perfectly. Now go to her. She needs you."

Jack nodded and walked into the other room. He found Denise staring out the window overlooking the courtyard. The moon shone down, illuminating a small fountain that lay still, its water flow shut down for the night.

"Hi," he said. "I'm sorry if I was unappreciative. But as soon as I saw that coin, I got scared. All I could see was you popping into an apartment swarming with SS."

She turned from the window, an impish smile on her face. "So you did miss me?"

"Hell yes," he said, taking her into his arms. They held each other tightly, both aware that a major corner had been turned. "What was it like?"

She pulled away from him, her eyes shining. "My God, Jack, it was like... like... I can't describe it. It felt like I was wired into the universe or something, like I became part of everything at once and for the briefest second knew everything there was to know. Does that make any sense?"

Jack nodded. "I think so. You just described my drug-soaked youth."

She socked him playfully. "Just like you to make fun of me."

"Chessman says you're ready."

Denise shivered involuntarily.

"I'm scared, Jack. Popping across a couple thousand miles is strange enough. But fifty years? I don't know."

"Well, don't forget. I'll be with you on this one."

She squeezed his hand. "Have you guys gone shopping yet?"

Jack smiled and nodded. "Wait till you see this stuff." Jack led her over to a pile of neatly folded clothes. Aside from a change of civilian clothes, there were two uniforms, that of a WAC sergeant and a full colonel in the Army Air Corps.

"I got us a couple of changes of clothes right down to the underwear," Jack said. "You realize they didn't have elastic waistbands then? Shorts just buttoned like everything else. It was also damned hard to find anything that wasn't full of moth holes. And shoes were a real bitch."

"You guys did great," she said. "How about weapons?"

Jack smiled like a kid in a candy store. "You must be rubbing off on me," he said, opening up a small satchel. He pulled out two Colt 1911-A1 model .45 automatics and two original Cross daggers, the kind that strapped to the forearm.

THE NORMANDY CLUB

"You found them!" Denise said.

She picked up one of the forty-fives and worked the slide. It slid back easily and snapped a round into place with a satisfying clack.

"How about papers?"

Jack reached into the bag and pulled out two sets of military IDs. "You were right on the money with the Lambda contact. They had them within two days. I don't know how they did them, but judge for yourself."

Denise opened hers and looked at the photo. Even the photographic style matched that of the mid-1940s. They were now Colonel Jack Brenner and his driver, WAC sergeant Wendy Younger.

"What's the cover story?"

"We're recent transfers from the States," he said. "Attached to SHEAF under Bedell-Smith. The forgeries are okay, but not perfect. With any luck we can neutralize Kruger and come back before anyone starts asking questions."

"You think we can?"

"It's all up to you, sweetheart. The closer you get us to the date and location, the less we have to worry."

"Hey, you guys, are we going to get some grub or what?" Wiley said, sticking his head into the room.

"Hold your horses," Jack said. "We'll be right with you."

Jack stuffed one of the guns into his belt.

"What's with the gun?" Denise asked.

"Maybe this psychic business is rubbing off, but I got a feeling. Maybe after all we've gone through, I'm just paranoid."

Denise smiled and stuffed the other gun behind her back. "Welcome to the club."

※　※　※

The Science & Mathematics building lay shrouded in total darkness save for the warm, yellow glow spilling out the windows of Chess-man's lab. From her viewpoint, Leslie couldn't see if anyone was there, but she knew they were in there just the same. She and Kruger had been watching them for three days, ever since picking up Jack's trail during his shopping spree through old thrift shops and cos-tume-rental houses. She turned and glanced at Kruger. He appeared so calm, so assured, staring up at the window, his eyes narrowed in-tently. She wished she felt the same way. But every time she caught a glimpse of Jack, her heart began to pound, and she felt light-headed and dizzy.

That, of course, was nothing compared to how she'd been af-fected by the "trip" to Canada. After Bock's little dinner party, Les-lie and Kruger dropped off Hannah and went straight to Leslie's condo on Biscayne. There, she changed into civilian clothes while Kruger stood staring out across the bay. They'd barely spoken five words since leaving Bock's estate. But the real surprise came when she emerged from her bedroom.

"Do you have a weapon?" he asked.

Leslie nodded, patting her abdomen.

"*Sehr gut.*"

Then everything got screwy. Kruger reached out and grabbed her hand. She started to fight back, thinking the bastard was trying to assault her, that this entire time-travel business was some elaborate ruse to get her alone. Suddenly, she felt as if someone were squeezing her head, and the room tilted oddly. She stared open-mouthed when Kruger began to glow a bright blue. A moment later, the pulsing aura surrounded them both. A second later everything whited out.

In the next instant, they stood in a dirty alley strewn with broken liquor bottles, shredded newspapers, and fast-food wrappers.

"Welcome to Canada," he said, a smug grin on his face.

"What?" Leslie said, her head feeling like it was stuffed with cotton.

"Come. We begin." He strode toward the mouth of the alley. Still reeling from the experience of being telekinetically transported, Leslie staggered after him, her legs rubbery.

After three days, they'd picked up Jack's trail and followed him. From their hotel in the morning, Jack, the Malloy woman, and the second man Kruger IDed as Wiley Carpenter, made their way to the university. After an hour or so, Jack, sometimes accompanied by Wiley, would begin scouring the antique stores specializing in militaria and war surplus. It was such a routine, Leslie got so she could predict where they were going. But now, standing outside the eerie, Gothic building on the darkened campus, she found her patience wearing thin.

"Why don't we take them now? You *know* they're up there."

Kruger turned and gazed at her with thinly veiled contempt. He'd made it clear very early on that she was with him only on Bock's orders.

"All in good time, *my dear.*"

Leslie resisted the urge to put a bullet in his brain. Doing so would leave her no way to get back to Miami, except, of course, by the conventional method. And that was no option at all. Here she was, illegally in Canada, with no passport and carrying an illegal weapon. They'd throw her to the dogs, especially after finding out who she really was. Outside of the Original Reich, Avalon, and the occupied countries of South and Central America, the SS were the targets of vicious reprisals. Canada was known for its long prison terms.

Leslie snapped out of her reverie when she spotted three figures emerging from the building out of the corner of her eye. It was them. Jack, the *lesbisch* cunt, and Wiley Carpenter. The three figures walked away from where she stood with Kruger, moving at a leisurely pace toward the corner. Leslie started to move after them, but Kruger grabbed her roughly.

"Let them go."

"What!"

"Let them go. They will be back, and we shall be waiting for them... upstairs."

Leslie watched as Jack and his friends turned the corner and disappeared from view. She felt an ache in her soul when he turned the corner. Shit. Why did she have to fall for the jerk? He'd caused her nothing but grief.

"Come," Kruger said. He stepped out from the shadows of the building and crossed the street. Leslie followed. Kruger slipped out a thin piece of metal the size of a credit card and slipped it into the slot between the door and the jamb. In a second, the door opened, and he slipped through it, striding purposefully for the wide, stone staircase. Leslie fumed. The man had absolutely no manners.

Hurrying, she followed him up the steps two at a time. On the second floor, Kruger turned and marched toward the lighted room at the end, stopping to listen at the door. Leslie placed her own ear to the dark wood and heard Chessman muttering to himself. Satisfied, Kruger reached out and tried the door, and found it unlocked. He smiled, pulled out his pistol, and threw open the door.

Chessman started violently as the door crashed against the wall. When he saw Kruger, all the color drained from his face, and he staggered back against some large piece of machinery. His mouth opened, but all that came out was a strangled croaking sound.

"Good evening, *Herr Doktor*," Kruger said, leveling the gun at Chessman. "I've come for my refresher course."

THE NORMANDY CLUB

Wiley shook his head in disbelief. "I don't see how you guys are going to do this."

They sat huddled in the booth of an ersatz English pub tucked away down a small side street. Being long after the dinner hour, only a few other patrons remained, and they kept to themselves, drinking their pints of bitters and staring at a soccer match on the large flat-screen opposite the bar. It was a comfortable place with dark wood paneling and decent food at cheap prices. Students jammed it on the weekends.

Jack took a sip of his Guinness and gave Wiley an impatient look.

"It's the only option we have. It's where Kruger went."

"This St. Peter's school?"

"St. Paul's in Hammersmith. West London."

"Why don't you run this by me one more time," Wiley said.

"All right. On May fifteenth, nineteen forty-four, Eisenhower and Montgomery gave a briefing to Churchill, King George VI, and all the major commanders involved, detailing the entire invasion plan. This meeting is unprecedented because at no other time were all who were integral to the plan assembled in one place. St. Paul's was the headquarters of 21 Army Group, Monty's command. It had a lot of advantages, including the fact that it was easily defended, somewhat out of the way, and didn't look like your typical army command post. Only someone who knew his history could take advantage of the situation. You know the rest."

"So Kruger, disguised as some limey lieutenant, plants ten pounds of Semtex with a digital detonator and blows them all to hell."

Jack nodded. "You got it. With everyone connected to the plan killed or severely maimed, the invasion was postponed indefinitely. With one masterstroke, Kruger altered the course of history—changed everything. He never had to go into Germany to convince Hitler of anything. Within days of the blast, *Der Führer* knew what had happened. Two months later, he invaded England, and the rest we know."

"But wasn't Kruger supposed to deliver the letter?" Denise interrupted.

"He was. We can only assume that the Nine Old Men got what they wanted without it. I've done a bit of research. All of them, including Bock, are far wealthier than they ever were in the other timeline, maybe ten times as much."

"Shit," Wiley said, draining his beer. He picked up the pitcher and refilled his glass. "So you guys are going to try and beat Kruger to the punch?"

"That's right."

"Everything you've said makes sense except how you're going to get into the school. You may have forged papers that'll get you into SHAEF headquarters, but you know damn well that meeting will be closed tighter than a drum."

"Kruger did it," Denise said.

"Hold on a minute," Jack said, raising his hand. "Wiley's got a point. Kruger did—does have an advantage we don't. Everyone was accounted for after the blast except for a Flight Lieutenant Liddington. Everyone assumed he'd been closest to the bomb and blown to bits, except someone saw a man in RAF uniform running from the building moments before the bomb went off."

"Kruger?"

Jack nodded. "From what I can gather, Flight Lieutenant Liddington actually existed and had recently joined the SHAEF staff, attached as one of Monty's aides. No one at SHAEF had known him prior to his posting there. I'll bet my life Kruger killed the man and took his place. You can't get much better credentials than that."

"So what are you guys going to do?" Wiley said.

Jack shrugged. "To be honest with you, I don't know. From what I've read in the books here at the university, the briefings on April seventh and May fourteenth remained top secret. Everyone, including Churchill, was notified the day before by hand-delivered, sealed orders and told to report to a certain classroom at the school at a certain time. They didn't even know what they were going there for."

"Then what do we do?" Denise said.

"We're going to have to get ourselves there and hope like hell we can bluff our way in."

Wiley raised his glass and said, "Well, I'm just glad it's you and not me, thank you very much."

"Yeah, well, you just better pray we pull it off, or it's good-bye Charlie."

Jack finished his beer and looked at his watch.

"Come on, let's get back to the lab."

Out on the street, Wiley bid them good night and headed back toward the hotel. Jack watched him stroll away and wondered if what he'd said was right.

"You shouldn't let him get to you," Denise said.

"Reading minds now, are we?"

Denise let out a sigh. "Jack, cut the crap. I know you're scared. Hell, I'm shittin' bricks, 'cause I'm the one everyone's depending on."

"I'm sorry, you're right. He did get to me," he said, shaking his head. "I wonder if it's possible to change everything back?"

"Kruger did it."

"I know. You keep saying that. But maybe time only gives you one shot, maybe this mixed-up world is all we'll ever have."

Denise shook her head, took him into her arms, and kissed him. He wrapped his arms around her and felt himself melting into her. Suddenly the world flashed white and they were now outside Chessman's door.

"How ya like them apples?" she said, grinning.

Jack felt slightly nauseated and his head ached.

"Goddammit, Malloy, you might've warned me!"

"And spoil all the fun? Come on, Dunham, chin up."

She chuckled softly, grabbed his hand, and they both walked into a nightmare. Every piece of equipment had been ruthlessly and completely smashed. Papers littered the room as well as broken test tubes and the like.

"Damn, I knew it," Jack whispered, pulling out his .45.

Denise flipped off the safety on hers. Both of them looked into the next room where the Psionic Wave Detector sat. From their point of view, most of the room lay out of sight, but Jack could smell an odor of burning plastic and a light flashed on and off, like a fluorescent with a faulty ballast, casting weird shadows across the room.

They crept along the wall, careful to avoid stepping on anything that might make a noise. When they reached the door, Denise held up three fingers. Jack nodded and Denise mouthed off the count. One... two... three. On three they sprang through the door, one high, the other low. It was a foolhardy way to enter a room, but there was no other way in.

The room lay empty, save for the smashed Wave Detector and the usual scattered notes and debris.

"Where's Chessman?" Denise said.

THE NORMANDY CLUB

"Oh God!"

Denise turned and followed Jack's gaze to a spot near the Wave Detector. The door stood open and behind it laid an outstretched hand. Jack reached him first, recoiling at the sight. Chessman had been systematically and brutally beaten. Jack felt his pulse and found it weak and irregular. The man's skin felt cold and clammy.

"He's in shock. Call an ambulance," Jack said.

"That will not be necessary, Mr. Dunham."

Jack and Denise whipped around. Werner Kruger stood in the doorway, aiming a pistol at them.

"Drop the guns," he said, his voice hoarse and menacing. "Now."

Jack thought about going for it but changed his mind. He put his gun on the floor, followed by Denise's.

Kruger smiled. "Good idea, Mr. Dunham. No sense in playing the hero now. Kick them over."

Jack kicked the guns. They skittered across the floor and came to rest against the far wall, well out of reach.

"*Ausgezeichnet*. For your reward, I have a little surprise for you."

Leslie stepped out of the shadows behind Kruger, a pistol gripped in her hand. Her eyes looked tired, and new lines etched her face where none existed the week before. She still looked beautiful, though, and Jack felt a curious mixture of hatred and desire.

Denise eyed her with open hostility.

"Leslie!" he said.

"Is this the one you prefer, Jack?" she asked, stepping forward, gun leveled.

She looked Denise over, her expression edged with contempt. Then, without warning, she hauled off and slapped Denise across the face, knocking her off her feet and slamming her into the Wave Detector.

"Come, come, my dear *Brigadeführer*," Kruger said, an amused grin on his face, "jealousy does not become you."

"Shut up, Kruger!" she snapped.

A glimmer of unbridled fury flashed in Kruger's eyes, gone an instant later. He smiled and chuckled.

"Women. What is it you Americans say? 'You can't live with 'em, can't shoot 'em'?" He laughed again. "Then again... maybe you can."

Spinning around, he pointed the gun at Leslie and fired it point-blank into her chest. She cried out and crumpled to the floor, her gun sliding across the floor, out of reach.

"You son of a bitch!" Jack said, lunging at Kruger.

The man re-aimed the gun, halting Jack in his tracks. "Tsk-tsk, my dear Mr. Dunham. I thought you had more sense than that."

Leslie groaned and Jack saw a steadily growing pool of blood spreading out beneath her.

"You may go to her, Jack," Kruger said, motioning with the gun. "It is time for the poignant good-byes so common to your lugubrious cinema. You see, I am a sentimentalist at heart."

Wasting no time, Jack bent over her. Her eyes fluttered open and filled with sadness. "I'm sorry, Jack... for everything."

"It's okay, Leslie, I..." He stopped, unable to think of anything to say.

"Was I someone you loved in your other life?"

Jack smiled, remembering. "Yes, you were."

"Good," she said, sounding weaker. "Come closer, Jack."

Jack bent over her and felt her press a small dagger into his hands.

"I hope she'll make you happy," Leslie whispered. "Believe it or not, I loved you in this life too."

Suddenly she stiffened, drawing her last breath in a halting gasp.

Then it was over. Jack stared at her now lifeless form, his eyes clouding with tears. Even after knowing who she was and what she stood for, he suddenly realized he still cared for her.

"Goddamn you, Kruger," Jack said, wiping away the tears so Denise wouldn't see.

"Your time is up, Mr. Dunham," Kruger said, sounding bored. "Come, we shall return to Miami. Herr Bock would like to meet you before we turn you over to State Security."

As unobtrusively as possible, Jack stuck the knife in his belt, covered it with his shirt, and stood up. After watching Leslie die, he didn't care what happened. Right at this moment he felt as if nothing mattered anymore, that everything had been a colossal waste. He turned to Denise and saw the same look reflected in her own determined eyes. Suddenly, Chessman groaned loudly. Kruger's eyes snapped over to the old man, giving Jack the opening he needed.

In a flash, Jack lunged at Kruger, knocking the gun out of his hands and sending them both sprawling onto the hard, linoleum floor. Scrambling to pin him down, Jack slammed his fist into Kruger's face, and felt the solid smack of flesh against flesh. Kruger snarled and arched his back, attempting to throw Jack off. Jack wrapped his fingers around Kruger's throat and squeezed. The man's eyes bulged out and he flailed at Jack, his fists landing powerful, crushing blows to his midsection. Jack grunted with each blow and squeezed harder. Kruger turned, his tongue bulging out, his breath a strangled gasp, as the cartilage of the windpipe began to crush.

"Break his goddamned neck!" Denise screamed.

Before Jack could even think, Kruger smiled and dissolved away, the telltale blue aura fading after him. Suddenly, he felt Kruger's weight slamming into him, pushing him to the floor. Now it was Kruger's vise-like grip around his own throat. Jack's vision blurred with tears. Kruger smiled, his eyes nearly glowing in the faint light spilling in from the streetlights outside.

"NO!" Denise screamed, and leaped onto Kruger's back. Suddenly she flew across the room, her body crashing into the wall, denting the plaster. She slid to the floor, coming to rest in a crumpled heap, groaning softly.

Kruger grimaced and redoubled the pressure around Jack's neck. "Telekinesis when developed properly has other uses as well, *ja?*"

All Jack could see were those glowing eyes, the world having shrunk to a pinpoint. With his last conscious thought, Jack remembered the small dagger. He let both arms fall to his side, pretending to succumb. Falling for it, Kruger lessened the pressure slightly, allowing Jack to catch a fraction of a precious breath. Grabbing the small dagger, Jack pulled it out and thrust it upward into Kruger's midsection. Kruger shrieked and let go of Jack's neck. Before he could pull away, Jack ripped the knife upwards, slicing the man's gut completely open. Dark blood gushed out of the wound and splashed over Jack. Kruger screamed, clutched his stomach, and toppled over.

Jack, slipping in the blood, scrambled over to Denise. She lay where she'd fallen, unconscious. He picked up her head and kissed her on the lips. In the distance he could hear sirens approaching. Someone had heard the shot. Denise groaned and opened her eyes. They widened as she recognized Jack.

"Kruger! What happened?" she said, her body convulsing. "Ohh, my head."

"Take it easy. Kruger's dead. Leslie slipped me a knife before she died."

Denise gripped his shirt, pulling him closer. "Are you sure he's dead?"

This annoyed him. The sirens grew louder.

"Of course, goddamn it! I gutted him like a fish. Look for yourself," he said, pointing behind him.

Jack helped Denise to her feet and turned. Instead of Kruger's inert body, all that remained was a large pool of rapidly congealing blood.

"SHIT!" Denise yelled.

"How the fuck?"

"Damnit, Jack!" she said, pounding his chest with her arms. "He got away, he transported."

"How? I disemboweled the man. Look at all the blood. How could he have lasted long enough to go anywhere? And what the hell good would it do? The damage was massive!"

The sirens got louder.

"I'll explain later. We've got to get out of here."

Racing to the window, they saw several Toronto Police cruisers, as well as campus security, screech to a halt in front of the building. Heavily armed men poured out of the cars and streaked toward the front doors.

"They'll be here any second," Denise said. "Take my hand."

"The uniforms, the papers!"

Denise shook her head. "Kruger destroyed them."

Knowing that their enemy had won the round, Jack grabbed her hand and braced himself for the transport. The room whited out and they were back in their hotel room.

Jack dropped onto the bed.

"We haven't got time, Jack, we've got to move. Go get Wiley."

Feeling his muscles already cramping up from the fight with Kruger, Jack pulled himself off the bed and trudged toward the door.

"Jack! Your clothes."

He turned to the mirror and recoiled from the sight. He looked like someone who worked in a slaughterhouse. Throwing off the clothes, Jack wet down a washcloth and wiped off the excess blood. He then dried himself and threw on his one change of clothes.

Going to the door, he opened it and glanced both ways down the corridor. Empty. He crossed the hall and knocked on Wiley's door.

Nothing.

"Come on, Wiley."

Still nothing.

Jack pounded on the door. "Goddammit it, Carpenter, get the lead out. We've got to go!"

At the far end of the hall, a maid turned the corner, pushing a cart laden with towels and linen.

"Excuse me. You have a pass key?"

"*No hablo inglés, Señor,*" she said.

Wonderful, he thought. He'd forgotten that most of the Cubans had settled in Canada after being driven from Mexico by the recent war. Instead of going to Miami after Castro took over, as they had in the other timeline, they'd gone west to Acapulco. In this timeline, Castro had mysteriously died a year after taking over the country and Cuba became an official protectorate of Avalon. Of course, Cubans were not allowed to reside within Avalon's borders.

"Pass key?" Jack said, making a turning motion with his hand.

The woman frowned then smiled in understanding.

"*Sí, Señor*, she said, reaching into her pocket. She pulled out a small card with a pattern of holes punched through it, inserted it in the lock, and turned the handle. The door opened.

"*Gracias.*"

"*Muy bien, Señor.*"

She returned the key to her pocket and resumed her way down the hall. Jack waited until she turned the opposite corner then crept into the room. The shades were drawn, but Jack could see a form under the covers.

"Jesus Christ, Wiley. How can you sleep through all of this shit?"

Flipping on the light, Jack walked to the bed and stopped. A pillow lay over Wiley's head. But something was wrong. The pillow had a black burn mark in the middle of it, and he realized the room was covered with feathers.

"Oh, God, no," Jack said.

Reaching forward, he ripped the pillow away and felt his stomach heave. Wiley lay there, eyes open in death, his expression one of profound surprise and regret. The sheets were covered with blood that had flowed out of a hole drilled though his forehead. Neat and round on the front, Jack knew it was far worse where he couldn't see it. Blind anger and hatred washed away the pain and sadness. There was no reason for this. None at all. Kruger had somehow come here and done this just for spite. He staggered to the window and stared out at the skyline. He tried to stop all the memories from coming, but they flashed across his mind like a torrent. Squeezing his eyes shut, Jack whimpered, struck out with his fist, and smashed it through the glass. A jagged shard cut into the back of his hand, slashing deeply. Blood flowed steadily and the hand throbbed dully. Jack ignored it.

"Jack!"

Stunned by the pain in his heart and his hand, he continued to stare out the window, even when he heard Denise gasp at Wiley's corpse on the bed.

"Oh no," she said softly.

Jack turned then, and she flew into his arms.

"I'm so sorry, Jack. I should have known. I—I should have seen this coming," she said, crying into his shoulder. Jack remained stoic, unaffected by her tears. He held her away from him.

"How could he do this, Malloy? How? He should be dead. I practically ripped out his guts."

Denise stared into Jack's eyes then noticed the blood.

"You're hurt! Give me your hand."

"I have to know," he said, tears coming into his eyes.

"You will."

Jack held out his hand and Denise took it in her own. Standing up straight, she closed her eyes and inhaled deeply. A moment later, Jack felt a curious warmth flow through his hand and halfway up his arm. He watched, awestruck, as the skin of his hand melted seamlessly back together. A moment later all traces of the deep gash had disappeared, including the blood. Jack stared, unable to speak.

"That was how Kruger survived," Denise said. "He had enough energy to repair himself. It's a side benefit of learning to use the ability."

Jack let out a sigh. "So this guy's immortal too?"

"No, Jack, not any more than you or me. Shoot him in the head or break his neck, anything to cause instant death, and he's finished."

At the mention of head shots, Jack flinched, remembering Wiley.

"We can't just leave him here," he said.

"We have to. There's nothing more we can do."

"AYYYYY!"

Both of them jumped at the scream. Turning, they saw the maid Jack spoke to earlier, standing in the doorway, her eyes wide with fear. The woman turned to run, stumbled backward, tipping over her cart and sending towels flying. Her scream echoed down the corridor.

Denise grabbed Jack's hand. "Come on, we're going."

"Where?"

"Back there."

Jack shook his head then realized what she meant.

"Wait a minute. We've got no papers, no uniforms, no nothing."

"Yeah, but we've got us. Until we're dead, we've got a chance."

Taking his hand again, Denise clamped her eyes shut and began to mouth her mantra rapidly. Seconds later, her blazing aura enveloped him, the lights dimmed, and the world, again, turned white.

17

London, England
13 May 1944

"**W**E HAVE DONE IT!"
Armand Bock's triumphant shout still rang in Kruger's ears as he appeared in the cobbled alley. Here, no lights dimmed because everything lay shrouded in darkness. A blackout. For a moment, Kruger felt a stab of pure fear. Had he failed, had he ended up in some purgatory for time travelers? His eyes adjusted to the gloom and Kruger found his bearings. Looking toward the mouth of the alley, he found himself surprised at the crowds of people walking on the street. The sidewalks teemed with all manner of soldiers: British, American, Polish, Norwegian, all laughing and joking, flirting with the hookers standing in doorways, and generally out to raise hell. Kruger glanced at his watch: 0300 hours. It was early yet. All these men were here for Overlord, though some participated unwittingly in Fortitude, SHAEF's wide-ranging deception to make Hitler and his General Staff believe the main thrusts would come at Pas de Calais and Norway. Kruger turned his attention back to his immediate surroundings and wondered where in the city, he'd appeared. And when. For all his training, for all his skill, transporting oneself across

time and space still held surprises. Squinting, he saw the outlines of fire escapes, dustbins, and the typical detritus of city life: empty cans, broken bottles, and newspapers.

Bending down, he grabbed the shredded newsprint and looked at the masthead. It read: The London Times, Saturday, May 13, 1944. He'd made it! But where? He scanned the alley further and spotted several posters plastered to the brick wall of the building abutting the alley. One of them appeared to be an advertisement for a music hall performance. The names of the performers meant nothing, but the name of the theatre made him smile again: The West End Theatre.

When he reached the mouth of the alley, he quickly melted into the hordes of drunken revelers. The streets themselves were choked with cabs and military vehicles. Horns honked and drivers screamed. He glanced inside a cab, looking for one without a fare. Up ahead, he saw an American officer alighting from one in front of another theatre. He caught up with it just as a middle-aged civilian was about to step into it. He saw Kruger's RAF uniform and smiled.

"You take it, Lieutenant. I'll get the next one."

"Thank you," Kruger said, his British accent flawless. "You're too kind."

The older man smiled, saluted, and melded into the crowd. Kruger crawled inside and slammed the door.

"St. Paul's School, Hammersmith. Please."

"A little late for school, Lieutenant."

Surprised by the soft, musical voice, Kruger looked toward the driver and saw, reflected in the rearview, the most stunning pair of green eyes. They gazed at him, amused, slightly mocking. The driver turned in her seat and Kruger caught himself before he could react. That this woman drove a cab was no great surprise. It had been a common enough sight in 1944 when most men served in the military. What did surprise and vaguely disturb him was the woman's uncanny resemblance to Helga, his first love, right down to the milk-white skin and flaming-red hair.

"It's all closed up. Are you sure you want to go there?" she asked.

"It's my old alma mater. I wanted to see it once more before shipping out."

The woman smiled, turned on her meter, and threw the car into gear. "St. Paul's it is."

The woman kept up a steady patter as they wound their way through the narrow streets, avoiding jaywalkers and other vehicles. At any other time, the sound of her voice would have consumed his attention, but now, while trying to memorize the streets, he found it an annoying distraction. After about fifteen minutes of fighting the late-night traffic, the cab pulled up to a large, wrought-iron gate set into a fence that rose over seven feet high and surrounded the three-acre campus. Built in the late 1600s, the school had attained that venerable, ivy-covered look that only time could bestow. Kruger surveyed the buildings. Which one could it be? The briefing would be in the school's model room, a sort of amphitheater where students heard lectures.

"You miss the place, love?" the driver asked. She stood next to him, her perfume tickling his nostrils with its soft, flowery fragrance.

"Hated every minute of it," he said, smiling his most rakish smile. He used the moment to look her over. She lacked the voluptuous proportions of Helga, but she looked eminently desirable with her tall frame and lithe curves. Besides, Helga was a long time away, not even born yet. Kruger winked at her, letting her in on his joke.

"Please allow me to introduce myself, Flight Lieutenant Arthur Liddington, late of St. Paul's School."

She stuck out her hand and took his. "Jane Summers, just plain late." She smiled at her own joke, revealing perfectly formed, dazzlingly white teeth. Kruger felt his groin twitch.

"Can you recommend a good hotel?" he asked.

Jane frowned. "The hotels are likely full by now, but we could try the Savoy."

Kruger nodded and they returned to the cab. When they pulled away, he turned and stared at the school receding in the distance. *Soon*, he thought.

Sometime later, they pulled up to the entrance of the Savoy Hotel. Even if there'd been no blackout, the Savoy would not have impressed him. The awning had a few rents, and the brass poles needed polishing. He could see the paint peeling around the edges of the large, heavy door. Even the famous lions flanking the entryway looked careworn.

The doorman, a rotund man in his late fifties, opened the cab door. "Good evening, Lieutenant, and welcome to the Savoy."

Kruger nodded to the man and turned to grab his haversack.

"Shall I wait for you, Lieutenant?" Jane asked, displaying that smile again. "Just in case?"

"Yes, please."

Slinging the sack over his shoulder, Kruger strode into the hotel. At this hour, the lobby lay deserted, save for the desk clerk, a gray little man in a mourning coat and striped trousers. He looked up and smiled as Kruger approached.

"Yes, Lieutenant, may I help you?"

"A room, please."

The little man's face lost its smile, becoming regretful. "I'm so sorry, sir, but we are full this evening. However, we expect several guests to depart by morning. If you would care to make yourself comfortable in the lobby?"

Kruger stared at the lumpy, threadbare couch and thought better of it. "Thank you, no. I believe I have a better offer." He smiled, turned on his heels, and walked back out. He could tell Jane was happy to see him, though she tried to appear nonchalant.

"Can you recommend another hostelry?" Kruger said, climbing back into the cab.

Jane started the cab and pulled out into traffic. Her eyes flicked up to the mirror. To Kruger, they appeared to study him. "I have a flat about a mile from here," she said, her voice betraying a hint of nervousness. "My roommate's in the country, we'd have it all to ourselves."

"Sounds inviting."

Jane shifted gears and honked the horn at someone who jumped out in front of her. "Least I can do for one of our boys."

Kruger smiled. "What makes you think you can trust me?"

The eyes smiled back at him through the mirror.

"Who said I did?"

※　※　※

Jane's flat, a third-floor walk-up, was situated in an unpretentious brownstone, above a greengrocer. They took the narrow stairs, stumbling a couple of times in the near total darkness.

"Sorry about the light, but the landlord's a right cheap bastard. Thinks the blackout is his excuse to put the screws on us tenants."

Reaching the third landing, Jane took out her key, slipped it in the lock, and turned it. The old mechanism turned with a loud, satisfying clunk, and she pushed open the door, hinges squeaking.

She crossed the room and Kruger heard the hiss of gas. A moment later, the warm glow of gaslight revealed the interior of the flat. Though only one room, with a bathtub and a tired old stove in plain sight, Jane had given the dreary place a feminine grace with lacy curtains on the wall, a vase of flowers on the small dining table, and stuffed animals covering her bed. Most of the furniture was battered and seedy—Salvation Army rejects. On a table next to the sagging double bed lay a photograph of a smiling man in RAF uniform.

"Sorry about the mess," Jane said, puttering about.

"Where does your husband sleep?"

Jane turned to him, her expression one of surprise. Her eyes flicked to the picture and back to Kruger.

She stared at him, saying nothing.

"Excuse me. I am intruding," Kruger said, bowing and turning to go.

"Wait!"

She came to him, her eyes wide with desperation.

"I know what you must think, but please don't go. I'm sorry I lied." She walked over, picked up the picture and stared at it, a tear rolling down her cheek. "My husband was a pilot, shot down in nineteen-forty. We had so many plans... I was just this close to coming home and turning on the gas... and then you got in the cab. For a moment... I saw John again and these feelings overwhelmed me. I just wanted you so badly... couldn't help it, really."

Kruger stared at her. She turned away from him and walked to the small, grimy window. He pulled the shade and gazed out onto the street.

"You must think me horrid, throwing myself at you like that."

Kruger smiled, letting the shade fall back. "Not at all. After all, I did come up here."

She turned and studied him. After a moment, she began to disrobe. Kruger watched, mesmerized, while she tossed away her clothes item by item, her magnificent, Junoesque body slowly revealing itself.

"Stay with me," she said, her eyes smoldering with desire.

In spite of her vulgar revelations, Kruger found himself entranced by her beauty. This woman might not be Helga, but she had much to offer. He smiled and began walking toward her.

"I like things a little rough."

She stared into his eyes, her expression betraying a hint of fear.

"Anything," she whispered.

18

London, England
14 May 1944

Kruger awoke to the singular sensation of Jane fellating him. The woman had surprised him, taking the belt with relish, begging for more. He watched her through slitted eyes and suppressed the wave of pleasure that coursed through him. There was definitely something to be said for desperate widows.

Reaching out to her, he caressed her silken, red locks, made fiery by the sunbeams streaming through the window. She looked up at him and smiled.

"We're awake, are we?" she asked.

"You do make it difficult to sleep."

She laughed and moved astride him. She moaned as she took him inside her and began to move. Kruger matched her thrusts and gazed again at her body, noting the welts crisscrossing her flesh. He'd left her face alone. After all, one did not desecrate a work of art, did one?

A moment later she came, arching her back and groaning loudly. Kruger followed suit a moment later. Spent and quenched, Jane collapsed beside him and laid her head on his chest. He could feel her pulse beating wildly in her temple. Could he trust her? Could he ask her the favor he needed and trust she would not betray him? Nothing was as powerful as the emotions of a desperate woman. But was it enough to overcome love of country?

"What would you like to do today?" she said, playing with his chest hairs. "I have the day off. Don't go on duty until six."

Kruger decided to chance it.

"How about we take a drive south to Dover?"

"Travel's restricted that way."

Kruger got out of bed and began dressing.

"Where are you going?"

"I do not wish to trouble you any longer," he said, buttoning his shirt. "I'll find my way about."

He pretended not to look at her as he completed dressing. He could easily transport where he needed to go, but not without knowing a precise location. It would be suicidal to go popping up without knowing exactly where he was going. One miscalculation and he could appear among people, or worse—inside a solid object, and that wouldn't do at all. For now, he needed to rely on this woman. He glanced at her and saw the war going on behind her eyes as she struggled with the notion of breaking wartime regulations or losing her new lover. As he suspected it would, love and lust won out.

"How about I pack us a lunch?" she offered.

Kruger smiled.

※　※　※

The cab swept along the two-lane road, the lone vehicle for miles. Kruger found the wide-open spaces and checkered fields of the various farms peaceful and reassuring. He patted the inside pocket of his tunic, feeling for the small Minox camera he'd brought with him. Somewhere out here lay Patton's phantom armies, whole bases that were phony, designed to look busy from the air. Armed with pictures of them, he would have no trouble convincing Hitler to move his armies. All doubt would be swept away by a few simple photos showing empty tents and inflatable rubber tanks, plywood planes, and armored vehicles.

"This looks like a good spot," she said, beginning to slow the cab. "How about here?"

"Let's drive closer to the coast. I want to smell the sea."

Jane smiled and nodded.

A few miles later, Kruger saw the beginnings of chain-link fencing. Every hundred yards or so a sign was posted, warning of dire consequences to the hapless trespasser. Kruger squinted, seeing tents and vehicles in the distance.

"Stop the car."

"What?"

"Stop the car, now, damnit!"

Jane screeched to a halt and turned to him, anger flaring in her eyes. "I may enjoy taking your abuse in bed, but I won't stand being yelled at."

Kruger smiled and grasped her shoulder and jabbed her pressure point. She gasped in pain, her eyes going wide with fear.

"Do not *ever* use that tone with me again. Am I clear?"

She nodded, tears in her eyes. Smiling, he relaxed his grip on her shoulder and kissed her lightly on the lips.

"I will return in fifteen minutes. Get out of the cab and raise the hood."

"Raise the what?"

Kruger looked momentarily startled, realizing his error. He recovered quickly, leaning closer. "Raise the bonnet," he said. "Make it appear you have broken down. If anyone happens by, tell them you have everything under control. Is that clear?"

She nodded again and threw herself into his arms, crying in earnest now. "You won't leave me, will you?"

Kruger suppressed the urge to slap her. God, she was such a spineless creature. "Never," he said, letting the lie roll easily off his tongue.

Opening the door, he stepped from the cab and quickly looked in both directions. Satisfied that no one approached, he strode to the fence and climbed over, careful not to snag his uniform on the barbed wire at the top. Curiously, Kruger felt his stomach flutter with butterflies, something he'd rarely felt in his life, and usually before something momentous. Here lay the proof that an invasion at Calais was a myth.

Breaking into a trot, Kruger bounded across the expanse, pulling out the small camera when he reached the first formation of armored vehicles. He nearly laughed when he saw them up close. Made totally of rubber, they looked like a child's toy, except they and hundreds like them looked totally convincing from the air.

Snapping off several shots, he moved on to the tents, opened one of the flaps and photographed its empty interior. Next came the rubber tanks and the wooden planes. He finished the last of the roll on the mess tent, where not a soul sat inside. And that was the greatest indictment of all, the sheer emptiness.

He stuck the Minox camera back in his pocket and walked back toward the fence. In the distance, he could see Jane standing over the engine. *She must suspect something*, he thought. He would have to watch her and dispose of her if need be. For now, she could be useful in a number of ways.

"You! Halt!"

Kruger froze as he heard the bolt of a submachine gun slide into place. He turned slowly and caught sight of an American soldier, a sergeant, fast approaching. The sergeant halted a few yards and stared at him, taking in the uniform and the rank.

"What are you doing here, Lieutenant? This area's restricted."

Kruger reached for his papers and stopped as the soldier snapped up the machine gun, his expression suspicious.

"I am going for my papers, Sergeant."

"Just do it *real* slow."

"Good show, Sergeant."

Kruger reached inside his tunic and pulled out his ID and handed it to the sergeant. Now he would know whether or not the forgers in State Security's archives knew their business. Of special note was the word BIGOT stamped in red ink on the first page. It meant that the bearer had *carte blanche* to be where others could not.

The sergeant frowned, studied the documents, nodded and handed them back, snapping to attention.

"Begging the lieutenant's pardon, sir, but I was not told anyone would be here."

"That is quite okay, Sergeant. I was ordered to make a surprise inspection. I suppose for you it was just that."

The sergeant grinned and offered a salute. "You got that right, sir."

Kruger returned the salute and the smile. "Carry on, Sergeant..."

"Mills, sir. Terence Mills."

"Very good, Mills. And you might want to start a fire in one of the cook stoves. We wouldn't want Jerry to get the wrong impression, would we?"

"No, sir," Mills said, smiling again, no doubt relieved he would not go on report.

Kruger turned and walked back toward the fence, his blood boiling. That his papers had passed muster meant nothing; that he'd been spotted could ruin everything. What would happen should someone else show up and the happy sergeant report the "surprise" inspection?

When he reached the fence, Kruger looked back and saw the soldier had disappeared into the mass of tents. He quickly climbed over and bounded up to the car.

"Drive," he said, slamming the door.

※ ※ ※

Jane looked at him, her expression unreadable, threw the car into gear, and sped off. Sensing that he no longer desired to have a picnic, probably never had, she turned the car around a little way up the road and drove back toward London. Ever since they'd pulled over, Jane knew that Arthur, if that was his name, was a spy. She'd suspected as much when he'd asked to drive out here. But the clincher came when he'd jabbed his thumb into her shoulder and hissed at her in that voice. He hadn't noticed that his accent had changed, ever so slightly.

When he'd gone into the base, she'd debated whether to drive off and leave him, but decided against it. And when the soldier had challenged him, she'd sat there, her heart in her throat, hoping that it would all end there in that field. But somehow, he'd convinced the man.

Now they drove back in silence. She could tell he seethed over something and avoided even small talk. What could she do? Hell, she'd been ready to throw all caution to the wind and fall in love again, had even let the man flog her with a belt, something that satisfied a deep craving inside her and something her dear, departed Freddy had hated. Christ. She was a bloody fool.

As the skyline of London appeared, Jane made a decision. She would keep up the pretense, act as if nothing had changed—continue to play the desperate widow until she could gather enough evidence to hang the bastard.

※　※　※

Kruger strolled through the evening crush of Victoria Station, oblivious to everyone but the man he waited for. His eyes, ever moving, roved over the sea of travelers alighting on every man in RAF blue. Presently, he spotted the man, struggling with his bag, as he stepped off the train compartment. Smiling, Kruger stepped forward.

"Flight Lieutenant Liddington?"

The man looked up and smiled quizzically. He stood about Kruger's height and had the look of an underfed schoolboy.

"I'm Captain Smythe," Kruger said, "SHAEF sent me to collect you."

"Jolly good," he said, smiling even wider. He had one of those detestable Oxonian accents that automatically made everyone who spoke it sound supercilious and arrogant. "I was wondering if HQ would send someone. Smythe, is it?"

"Quite. Here, let me take your bag," Kruger said, reaching out.

"Nonsense, old boy. I'll be fine. Wouldn't be cricket, anyway."

He hefted his bag over his shoulder and began striding toward the exit. Afraid his quarry would get away, Kruger caught up with him.

"You mind if we detour to the Gents?"

"Not at all," Liddington said. "Need to go myself."

As he'd hoped, the men's lavatory stood momentarily deserted. Liddington headed toward one of the urinals. Kruger crept up behind him, flexing his fingers, preparing himself.

"Oh, Arthur," Kruger said.

Liddington turned, about to reply, when Kruger's fist smashed into his throat, crushing his larynx. He gasped, his eyes bulging out.

He clutched at his throat, began turning red, then blue. This was taking too long. Lashing out again with the flat of his palm, Kruger struck upwards and jabbed his hand into Liddington's nose. The man stiffened and dropped like a stone, dead from a thin shard of bone piercing his brain.

Suddenly, Kruger heard the sound of the door's rusty hinges creaking open. Quickly, he grabbed Liddington's bag, then reached for Liddington's hand and closed his eyes in concentration. The transport only took seconds this time. Opening his eyes, he found they were in a copse of trees near the base at Dover. There was a small depression in among some bushes, and he set about covering the body with dead leaves and small branches. With luck, Liddington would not be found for at least a week. By then, it would be far too late. Satisfied the body could not be seen by the casual eye, Kruger grabbed Liddington's bag and closed his eyes again. In a moment he was back inside one of the stalls. The lights flickered rapidly, giving the place a bizarre stroboscopic look.

Kruger stepped out of the stall and saw an old man washing his hands at one of the sinks.

"Bloody lights. You'd think the bloody boffins in Whitehall could at least keep 'em working when they're supposed to be on."

Kruger smiled noncommittally and washed the dirt from his hands. This only made the old man more querulous.

"It's all bloody Churchill's fault, you know. He's the one who got us in this mess. We could've joined with Germany and had it good."

Kruger dried his hands and turned to the old man. "Who knows. Maybe someone will put a bomb in one of his cigars."

The old man roared.

"That would serve the old blighter! Hah, hah, a bomb in his cigar!"

THE NORMANDY CLUB

Kruger smiled dryly and walked out of the lavatory clutching Liddington's bag. Now came the true test: reporting to SHAEF in Grosvenor Square as Liddington. The one detail no one could research was whether anyone knew the man from a prior assignment. Kruger prayed no one did. He grabbed a cab in front of the station, growing nervous as they approached the square. It would all stand or fall in the next few moments. He paid the driver, giving him a generous tip.

"Thank you, Guv'nor. Good luck."

The cab sped off, leaving Kruger standing in front of the six-story Georgian brick building. In spite of the fact it was May, he could see his breath in the cool night air. A fog had crept in, giving the immediate area the look out of an old movie. Shaking off the cold, Kruger walked up to the innocuous-looking white door, taking note of the sandbags that ringed the building, piled waist high. No doubt there was an Ack-Ack battery on the roof.

"Halt. Who goes there?"

An armed sentry stepped out of the gloom, his face rigid and unemotional.

"Flight Lieutenant Arthur Liddington, reporting as ordered."

"Your papers, sir?"

Kruger pulled out his ID and Liddington's orders and handed them to the sentry. The man turned on an electric torch and examined them. Kruger felt a bead of sweat run down his back and his heart pounded in his chest, making his knees shaky. The sentry looked at the photo on the ID and then stared at Kruger, shining his light into his eyes. Kruger resisted the urge to squint. *Blast it, man, get on with it*, he thought, ready to scream.

The light clicked off.

"Right. The officer of the day is Major Crutchins. He's inside.

Go left off the foyer, third door on your left. He'll have your new orders and a place for you to billet for the night."

The sentry saluted and disappeared back into the shadows. Relieved, Kruger picked up his bags and pushed through the door.

Inside, he followed the sentry's instructions and soon found himself in front of a large mahogany door. He knocked and a gruff voice ordered him inside. The office looked like every other office in a military establishment: heavy, wooden, utilitarian furniture and wall-to-wall file cabinets. The room itself, once the house's library, still held leather-bound volumes on the shelves. Kruger dropped his bag and snapped his arm in a perfect salute, palm facing out.

"Flight Lieutenant Arthur Liddington reporting as ordered, sir!"

The older man scowled, his eyes narrowing to slits. "You're late, Lieutenant."

"The trains, sir. They were running a trifle behind."

The man grunted and looked down at his desk. "Tell me, Lieutenant, how is your father? Haven't seen the old scrapper since the last regimental reunion."

Kruger showed nothing outwardly, but his heart skipped a beat and a cold sweat broke out all over his body. Somehow this old windbag knew Liddington's father. Then he realized he had nothing to fear. If the old man had known *him*, he would be under arrest by now.

"I'm sorry, sir, he passed away last year. I thought you knew."

A flicker of sadness passed over the major's features and was gone a moment later. Reaching into the pile of papers, he pulled out an envelope and handed it to Kruger.

"These are your orders for tomorrow. You are to report to 21 Army Group HQ and assume duties as the general's new aide."

"Montgomery, sir?"

"Who bloody else?"

"Begging the major's pardon, but doesn't the general have an aide?"

Crutchins looked at him and sighed. "You're just like your father, Liddington, always asking questions. General Montgomery deems it necessary to add you to his staff temporarily."

"Right, sir."

"Now as to your quarters—"

"Sir?"

"What is it now?" he said, becoming annoyed.

"If it's all the same, I have quarters arranged."

"Where?"

Kruger smiled conspiratorially. "A certain lady friend has extended the hospitality of her modest home to a needy soldier."

As Kruger had hoped, the old man echoed his smile, picking up on the not-so-subtle hint of debaucheries to come.

"Aye, just like your father, all right." He stood and saluted. "Can't keep the lady waiting, Lieutenant, eh, what?"

"No, sir," Kruger said, returning the salute.

He turned to leave but stopped when the major called out.

"Lieutenant?"

"Yes, sir?"

"Your car will be leaving from here precisely at oh-eight hundred. Don't be late."

Kruger smiled. "Have no fear, sir. I wouldn't miss this for the world."

"Miss what?"

"Whatever it is," Kruger said, recovering nicely.

Picking up Liddington's bag, Kruger strode out the door. He

retraced his steps and passed the sentry, who paid him no mind this time. Reaching the street, he turned and began whistling a jaunty tune, his footsteps marking cadence. A moment later he was swallowed by the swirling fog.

19

London, England
14 May 1944

The icy wind whipped across the Thames, blowing away the last of the fog. The sky in the east turned gray, signaling the dawning of a new day. Jack and Denise snapped into existence in the shadow of the Tower Bridge, hidden by one of the monstrous abutments. Jack leaned against the venerable stone and tried to keep his head from spinning. The move they'd just made in both time and space made him want to throw up. Like Denise had described, for the briefest of moments, he'd felt wired into the pulse of the universe, stretched over eons of time and infinite miles of space. The price for that experience was a throbbing headache and a woozy stomach.

"You okay?" Denise said, putting her arm around him.

"I feel like I've been put through a cosmic meat grinder." His teeth chattered and his lips felt raw and chapped. "How 'bout you?"

"Freezing, tired, and I need a goddamn drink. Let's find a hotel."

"*Scheiss*, Malloy, you drink too much."

She laughed. "You better lose those German curse words, if you know what's good for you."

"Yeah, yeah. Let's just get out of this wind before I catch pneumonia, all right?"

"You sure are a fussbudget, aren't you?"

He snarled, half in jest, and began walking along the riverbank, huddled against Denise. About half a mile on, they spotted a lone taxi and took it to a small hotel near the West End. There'd been a near panic when Denise realized they had no money, but the kind driver waved them out of his cab with a cheery good night.

The hotel, The Royal Arms, had seen better days. The lobby was seedy, run-down, but it somehow added to its charm. Both Denise and Jack were taken aback by the number of people, some in uniform, who slept on the various chairs and couches. The air smelled of cigar smoke and cheap perfume.

"They must be full, Jack."

"They also don't appear to mind if people sack out in their lobby."

Jack glanced over at the registration desk and saw no one there. Even clerks had to sleep, and manpower was in demand elsewhere. Scanning the room, he spotted an empty love seat.

"Come on," Jack said, pulling Denise with him.

"What if these people are paying?" she whispered.

"We'll find out, won't we?"

"Damn!" she hissed after tripping over a soldier's duffel bag.

"Ssssssh!"

Denise gave him the eye, as if to say, "No kidding!"

They both fell into the small couch, exhausted. When a sailor seated nearby offered Denise a pull from his flask, Jack resisted the urge to rip it out of her hands. *Let her have it*, he thought. After what she'd done, maybe she deserved a whole case. He shifted in his seat and his eyes grew heavy. Even the spring he felt digging into the small of his back did not keep him from falling into a deep and immediate sleep.

⚜ ⚜ ⚜

"Hey, shithead. How are you?"

Jack's eyes snapped open as Wiley's voice faded into his subconscious. The dream shook him to the core. He'd been back in the hotel room again, only this time, he'd seen Kruger pop in, place the extra pillow over Wiley's head, and pull the trigger. Feathers flew about the room, the report like a muffled cough. Wiley's body jerked once and lay still. Jack had tried to scream, tried to move, do anything to stop it, but it had felt like he was chained to the spot, forced to watch as some sort of ghoulish penance for some unknown sin.

He closed his eyes and inhaled.

"Excuse me, sir?"

Jack opened his eyes to find the hotel clerk standing above them. Pert and petite, she exuded the studied charm of someone accustomed to dealing with the public all day long.

"Yes?"

"You and your lady friend will have to vacate the lobby, sir."

"Why?"

"It's past six."

Shaking the grogginess from his mind, he looked about the lobby and noticed they were the only ones left.

"Sorry," he said, sitting up.

"That's okay, sir. It's hotel policy. All transients out by six."

Awakened by Jack's movement, Denise groaned as she stretched her body.

"Cute ass," she said, watching the departing clerk.

Jack shook his head.

"Get your head out of the gutter, Malloy. Time to move out."

She smiled lazily and saluted. "Yes, sir, General."

Out on the street, they found themselves overwhelmed by the pandemonium. Cars vied with military vehicles in a never-ending stream. Cabbies screamed out invectives that made even Denise blush. Horns honked incessantly while unflappable Bobbies directed traffic, making their directions known with abrupt hand signals and piercing blasts of their whistles.

"Where do we go from here?" Denise shouted.

Jack studied the street, trying to get his bearings based on a London he'd visited only once, and one that wouldn't exist for forty years. Suddenly, he remembered.

"SHAEF headquarters!" he said.

"How far is it?"

That was something he couldn't guess at. He shrugged and started to walk. Frustrated, Denise followed.

"You mean you don't know?"

"No, I don't. All I know is it's in Grosvenor Square. That help?"

Denise shook her head and muttered something Jack could not hear over the street noise. Up ahead, he saw a familiar sign. It read: London Underground.

"Come on!" he said.

Taking the stairs two at a time, Jack descended into the tube station, his eyes ignoring the quaint old advertisements, on the lookout for something far more important. A second later he spotted it behind a knot of passengers waiting for the next train: a map of the subway system.

It took only a minute to find out that Grosvenor Square lay a little over a mile away, only two stops on the tube. Again, the problem of money arose.

"How about I do my impression of Bing Crosby," Denise said. "Maybe people will throw money in our hat."

"We don't have a hat. Besides, you sound more like Bob Hope. They'll probably arrest us for disturbing the peace."

Denise frowned. "And I suppose you could do better?"

"Never mind, I'm sorry," he said stepping over a sleeping woman wrapped in a frayed blanket. The entire station appeared to be a home away from home for dozens of people lounging about, waiting for the next air raid. Whole families sat huddled together, boiling pots of tea over small alcohol lamps.

"Well, I'm waiting for one of *your* bright ideas," Denise said, nearly tripping over a small boy playing with a set of lead soldiers.

Jack scanned the crowd, wondering what to do. Despite the depression and the wartime shortages, panhandling was not a common sight in Britain. He had no idea how anyone would react. Would they scream at him to get away or ignore him completely like some insignificant piece of trash?

He spied a young couple alighting from one of the trains. The young man looked snappy in his Royal Navy uniform and the young woman stared at him, her eyes filled with love. No doubt they had spent the night together. Jack started to move toward them, figuring they might be sympathetic, when from out of the crowd behind them, a man ran out and grabbed the young girl's purse. She screamed, startling her boyfriend, who stood rooted to the spot, his mouth gaping.

Jack ran toward the thief and hit him with a cross-body block, the kind he'd learned in high school football, and knocked him flat, then ripped the purse out of the man's hand. Stunned for only a moment, the snatcher grimaced at Jack, his ferret-like features taking on an expression of pure venom. Before he could do anything, Denise ran up. Now that the odds had changed, the little man scrambled to his feet and melted into the crowd.

The couple ran up, breathless.

"My God, I've never seen anything like it. Are you all right?" the man asked.

"Yes, I'm fine. Here's your purse."

"You're American, aren't you?" the young woman asked.

"Guilty as charged," Jack replied.

The young woman smiled, relief spelled out all over her face. "We can't thank you enough. I don't know what I would have done. All our savings are in here. We're off to buy a ring."

She smiled again at her fiancé.

"Excuse us," he said, sticking out his hand, "Roger Demming, and this is my fiancée, Honoria Williams."

Jack grinned and made the introductions.

"I had to do something," Jack said. "The same thing happened to us."

He ignored Denise's puzzled expression.

"Oh my! What did you do?" Honoria said.

"There wasn't much we could do. He got clean away."

Honoria opened her purse and pulled out two five-pound notes and handed them to Denise. "You must take these. Roger and I insist on it, don't we?"

Roger nodded, but Jack could tell he was less than enthusiastic.

"I can't take this," Jack said, playing it out.

For a moment he thought Roger would overrule his fiancée, but he shook his head. Obviously, he knew when to keep his mouth shut.

"Nonsense. And you'll join us for breakfast."

Rather than argue, Denise pocketed the money and the four of them went above ground and took breakfast in the station café. The food, typical English fare, tasted bland and greasy. Still, he was hungry, and had to force himself to eat slowly, for fear of looking boorish. Their conversation tended to the banal until Roger brought up the invasion.

"It'll be soon, mark my words. We can't let Jerry go on with this mess, that's for sure."

"I don't doubt it, Roger."

Of course, Jack could not tell him what he knew about Overlord. He wondered what lay in store for the young sailor. Would Honoria end up a widow after only a few scant weeks of wedded bliss? Jack preferred not to think about that.

"How come you're not in uniform, Jack?"

Jack felt a stab of panic.

"Punctured eardrums," he said, spouting out the first thing that came to him.

"Sorry, old chap, bad show. By the way, those are smashing shoes you have on. Where did you get them?"

Jack looked down and saw the white running shoes and felt panic lance through him again. The rest of his clothes were nondescript, more or less blending with the fashions of the day. But how the hell was he ever going to explain a pair of Nike jogging shoes? He had to get rid of them.

"Jack?"

"What?" he said turning to Denise. She nodded toward Roger, frowning with concern.

"Oh, I'm sorry, you were asking about my shoes. Uhh, They're an experimental athletic shoe. I used to work for a shoe company back in the States. Never caught on, I'm afraid."

Roger smiled. "Too bad, they look quite practical."

After breakfast, they parted ways. Jack tried to give back the money one last time. Fortunately, Honoria stuck to her guns. Jack and Denise watched them disappear down the block.

"I wonder if—"

"Me too," Jack said.

"Well, at least we have some walking-around money. Not much, though."

"You're forgetting your history, Malloy. A British pound was worth about five bucks in nineteen forty-four."

Her eyebrows shot up. "What?"

"Yeah, they gave us the equivalent of fifty dollars, nearly two weeks' salary for most working people these days. It'll get us around for quite a while."

"No wonder you were trying to give it back. God, I feel awful."

"I know. That story I gave them obviously hit the spot."

"You should be ashamed."

"I was, for about a minute—until I remembered Kruger. Come on. We've got to go," he said, grabbing her hand.

Their first stop was a secondhand store where they bought clothes more apropos to the period. The clerk eyed Jack's running shoes like they were some grotesque artifact from a far-off world. Jack told him to keep them. The whole bill came to £1.15.0. He still couldn't get over how far money went even in an economy plagued with shortages.

Now dressed in the height of 1944 fashion, Jack and Denise dashed back to the tube station, jumping on a train just as the doors slid closed. It was crowded and smoky, so Jack let Denise take the last remaining seat and stood next to a man reading *The Times*. He scanned the front page, seeing nothing about any murders or disappearances. Liddington was either still alive, or his body still lay undiscovered.

THE NORMANDY CLUB

After the first stop, the train emptied out, allowing him to take the seat next to Denise. She rested her head on his shoulder and fell instantly asleep. Jack chuckled softly, wondering how she could do it, and desperately wished he could do the same. Moments later, the train pulled into their stop: Bond Street. Emerging at street level, they strolled toward Grosvenor Square and into the full bustle of downtown London. He heard a clock chiming the hour: 0800.

"Which building is it, Jack?"

Jack squinted, trying to see through the bright haze of reflections bouncing off the hundreds of cars thronging the square.

"Over there," he said, pointing to a red brick building across the square. "The one with all the sandbags."

The adrenaline began to flow when they dodged through the traffic. Even with its minimal fortifications, the building looked like a hundred others, had no sign to signal its importance, yet it contained men and women who held the future in their hands.

"Halt!"

They stopped in their tracks. The sentry stepped forward, a sergeant in the Military Police. His waxed mustache looked comical, but Jack wasn't laughing.

"State your business," the MP said.

Momentarily startled, Jack remained speechless.

"We've come to see General Eisenhower," Denise said.

If the request appeared out of line, the soldier didn't react. He snapped out his hand.

"Your papers, please."

Jack felt his heart sink. They had nothing to identify themselves. What they did have now lay in tatters, fifty years in the future.

Denise made a great show of looking for their ID.

"Oh, honey! How could we be so stupid? We passed right by the front desk and forgot to get our passports. Mamie is going to kill us if we don't stop by and see how Uncle Ike is doing."

Jack thought he saw something flicker in the MP's eyes. Could it be worry? Denise turned to the sentry and turned on the charm.

"Couldn't you let us in just this once? I'm sure Uncle Ike wouldn't be mad."

Her bedroom eyes would have melted stone, but the MP's features hardened, and he thrust his rifle to port arms.

"These are restricted premises, ma'am. Military personnel only," he said, his tone clipped and strident.

It was completely obvious they would get nowhere with the guard. Frustrated, they turned and walked back to the sidewalk.

"Well, it was worth a try," she said. "Why don't we hang out and wait? Maybe someone important will come out?"

"And then what? We start babbling about time travel and a Nazi America? They'll lock us up. At the very least, they'll ignore us."

Denise sighed. "What'll we do?"

"I don't know about you, but I'm tired of walking and taking trains. Let's grab a cab and get to the school."

"Where is it?"

"In Hammersmith. About six miles that way," he said, pointing west.

"Why spend the money?" Denise said, grabbing his hand and pulling him into a nearby alley.

"Oh, no, Denise!"

Before he could stop her, he felt the familiar flash and they landed on the corner of Hammersmith and Blyth Roads. The school grounds lay a quarter of a mile away. Jack wanted to throw up.

"Damnit, Denise! Why do you keep doing that to me?"

She laughed, a deep, throaty laugh he found appealing in spite of his anger. "We're here, Dunham. What's the beef?"

He shook his head and stalked off toward the school.

Set off on about five acres, it appeared to be no different architecturally than a thousand other places in London. Jack remarked that it looked remarkably like a smaller version of Harvard University. Surrounded by a wrought-iron fence, there was a sentry box with two MPs standing guard, one American and one British.

There also appeared to be a hive of activity as dozens of personnel crisscrossed the grounds, intent on business no doubt pertaining to the next day's historic briefing. What Jack found amazing is that none of these people knew what they were preparing for. Compartmentalized totally, these men and women did their jobs without question, and very likely, without much curiosity. Certainly, none of the burning desire he felt.

"What now?" Denise said.

Jack knew it would be no easier getting in here than into Grosvenor Square, harder in fact. For a brief moment he thought of having Denise pop them into the middle of the meeting and pointing the accusatory finger at Kruger. It satisfied his sense of the dramatic, but would it work? More than likely, their appearance would give the old generals coronaries and accomplish Kruger's mission for him. And that was assuming they could pinpoint the right classroom.

"Well, we can't stay here, or someone may get suspicious seeing us waiting around," he said, turning his head from side to side. "Let's go back to that hotel and see about a room. We'll come back tonight. I have an idea."

"Jack? What are you thinking?"

He grabbed her hand. "You'll just have to wait. Come on, let's go... and *no* transporting."

"You're no fun, Jack Dunham."

"Right. Come on," he said reaching for her.

BILL WALKER

Hand in hand, they ran back down Hammersmith Road and grabbed the first available cab back to the Royal Arms.

20

For the first time in a long while, Werner Kruger allowed himself to feel the giddy sense of excitement bubbling within him. The importance of the mission had taken precedence at all other times, stifling any expression of happiness, fear, or any other judgment clouding emotion. For the first time in a long time, he allowed himself to enjoy a degree of pleasure, and strolled through London's historic and stately government district. He watched the changing of the guard at Buckingham Palace, stared resolutely at the black door of number 10 Downing, and fed the pigeons flocking around Nelson's Column. Yes, for the first time, he felt completely at home.

What made his stay in London especially sweet were the admiring glances he received from pretty girls and the scarcely disguised envy of other men both young and old. Remarkably, the uniform had other benefits. While shopkeepers sometimes overcharged the boisterous Americans, not a single shopkeeper, public house, or restaurant owner would take his money. Discreetly, with a nod and a wink, they would slip him a glass of beer or a filling meal.

This was what a king felt like, he thought.

BILL WALKER

Jumping on a double-decker bus just as it pulled away from the curb, he climbed the spiral stairs and sat on a seat near the front, right above the driver. As ungainly as they looked, he'd always wanted to ride one of London's famous buses, but never had. Now he found himself enjoying the ride much as a small boy would. The route took them westwards down Kensington Road.

Glancing out the window, he caught a glimpse of red hair and found himself inexorably drawn to it. The woman talked animatedly to her beau, who looked oddly familiar. With a sickening twist of his stomach, he knew who it was.

Jack Dunham and that woman!

The bus flashed by the corner and Kruger raced toward the back of the bus and down the spiral stairs. He pulled the stop-cord and braced himself as the bus screeched to a halt, then jumped off and ran back to the corner, his eyes searching the crowd, head turning in every direction.

Nothing. Nothing at all.

"Damn you, Dunham!" he screamed, oblivious to the stares he drew from passersby.

Suddenly realizing the spectacle he'd made of himself, Kruger walked on, trying to sort things out. Perhaps he'd been mistaken. Perhaps it was some kind of bizarre mirage brought on by pre-mission jitters. But that was ridiculous. Everything had been planned meticulously down to the finest detail. Nothing left to chance.

Dunham.

It *had* to be him.

He marched off toward Jane's flat. She wasn't due to go back to work for another few hours. Time enough for some fun and games.

※　※　※

Ever since that moment in her cab when Jane had seen those eyes burning with repressed fury and heard that voice with its unmistakably German accent, she was desperately afraid.

When they returned to her flat, she'd run everything over in her mind about the drive out to Dover. She felt like a fool for letting her lust get the better of her. She'd let the bastard con her into breaking wartime restrictions. If they'd been caught...

But they hadn't. He'd gotten his pictures—she was sure there'd be a camera hidden in his bag, somewhere—and now he'd be leaving. And taking the bag with him. Funny, he hadn't taken it with him on his outing. He'd hidden it after he'd thought she was asleep. Through slitted eyes she'd watched him remove a small bundle and place the haversack deep inside her closet behind several boxes containing her dead husband's effects. Then he'd slipped out the door. Returning without the bundle several minutes later, he'd slipped back into bed and "awakened" her to make love for the third time that day.

In spite of what she suspected, Jane found herself replaying their sexual escapades in her mind. The pain and pleasure had been exquisite.

She shook herself from her masochistic reverie, glanced toward the closet, and made a decision. If there was anything in that bag that could hurt her country, she would destroy it. Climbing off the bed, she crossed the room and tore open the closet door. It took only a moment for her to find the bag. She unzipped it and dumped all the contents on the floor. Amongst the socks, underwear, and other sundries, she spied the small Minox camera and a round can that appeared to hold movie film.

A door slammed in the hall, startling her. Whoever it was swore in a loud, gravelly voice and tromped down the stairs to the street below. Knowing that she was vulnerable, that Arthur, or whatever his name was, could return at any moment, she grabbed the small camera and tried in vain to open it. Failing, she grabbed a brick she used as a doorstop and bashed the camera until it broke open, spilling tiny gears and pieces of glass. She then threw it into the dustbin, covering it with the newspaper that had come with her lunch of fish and chips.

Next she picked up the film can and opened it. Inside, lay a small reel of 35mm black and white film. She knew she should destroy it but couldn't resist looking at it. Spooling off a bit, she held it over her bedside lamp and found the tiny images far too small to see without magnification. She walked over to the bureau and dug out an old magnifying glass. The first thing she noticed was the Fox Movietone logo, a familiar sight even to Londoners. But what followed both intrigued and frightened her. Without the familiar narration to go with it, all she could glean was that it showed some kind of criminal trial. The superimposed titles gave the location as Nuremberg, Germany, 1946. For a moment she stood rooted to the spot, not really grasping what she held. Was it a hoax—some kind of joke? But those burning eyes came back to her and she realized nothing about this man could be construed as a joke. Then what was this?

She spooled out the reel and found a close-up of a fat man glaring at the camera as he listened to something on a pair of headphones. At that moment, her blood froze. The man was Hermann Göring! Even she knew that corpulent face seen strutting about in ridiculously opulent uniforms in countless other newsreels. Here he sat, stripped of his gaudy medals and his swagger—beaten. Here he was, yet this she knew could not be!

Stunned, she dropped the film, cursing as it rolled under her bed. Not bothering to roll it back onto its reel, she gathered it all up into her arms and took it to the fireplace. The coals still glowed from the fire she'd started that morning. She tossed in a few more lumps of coal and fanned them into a small blaze. She then threw the film into it, watching as the thin nitrate film burst into a brilliant flame. It didn't burn so much as explode. Regardless, it could now do no harm.

She thought she heard something and dashed to the window and gasped. Arthur Liddington was no more than half a block from the flat, walking determinedly, his expression dark and troubled. For a fleeting moment, Jane had the urge to run, to get out and never come back. But something told her it wouldn't do any good. Acting quickly, she threw more kindling and a couple of medium-sized logs onto the fire, hoping they would cover the remnants of her treachery. She heard Liddington's feet on the stairs and stuffed everything back into the haversack as she found it. When he stormed into the room, he found her puttering in the kitchenette.

"Arthur, what's wrong?"

He barely glanced at her as he paced the room, snarling under his breath.

"What is it, please tell me?" she said.

He stopped pacing and smiled, as if nothing at all bothered him. The abruptness of his transformation unnerved her. He came to her and took her into his arms, kissing her savagely. She responded to his burning lips in spite of herself.

"I want you," he whispered. "I'm going to spank you just how you like it."

He reached for her blouse, then stopped, his face clouding. Shoving her aside, he rushed to the fireplace, and peered into the pulsing flames. There was no doubt. It was the reel of newsreel film, the twisted metal now glowing a fiery red. He whirled, his eyes filled with fury.

"WHAT HAVE YOU DONE!"

Jane flinched, her eyes looking guilty.

"I-I haven't done anything," she stammered.

Without answering her, he raced to the closet, pulled out the haversack, and dumped it onto the floor, much as she had done. The two halves of the empty film can rattled noisily on the floor. He appeared to swoon for a moment before his anger returned. He crossed the room and grabbed her around the throat.

"Where is the camera?" he hissed.

Jane felt blind panic at that moment, but her mind held on to one unshakable truth: she stood no chance if she admitted anything.

"I don't know anything about your camera. I didn't know you had one."

"Lying *hündin*," he said, backhanding her across the face.

She tried to pull away from him, but he grabbed her by the hair and threw her across the room. She slammed into the bureau and crumpled to the floor.

"Where is it?" he demanded, approaching her.

Dazed and disoriented, Jane again tried to get away, quite unprepared for the kick that now struck her full in the face. She crashed into the dustbin, knocking it over. Kruger made for her again and halted. He could see the remnants of the Minox. Reaching into the garbage, he pulled it out. Trembling, he sank to the floor.

"NO!" he wailed, almost crying from frustration.

Jane took that moment to scramble to her feet and lunge for the kitchen knife lying on the table. Grasping it, she turned and ran for him. In the last second before she could plunge the knife into his back, Kruger turned and grabbed her hand. Drawing back his fist, he punched her in the face, breaking her nose. She flew back, hitting the table, and let go of the knife. Blood gushed from the crushed cartilage, splashing her clothes as she crumpled to the floor.

Kruger took the knife and approached her. In spite of the beating, Jane was conscious and alert.

"Is this what you want, my dear?" he said, holding the knife to his body.

Jane watched him, now devoid of fear, accepting the inevitable.

"Is this what you want?"

"Go to bloody hell," she said, her voice sounding muffled through her ruined nose.

Kruger laughed. "I've already been there."

Laughing again, he plunged the knife into his abdomen. Jane screamed as the blood gushed.

"What are you doing?" she shouted, shocked to the core.

"Isn't this what you want, Jane?" he said, slicing a deep gash into his arm. "Don't you want to see me bleed?"

Again, the knife flashed, opening up an artery in his other arm. It spurted rhythmically in time to his rapidly beating heart. Was he mad, after all? Kruger dropped the knife and Jane watched transfixed as the man she knew as Arthur Liddington closed his eyes and began to chant. The words sounded ancient, formidable. A moment later, the air around his body glowed a deep, fluorescent blue, crackling with a kind of static electricity. Awestruck, she saw all the cuts and stab wounds melting away, knitting themselves back into seamless, unblemished skin.

He knelt down and took her head in his hands.

"You think you can beat me, my dear Jane?" he asked, staring into her frightened eyes. "Think again." With a savage twist of his hands, he heard her neck snap and felt her body go limp. Clamping his eyes shut, he began to chant again. A moment later, Jane's body glowed, then imploded into nothingness.

Dressing quickly, Kruger gathered his things. Jane's naive patriotism had been a bad miscalculation on his part, one that had cost him priceless proof, proof needed to convince *Der Führer* of the veracity of his claims. Leaving the flat momentarily, Kruger scanned the deserted hallway, listening for any clues that someone might have heard—might be watching. He heard someone screaming, a child crying, and smelled the odor of boiled beef and cabbage. But the hall remained empty. Closing the door, he padded down the hall to the small lavatory and went inside.

After locking the door, he used a sixpence to unscrew the grating covering the heating vent. With the last screw removed, he pulled off the grate and saw the Semtex and detonator. He sighed with relief. Something had told him to separate the explosives from the rest of his gear, and that blind foresight had saved the present mission. Too bad he had not done so with the rest. Now his mission in Germany would stand in greater peril. For a fleeting moment he considered returning to the future and obtaining another Minox, a new copy of the newsreel and starting all over again. He could have the pleasure of killing this bitch twice. This time *before* she could become a problem. But Kruger realized he would have to face Armand Bock's withering criticisms. And his ego would never allow that. No. He would continue on with the original plan. Newsreels be damned.

Gathering up the material, he returned to the flat and packed it inside the haversack. Tomorrow, he would enter St. Paul's with both the plastique and the detonators strapped around his waist.

Satisfied that everything stood in order, Kruger scanned the flat. He found what he needed under the small sink: an old lamp filled with kerosene for those nights of enforced blackouts. He unscrewed the top and poured the oily liquid out onto the bed and the surrounding floor, leaving enough to form a trail to the door. He then smashed it to look as if it had fallen off the nightstand.

Looking out the windows, he saw the street was quiet. He pulled the shades, gathered up his haversack, and walked to the door. Reaching into the pocket of his uniform tunic, he pulled out Liddington's trench lighter and struck the flint. The flame sprouted immediately. He reached downward and touched it to the trail of kerosene and watched as it caught. The flame moved lazily back along the trail toward the bed.

Kruger closed the door and left, taking the stairs at a leisurely pace. Out on the street, he walked briskly, turning around only once to see the faint orange glow behind the drawn shades. He smiled. With luck, this would only rate a small footnote in the morning's paper, something quite unimportant compared to the deaths of Winston Churchill, Eisenhower, and the rest. He looked forward to those headlines with undisguised relish. If nothing else, he would see those bastards roasting in the flames. He knew Dunham would come for him there. He knew the smarmy shit would try and stop him. *Let him come*, Kruger thought, *let him come and be damned.*

Kruger smiled again and thought of the perfect solution to annoying pests. In his foolishly valiant attempt to stop him, Jack Dunham would get the surprise of his life.

21

London, England
14 May 1944

> *Don't sit under the Apple Tree,*
> *With anyone else but me,*
> *With anyone else but me,*
> *With anyone else but me, no, no, no,*
> *Don't sit under the Apple Tree,*
> *With anyone else but me,*
> *'Til I come marching home...*

The crowd stood shoulder to shoulder inside the crowded pub, their voices raised in joyous song, the atmosphere made even more romantic by the dim candlelight. Songs like "Don't Sit Under The Apple Tree" competed with "Tangerine" and others Jack didn't recognize. The piano player, an American army sergeant, banged out the tunes on a battered, out-of-tune upright, a Lucky Strike hanging from his smiling lips. The smoke hung thick, and the booze flowed freely among the civilian regulars and the military personnel from all the different branches and armies stationed in England. They smiled, laughed, cried, and hollered with a kind of deliberate abandon. Their boisterous din was guaranteed to drive away all cares. From Jack's point of view, they all looked like they were trying very hard to forget what lay just beyond the door: death, destruction, painful memories, and dreadful uncertainties.

In a way, he envied them their frenzied good humor, their defiance in face of all they had to deal with night and day. He and Denise had come back to Hammersmith in a desperate attempt to find some way to get into St. Paul's. Tired of going back and forth to a hotel where they still could not get a room, Denise had come into the Roundhead Tavern and played the part of a war widow looking for lodging. The kindly barkeep took pity and gave her the spare furnished bedsitter over the pub. This surprised Jack. Between the bombings over the past few years and the thousands of soldiers clogging the city, to find *any* available housing amounted to a small miracle. Now they sat there in the thick, hazy atmosphere, drinking their third warm beer, totally frustrated.

"What now?" Denise said, draining her beer. Her words slurred.

"Ease up, will you? We've got a big day tomorrow."

She shrugged. "For what? Sightseeing? How the hell are we gonna get in there?"

Jack sighed and decided to go with his last-ditch plan. "We're going to use your newfound talent and pop in on Winston and his friends, that's how. But if you keep pounding back those pints of Guinness, you're going to be no good to anyone."

Denise smiled a lopsided grin. "I know one thing I'm good for," she said, looking seductive. "How 'bout a roll in the hay, soldier?"

"For Christ's sake, you're plowed."

"Me and everyone else here," she said, waving her arms expansively.

"In case you've forgotten, we've got a nutcase out there with a bomb who's going to blow up a lot of very important people tomorrow at that briefing!"

"I haven't forgotten. But I'm not going to get all bent out of shape over something I can't do anything about tonight."

"Why do you have to drink so damn much?"

"I like it. That good enough for you?"

Jack fumed. What the hell was wrong with her? Getting up from the table, he fought his way through the crowd and went into the men's room. He stood at the urinal and let his bladder go, feeling immeasurably better. Staring at the wall in front of him, he read some of the graffiti. One in particular caught his attention:

> *Whistle while you work,*
> *Hitler is a jerk,*
> *Mussolini bit his wienie,*
> *Now it doesn't work.*

Seeing the familiar schoolyard refrain here and now made Jack burst out laughing. He turned and noticed a soldier staring at him from one of the other urinals.

"Just a funny thing written on the wall," he said, shrugging.

The soldier, a young lieutenant, stared at him, his eyes cold. Jack suddenly felt self-conscious.

"Guess you had to be there," he said, buttoning up and leaving the lavatory. He pushed his way back to the table and found Malloy with a fresh pint, in earnest conversation with another woman at a nearby table. Jack felt a tiny stab of jealousy as he sat back down.

"Hi, sweetie, this is Maude!" she said.

"Hi," Jack said, immediately turning away.

THE NORMANDY CLUB

"That was rude," Denise said.

"Never mind that. I was taking a piss and some guy was giving me the eye."

Denise grinned and Jack held up his hand.

"Forget it. It's not what you're thinking. This guy was an officer, and if looks could kill, I'd be on a slab. I think we'd better leave."

"Oh, Jack, you're just paranoid."

He was about to come back with a smart remark when he felt someone come up from behind him. A chill ran up his spine when he heard the voice.

"Excuse me, sir."

Deciding not to be intimidated, Jack turned, a nasty remark on his lips. He lost all his steam as he spotted the three soldiers standing by their table. Two military police, one British, the other American, stood flanking an American lieutenant. The same lieutenant from the men's room. The noise inside the pub died to a soft murmur as all eyes turned toward them.

"Excuse me, sir. But I'm going to have to ask you and the lady to accompany us."

"Uhh, what seems to be the trouble, Lieutenant?"

"No trouble, if you come quietly," the lieutenant said. The man looked barely older than twenty-two. Something felt very wrong.

"May I ask why?"

"No."

Denise whispered to him, "Let's go, Jack. I don't think they're kidding around."

Jack eyed the two MPs. Both were strapping men with bull necks and steely expressions. Both would have made great bouncers for the pub. Each of them gripped the holsters where their pistols resided.

Seeing no other choice, Jack and Denise rose from the table and were hustled from the pub, out onto the sidewalk, and into a waiting half-ton truck. The MPs sat in the back watching them while the lieutenant climbed into the cab with the driver. The engine started with a throaty roar and lurched from the curb.

"So where are we going, handsome?" Denise said to the American MP. He stared through her as if she didn't exist.

"Forget it, Malloy, he isn't talking," Jack said.

"Can't say the same for you," she said, ignoring him.

Jack shook his head and watched the receding road out the back of the truck, noting the slightly noxious odor of gasoline and stale vomit. *They must make a sweep of all the pubs*, he thought.

Hardly on the road for more than a few minutes, Jack felt the truck slow as it pulled through a gate. Though an especially dark night, Jack could still see they had entered the grounds of 21 Army Group, St. Paul's School. His lips curled in a wan smile. They'd made it onto the grounds, but not the way they'd intended.

The truck, its breaks groaning as it slowed, jerked to a stop up in front of one of the buildings. The MPs hustled them off the truck and into the building. Though now an army headquarters, the interior of the ivy-covered walls still held the looks and smells of academia. The MPs guided them down a flight of stairs into an area that in no way resembled anything like a school. They'd reached the brig.

After passing a guard sitting at a desk piled high with paperwork, they passed through a steel door and into the holding cells, two on each side of the narrow corridor.

The British MP opened the cell farthest from the door and shoved Jack inside, slamming the door behind him. Denise got the adjacent cell and more gentlemanly treatment. After checking that their cells were locked, the MPs turned heels and marched out, their hobnailed boots clacking cadence as they faded into the distance.

"Nice work, Dunham," Denise said, giving Jack one of her patented looks of disgust. She turned and flopped down onto one of the bunks, her back to the bars dividing their cells. Jack sighed, sat down on his bunk, and tried not to notice the overpowering odor of feces and ammonia.

"Hey mate, what're ya in for?" someone called.

Jack shot a glance toward the cell across the hall and spotted a British corporal peering at them through the bars. Wearing a wrinkled uniform and a black beret pushed back on his balding pate, he smiled, revealing a missing front tooth and deep laugh lines etched into the nut-brown skin around his piercing, slightly oriental eyes.

"Yeah, over here, Guv," he said.

The man smiled again and held out a pack of cigarettes in a hand crisscrossed with calluses and scars and nails chewed to stumps.

"Uhh, no thanks. Don't smoke," Jack said.

The corporal shrugged and lit one for himself.

"The name's Harry, Corporal Harry Gordon, Royal Fusiliers at your service."

Jack didn't feel much like socializing, but the little man's infectious grin and cockney accent broke the ice.

"What are *you* in for, Harry?"

"What you might call a little extracurricular activity after hours. In short, absent without leave. I was supposed to be on guard duty."

"Sorry."

Harry smiled slyly. "Nothing to be sorry about. At least the buggers let me finish with the dolly before they broke in."

It was Jack's turn to smile.

"So…"

"I'm sorry," Jack said, feeling foolish. "I'm Jack Dunham and this is my friend, Denise Malloy."

"Nice to make your acquaintance, Jack, Denise."

Denise, still angry, waved curtly from her bunk, saying nothing.

"So, Jack. What're ya doing in this fine establishment?"

"To tell you the truth, I don't have a clue. Denise and I were having a pint or two and a nice conversation and, wham, these MPs grabbed us and hauled us out of the pub and brought us here."

"Cor," Harry said, his eyes wide. "You blokes must have ruffled someone's feathers to get put in here. You're not even military, are ya?"

"No, we're not!" Denise said, speaking up for the first time. "Jack was shooting his mouth off about things he shouldn't."

That pissed Jack off. "Can it, Malloy."

"Fuck you, Dunham."

Harry whistled, long and low. "And a lover's quarrel to boot. Not good. Not good at all."

About to explain, Jack's attention was caught by the opening of the steel door leading into the brig's outer office. The American lieutenant had returned with two different MPs, both American. One of the MPs unlocked the cell door and swung it open.

"You two. Come with me."

Jack and Denise followed the lieutenant out and Jack caught Harry winking at him. He wasn't sure what that meant, but he took it as a sign of encouragement. The lieutenant led them through the outer office and down the basement hallway, reaching an open doorway. He beckoned them both inside.

The room, except for three battered chairs and a table, stood empty. The lieutenant pointed to the chairs and both Jack and Denise sat. The lieutenant remained standing.

"Cigarette?"

"No thanks," Jack said.

"Do you know why you two are here?"

"No, we don't," Denise said.

The lieutenant closed the door and leaned back, casting his face in shadow.

"I think you do. And we'll get along a lot better if you cooperate."

"I have no reason *not* to cooperate, Lieutenant...?"

"Simmons."

"Why are we here, Lieutenant Simmons?"

Nodding as if to acknowledge their decision to play the game their way, the lieutenant sat down on the chair in front of them.

"We have reason to believe you are involved in a plot to assassinate Eisenhower and Churchill. You were spotted outside the school yesterday afternoon." Jack looked at Denise, who shook her head in disgust. Simmons continued.

"Thinking that someone standing around for so long was up to no good, I had one of our undercover men follow you. Last night in the pub, he overheard you talking about a bomb and called me. That's why you're here."

"That's ridiculous," Jack said.

The lieutenant pulled out a small notebook and flipped it open. "Then why were you talking about, and I quote, 'a nutcase with a bomb who's going to blow up a lot of very important people at that briefing.'"

"Doesn't that prove we're not the ones to worry about?" Denise said.

"That proves nothing except you are aware of top-secret information. And since you are dressed in civilian clothes, we can assume you are German spies."

"Oh, for crying out loud! We are *not* spies!" Jack shouted.

"Tell him, Jack," Denise said.

"Tell me what?"

Jack looked at the man, wanting to hate him, but instead saw a dedicated man trying to safeguard a very important operation. He decided to come clean.

"All right," he said, taking his seat once again. "But you're going to think we're nuts."

"Try me."

Jack glanced at Denise, who nodded. Turning back to Lieutenant Simmons, he began to tell the whole story. As incredible fact followed incredible fact, Simmons's eyes never wavered, never changed expression. He sat there and listened intently.

"And that's it. If we don't stop Kruger tomorrow at the briefing, he will kill everyone in that room. Hitler will win and everything that I told you about the future *will* come true."

After Jack finished speaking, a silence fell over the room. For a long, pregnant moment, nothing was said. Jack felt like screaming.

"And that's it?" Simmons said finally.

"Isn't that enough?" Jack said.

"Let's show him, Jack," Denise said.

Jack sighed and nodded. He hadn't wanted Denise to use her power unless absolutely necessary. Now they had no choice. Denise closed her eyes and began to chant. Simmons sat forward imperceptibly, waiting. But, after a couple of minutes, nothing happened. Denise's eyes snapped open in shock.

"What's wrong?" Jack asked, sweat beginning to pop out on his face. "Try it again."

Again, Denise closed her eyes, her concentration redoubled. Again, nothing. At that moment a sharp knock sounded at the door.

"Yes?" Simmons said.

"Begging the lieutenant's pardon, but the general is requesting your presence."

"Very good, Corporal. Tell the general I'll be along." He stood up and gave them a vaguely contemptuous look. "You two will be staying with us for a while. I suggest you think of a better story and be ready to explain how you know so much about Overlord."

The lieutenant opened the door and signaled the two MPs to return the prisoners to their cells. Too shocked to protest, Jack trudged back to the cell and sat on his bunk. Denise sat on hers, equally shocked.

"I don't understand, Jack. It should have worked. It always works."

She began to cry, prompting Jack to reach through the bars and take her hand in his.

"I love you, you know that?" he said.

She nodded through eyes clouded with tears.

"I think I know what it is."

"What?"

"The Guinness. I think getting drunk blunts the power. Tomorrow, you'll have a hell of a hangover, but I think you'll be back to normal."

Denise looked hopeful for a moment then began to cry again.

"But what if I'm not? What will we do?"

"I don't know. We'll have to wing it somehow. We'll make it, okay?"

Denise nodded and wiped the tears from her face.

"Okay."

Pushing her face as far as she could through the bars, she kissed Jack passionately.

"Awww, now ain't that ducky," Harry said.

"Harry! Do you mind?" Jack said.

"Excuse me, Guv, but this ain't exactly the Ritz, ya know. Not the most private of accommodations."

Jack chuckled and was joined by Denise. The humor was a badly needed respite from all the anger and frustration. It also gave Jack an idea. If Denise was not back to normal in the morning, it would be their only shot. It was audacious, crazy even, but Jack liked it the more he thought about it.

"Say, Harry. Do you know the school grounds well?"

"I should say so. I've been stationed here ever since Monty took the place over in 'Forty-three."

"Do you know where the model room is? It's sort of a classroom shaped like an amphitheatre."

Harry beamed. "That's a right tight room, that one is. But I do know where it is."

"Where?" Denise said, trying to catch the drift of Jack's thoughts.

"About twenty feet straight up."

Jack went to the bars, excited. "You mean it's in *this* building?"

"Right you are, Guv. Right you are."

"YES!" Jack shouted.

"What?" Denise said.

"I have a way in," he said.

"A way into what?" Harry asked.

"The top brass are having a little soirée tomorrow and they forgot to invite us," Jack said, rubbing his hands together.

Denise narrowed her eyes. "Jack? What're you planning?"

"Nothing we aren't already prepared to do. Besides, Harry's going to help us."

"And how am I supposed to do that in here, Guv?"

Jack smiled and put his arm around Denise. "Let me tell you a story, Harry. It's one that's guaranteed to curl your toes and put hair on your chest."

Harry chuckled. "I could use one of those, mate."

The little corporal leaned forward, pressing against the bars of his cell while Jack retold their story and then outlined their plan for the following day.

The more he heard, the more Harry smiled.

22

London, England
15 May 1944

Kruger's eyes snapped open precisely at 0700, just as the phone next to the bed rang.

"It's seven, sir," the voice said.

"*Dank*—Thank you."

He slammed the phone down, cursing under his breath. He'd nearly blown it right there. What was wrong with him? Climbing from the feather mattress, he padded over to the window and threw open the drapes, staring out over the city. After leaving Jane's flat, he'd taken a cab to Claridge's Hotel and gotten the last room available. The hotel manager had been most insistent that the room was reserved for a colonel and his bride, but Kruger quickly changed his mind with two five-pound notes slipped into the obsequious bastard's hand. After that, it had been "Yes, sir" this and "Anything for our fighting men" that. All such rubbish.

Kruger looked toward the west and felt the return of the old excitement. He hadn't slept much, kept up by the thoughts raging through his mind. He was ready for whatever Dunham could dish out. Kruger smiled, remembering his little plan for the man. He could hardly wait to see his face.

Stepping away from the window, he walked into the bathroom and turned on the shower and stepped under the icy spray. Immediately, he felt his mind and body become alert, fresh for the day's events. He toweled off, heard the light tapping at the door, and opened it. The waiter smiled and wheeled in a covered tray.

"Good morning, Lieutenant," he said cheerily. "I do hope you slept well."

Kruger had no patience for the man's pathological cheekiness. He paid him a ridiculously large tip and practically pushed him out the door. Pulling off the covers on the plates, Kruger scowled: runny eggs, limp bacon, and something that could only be kippers. He shivered involuntarily and grabbed a piece of toast from the rack and stuffed it into his mouth. About to return to the bathroom, he thought better of it when he spied the copy of *The London Times* tucked neatly between a basket of muffins and the teapot. He scanned it and smiled. There it was, buried on page ten: TWO DIE IN FIRE ABOVE GREENGROCERS. The one-column article went on to say that witnesses were being sought and that the fire had started in the flat above the store. Nothing was mentioned about Jane. Who the other bodies were didn't matter. Happy for the first time, Kruger dressed and descended the stairs into the lobby.

He could see the hotel manager arguing heatedly with an officer. The man looked apoplectic, while the woman with him looked as if she'd slept in the lobby. No doubt the unfortunate groom and his bride. Striding past the desk, Kruger crossed the lobby and headed out onto the streets. He nodded to the doorman, who blew his whistle and waved for a cab. One immediately pulled up from a long line, and the doorman held open the door.

"Grosvenor Square," he said, sliding into the seat.

"Bloody hell, Guv. I've been waiting two bleeding hours for a fare, and now I'm going to have to wait in the queue again!"

"What's the problem?"

"The problem, Guv, is Grosvenor Square is right over there," he said, pointing down the road.

"Quite," Kruger said, pulling out a one-pound note. "Officers do not walk. Drive."

The cabbie shrugged and snatched the bill from Kruger's outstretched hand. "Your money, Guv."

The cab lurched away from the curb and joined the morning traffic.

※　※　※

Lieutenant Simmons sat in his office and stared out the window, waiting for his coffee to cool. He'd slept badly the night before, haunted by nightmarish visions of a world fifty years in the future. The story that Dunham—or whatever his name really was—gave him clearly could not be believed. It was absurd, preposterous, yet one thing weighed heavily on him: Dunham insisted someone planned to bomb the briefing. How did he know about the briefing, something only he and a handful of the top brass knew about? Even General Patton had not known until just yesterday. And that amounted to sealed orders merely telling him to report to 21 Army Group at 0900. They said nothing about the nature of the meeting. That was known by even fewer people.

Perhaps Dunham and his lady accomplice were members of a ring of saboteurs and it was their job to sew discord and disinformation, keeping everyone off-balance. But then why give away the store? Why reveal exactly what it was they planned? It didn't make sense.

That Dunham and his woman were trouble, he couldn't deny. The phone rang at that moment.

"Yes... I understand. Tell the general I'll be right along."

He hung up the phone and picked up his cap, the coffee forgotten. All the way down the hall, he debated whether or not to tell Montgomery about his two prisoners. He decided to keep it to himself a while longer. They weren't going anywhere, and security today had been doubled. No one would get past the guards without an invite. He stopped at the intricately carved door and stared at the nameplate:

GENERAL BERNARD L. MONTGOMERY

He could hear the general berating someone for some slip-up. That made the decision a firm one. No way would he bring up fantastic stories about time travel and Nazi futures. He would, however, keep his eyes and ears open.

※　※　※

"Hey, Guv! Wake up."

Jack opened his eyes and saw Harry's smiling face beaming at him from across the narrow hallway.

"What time is it?" Jack said.

"Breakfast."

Jack concealed his annoyance and glanced over to Denise's cell. She slept like a stone, oblivious to the bright light in the cell, on twenty-four hours a day. He shook his head in wonderment. How the hell did she do it?

"You ready, Harry?" Jack said.

"Ready, steady, and right as rain."

A moment later, the metal door leading to the outer office swung open and a guard came through pushing a breakfast cart. Without speaking, he pulled out three trays and slid them through the slots in the cells. He then turned and retraced his steps. The door clanged shut, echoing slightly. That sound still gave Jack a chill.

"Hey, sleepyhead, get up," Jack said, gently shaking Denise's shoulder.

She bolted from the bunk, her muscles tense. "Huh, what?"

"Take it easy. It's breakfast."

She sighed then frowned. "Oh, shit, my head is killing me."

Jack smiled in sympathy. "I told you."

"Yeah, yeah," Denise said, waving him away.

"Eat something. You're going to need your strength," he said, pointing to her tray.

She curled her lip in disgust. The sectioned metal tray held a huge mound of lumpy porridge, a burnt piece of toast with a dollop of marmalade, and a mug of tea. The tea had the leaves floating in it.

"Man, I hate marmalade," Denise said.

"Mm... and how about this lovely mush?"

Denise stuck out her tongue and Jack laughed.

"Are you always so chipper in the morning?"

"Only when I sleep with motormouths," she said, taking a bite of the porridge. She grimaced but kept eating.

Jack's annoyance came back. "Come on, you're not still angry about that?"

Her warm smile and soft chuckle answered his question. "I just had to pull your pud one last time."

"Oi, she is one salty skirt," Harry said.

"Yeah? You should see her with a machine gun."

It was Jack's turn to smile until a spoonful of porridge landed on his shirt.

"I can't take you anywhere," he said, wiping it off and putting it in his mouth. He shivered. It tasted like warm cardboard. "How can you eat this?"

"It oughta make Harry's job easier," Denise said, tossing her empty tray to the floor.

Jack nodded and turned to the little corporal. "Let's give it two hours. The briefing should have just started by then. All right?"

Harry leaned back on his cot, his hands behind his head and a sly grin on his face. "Don't you worry, Guv. Old Harry will make the Old Vic right proud, you'll see."

Jack turned to Denise, the question on his lips echoed in her eyes. "I don't know, Jack, I'm scared."

"You feel up to trying?"

Denise nodded, climbed off her bunk, and sat on the concrete floor in a rough approximation of the lotus position. Harry pressed his face to the bars of his cell and watched. Denise closed her eyes and began to chant, her lips moving silently. Sweat beaded her brow and she frowned. Nothing happened. Her eyes slowly opened, filling with tears. "I'm sorry, Jack," she said, throwing herself back onto her bunk.

For the first time since all of this began, Jack felt blind panic shooting through his body. He'd been sure that once the alcohol had worn off, she would be back to normal. And no doubt she would be after more time had passed.

Ironically, there was little time left. The briefing would be starting in a little less than two hours. Something had to be done.

"Is everything all right, Guv?" Harry asked, his beetled brow furrowed with concern.

"Change in plan, Harry. I'm afraid the Old Vic will have to wait."

The car sliced through the morning traffic effortlessly. Kruger noted how the other cars moved aside with nary a honk on the horn. It helped to be riding in a general's staff car and one that proclaimed that fact with bright-red pennants flapping from either side of the hood. He glanced at his watch and noted it was now 0830. Half an hour until the beginning of the end. As he recalled the reams of re-search Armand Bock had provided, he knew that the meeting would go on all day with a lunch break at noon and tea at four. He planned to excuse himself just after the noon break, pretending a need for the lavatory. He would place the explosives in the adjoining classroom. Two shaped charges to blow in the wall and another, larger one to create a concussion that would kill anyone left alive. Classic demoli-tions technique.

Kruger shifted in his seat and felt the Semtex dig into his ribs. He only hoped he could sit there for three hours. And what if Mont-gomery decided to send him out on some errand? What then? He stifled the thoughts and turned his attention to the passing buildings and people. That would not happen.

The car stopped momentarily at the front gates of St. Paul's. The two MPs, both British, took his and the driver's IDs, scrutinized them for what felt like hours, then returned them with a snappy sa-lute. Kruger let out his breath. He was in.

The car pulled to a halt in front of the main building. The driver, a British sergeant, got out and opened the door. Kruger stepped out and scanned the grounds.

"The general's office is the corner office on the north side. Just ask anyone if you get lost, sir," the driver said.

"Thank you, Sergeant. Carry on."

With his briefcase in hand, he marched up the steps and into the venerable building. Without thinking, he patted the inside pocket of

278

his tunic for the fifth time that morning. It contained Bock's letter to his uncle. After his mission here, he would leave immediately for Germany. Aside from the Semtex, this letter was the most important item on his person.

He saluted when two American colonels passed him in the hall, and he nodded at another captain who came out of an office just ahead of him.

"Oh," the captain said, "you must be Liddington, right?"

"Quite."

The officer smiled and extended his hand. "Good show. I'm Breckenridge, the general's other aide."

Kruger pretended to be uncomfortable. "I hope I'm not stepping on any toes here."

Breckenridge smiled. "Not at all, old boy. The general's got a lot on his mind and a lot to delegate. There are three more of us."

"Any idea what he's got in store for me?"

"Looks like you get the brass ring, Liddington. The old man wants you in with him today."

Kruger could barely contain his excitement, but he continued to play dumb.

"But aren't you and the others more familiar with everything?"

"Precisely the point. Monty wants fresh blood in there, someone without preconceptions and who'll be a little off-balance. He likes it that way."

Kruger shrugged. "It's his show. Can you direct me to his office?"

"Right. Go to the end of the hall and go right. It's four doors down. You can't miss it."

"Thank you," Kruger said, moving off.

"Not at all. Welcome to the club."

Reaching the end of the hall, Kruger turned and walked toward the imposing door at the end of the short corridor. Even from where he stood, he could see the nameplate. His pulse quickened with anticipation. About halfway down the hall, the general's door opened, and an American lieutenant exited. The man stared at him, making him feel like a lab specimen. He also blocked the way in to the general's office.

"Excuse me, Lieutenant," he said.

"You are?"

"Pardon?"

"I don't believe we've met."

Kruger didn't like the man's attitude one bit and decided to play up his part a little.

"Do you always forget to salute a superior officer, Lieutenant!" he said, his voice rising. "In answer to your question, Lieutenant, I am General Montgomery's new aid, *Flight* Lieutenant Arthur Liddington, and you will salute me!"

He thought he saw the man's eyes widen, as if he recognized the name, but the reaction was gone in an instant. Just then the door flew open.

"What is going on here! It sounds like a bloody barroom!"

There stood General Bernard Law Montgomery, Commander of 21 Army Group.

Both men snapped to attention.

"Begging the general's pardon, but I did not recognize this officer, sir," Simmons said.

Montgomery turned to Kruger.

"You must be Liddington."

"Yes, sir."

A hint of a smile flashed across the hawk-like features. "You must forgive Lieutenant Simmons. He is our security chief and a little overzealous at times. Right, come in. We have things to go over."

Liddington saluted and walked inside. Montgomery turned to Simmons. "Carry on, Lieutenant."

Simmons saluted and stood there as the door slammed in his face.

※ ※ ※

Simmons returned to his office feeling like a fool. He'd let the shock of the man's face and name make him forget common military courtesy, something Montgomery frowned on. Still, forgetting to salute was the last thing on his mind. Liddington! The man was exactly as this Dunham character had described him. And how could Dunham have known the man's name in advance? Even he hadn't. In the hectic events of the last few hours, he'd neglected to study the duty roster. He glanced at it now and saw that Liddington had been ordered to report this morning. If he'd bothered to look at the sheets as he always did, he would not have acted like such a bleeding idiot. Still, something bothered him about the man, but he couldn't put his finger on it.

And that was not the only thing that bothered him. Only that morning he'd received a garbled report about a corpse being discovered in a copse of trees on one of the Fortitude bases. No ID and stripped naked. The body even now was on its way to army pathologists, but after being exposed to the elements, the body had begun to decompose. It would make the ID process longer.

Problems. Nothing but problems.

Simmons leaned back in his chair and stared at the clock. The briefing would start in a few minutes. He needed to make sure all the arriving parties were properly checked. He grabbed his cap and walked out of the office. After the briefing began, Simmons decided he would pay his new prisoners another visit. Maybe this time he would get some answers that made sense.

※ ※ ※

Kruger stood at attention while Montgomery closed the door and strode over to his desk. "At ease, Lieutenant."

"Thank you, sir," Kruger said, taking a seat after Montgomery seated himself.

"Crutchins tells me you're 'Doubting Tommy's' son?"

"Yes, sir."

The general's expression saddened.

"He was a bloody great soldier. One of the best officers I ever served with. Asked too many bloody questions, though. Not like that, are you, Liddington?"

"Uhh, no, sir."

"Too bad. Could use a man with some brass in his sack."

Kruger felt like an idiot but had to admire the old man. A master manipulator. The general's smile told him it had all been in jest.

"Right. Let's get to it. What you are going to witness today is nothing short of historic, Liddington."

"Yes, sir."

The general stood up and began to pace. "After this war is all over, I expect my account of this great conflict will be in high demand. I want you to transcribe today's events for inclusion in my memoirs. Not a detail is to slip by you."

"Never, sir," Kruger said.

Kruger could barely contain his mirth. Here he was, about to participate in one of history's greatest moments—as a secretary to a popinjay with delusions of grandeur.

"You *do* take shorthand, Liddington?"

"Yes, sir, General."

"Good. I expressly ordered they send me someone who could write that nonsense. History waits for no man."

"So I'm told, sir."

"Right. And after today, you'll be taking over for Breckenridge. Man can't write a bloody word."

The general glanced at his watch. "Come, Liddington. Let us make our mark."

Montgomery turned on his heels and marched to the door. He stood there waiting for Kruger to open it. Scrambling out of his seat, Kruger held open the door and followed the rapidly striding general down the hall.

23

London, England
15 May 1944

Jack glanced at his watch. It was now 0845. The meeting would begin in fifteen minutes. If all went as planned, Jack would be there waiting for Kruger. He nodded to Harry and then grabbed his abdomen.

"Ooooohhhh! My stomach! Oooohhh. Someone! Guard! Get me a doctor! Oooooohhhhh!"

Jack writhed on the bunk, his face contorted in pain, and yelled as loud as he could. Out of the corner of his eye, he could see Denise watching him, her expression doubtful. On cue, Harry screamed for the guard, adding to the noise.

"Guard! Guard! Get your bloody arse in here!"

The metal door banged open.

"Shut your fucking mouth!" the MP said.

"Oi!" Harry said. "Can't you see this bloke's sick as a bloody dog? I think he's got food poisoning."

The guard sneered at Jack. "Poisoning's too good for guys like him."

Denise joined in. "If you don't help him, Lieutenant Simmons will have your balls for breakfast."

The mention of Simmons's name had the desired effect. Fumbling with the ring of keys, he unlocked Jack's cell door and walked in. Jack continued to moan softly, his eyes squeezed shut.

"You really look like shit, Mack," the guard said, shaking his head.

In a flash, Jack grabbed the MP by his shirt and slammed his head into the cinder block wall, knocking him out. Jack leaped to his feet, threw Denise the keys to their cells, and began exchanging clothes with the unconscious guard.

"I still don't like this, Jack. What if you get caught? What if—"

Jack buttoned up the MP's britches, noting that they were two inches short. "Look, we've been over this a hundred times. You can't help at this point. The best thing you can do is let Harry get you off the grounds and back to the Roundhead. If something happens to me—"

"Don't you dare say that!" Denise said, her eyes aflame.

Jack buttoned up the shirt and put on the tie. "*If* something happens, you've got to follow Kruger and get him."

"What if they won't let Harry and me out?"

Harry chimed in. "Not to worry, love. I was due to be sprung this morning, anyway. As for you, I'll tell them that Simmons has released you."

"Won't you need some kind of official release?" Denise asked.

Harry shook his head. "It being Monday, Smithers and Walston will be on guard. They both owe me big favors. You see, I'm also what you might call the procurement officer."

Jack put on the finishing touches to his MP uniform and stood at attention. "How do I look?"

"Like a damn fool," Denise said, flying into his arms. She kissed him. "You be careful, you hear?"

Jack nodded. "I will."

Jack watched Harry escort Denise out the door, his body trembling with nervous energy.

Now came the tough part. Straightening his uniform, Jack walked out into the main office, profoundly relieved to find it empty. As he suspected, with the briefing occurring, they rated only the one lone guard. Too many important people about to worry about two prisoners who weren't going anywhere. He grabbed the guard's M1 Carbine and walked out. Taking the stairs, he marched nonchalantly up to the first floor and spotted a contingent of ten MPs marching up the next flight. He fell in behind them, hardly believing his luck. They were leading him right to the classroom. The good feeling died as quickly as it had come when he saw the sandy-haired lieutenant waiting outside the door.

Simmons.

What could he do except keep walking towards his doom? If he peeled off, he'd attract attention to himself. If he got too close to Simmons, it would all be over. Fortunately, the man looked down at a clipboard and spoke. Taking no chances, Jack positioned himself behind a particularly beefy soldier. Simmons looked up, scanning the MPs.

"All right, men, listen up. Two of you will be stationed outside. Once the meeting has started, no one is to enter or leave until the specified break times. Is that clear?"

"Yes, sir." The response was in unison.

"Good. Haskell and Leavitt, you guys get the door. The rest of you deploy yourselves every ten feet around the top rim of the seats."

THE NORMANDY CLUB

"Sir?"

"Yes, Connors?"

"What about latrine breaks?"

The rest of the group began to chuckle.

"All right. All right, you guys, knock it off. Those of you inside may do so one at a time after signaling the others. Make it subtle—a touch to your helmet brim.

"Haskell and Leavitt will have to hold it until the scheduled breaks."

Jack saw the expressions on the two men fall as they took their positions. He managed to avert his face when he passed Simmons.

Shaped like an amphitheatre, the room sloped upward like a large bowl with hard wooden step-like seats ending about eight feet from the ceiling. They were stained a deep walnut like the rest of the wood in the room and looked aged and worn smooth by countless derrieres over the years. He climbed them to take his position, and noticed a few initials carved here and there. It appeared students were the same everywhere.

The most imposing aspect of the room had nothing whatsoever to do with its architecture. Near the front row of seats lay one of the most impressive dioramas Jack had ever seen. Measuring twenty-five feet in length, it rested at an angle, tilted so the spectators could get a view of the proceedings. It took Jack's breath away. In every exacting detail lay a perfect model of the Normandy coast complete with all of the German fortifications.

"You!"

Jack turned to the source of the voice, suddenly nervous. He saw one of the MPs, a sergeant, beckoning to him. "Let's not lollygag. Take the far position," he said, pointing to the opposite wall. From there he would be able to watch Kruger's every move.

"Yes, sergeant," Jack said, taking the steps two at a time.

He watched the other MPs and imitated their rigid stance, their carbines at port arms. Just as he got into position, the door swung open and history walked in. First through the door was Montgomery, nattily turned out in custom-tailored battle dress. He was followed by Kruger. Jack's knuckles turned white as he gripped the gun.

One shot.

One quick shot and Kruger was done for. Jack made himself relax, knowing it would be sheer suicide to make any such move. Montgomery took a position behind the huge diorama while Kruger sat in one of the front-row seats. Curiously, he opened his briefcase and took out a steno pad and pencil. Jack's attention wavered when he caught sight of the next group entering the room. They were various generals and top brass. Among them Jack recognized Generals Hap Arnold and Carl Spaatz of the USAAF, General Walter Bedell-Smith, and General Omar Bradley. The few he did not recognize were British. All of them sat with their aides in the first few rows.

Jack's heart beat faster when he spotted Eisenhower enter the room. As always, the general beamed that warm smile of his, greeting everyone and shaking hands. Churchill appeared next, his bulldog face swathed in wreaths of pungent cigar smoke. With great purpose, he strode into the room, pausing only to gaze at the great three-dimensional map of Normandy. He puffed his cigar, nodded his approval, and took a seat.

"His Majesty, the king," a voice rang out.

Everyone stood as King George VI glided into the room, looking regal and somewhat preoccupied. He nodded and his subjects bowed. The Americans looked a little uncomfortable, not sure whether to bow or offer their hands. As if sensing this, the king held out his hands to Eisenhower and the others.

Somewhere on the campus a bell chimed, prompting Jack to glance at the wall clock.

0900 hours.

"If you will all take your seats, please," Montgomery said, pointing to the gallery, "it's time to begin."

Everyone stopped talking and quietly sat. Montgomery nodded to the two guards at the door.

"Right. Lock the doors. No one in or out until my orders."

The two beefy MPs saluted and swung the double doors shut. The bolt shot, echoing through the silent room. In spite of the windows, the whole room had a dark, gloomy feel that even the lights couldn't dispel. Jack shivered from a draft through one of the windows. God only knew when Kruger would make his move, but he was here and ready. Montgomery cleared his throat and began his introductory remarks.

"Very good. Your Majesty, Prime Minister, fellow officers and esteemed Allies. We are here to rehearse and finalize plans for the greatest amphibious assault in modern times. In no way can we—"

Montgomery stopped in mid-sentence as a terrible pounding began on the doors. Churchill puffed on his cigar, his eyes betraying a hint of amusement. The others began murmuring. The pounding increased and Montgomery nodded to one of the MPs near the door.

"Open it," he said.

The MP ran over and relayed the order through the door. Immediately, the doors swung open, revealing General George S. Patton resplendent in his jodhpur trousers, olive drab, *Eisenhower* jacket, and his pearl-handled .357 magnums. His spotlessly shined riding boots clacked across the hardwood floors. He carried his four-starred helmet liner under one arm and a riding crop in the other.

His steely-blue eyes shone bright with the promise of conflict. He smiled, appearing to relish his moment of theatre.

"Starting without me, Monty?" he said, his jaunty, high-pitched voice filling the room.

A scowl flashed across Montgomery's face. It was no secret that Montgomery and Patton disliked each other intensely. He never let the flamboyant American general forget that it was he, along with Eisenhower, who held the cards to Overlord. Given the ignominious role of commanding the false armies of Fortitude, Patton had surprised everyone by diving into the deception with undisguised glee. Now, he would command the Third Army to come in behind the invasion force.

Montgomery smiled and waved him to an empty seat and began again.

"Now that we are all here, may I present General Dwight D. Eisenhower." With that, Eisenhower rose and walked to a spot in front of the diorama and stared for a moment at all the faces in front of him.

"We are here on the eve of a great battle to deliver to you the various plans made by the different Force Commanders. I would emphasize but one thing," he said, pausing for effect, "that I consider it the duty of anyone who sees a flaw in this plan not to hesitate to say so. I have no sympathy with anyone, whatever his station, who will not brook criticism. We are here to get the best possible results, and you must make a really cooperative effort."

All through Eisenhower's remarks, Jack kept his eyes riveted on Kruger. The man appeared intent on taking notes, and from the speed he wrote, it had to be shorthand. After Eisenhower, Bradley and two others spoke and then the briefing began in earnest. With two officers as helpers, Montgomery explained how the US First

Army would land at both Utah and Omaha beaches, while the combined British 50th, 3rd, and Canadian 3rd Infantry Divisions would simultaneously assault Gold, Juno, and Sword Beaches. In all, over thirty-five miles of beachhead.

As the day wore on, the models of landing craft and ships were shifted around on the board as plans were revealed and sometimes modified.

"As you can see," Montgomery said, "this plan requires a robust mentality on all who will execute it. We cannot falter."

"Excuse me, General."

Everyone's eyes turned to Churchill, who had lit a fresh cigar. "At Anzio, we put ashore one hundred sixty thousand men and over twenty-five thousand vehicles and advanced twelve miles in one day. Certainly, we can afford the risk here. We must, I pray."

Montgomery nodded soberly.

"Quite right, sir. Rommel is the man we must reckon with. I have studied the man and his tactics quite thoroughly. I believe I know the measure of the man."

"What about Hitler?"

"What? Who said that?" Montgomery asked.

Jack stared in disbelief as he saw Kruger raise his hand. The man either had brass balls or was crazier than he thought.

Montgomery appeared both annoyed and pleased.

"Yes, Lieutenant?"

Kruger stood, the steno pad now resting on his seat. "Begging the general's pardon, but my question is this. What if Hitler moves the Fifteenth Army?"

Montgomery stared at his new aide, trying to figure out what his game was.

Kruger continued. "From the intelligence, it is well-known that

Rommel believes the invasion will come in Normandy, while Hitler believes it will be Calais. What happens if the man changes his mind?"

"Then, my dear boy," Montgomery intoned, "we are all up the creek."

※ ※ ※

Denise stared at the pencil sitting on the table, sweat popping out on her brow. She'd been trying for hours to move the damn thing without so much as a quiver. Never. Never again was she going to take a drink, at least not until all this was over, and certainly not that awful Guinness. There had to be something about that particular brew that made her system go haywire. After all, she'd had wine during her training, and Chessman had never objected, nor had anything happened. Then again, she'd never gotten stinking drunk either. She stood up and began pacing. Her feet made the floorboards squeak in a rhythmic cadence that soon drove poor Harry to distraction.

"Blimey! Will you stop that bloody pacing," he said, burying his face in a pillow.

He lay on the rumpled bed in the tiny room above the Roundhead Tavern, watching Denise become more and more agitated.

"I'm sorry," she said, chewing her nails. With nothing else to do, she went back to the table and resumed her duel with the stubborn pencil.

"Give it a rest, love. You'll drive yourself bloomin' loony."

"I can't!"

"Look, Jack's a big boy. He'll do fine. Give him a chance!"

Denise turned, her eyes blazing. "Are you psychic now? Can you see the future? If not, then shut up!"

"Christ. Who made you bloody Queen Victoria? I may not go around walking through walls and popping into strange places, but I can think. If there were trouble, Simmons and his goon squad would have come for us by now."

Denise clamped her jaws together and stared out the window. Maybe Harry was right. Maybe it was all going to be okay. Then she remembered Kruger, and the knot in her stomach twisted anew.

"What time is it?"

Harry sighed. "Five minutes since the last time, love."

Denise strode over and grabbed his wrist.

The watch read 1225.

"We're going back," she said.

"WHAT!"

"I said we're going back. You deaf?"

"No. Are you crackers? We can't go back there. Simmons will crucify us."

"Maybe. Then again, if we 'pop' into his 'bloody' office, he might listen this time."

"You can't even move that bloody pencil."

Denise scowled. "We'll see about that!"

She returned to her seat at the table and forced herself to relax. Breathing evenly, she stared at the pencil and said, "MOVE!"

As if rocket propelled, the pencil flew off the table and rammed itself into the wall about six inches from Harry's head. His eyes widened, a mixture of awe and terror.

Denise leapt to her feet, pumping her fist into the air. "Yes, yes, YES!" She ran over to Harry, pulled him to his feet, and danced him around the room. "I'm back, I'm back, I'm back," she sang, giggling hysterically.

"Let me go, you're making me bloody dizzy!" Harry yelled. Denise let go of him and watched Harry wobble back to the bed.

She stifled a giggle. "I'm sorry, Harry. Are you all right?"

"Well, aside from the fact that you almost took me head off with that pencil, I'm right as rain."

"Good enough to take a little trip?"

Harry's eyes bulged.

"Oh, no," Harry said, leaping off the bed and shrinking into the corner. "You're not scrambling up me atoms!"

She grabbed his hand. "Sorry, Harry, Jack needs us," she said. A moment later, the room flashed blue and they both disappeared.

※　※　※

The room smelled of cigar smoke, making Kruger want to retch. He continued to take down all the words spoken but ceased to be interested in the proceedings. Yet another commander, this one a Canadian, went on and on about his armies' landings on Sword Beach. All the jargon and detail began to blur in his mind. Glancing at the wall clock, he saw that it was nearly 1230 hours.

Time to move.

In a little more than one hour, they would break for lunch, and by then the room would be a raging inferno consuming all who now resided within. He would be safe in Germany. Putting down his pad, Kruger sauntered over to Montgomery, who bent his head to listen.

"Excuse me, sir, but I need to use the facilities."

Montgomery nodded without speaking. Careful not to disturb the Canadian general's monologue, Kruger padded to the main door and knocked softly. He could hear the bolt scraping as it moved. The door cracked open and the MP stared at him, his eyes devoid of curiosity.

"Toilet," Kruger said.

The MP snapped his head forward in assent and pushed the door open to allow Kruger to slip out. The bolt slid home immediately. Not looking back, Kruger strode down the hall and ducked into the bathroom for a brief moment. Sticking his head out the door, he crept back toward the classroom, all the while watching to see if the MPs would turn their heads and see him. But the big, beefy automatons stood rigid with their exaggerated sense of duty. When he reached the classroom next to the briefing room, he ducked into the doorway's alcove. Now he could not be seen unless someone stood directly opposite. He grabbed the handle and turned. The door remained closed. Only momentarily annoyed, Kruger closed his eyes and began to chant. Then he stopped himself. Transporting here would attract attention. Reaching into his pocket, he removed a small set of lock picks and made quick work of the ancient tumblers. The door creaked slightly and swung open. Kruger froze. Did someone hear? The noise had sounded like the crack of doom in the cavernous hallway. But no one came running. There were no shouts of alarm. Nothing.

Relieved, he slipped inside. The classroom was about half the size of the briefing room next door. The wall it shared with the briefing room was paneled in dark mahogany about waist high. From there to the ceiling was ancient plaster, now cracked and yellowed in a few spots. Behind that plaster, he knew there were stout support beams that, once blasted by the Semtex, would transform into thousands of lethal projectiles.

Working quickly, he tore open his tunic and pulled out his shirt. Underneath was a large money belt. Each of its six compartments held a portion of the plastic explosive, totaling nearly eight pounds, as well as three detonators and the digital timer. Stripping it off, he ripped open the pouches and pulled out the plastique and molded them into rough conical shapes. They would be placed on the walls and joined together. The timer would trigger these first, blowing the wall into the briefing room. The final, larger blast would send a powerful concussive wave that would kill anyone else left alive and bring down the roof on their heads. Chuckling to himself, Kruger picked up the two shaped charges and began looking for the perfect spot to place them.

⁂ ⁂ ⁂

Lieutenant Simmons put down the report he'd been reading and glanced at his watch.

1224.

Damn. He'd been so absorbed in paperwork that he'd forgotten to call down to the brig and check on the prisoners. After the briefing was safely over, he intended to sort all this mess out. He grabbed the phone and immediately heard the switchboard operator.

"Put me through to Patterson."

"Right away, sir."

The phone rang and rang.

Simmons scowled. The goldbricker was sleeping again. He would see to putting the man on report personally if anything was amiss. He slammed down the phone and reached for his cap. When he stood, the pressure in the room dropped, making him feel dizzy and slightly sick to his stomach. Reeling, he collapsed in his chair. He watched, overcome with nausea, as the room took on a hazy glow. A moment later he heard a large hum and an electrical crackle. Instantly, the room filled with light and his ears roared as the air snapped. When his eyes cleared, he saw Denise Malloy and Harry Gordon standing in front of him. Harry plopped into a chair, trembling, totally forgetting about military etiquette. Denise remained where she stood, defiant. For a moment, Simmons sat rooted to his chair, a stupid look of surprise on his face.

"Didn't your mother tell you it's not polite to stare?"

"My God," he croaked. "You... you..."

"...were telling the truth. Yes. Jack figured it was all that beer I drank. Funny, huh?"

"Then what you said about nineteen ninety-four and all that is..."

"True as well."

Simmons tried to assimilate everything. He rubbed his eyes and attempted to pour a glass of Scotch from a decanter with his trembling hands. He gave up and drank directly from it. He coughed as the fiery liquid coursed down his throat. Sensing his mental inertia, Denise moved forward and planted herself on his desk, her face inches from his.

"Pull yourself together, Simmons. Jack's in over his head. We've got to get in that room and clear everyone out."

At the mention of the briefing, Simmons became alert, his eyes widening. "Shit!" he said, grabbing his cap

Denise turned to Harry and winked. "Let's go, Harry. Time to party."

Harry smiled and all three ran for the door.

※　※　※

Jack's pulse quickened when Kruger whispered to Montgomery and then left the room. As instructed, Jack reached for his helmet and touched the brim. It was the agreed-upon signal that he would be going on a bathroom break. He saw the others nod and he began moving. He descended two steps and walked the length of the seats until reaching the area near the door. He then climbed down as quietly as possible and knocked on the door. The MPs nodded and let him through.

Barreling down the hall, Jack burst into the lavatory, the M1 raised, his heart pounding. One by one he bashed open the stalls.

Empty.

Where the hell was he? Had Kruger given him the slip again?

He remembered passing another classroom door. Bolting into the hall, he crept up to the classroom door and placed his ear against the wood. He listened. Through the thick mahogany, he heard what sounded like a faint, high-pitched beeping.

A timer!

Wrenching open the door, Jack saw Kruger putting the final sequence of numbers into a compact digital timer held in the palm of his hand. From it snaked wires that terminated at two beige-colored mounds pasted against the paneling. A third wire ran into a hemispherical-shaped charge that rested on the floor ten feet from the wall.

"Hold it right there!" Jack said.

"So glad you could make it, Dunham," he said.

Kruger laughed and pushed the final button. A series of tones emitted from the timer and the clock began running. Kruger placed it gently on a nearby table and began moving toward Jack.

"Turn it off."

Jack raised the carbine and pointed at Kruger.

"Turn the goddamned thing off. Now!"

"Sorry, old friend, but once the sequence begins, it cannot be stopped."

He kept approaching, causing Jack to retreat.

Feeling himself losing control of the situation, Jack turned the gun toward the timer. The numbers glowed brightly, the last two digits a crimson blur.

"I would not do that, Jack. You will turn us into *hundefleisch*." Kruger smiled again and moved toward Jack.

The gun came up again. "Stay right there."

"What are you going to do, *Herr* Dunham. Shoot me? Aim true, old friend," he said, pointing to a spot between his eyes.

He never stopped moving. He crept closer and closer.

Jack wondered if all the time traveling had loosened the man's screws. "Fine, dickhead. You got it."

Jack raised the carbine, flicked off the safety, aimed, and pulled the trigger.

Click.

He lunged toward Kruger, holding the rifle in front of him with both hands. He caught the man head on and smashed him against the wall. He pushed with all his strength, wanting to crush the life out of him. But Kruger fooled him again. A bright flash and suddenly the roles reversed. Jack was on the floor, Kruger's hands clenched about his throat. The room began to turn gray and bright flashes swam before his eyes. Desperate, he fought back, hitting Kruger about the head with his hands. But his blows landed ineffectively. He began to lose consciousness. With unconsciousness and death rapidly approaching, he thrust his hand upward and dug his thumb into Kruger's left eye. The man screamed and fell back. Instantly Jack fell upon him and pummeled his face with his fists. With one final roundhouse, Kruger went slack. Jack took the man's head in his hands. This time, Kruger was his.

One hard twist and it will all be over, he thought.

Suddenly, the small hairs stood up on his body and the air in the room took on an electric smell. He knew what that meant. Kruger was not unconscious. Had only faked it.

"NO!" Jack said.

With a loud snap, the world turned white, and when his vision cleared, he was inside a darkened room. Constructed of poured concrete and bare of any ornament, it stank of stale cigarettes and rancid urine. The only furnishings were a scarred wooden table and two matching chairs. The only light spilled from a bare fifteen-watt bulb hanging from a braided cloth-covered wire. It barely dispelled the shadows. Kruger stood away from him, smiling as he buttoned up the tunic of an *SS-Obersturmführer*.

"Finally awake, are we?" Kruger said. The man's puckish grin made Jack angry all over again. He tried to rise, but his vision blurred, and he fell back against the wall, fighting the urge to vomit.

"I am sorry, but you materialized 'head-first,' so to speak."

Jack shook his head, trying to clear his vision.

"The uniform... How—"

"Did I come by this? The previous owner won't be needing it."

Jack followed his gaze to the corner and saw a man lying there dressed in Kruger's RAF uniform. The man stared sightlessly at him, his eyes and tongue bulging from his face, the skin a darkening purple.

Kruger walked over to the corpse, closed his eyes, and chanted softly. A moment later the body glowed and snapped out of existence. The subtle odor of ozone permeated the room.

"You won't get away with this," Jack fumed. "I'll find you."

"I doubt that very much, old friend. You see, we are now in the basement of *Prinz Albrechtstrasse* in Berlin. You would know it better as Gestapo Headquarters."

With a growl in his throat, Jack rose, ready to rush Kruger, when the door bashed open. In walked two men in field-gray SS uniforms like the one Kruger now wore. The two SS men appeared surprised to see them both.

"Who are you?" the officer barked in German.

Kruger instantly snapped to attention and gave the Hitler salute. "*Heil* Hitler!"

The SS officer, a *Hauptsturmführer*, ignored the salute and motioned for Kruger to move back, away from the door. The other German, a *Scharführer*, stood with his back to it, barring any chance of escape.

"I asked you a question," the officer said, his tone threatening.

"Begging your pardon, sir," Kruger said. "I am *Obersturmführer* Werner Kruger. I have been on assignment in Paris. This man here is my prisoner. I have brought him back for questioning."

"How did you get in here? This room is supposed to be empty."

"I am sorry, sir. I assumed it was free for my use. Here is my identification."

Kruger reached into his tunic and pulled out his Gestapo ID, an oval metal disk. Stamped on one side was the *Wehrmachtadler*, the eagle and swastika emblem. On the other side, presumably, was Kruger's name, rank, serial number, and blood type. The *Hauptsturmführer* glanced at the disk, grunted, and handed it back.

"Where are your orders, *Obersturmführer*? I should have been informed of your arrival. Instead, I find you in a room that is supposed to be empty."

"I am sorry, *Hauptsturmführer*. My written orders were lost during an Allied strafing run on my way here from Paris. My orders stated I was to deliver this man to *Prinz Albrechtstrasse* for questioning. We believe he is OSS, part of an advanced unit paving the way for the invasion."

This got the man's attention.

"*Ja?*" he said, his eyebrows shooting up. "Good work, *Obersturmführer* Kruger. I shall see your commander receives word of your fine achievement."

"Thank you, sir," Kruger said, bowing and clicking his heels. "I assure you, he already knows. May I tell him your name as well?"

"*Hauptsturmführer* Johann Streicher, at your service."

"You're not letting him walk out of here, are you?" Jack said. "This man's a fraud!"

"SILENCE!" Streicher screamed.

"I leave the prisoner in your capable hands, *Hauptsturmführer*. I regret I must catch the next train back to Paris. *Guten Abend*."

Again, Kruger bowed and clicked his heels.

"*Heil Hitler!*"

"*Heil Hitler*," Streicher responded. A moment later, Kruger was gone, the steel door slamming behind him.

"STOP HIM!" Jack screamed, leaping to his feet. Streicher turned and shot him a murderous look. He then shouted an order to the sergeant who stepped forward, clubbed Jack across the face, and threw him down into one of the chairs.

At that moment, Jack felt the walls close in on him. He knew deep in the pit of his soul that all was lost. Without Denise to help him, he would end his life in the bowels of this infamous building, the plaything of sadistic men bent on extracting every tidbit of information they could.

"Who are you?" Streicher said.

"You wouldn't believe me if I told you."

Scowling darkly, Streicher stepped forward and backhanded Jack across the face. The blow stunned him.

"You will tell me!"

"I know... 'You haf vays of making me talk,'" Jack said, rubbing his mouth. The man stared at him blankly. The humor of the old Hollywood cliché rang hollow in this shadowy room. He knew he was in dire trouble, something he could not talk his way out of, even if he told the improbable truth.

Where are you, Denise?

About to speak, Jack held back when he saw Streicher make for the door.

"Think long and hard, my *Americanische freund*. I will return and I shall expect answers." He turned and, followed by the sergeant, marched out the door. An instant later, he heard the tumblers click on the lock.

Jack began to tremble, and he had to fight to keep the tears back. How long could he last before he broke? And what of Kruger? The man no doubt was laughing at his cleverness. Even now he would be on his way to the residence of Armand Bock's uncle, Field Marshal Fedor von Bock, and through him, Adolf Hitler. And the worst of it was, the bomb still sat there in London, ticking away. He hadn't prevented a thing. All he succeeded in doing was putting himself into a world of shit, a world destined to remain as screwed up as the Nine Old Men wanted it.

24

London, England
15 May 1944

Denise, Harry, and Lieutenant Simmons raced across the immaculate green lawn of St. Paul's, picking up two bewildered MPs on the way. In front of them lay the large, barrack-like school building where Monty had his headquarters, the same building where the briefing was now going on. Denise found her breath coming in ragged gasps, a vestige of her childhood asthma. Even now she could taste the familiar coppery taste in the back of her throat. Simmons stabbed a finger at the two MPs.

"You two take the back way," he ordered. "Check the brig and release anyone inside!"

The soldiers ran around the side of the building as Simmons and Denise banged through the front door. Following him up the wide staircase, Denise began to feel afraid for the first time. Was she too late? They reached the second floor and Simmons tore down the hall, his cap flying off his head and rolling to a stop against the mahogany wainscoting.

Not waiting for him, Denise began running from room to room, opening doors, and scanning the interiors. She felt a mounting sense of panic. Where was the bomb? Where was Jack? She burst into the room next to the briefing and stared, wide-eyed with fright. In a flash, she took in the three mounds of plastique, the wires, and the timer with its red numbers flashing. Running to it, she grabbed it, wanting to rip out the wires, but something stopped her. How many movies and books had she read where tampering with the timer or the wires made the device detonate? She had no idea what to do, whether she *could* do anything. Her heart pounded when she read the time left: 3:07... 3:06... 3:05...

Stifling a scream, she ran out of the room and down the hall toward Simmons and the four MPs. He looked angry, panicked.

"This is an emergency, Corporal. I'll take responsibility."

"Sorry, sir. I've got my orders."

Simmons's face turned beet-red and his neck appeared to swell with unseen pressures. "I am countermanding those orders!"

The MP squared his shoulders and stared straight ahead, his expression blank, save for a tiny spasm in his left eye.

The two MPs they'd brought stood by, not knowing what to do, their expressions wide-eyed.

"Goddammit! You will listen to me!"

The MP remained frozen, immovable.

"Shit," Denise said, stepping forward.

In a flash of movement, she plucked the rifle from one of the other MPs and snapped back the bolt.

"All right, shit-kicker, open the fucking door!"

A pounding sounded on the door from the inside.

"Hey, Leavitt, what gives?" someone whispered. "The brass are getting all bent out of shape."

Denise could tell Leavitt was sweating bullets as he tried to reconcile his orders with the immediacy of the situation.

Denise raised the carbine. "We don't have much time."

"Fuck it," Leavitt said, turning to the door. He slid back the bolt and both Simmons and Denise rushed into the room. The MPs along the top of the seats reacted as one, their rifles aimed at her.

"What is the meaning of this!"

Denise jerked her head toward the man who'd shouted. General Montgomery.

"BOMB!" she shouted.

At first, no one moved. Incredulous, Denise pointed the gun into the air and fired. "BOMB!"

Far from a panicked stampede, the men rose and filed quickly out of the room. It was as if four years of war and bombs falling every night had blasted the fear out of them. As they exited the briefing room, their pace picked up and they clattered down the flight of stairs, out the front door, and onto the lawn.

Denise and Simmons brought up the rear. The lieutenant looked both relieved and apprehensive.

"I hope the hell this isn't all some sick joke. They'll have our hides," he said, nodding toward the group of dignitaries huddled together on the grass.

Denise stared back at Simmons and smiled. "I don't think you'll have to worry about that.

The first explosion blasted out the windows as it roared through the venerable building. The second and larger of the two rumbled through the ground, rattling the windows of the neighboring building. They watched as the roof collapsed, belching thick smoke and the beginnings of what would be a raging blaze. An air-raid siren wailed, and troops poured out of yet another building now converted to barracks. Already in the thick of the action, General Patton shouted orders to the troops bringing up the firefighting equipment; his salty expletives carried over the siren's ululant cry.

Denise watched the burning wreckage, unable to stop the tears. "Oh, Jack."

"My God," someone said.

Denise turned and saw a man approaching, his face knotted with rage, his cigar puffing like a steam engine full throttle. She felt a moment of panic as she came face-to-face with none other than Winston Churchill. In spite of all she and Jack had gone through, all the training and the trip through time, nothing prepared her for meeting a man she knew to be long dead and familiar only through old films and television documentaries. Yet here he stood, alive, vital, and totally livid!

"You are the man in charge of security?" he snapped.

"Yes, sir," Simmons said, his voice cracking.

"How on earth could you allow something like this to happen?"

Simmons appeared to deflate as he tried to come up with something that would satisfy this irascible old warrior.

"Sir, I... uhhh."

"He didn't know until just now, Mr. Churchill," Denise interrupted.

Churchill turned toward her, and in spite of his anger, she could see a twinkle of male appreciation in his eyes. "Damned handy with that carbine, aren't you, my dear? Wish I could say the same for myself."

Denise opened her mouth to speak, but the Prime Minister rolled right on, his manner hardening again. "He bloody well should've known. It's his job."

"He couldn't have known, sir, because the bomb was brought in by someone with top-secret clearance."

"Who?" he said, chomping on the cigar. Even in the open air, the stench made Denise want to retch.

BILL WALKER

"Flight Lieutenant Arthur Liddington, General Montgomery's aide. If you check with the general, you will find out the man reported for duty only this morning. In reality, he is a German spy by the name of Werner Kruger."

"And how do you know this, young lady?"

Denise hesitated, looking to Simmons. The lieutenant blanched and turned away to stare at the burning building. Also drawn to the blaze, Denise was hypnotized by the undulating fire. The heat made her face flush and her skin had a parched sensation, as if the flames had robbed her flesh of all its moisture. Suddenly, timbers from the ruined roof crumbled in, causing a great shower of sparks and collapsing the floor of what was once the briefing room. Black smoke curled skyward. Patton now stood up on one of the fire trucks, gesticulating with his swagger stick.

"Come on, you sons of bitches. Move those butts!"

The soldiers scrambled back and forth, laying out the hoses. Despite the general's able directions, the building was clearly lost.

"My dear..." Churchill began, his tone sounding annoyed.

Denise whirled to face him, embarrassed.

"I'm sorry, sir. There was someone else in there trying to help us. I didn't see him come out... I..."

Denise began to cry in earnest. Instead of becoming flustered like a lot of men do when women cry, Churchill stepped forward and put his arm around her.

"There, there, my dear," he said. "I'm sure he got out. No one was in the room after us."

Denise clung to the old man, reminded of her grandfather and the nights she would sit in his lap, listening to the gilded stories of his youth.

"Please forgive me, Mr. Churchill... I—"

"Nonsense, child. It is we who should forgive you. Were it not for your valiant impertinence, we should all be smoke and ash. And no doubt *Herr* Hitler would be having a jolly laugh over our charred remains."

Just then one of Eisenhower's aides approached, a look of concern etched on his young face. "Excuse me, Mr. Prime Minister, but General Eisenhower wishes to continue the briefing. We have another room ready."

Churchill nodded and the aide trotted back to the group of commanders. All business again, he turned to Simmons.

"Bring her to Downing Street this evening," he said. "I should like to speak with her further."

Simmons looked positively relieved at having escaped a further reprimand.

"Yes, sir," he said.

▘ ▘ ▘

The guard around the prime minister's residence at Number 10 Downing Street had been doubled. Both London Police and British troops stood at attention, eyes scanning everyone who walked by. The Willys jeep pulled up and both Denise and Simmons got out.

"Wait here, Private," Simmons told the driver.

The young man nodded and switched off the motor.

In spite of the extra security, Denise and Simmons passed through with only a cursory glance at his papers. They were expected. The London bobby nodded and opened the black-painted door. A liveried butler took Simmons's cap and led the way up the narrow stairs and into the prime minister's living quarters. Unlike Chartwell Manor, his famous estate in Westerham, Kent, Number 10 Downing appeared almost threadbare and common. Besides the bookshelves lining the walls, the furnishings were sparse: a small couch, a couple of freestanding lamps, a coffee table, and two overstuffed chairs with the most hideous slipcovers Denise had ever seen. Yet, somehow, it all seemed to fit the aura of the place and the man who occupied it: no-nonsense and practical.

Churchill stood gazing out one of the windows, the blackout shade lifted. The streetlights outside shone against his face, throwing a theatrical slash of light across his formidable features. The rest of the room lay in shadow, lit only by a fire crackling in the hearth.

"So glad you could come," he said, turning to face them. "Please sit down."

Simmons and Denise each took one of the repulsive chairs, leaving the couch for Churchill.

"May I offer you some sherry?" he said, sitting down. "Or perhaps a Courvoisier?"

"Make it a double, sir," Simmons said.

Denise hesitated, her body crying out for its daily deluge of alcohol. Her breath grew short, and her mouth suddenly tasted of old socks. God, how she wanted that drink. She shook her head. "Nothing for me. Last time got me into a bit of trouble."

Churchill smiled. "Ah, a woman after my own heart."

The old man turned to the butler who hovered just inside the room. "Bring in the Courvoisier, Jeffries."

"Very good, sir."

The butler vanished, appearing scant moments later with an ornate silver tray. On it lay a crystal decanter of brandy, a seltzer dispenser, and two snifters. Bowing from the waist, Jeffries deposited the tray on the coffee table. Churchill picked up the decanter, lifted off the stopper, and sniffed the rising vapors.

"My father gave me a case of this special brandy shortly before he died. This is the last of it. When the war began, I vowed not to drink any until that bloody paperhanger had gotten his comeuppance. After today, I think perhaps we can make an exception. Soda?"

"Straight up," Simmons said.

Churchill nodded and poured a generous three fingers into a snifter and handed it to him. He took the proffered glass and gulped it all in one swallow, his eyes watering as it burned its way down his esophagus.

Denise watched the prime minister pour the brandy into his snifter and give it a dash of soda. He took a sip and sighed softly.

"So, my dear, please tell me how you know so much about our affairs of state."

Simmons closed his eyes and took a deep breath.

Denise smiled, remembering something Jack had said. "Well, Mr. Churchill, let me tell you a story. It'll curl your toes and put hair on your chest."

The old warrior chuckled. "Well, that might be just what the doctor ordered."

※　※　※

"Incredible," Churchill said, lighting one of his cigars. The decanter lay on its side, empty. Simmons had sprawled out in his chair and now snored softly. Denise was galvanized, her mind racing in anticipation of the prime minister's questions. A small clock chimed 0100 hours, and the fire had long since dwindled to softly glowing embers.

"So, in your time, the bloody Hun got his way."

"Yes, sir."

"Please, we've come too far for all this formality. You must call me Winston."

"How about Uncle Winston?" she said, a warm smile on her lips.

Churchill smiled as well. "You know, you remind me of my daughter, Sarah. She has the same fire. Always putting me in my place."

He chuckled and reached for his snifter of brandy, finding it empty. "I should be far drunker than I feel," he said, suddenly melancholic.

Denise was sad for the old man. He had come back from political oblivion time and time again and now stood on the brink of immortality, yet here he looked like someone's lonely grandfather. She knew from her history that he could be the lion everyone thought him to be. In spite of his conciliatory attitude and all that had happened, Denise sensed that Churchill still doubted the whole story. Perhaps he'd gone along and listened as a child would to a fairy tale: not judgmental, but not truly believing either.

"Are you all right?" she said.

"Quite, my dear."

She took a deep breath and plunged ahead.

"I want to thank you for being so kind to me, but I know you're just humoring me. Everything I've said to you is true."

"But how can I be sure?" he asked, leaning forward and fixing her with that famous glare. "You may be a part of this Kruger's plot, the bomb only a diversion."

"Do you really believe that?"

"No."

"Then listen to me. In Bletchley Park, there are a group of cryptographers who, with a captured German Enigma coding device, have succeeded in breaking the German code. They have been intercepting messages for the last couple of years. It is the most closely guarded secret of the war, even more so than Overlord. You call it ULTRA."

Churchill's eyes widened. Denise could not tell whether he was angry or shocked.

"My God," he said finally. "How could you know? How could you?"

Denise smiled sadly. "History, Uncle Winston, history."

The old man stood and began pacing, his energy level in top gear.

"Then if everything you said is true, we must stop this man, Kruger, or—"

"Everything turns to shit."

He stopped and looked at her.

"Sorry."

He laughed. "For what? You called it for what it is. Come, I want to show you something."

The old warrior pushed himself out of his chair and Denise followed suit. He led them out into the hall where they found Jeffries slumped in a straight-backed chair, snoring contentedly. Churchill smiled and raised a finger to his lips.

"Take care on the second step," Churchill whispered. "The noise it makes will wake the dead, and Jeffries needs his sleep."

Denise looked at him strangely, then smiled when she saw him wink. Shaking her head at his eccentric humor, she followed him down the stairs to the front door. The bobbie jumped to attention when he saw his charge exiting the house.

"Sir!" he said, snapping a salute.

"Carry on, Hargreaves, it's much too late for all that bunk. Have Putnam bring round the car."

"Where are we going?" Denise whispered.

"Won't you allow an old man some secrets?" he asked, a twinkle in his eyes.

A few moments later, a large Daimler appeared on the street, its engine purring so quietly, Denise had to look at the exhaust pipe to tell it was running. Churchill held out his arm and Denise slipped her arm through it. Together, they walked to the waiting car and climbed in. The driver, a woman, held the door for them.

"Take the 'Grand Tour,' Putnam," Churchill said.

The driver smiled, climbed back in the front, and put the car in gear. Like a metallic ghost, it glided away from the curb.

❊ ❊ ❊

The car turned left out of Downing Street, heading down Whitehall, past Parliament and Big Ben. Churchill, ever the voluble host, pointed out the sights. Denise watched his eyes sparkling as they moved through Trafalgar Square. She could plainly see he dearly loved this sprawling city by the Thames.

From the square, they turned left into The Mall and passed under the Admiralty Arch. In the distance, she could see Buckingham Palace, the king's standard snapping in the breeze. A moment later they turned again, and Denise saw a squat, red brick building, a few spidery tendrils of ivy beginning to creep along its walls.

"Here we are," Churchill said expansively. "My home away from home."

The Daimler eased to a stop and the driver held the door for them. Denise got out and waited while the driver helped Churchill. She noted the steel door and the guard standing at attention. She also noted they'd made a complete circle, for the rear of 10 Downing sat not more than fifty feet away.

"Kind of a long drive for such a short distance," she said.

Churchill smiled enigmatically and walked toward the heavy door. The guard, a British MP, snapped to attention and brought his rifle to port arms in salute, then reached for the door. It swung open, revealing a hallway that ended at a set of sliding doors. A lift.

The lift, though superior for its time, nevertheless made Denise nervous as it slowly descended into the concrete shaft. It was no bigger than a small closet and rattled and creaked and shimmied from side to side, forcing her struggle to keep from bumping into the walls or into Churchill. She was uncomfortably close to "Uncle Winnie" as he stood staring past the lift's female operator, a far-off look in his eye. This close, Denise could smell the brandy on his breath and the cigar smell emanating from his clothes, something that would normally have made her ill, but somehow now felt reassuring.

The lift operator stole a glance at them, but the woman's skinny, horse-like features betrayed nothing. Denise wondered whether the woman thought her Commander-in-Chief was off on a romantic tryst and had chosen his underground bunker for the occasion. The very idea evoked a smile.

The lift came to a groaning halt and the operator pulled open the doors, allowing her and the Prime Minister to exit.

"This way, my dear," he said, taking her arm and guiding her along the concrete hallway that resembled a sewer conduit with incandescent bulbs jutting from junction boxes every ten feet overhead. Despite the almost antiseptic look of the place, it held a trace of dampness.

Churchill began to describe the bunker, a note of pride sneaking into his voice. "We spent the better part of a year working round the clock, throughout the Blitz, building this bunker. It lies seventy feet below the surface and can accommodate one hundred people at any one time for a period of thirty days before needing resupply. *Herr* Hitler has one of these in Berlin, I am told," he said, chuckling softly. "If all goes well, he'll be spending a lot more time down there. By then it will be a great deal quieter than above ground."

They turned several corners and Denise lost her bearings as they passed room after room. Suddenly, they stopped in front of another steel door guarded by yet another lone sentry. Like his counterpart above ground, he came to full attention.

"At ease, Collins, it's only me."

The man appeared to relax yet stayed rigidly still. Churchill removed a key and opened the door. It swung out with the hiss of oiled hinges. He beckoned her inside and closed the door.

"Welcome to the War Room," he said, motioning expansively.

Denise had read of the place in history books but was not prepared for the sight that met her eyes. The room was at least thirty by forty feet, the walls covered by maps of every theatre of the war: Europe, Burma, the Pacific Rim. She and Churchill were not alone. The place was jammed with desks staffed by men and women huddled over wireless radios and typewriters, busily going about the business of running a war.

"What are they doing?" Denise asked.

"Decryption. With the invasion so close, we are frightfully busy collecting the latest intelligence from our agents in Europe. As precise as our plans are, there will need to be minute adjustments. Our biggest concern is the Channel weather. It's so unpredictable this time of year. Come."

He led her through the maze of desks, winding their way toward another door. Denise marveled that no one paid them the slightest attention, so focused were they on the tasks at hand. She could feel their excitement, their vitality, their commitment, and envied them their place in history. She knew that unless she could succeed where Jack had failed—she refused to think that he was dead—their gallant efforts would be for naught, a curious footnote lost in the dusty archives of a cold-blooded Nazi future.

Churchill unlocked the door and snapped on the lights. From its homey, well-worn disarray, Denise instantly knew the place to be the man's inner sanctum. And like every place he lived and worked, the room reeked of his trademark cigars. The brick walls and support poles were painted a cheery white, as were the stout wooden beams crisscrossing the ceiling. The wall shared with the War Room held maps covered with Churchill's studied notations.

At one end of the room lay an austere mahogany desk covered with a blotter, two ink wells, a banker's lamp, and a decanter—presumably filled with brandy. A tired-looking leather swivel chair sat behind the desk, and two wooden chairs sat facing it. At the opposite end of the room, perpendicular to the door, laid a sagging military cot made up with a thin wool blanket and a rumpled pillow. A water cooler stood nearby, its compressor humming quietly.

"Please, sit," he said, indicating one of the wooden chairs in front of his desk. Denise sat down and waited. She felt a giddy sense of excitement, palms sweaty, chest tight, eyes alert. Churchill stood for a moment staring at her, as if he were reassessing her, as if all she'd said, and the bond they'd forged, meant nothing.

"I want you to know that I do not believe you to be a deceitful person, but you must understand that I need further proof of your story. That you know of ULTRA is both mind-boggling and frightening, but could easily have resulted from the loose tongue of some lovesick soldier too drunk to know any better..."

Denise smiled and nodded knowingly. "I think I can help you there."

Churchill inhaled sharply while Denise closed her eyes and began mumbling softly. In a flash of bright blue light, she snapped out of the room. Before he could react or move, she returned as dramatically as she'd left. In her hands she held a simple yellow rose. Churchill's eyes widened as he stepped forward to grasp it, faltering. Denise grabbed his arm and helped him to one of the wooden chairs.

"There is more brandy on the desk," he said, gasping.

She returned with a snifter of the fiery liquid and watched as he gulped it down.

"This rose... is it—"

"From Chartwell? Yes," Denise said, not able to hide her triumph.

"If I had not seen it with my own eyes, I never would have believed it," Churchill said, shaking his head. "Tell me. Can you succeed? Can you stop this man?"

It was Denise's turn to doubt. "I don't know. Every time Jack and I try, the bastard slips away. He's done it again, and God only knows what he's done to Jack."

The long day and her fears combined to push her over the edge. She began to weep. But instead of comforting her as before, Churchill went over to his desk and picked up the phone.

"Yes, tell Barrows and Finley to report here at once... Never mind. Their leaves are canceled as of now. I have a rush job for them... Yes, goodnight."

He walked back and pulled up the other chair, his face stern and forbidding.

"My dear, this is no time to cry. I've had a feeling about you from the moment you barged in on our little soirée with your blazing carbine. You are not a shirker. You have what few men have and what fewer know what to do with..."

Denise had stopped crying, her eyes drawn to the Prime Minister's intense stare, his words burning into her brain.

"...What you Americans call 'guts.' If I know you at all, I suspect the man you've chosen is equal to the task as well. He is alive. I'm sure of it."

"How *can* you be sure?" Denise said, wanting to grasp at any straw available.

"My people have been all through the wreckage. There were no bodies found."

Tears of joy stung Denise's eyes. Jack was alive!

Churchill stood and paced. "It is my estimation that your man, Jack, is now in the hands of the Gestapo."

Denise gasped. "Oh God, no."

Churchill waved away her outburst. "You have to continue with or without him. All of us... all of the future depends on you now. You cannot falter."

"Wait a minute. If Kruger put him there, I can get him out!"

Churchill smiled. "Quite so."

Denise's eyes widened in surprise. "You knew—that phone call—"

"—Was to two men in our Forgery Bureau. By tomorrow you will have new documents and clothing that will get you into any place in the *Reich*, including Gestapo headquarters. After that, you will be on your own."

Denise wanted to scream with joy but held herself in check. Instead she said, "You know, Uncle Winston, I could kiss you."

The old man's face flushed with color and he smiled slyly. "If I were thirty years younger, I might take you up on that."

"Age before beauty," she said, coming forward and planting a tender kiss on his cheek. She pulled back just as the door opened and the lift operator, now bearing a pot of tea, entered the room. She blushed, put down the tray, and scurried from the room.

Churchill burst out laughing, the jovial baritone cackling filling the room. "Now my reputation as a ladies' man is assured!"

glass. At the sound of the cell door's bolt sliding back, Jack scrambled to his feet, ready for another onslaught, but the two guards only stood there motioning with their MP40 submachine guns.

"*Raus. Kommen Sie,*" one of them said.

Jack stood there a moment too long and the guard reached in and yanked him out by his hair. His momentum carried him into the opposite wall of the hallway, stunning him. His legs were rubbery, and he wondered if he was about to faint. The two Germans came up on either side of him, grabbed his arms, and hauled him down the narrow hall to the room where Jack had first appeared with Kruger. Streicher sat behind a small table, smoking a cigarette, watching him with hooded eyes. The smoke curled upward through the harsh lighting, giving the room a diffuse softness it did not warrant.

"*Guten Abend, Herr* Dunham," he said, his voice soft and silky. "And how are you today?"

The guards thrust Jack into the chair opposite the table. He winced as a bolt of pain shot up his spine through the coccyx. He squeezed his eyes shut and inhaled sharply. "I've been better."

"Quite so, *Herr* Dunham, quite so. Are you ready to tell us what you know of the invasion?"

Jack stared at him, but what had captured his undivided attention was a plate of food, *Wienerschnitzel,* if he was any judge. There was also boiled red cabbage and potato pancakes. Next to it sat a frothy stein of beer, the ceramic glistening with beads of condensation. He could actually hear the bubbles popping on the mountainous head.

"You need not tell us everything at once. Just the day and hour of the landings. Tell me that and you may eat."

Jack drooled and hated himself for it. But his body had no pride and only reacted to the stimuli it received. The heavenly odor of the breaded veal and potato pancakes wafted into his nostrils and made him want to swoon.

"Sleep?"

"That, too, *Herr* Dunham."

For the first time in his life, Jack knew what it meant to be caught in a dilemma. If he succumbed to his body's cravings, he would betray everyone who sought to destroy the Third Reich, everyone who had already fought and died to make Overlord happen. He would be accomplishing Kruger's mission. Then it hit him. Hitler already believed the invasion would come from Calais. Why not tell Streicher that and help reinforce the Fortitude deceptions? Jack almost smiled, but he maintained his composure. He decided to play out the drama just a little longer.

Jumping to his feet, he charged the table before the guards could react. Picking up the plate, he hurled it at Streicher, who snapped his head out of the way. The plate smashed against the concrete wall, splattering the food every which way. A small piece of cabbage landed on Streicher's tunic. Apoplectic with rage, he grabbed Jack, punched him in the gut, and brought his knee up into his face. Blood gushed from his nose, staining Streicher's jodhpur trousers. This only enraged him further.

"Take this filthy swine back to the cell and send in the X-team!" he bellowed and stalked from the room.

Jack feared he'd gone too far. Through his bleary eyes, he could see the look of fear on the guards' faces when they picked him up off the floor. They dragged him down the hallway and threw him into the cell, and he thought he heard them speak the word *kaput* a couple of times. Apparently, Streicher was calling in heavier guns.

Jack had no idea how long he sat in the cell before they came for him again. It could have been twenty minutes or several hours. It all felt the same. The guards were different ones, indicating he was now on the late shift. He did not wait to be dragged from the cell but marched resolutely between the two SS men. The one behind him continually prodded him forward with the barrel of his MP40, no matter how briskly he walked. They passed the familiar room, took a right down another hallway and a left into another room. Inside, two men in hospital whites stood next to a tilted gurney. They watched him, their cold, fish-like eyes betraying no emotion. Jack suddenly realized what this meant: truth drugs.

"NO!" he said, trying to tear himself away. "Tell Streicher I'll talk. Tell him I'll talk!"

The guards pulled him towards the table and Jack fought harder. He couldn't allow himself to be drugged. If that happened, he would not be able to keep from telling them the truth about Overlord. The guards slugged him and threw him down on the gurney. It rolled slightly, prompting the two "doctors" to hold it steady while the guards strapped him in.

"Tell him I'll talk," Jack said weakly.

The doctors said something in German and one of the guards tore open the sleeve on his right arm. Jack continued to struggle, but soon realized the straps held him fast and he had no hope of avoiding the inevitable. One of the men, a tall, reed-thin man with a shock of reddish-brown hair, went over to a tray and picked up a hypodermic needle. Used to the plastic disposable syringes of another era, Jack's eyes bulged at the steel and glass monstrosity the doctor held.

The man then picked up a bottle of clear liquid, plunged the needle through the rubber top, and drew in several cubic centimeters of whatever it was. Jack strained his eyes to read the label. All he could see were the characters: S... o... d... Sodium Pentothal. Could it be? Could he be that fortunate?

THE NORMANDY CLUB

He knew Sodium Pentothal was practically all they had to use in the mid-1940s. And he'd been under its influence several times for operations. Once, the anesthesiologist had given him too little, allowing him to remain conscious longer than the surgery team would've wanted. He remembered feeling like he was floating on a warm cloud without a care in the world. He didn't care if they sawed off a limb at that point. Remembering that experience convinced Jack that he could beat Streicher at his own game, supply the false information and have it carry even more weight than given freely under other circumstances.

The gaunt man, who resembled Raymond Massey, came forward, the syringe aimed upward, its steel gleaming in the harsh light. The second man, stout and hairless, said something. The thin man nodded and squeezed out the air bubble in the syringe. Then, without swabbing Jack's arm with alcohol, Raymond Massey stabbed the needle into his bicep and pushed the plunger home. Seconds later, Jack felt the familiar warmth flood through his body. This would be a piece of cake. He smiled and giggled.

"Hey, Raymond. You know you could have a career haunting houses?" Jack burst out laughing, the thought popping into his mind, causing tears of mirth to roll out the corners of his eyes. The doctor remained impassive. After a minute Jack began singing an old song he remembered—"Purple Haze"—at the top of his lungs.

He began playing air guitar in spite of the straps, howling in imitation of Jimi Hendrix's flights of feedback. The guards looked at each other and shook their heads.

"*Verrückt*," one of them mumbled, twirling his finger next to his head.

The other smiled and was about to offer another comment when Streicher marched into the room, the glow of triumph on his face.

"I see our patient is ready," he said in German to no one in particular.

The two doctors began speaking at once. Streicher ignored them and held up his hands for silence. They shut up immediately.

"Ahh, I see you are enjoying yourself, *Herr* Dunham, *ja?*"

Jack saw Streicher's smiling face and broke into a rash of giggling. "Streicher, the Streicherman. King of Goon Squad!"

"Well, do you feel like talking, *Herr* Dunham?"

"Sure," he said, drawing out the word to ridiculous lengths. "Say, Streicherman, you any relation to Julius?"

Streicher's face clouded for a moment, then cleared, the frown instantly replaced with a warm smile.

"Tell me about yourself, Jack," he said, dropping into a dead-on American accent. "Where were you born?"

"Wilton, Connecticut-ticut-cut-cut."

"Ahh, that's a great town. Isn't it near..."

"New York. Used to go there every weekend—go to the clubs."

"Nightclubs?"

"Yeah..."

"Who did you see? Glenn Miller, Tommy Dorsey?"

Jack frowned. "No. AC/DC... Blue Öyster Cult... Ramones."

Streicher's eyebrows shot up. "*Was ist* Blue Öyster Cult?" he said to Raymond Massey. The man shrugged.

"And when did you join the service, Jack? Were you drafted?"

"No...Vietnam was over by then."

Streicher began to lose patience.

"What is your date of birth?"

Jack screwed up his face as if trying to remember.

"August third, nineteen fifty-six."

"*Scheiss*! What did you give this man?" Streicher yelled at the doctors. The short one recoiled, deferring to the other, who remained calm.

"Sodium Pentothal, *Hauptsturmführer*."

"Then what is all this Blue Öyster nonsense and this birthdate that is obviously impossible? I want him to tell me of the invasion!"

"Overlord?"

If Streicher had turned any faster, the man would have snapped his neck.

"What did you say?"

"Uhhh... Overlord?"

Streicher began to salivate, no doubt thinking that if he could deliver the time and date of the Allied invasion, his rise through the ranks would be assured.

"Yes, Jack. Tell me about Overlord."

Jack frowned again, as if trying to resist the question.

Streicher leaned forward. "Come on, Jack. Come on."

Jack's face went slack as he appeared to pass out.

"*Nein!*" Streicher screamed. "Awaken him. Give him more!"

"We cannot risk an overdose, *Haupsturmführer*," Raymond Massey said.

Impatience overcoming good judgment, Streicher reached forward and slapped Jack across the face three times. Jack stirred, opening his eyes to half-mast. "Hey there, Streicherman, the baddest man in the whole damn—"

"Right, right, Jack, it's me. Can you tell me about Overlord, Jack?"

Jack smiled and giggled. "They all think it's going to be Normandy, but I know better. I know what they don't know. Nyah, nyah, nyah, nyah, nyah."

"Where, Jack? Where and when?"

"Calais... Moon in June."

"June what, Jack? It is very important that you tell me. June what?" Streicher leaned forward, his breath smelling of garlic.

"June... June... June..."

"WHAT?"

"Seven-Eleven."

"Which one, Jack?"

"Seven-Eleven. Great slurpies."

Streicher appeared about ready to pull his hair out.

"Seven."

"June seventh? Is that the date, Jack? June seventh?"

"That's it, daddyo. The big surprise for Adolf." Jack dissolved into uncontrollable giggles, then pretended to pass out again.

"*Wunderbar!*" Streicher said, pounding the side of the gurney. He began pacing. Finally, he stopped and pointed to Jack.

"Take him back to his cell and when he awakens, feed him. Then take him into the courtyard at sunrise and shoot him."

Jack's heart skipped a beat. For all his efforts and Academy Award performance, he was to be shot down like a dog. Again, he'd gone too far.

Where are you, Denise?

26

The two men she dubbed Mutt and Jeff labored all the previous day and through the night on Denise's new documents. First came the photograph. They'd dolled her up in a field-gray SS uniform, complete with party badge and the rank insignia of an *SS-Sturmbannführer*, given her the latest coif and the requisite amount of makeup.

"Frown, dear, you look too nice," Jeff said. "These SS dollies are not known for their personality."

Denise scowled, trying to keep from laughing.

"Right. Perfect. You've got it."

The bulb on the Speed Graphic flashed, creating a flurry of spots swimming before her eyes. She blinked furiously. After that, the two men packed up their gear and took the elevator up to the surface.

Now came the waiting. Expertise required time, lots of time. The problem was Denise didn't feel she had any. But to appear at Gestapo Headquarters without the proper authorization would be tantamount to suicide. And the worst part about the waiting was

329

that she could not go anywhere or do anything. She was trapped, as surely as Jack.

Churchill had gone back to Downing Street at around 0400 hours to take a nap and get ready for a meeting with his staff. Denise spent the night on the sagging cot, an accomplishment that deserved a medal. She awoke when the spinster lift operator brought in a tray consisting of tea and cakes.

"What time is it?" Denise asked.

The woman looked at her, barely able to conceal her disapproval. "Half past nine."

She then turned and walked out, her gait one of supercilious disdain.

"Get a life, bitch," Denise said after the door clicked shut. Wolfing down the cakes, she poured a cup of tea and gulped it down. Its orange-accented flavor soothed as it rushed down her throat. A moment later, she felt dizzy as her stomach roiled and twisted. Bolting from the cot, she ran over to the small sink and threw up, heaving until nothing of the tea and cakes remained. That was strange. She hadn't had anything to drink, and even when she did, she rarely threw up. A sudden thought occurred to her, which she immediately buried, the images it conjured too disturbing to contemplate. A moment later she felt better and decided to go out into the main room.

Unlike the graveyard shift the night before, the room now buzzed with frantic commotion. The noise level was appalling. Teletypes clattered, endlessly spilling out reams of gibberish that only trained cryptographers could decipher. The hive of activity both exhilarated and frightened her. All this depended on her.

Just then, the outer door opened, and Churchill walked in flanked by two officers, one British, the other American. She recognized the American as Lieutenant Simmons. Churchill appeared completely normal, brimming with vitality.

"How the hell does he do it?" Denise mumbled, her head answering with a painful throb.

"Ahh, Denise, my dear," Churchill said as he approached her. "Slept well, I hope?"

"Whoever designed that cot should be court-martialed," she said, a lopsided smile on her face.

"Quite. Come. I have a surprise for you."

He led her back into his private office and pulled something from the inside pocket of his jacket and handed two items to her. One was the Gestapo disc ID, a sort of Nazi version of dog tags. The other was a small book, field-gray in color, with an SS eagle clutching a swastika and, underneath, the lightning runes of the SS printed in black. She opened it, her gaze immediately drawn to the stark picture.

"God! I look awful," she laughed.

"You are now *SS-Sturmbannführer* Greta Faust of the *Sicherheitsdienst*. As you can see, your total 'history' is in that book. Do not lose it."

At first, she did not understand what he meant by history until she began turning the pages. She marveled at the dozens of overlapping imprints of various-sized rubber stamps in a rainbow of colors. From the time of her "entry" into the SS in 1940, until now, it had her traveling all over Germany in her duties as a professional "interrogator." Mutt and Jeff had done a masterful job of aging the stamps. The closer to the beginning, the older and more faded they looked. There was even a coffee stain covering half of one page.

"This is amazing!" she said.

"Our boys are the best," Churchill said, his voice filled with pride. "How soon will you go?"

Denise was taken back by the question but realized that Churchill was anxious that she complete her mission.

"No time like the present."

Churchill nodded and reached into his jacket again. Out came a stack of *Reichsmarks* and another envelope. The latter bore the official RSHA/SD letterhead.

"These are your orders to question the prisoner, Jack Dunham, after which you are to take charge of him for 'final disposition.' If I know our boys' work, everything should hold up under scrutiny."

Denise opened the envelope and pulled out the orders. As horrible as it was to grow up in a world run by the Nazis, she thanked whatever god watched over her. The Nazi-run schools had thoroughly indoctrinated the young to the new mother tongue: German. No amount of skillful forgery or well-tailored uniforms would hide awkward phrasing or a faulty accent. Her eyebrows rose when she caught sight of the expertly forged signature of Ernst Kaltenbrunner, head of the RSHA, Gestapo, SD, and the *Abwehr*, successor to the assassinated Reinhard Heydrich, and a name both feared and hated by many.

"Looks like I have friends in high places," she said.

"Kaltenbrunner is a nasty sort and not one any subordinate is likely to question."

Denise picked up the stack of money and Churchill answered her unspoken question.

"That's about ten thousand *Reichsmarks*. Equal to about five thousand American dollars. It should tide you over."

"Quite," Denise said, poking gentle fun at Churchill's stuffy accent. He smiled and an awkward moment passed as she realized nothing else held her back. Though she desperately wanted to rescue Jack, a part of her wanted to remain here, safe with this remarkable man. Perhaps sensing her mood, Churchill bowed slightly.

"I'll leave you alone to change."

When he walked out of the room, Denise felt all the old doubts come flooding back. They came on so strong, she nearly cried out. This time she wouldn't let herself fall prey to them.

"Can it, Denise. Time to get your butt in gear," she said.

Five minutes later she heard Churchill knock softly.

"Are you decent?"

"For you, never," Denise said, fastening the last two buttons on her tunic. "Come on in."

The one concession to vanity in the small cubbyhole of an office was the mirror hanging on the far wall. Studying her reflection, she had to admit the damned Nazi creeps knew how to design uniforms. She noted the crisp lines of the field-gray tunic, and the distinctive, diamond-shaped, black and silver SD patch on the left sleeve just above the cuff band. In her *Feldgrau*, Denise looked and felt invincible. Churchill appeared behind her, nodding his approval.

"You are quite the Hun, my dear," he said, smiling indulgently.

She turned and clicked her boots together and raised her hand in a Hitler salute.

"*Heil Hitler!*"

"Perfect," he said.

Denise noticed a small leather box in his hands.

"What's that? You giving me a medal?"

Churchill smiled, but there was no humor in it.

"I'm afraid it is something decidedly less pleasant." He opened the box and handed it to her. On the red satin lining lay what looked like a Derringer.

"Nice... what is it?"

"That is something the boys in MI6 came up with. I am told it is quite sophisticated and took thousands of pounds to develop. It fires a small, poisoned pellet by compressed air, and is powerful enough to pierce clothing. The poison acts instantaneously. Use it wisely."

Denise picked it up and hefted it in her hand. It felt comfortably weighty.

"How many shots?" she said, placing it in the inside pocket of her tunic.

"Just one."

Churchill came to her and took her hands in his. "I *know* you shall succeed," he said, his warm voice filled with emotions. "Know that here and now, the hopes and dreams of a million hearts go with you."

Denise smiled, trying to hide her anxiety.

"You really know how to make a girl nervous, don't you?"

He scowled at her mockingly. "You? *Never*."

They both laughed.

"Godspeed, and may you find what you seek," he said, kissing her on the forehead.

"I'll miss you, you old coot."

He chuckled softly. "Lucky for you that I *am* an 'old coot,' or Mrs. Churchill would have your hide."

Before she could begin to cry, Denise hugged him and then backed off, closing her eyes. She began to chant, and a moment later the room filled with that awesome blue light. Churchill watched as she faded from view, his eyes moist with emotion.

"Good luck, my dear."

* * *

Werner Kruger breathed in the fragrant air, his nose wrinkling at the faint order of smoke in the air. A stray bomb from an air raid the night before had hit one of the expensive homes in the neighborhood and flattened it. A moment later, the odor was gone, replaced by the aroma of blooming flowers. Trees hung over the road from both sides, creating a sun-dappled canopy whose shadows flitted across the swiftly moving Mercedes.

"How much further?" Kruger asked.

The field marshal's driver flicked his eyes to the rearview mirror. "About a kilometer, sir."

Kruger nodded and picked a piece of lint from his clothes. After leaving Gestapo Headquarters, he had visited an expensive men's haberdashery and bought himself a new suit in dark blue worsted wool. He had the clerk place the SS uniform into a suit bag, which now lay inside the car's trunk. He would need it for later, when he was meeting with Hitler. For now, he needed to make a good impression on Field Marshal Fedor von Bock. Known as a hard taskmaster and a tough soldier, it was also well known that von Bock despised the SS with a passion. It was part of the reason Hitler had fired the old soldier, besides the debacle the Russian campaign had become. But von Bock still enjoyed some favor, as evidenced by the expensive Mercedes limousine and his lavish home in the exclusive Dahlem district of Berlin, still largely untouched by Allied bombing.

The car slowed, prompting Kruger to return his attention to the road. They turned into a driveway that reminded Kruger of the entrance to The Normandy Club. Indeed, the house itself, as it came into view, looked much the same, except for the European styling. Dark and imposing, the house no doubt reflected the personality of its owner. For the first time since the mission started, Kruger wondered if he would succeed. The phone call to von Bock had been brief and to the point. At the mention of Armand's name, the older man had told him—no, ordered was more like it—to come over the following day.

The car halted in front of the wide porch, and the driver hopped out and ran around to open the door.

"*Danke schön,*" Kruger said.

The driver clicked his heels and bowed stiffly. Kruger marched up the steps and pulled the bell. He could hear the chimes pealing deep within the house. He waited, hearing the clacking of heels approaching. The front door swung open, revealing a sour-faced butler.

"Yes?" the man said, the disdain dripping from his voice.

"I am Werner Kruger. I am expected."

"Follow me, sir."

No change of expression, no sign of deference. Kruger wished he could wrap his hands around his desiccated neck. Though the house had large windows on all sides, the interior remained gloomy and foreboding, made more so by the hundreds of hunting trophies sprouting from every surface. The man obviously loved to hunt, both in war and peace. Kruger smiled. This was a man to whom he could relate.

The butler halted in front of a pair of sliding doors and pushed them open into an expansive library. More trophies, some full-body mounts, lay strewn about. Von Bock, dressed in a dove-grey, double-breasted suit of exquisite cut, stood ramrod straight staring at Kruger as he walked across the luxurious Persian rug covering the floor. The man's hawk-like gaze never wavered, as if somehow he could, by sight alone, drill into the dark recesses of a man's heart.

"So, you are Armand's friend?" he asked, the voice as dark and grave as the man's surroundings. "How is my nephew?"

Kruger sensed a trap. "He is well, *Herr* Field Marshal, though he finds the Yugoslavian climate much too damp for his liking."

Kruger saw the hint of a smile on the man's face. "The boy needs some toughening up. Always too frail, that one. Would you like a brandy?"

"Please."

Von Bock turned to the butler who hovered in the doorway. "Two brandies, Hans. Make it the Louis XIII. This is a special occasion."

"Very good, sir," he said, and bowed out of the room.

"Please, sit." Von Bock pointed to a comfortable stuffed chair. Kruger nodded and sat. Von Bock took the matching chair across from him.

Hans appeared moments later bearing a silver tray laden with two large snifters half-filled with brandy. He served the drinks then left the room, closing the double doors behind him.

"Now," said von Bock, his eyes narrowing, "what has my idiot nephew done this time?"

Kruger maintained his composure, his spirits plummeting. It looked like an uphill battle after all. He took a sip of brandy to hide his annoyance then pulled out the letter. Von Bock took it, opened it up, and squinted. He patted the pocket of his suit jacket and scowled.

"Ach, I never have my spectacles when I need them."

He got up and looked around the room. Kruger watched him with growing impatience. Finally, the old goat found them on a small tea table, stuck inside a book on Teutonic knighthood. Putting them on, he scanned the letter where he stood, grunting every now and then as he read something that either annoyed or pleased him, Kruger could not tell which.

"It says here you have vital news concerning the war and that I am to accord you whatever help I can."

Kruger nodded.

"It is just like Armand to assume I will do whatever he asks. The boy is a pompous ass."

Kruger smiled in spite of the situation. Von Bock had his nephew nailed dead to rights. But it was time to put his cards on the table.

"Your nephew may be a pompous ass, but in this case, he is a loyal citizen of the Reich. I have just come back from England and have news of the invasion. I must gain an audience with the *Führer*. It is vital."

Von Bock looked at him, a look of incredulity on his face that transformed itself into one of mirth. His loud, grating laughter echoed through the large room.

"My nephew seems to have forgotten that the *Führer* relieved me of my command. I have a less than favorable reputation with the man. And even less influence. What makes him think I can do anything?"

Kruger's patience was at an end. Leaping to his feet, he crossed the room and put himself nose to nose with the old field marshal, his eyes burning with fury. "Because, my dear Field Marshal, in less than three weeks the largest armada in recorded history will put ashore on the coast of France, and I know *precisely* where and when that will be! Because if the Fifteenth Army is not moved from its present location, the war will be lost! Do you understand?"

The old man stood rigid with anger at the impertinence of this young upstart. But something held him in check.

"How do you know this?" he asked, his voice even and controlled.

Kruger had dreaded the question, but now realized that answering it was the only way he could convince the man.

"Because I come from a future time, a time where all of this is dusty history. The war will be lost within a year, and the thousand-year *Reich* will be swept away, Germany divided between the Allies. Russia will take half our country and turn it into one of their puppet states. Your precious Silesia will be in those barbaric hands. Berlin will have a wall cutting it in half. It has to be stopped!"

THE NORMANDY CLUB

The old man's anger boiled over. "How dare you come here and perpetrate this garbage! I should have known better where Armand was concerned. He was always playing his practical jokes. Well, you can tell him for me that he is no longer welcome here. Now leave this house before I call the Gestapo!"

Before von Bock could back away, Kruger grabbed his hand, his grip like a vise.

"What are you doing! What is the meaning of this?" von Bock blustered. But his voice soon dissolved into a frightened whimper as the air around them turned bright blue and the world snapped white.

The old field marshal looked ill when they appeared inside a large men's lavatory. He staggered over to one of the sinks, grasping the porcelain and gulping huge breaths of air.

"How... what... what happened? Where are we?"

"Are you all right, sir?" Kruger asked.

"Yes, I think so."

Von Bock trembled, bent over the sink, turned on the tap, and threw cold water onto his face. Kruger handed him a towel. The door to the lavatory swung open and an American sergeant stuck his head inside.

"You people better get a move on; the sentences are coming down." The door swished shut. Von Bock looked aghast.

"An American! What did he mean? Where are we?"

Without a word, Kruger grabbed von Bock by the arm, shoved him out of the lavatory and into a hallway choked with dozens of people, all chattering excitedly. Everywhere he looked, Kruger saw officers and enlisted men from the British, American, and Russian armies. White-helmeted MPs, carrying M1 carbines and .45 semi-automatic pistols, stood in strategic places, scrutinizing the crowd with steel-eyed suspicion.

The mob jostled and pushed them forward. Kruger eyed von Bock, noting the older man's frightened expression. Like a timid schoolboy, his wide, anxious eyes darted about, taking in the all-too-familiar uniforms of his bitter enemies.

Up ahead, the massive walnut-stained doors of room 600 stood open. Part of the crowd poured into the room, while others peeled off and took a staircase to the visitors' gallery. Kruger directed von Bock toward the staircase. The old man halted in his tracks and turned to Kruger. The schoolboy had fled, replaced by the haughty arrogance of the Prussian officer class.

"I demand to know where you are taking me!" he said, glaring at Kruger.

Kruger found the pressure point on the old man's shoulder and jabbed his thumb into it. Von Bock winced but kept his composure. Kruger felt a twinge of admiration for the old bastard.

"Be quiet! You are in no position to demand anything. Move."

Kruger yanked him forward, causing von Bock to stumble. He grabbed the railing, scowled at Kruger, then stoically marched up the steps, his face a hardened mask. A moment later, they were in the small gallery overlooking the room. The seats had been taken from a local cinema and helped give the whole atmosphere a theatrical air. Kruger smiled, for that was exactly what it was. Most of the 150 seats were filled with military men, secretaries, and reporters spilled over from the press gallery downstairs. Kruger and von Bock took two of the remaining seats in the back row.

Von Bock stared at the room, a sign of recognition in his eyes.

"I know this place," he said. "This is the Palace of Justice in Nuremburg... This is where that fiend, Roland Freisler, holds court. But why are all these Americans and Russians here? I do not understand."

THE NORMANDY CLUB

Kruger's only reply was a sly smile.

Toward the front of the room stood a dais with nine empty chairs. The docket, which sat directly across from the dais, also stood empty. Reporters on the floor jabbered among themselves, the atmosphere electric.

A door opened up near the dais and nine judges, representing the Allies, walked in and took their seats with a studied solemnity. The buzz in the room dwindled to an excited hush.

When the last whispers died away, the president of the court nodded to one of the white-helmeted MPs, who slid open a door behind the dock, revealing the first prisoner. The man's sky-blue uniform held razor-sharp creases yet hung on what was once a much larger frame. Defiant to the last, Hermann Göring held his head high in icy disdain.

The effect on von Bock was immediate. "*Mein Gott!* Göring! What is going on here?"

Kruger relished the moment. "My dear Field Marshal. As you so cleverly surmised, this is indeed the Palace of Justice in Nuremberg. It is October first, nineteen forty-six. and this is the War Crimes Tribunal. The war has been over for more than a year. Look well, Field Marshal... for this is the legacy of failure."

Von Bock paled as he watched the proceedings.

One by one the surviving leaders of the Third Reich stood in the dock, their faces ashen as they learned their fates:

Göring... Death.

Kaltenbrunner... Death.

Keitel... Death.

Speer... Life imprisonment.

Frank... Death.

Frick... Death.

von Ribbentrop... Death.

On and on the names were read, their fates intoned in a sepulchral voice that rolled through the room like an invisible juggernaut. The sentences appeared to weigh on von Bock like lead. He slumped into his seat, a look of utter despair on his haggard face. He turned to Kruger.

"And what of Hitler?"

"Dead, by his own hand."

"Take me back. I cannot stomach any more of this."

The two men fought their way through the pressing crowds and reentered the lavatory. Moments later they appeared back within the walls of von Bock's library. Staggering like a man in a daze, the field marshal went straight for the brandy, pouring himself a generous measure of the fiery liquid. He gulped it down and turned to Kruger, his eyes burning with a new light.

"I do not know how you came by this power of yours, and I do not care. But I will do what I can to get you in to see Hitler. Beyond that, I can promise nothing."

"That is all I ask, *Herr* Field Marshal."

With the glow of the self-satisfied, Kruger watched von Bock walk to the phone and pick it up.

"*Ja*. This is Field Marshal Fedor von Bock. Please connect me with *Parteigenosse* Martin Bormann at the Chancellery... *Ja*, I will hold."

27

Berlin, Germany
17 May 1944

The cellar stank of rotting garbage and stagnant pools of brackish water, its walls half caved in. Through the few beams that crisscrossed the patch of sky above her, Denise could see the moon hanging just above the other buildings, a luminous ring around it. It would rain soon. She squinted in the murky light and tried to gain her bearings. Ahead, barely discernible, lay a rickety staircase that led to what was once the ground floor.

Without intimate knowledge of the city's streets, she ended up in the cellar of a bombed-out building, a residence from the look of it. That was the one thing about transporting that made her nervous, the one aspect that held a random note, which frightened her. What if she had appeared in a crowded theatre among the startled patrons, or in the middle of a busy thoroughfare with a two-ton truck bearing down on her? Or what if she simply reintegrated inside a wall? She stumbled, her boot caught between two fallen beams.

"Shit," she said, yanking out her foot. Avoiding a wide, standing pool of water, she edged around it and found herself in front of the staircase. It looked even less able to bear her weight than it had from a distance. Moving forward cautiously, she stepped on the first step and startled an angry rat, which scurried off.

"Take it easy, Malloy. It's only a rat."

She began to climb, aware of every creak and groan of the blasted wood as she crept slowly upwards. Five, four, three more to go.

CRACK!

The stairs lurched sideways, threatening to pitch her back into the hole and into a pile of debris with any number of sharp objects to impale her. Steeling herself, Denise tore up the remaining three steps, out the battered doorway, and staggered onto the sidewalk. Breathing heavily, more from adrenaline than from fright, she took a moment to scan her surroundings. The streetlights, dim and a sickly green in color, cast pale pools of light that did little to dispel the gloom. The air felt damp and smelled of diesel fuel. By the looks of it, she'd appeared in one of the working-class neighborhoods on the outskirts of Berlin. The block had a dreary, seedy feel that no doubt existed prior to the bombings; but now a veil of despair hung over it like a poisonous fog. It made her shiver.

She began to wander west, hoping to find a cab or a bus. The cab would be preferable since her uniform and station would draw attention on a public conveyance. Gestapo Headquarters would be a good distance away. Turning at the sound of an engine, Denise spotted a *Wehrmacht* truck as it lumbered by. One of the soldiers, a young one by the looks of his fresh face, called out to her.

"Hey, *Fräulein*, how about a night on the town? You me and a bottle of *Schnapps*?"

He paled when he saw her uniform and quickly ducked back inside the bed of the truck. It appeared she would have little chance of a friendly encounter.

Rounding a corner, she came upon a newsstand. Her eyes hungrily scanned the various papers for anything about Jack, but it was useless. How could she expect truth from a dictatorship?

Traffic was heavier on this street, and Denise spotted a cab. Stepping to the curb, she held up her hand and the cab pulled up immediately. The driver smiled nervously, eager to please an *SS-Sturmbannführer*.

"Where may I take you, *Sturmbannführer?*"

Denise climbed inside, slamming the door behind her. "*Prinz Albrechtstrasse, schnell.*"

She could see the man shudder as he put the cab in gear. He pulled out into traffic, lurching past a couple of elderly women who screeched at him angrily. He ignored them, pushing the throttle down and speeding through an intersection, past a bewildered *Verkehrspolizei* directing traffic. The driver flicked his eyes up to the rearview and saw his passenger meet his gaze.

"My son is with the *Waffen-SS* on the Eastern Front. He came home last month on leave, but I have not heard anything since then."

The man was pathetic in his attempt to ingratiate himself. Not so much that he was doing it, but because he had nothing to fear. Yet with someone he thought held the power of the State behind her, the man turned to jelly. No doubt he would tell his cronies how he handled the "SS bitch." Still, Denise felt sorry for the man.

"What is his name?" she asked.

The cabby brightened immediately. "*Sturmmann* Johann Brenner, *Wiking* Division under *Obergruppenführer Gille*. He has received both classes of the Iron Cross and the Wound Badge in gold!"

The man beamed with pride, and Denise saddened. At this point, the Germans were sustaining heavy losses on the Russian front. It was likely the man had heard nothing from his son because he was dead. Somehow the notification had gotten lost inside the dizzying bureaucracy.

"Your son is a brave soldier, *Herr* Brenner. The *Reich* could use more like him. I will see if I can find out anything."

"You will have my undying gratitude, *Sturmbannführer*."

The rest of the ride went on in silence. Brenner was lighthearted and carefree racing through traffic. She hoped the man wouldn't get them killed. Twenty minutes after she got into the cab, it pulled up in front of the stone facade of *Prinz Albrechtstrasse*.

Denise reached into her briefcase for money, but Brenner waved her away. "No, no. It is my pleasure."

"Nonsense. You work hard. It is *my* pleasure," she said, and thrust a hundred-mark bill into his hand and walked away before he could hand it back.

The man looked at the money, gasped, and smiled. He leaned out his window and called after her.

"*Danke schön, Fräulein, danke schön!*"

Denise couldn't help the grin that broke out on her face as she mounted the steps of Gestapo Headquarters. In a world gone to the devil, it still felt good to do something nice.

She passed the two guards dressed in the black uniform of the *Leibstandarte*-Adolf Hitler regiment: an elite bodyguard formation dedicated to protecting the *Führer* at all costs. Even in their state of immobility, Denise could detect their watchful eyes taking in her every move. Through the doors she entered a large lobby. The floor was marble inset with the lightning runes of the SS. On either side of the wide expanse, a staircase led up to a mezzanine level. Straight in front of her was a huge desk, behind which sat a harried receptionist, a young man with the rank of *SS-Sturmscharführer*. Behind him, on the wall, hung life-sized portraits of both Adolf

Hitler and Heinrich Himmler, flanked by the swastika flag and the SS banner.

The receptionist argued with an insistent *Wehrmacht* officer.

"I am sorry, sir, but you need to make an appointment. We can't have people dropping by unannounced."

The officer, beet red from anger, began yelling.

"This is an insult! Heinrich Müller and I go back to Gymnasium together. Just tell him Heinie Berger is here. He'll remember me. The Two Heinrichs. *Mein Gott!* How could he forget?"

To the receptionist's credit, he remained cool and calm, his gaze level. "I will be glad to give you an appointment for next Tuesday at thirteen hundred."

"*Ach! Scheissekopfen! Bürokraten!*"

The officer continued hurling invectives but turned and stalked out of the building. Denise, wearing a wry smile, took the officer's place in front of the desk.

"*Guten Morgen, Sturmscharführer,*" she said, pulling out her papers and orders. "I am here to see the prisoner, Jack Dunham."

The receptionist, obviously struck by Denise's beauty, took the papers and the orders with a lecherous smile.

"Well, now. You are certainly much more agreeable than that *verdammter* idiot."

"I will need to see him immediately to determine whether I should remove him for further disposition."

"Well, *Sturmbannführer*, there are procedures..."

Denise took great pleasure in popping the man's bubble. His smile became an expression of alarm when he read the orders signed by Kaltenbrunner.

"Uhh, excuse me, *Sturmbannführer*," he said, scrambling for the phone. "Get me *Hauptsturmführer* Streicher. Yes, interrupt him!"

❋ ❋ ❋

The door to the cell burst open, catching Jack as he drifted in a kind of half sleep. The food they'd given him, stale black bread and potato soup, in no way resembled the mouth-watering meal Streicher had tempted his loyalties with. He'd eaten it gladly, his stomach growling as the first few bites touched his tongue. He ate with the air of one secure and satisfied. He'd beaten the bastards at their own game. Let them shoot him. Let them do whatever the hell they wanted; he'd steered them exactly in the wrong direction just as hundreds of agents and members of the Fortitude Deception had been doing for months, and it felt great.

Two guards pulled him roughly to his feet and dragged him down the long corridors, turning left, then right, then left again. He passed locked steel doors much like the one he'd been behind. He could hear the faint whimpers of other lost souls, crying for some measure of mercy. It made his blood boil. He decided he wouldn't go so blithely to his death.

In a surprise move, he rammed his elbow into the stomach of the guard on his right, stunning him. Ripping the MP40 out of his hands, he whipped it around, catching the second guard across the face. He dropped like a stone, his helmet falling off. Jack silenced the second guard with a quick punch to the throat. The guard coughed once, turned blue, and collapsed. Jack spotted the keys to the cells on the second guard's belt and tried one to open a nearby door. It worked. He dragged both bodies inside and closed the door. Next, he checked their pulses, and found the one he'd punched in the throat was dead. He was the right size. Stripping quickly, Jack donned the uniform, chafing at the rough, itchy fabric. The boots were slightly big but fit enough to get by. After tying up the unconscious guard with his own belt, Jack grabbed the MP40, extra magazines, and left the cell, locking it behind him. He retraced his steps through the labyrinthian maze that was *Prinz Albrechtstrasse*.

❋ ❋ ❋

"I am not accustomed to being kept waiting," Denise said, putting on a brave front. In reality, she was scared witless. It had been more than ten minutes since the receptionist made the call upstairs and still no one had come down to meet her.

"I am sorry, *Sturmbannführer*, *Hauptsturmführer* Streicher will be with you in just a moment." The phone rang and the receptionist appeared relieved to answer it and get out from under her blistering stare.

"Ahh, *Sturmbannführer* Faust..."

Denise turned and saw a man approaching her. He was of medium height and build, and walked with a rolling gait, his mannerisms clipped and efficient. There was a burning intensity about him that his hatchet face made even more intense. Denise disliked him immediately.

"You are *Hauptsturmführer* Streicher?"

He bowed stiffly, taking her hand in his. His skin was dry and scaly, like a lizard's.

"At your service."

"Then you will release your prisoner to me immediately," she said.

"That, I regret, I cannot do."

"I have orders signed by Kaltenbrunner himself. I am to take him into custody."

Streicher did not appear to be intimidated by Kaltenbrunner's name, which made Denise even more nervous.

❋ ❋ ❋

Jack began sweating when he realized he'd passed the same doorways

349

moments before. He was lost. How did anyone find his way around down here? Taking another corridor, he spied another contingent of guards leading a prisoner. He fell in behind them. They approached a large steel door, a desk to one side of it. An officer checked the paperwork and passed them through. Jack breathed easier when the door clanged shut behind him. He continued following the guards and split off when he recognized the stairs leading to the ground floor. Taking them two at a time, he reached the landing and faced an *SS-Brigadeführer* making his way downstairs. Thinking quickly, Jack saluted. The SS general returned the salute and continued on his way. From his vantage point, Jack could see the front entrance of the building and began walking purposefully, but not too fast, lest he attract attention.

※　※　※

Streicher smiled, allowing a measure of feigned remorse to cross his features.

"I regret that you have arrived too late. The prisoner, Jack Dunham, has been executed as of a few moments ago."

Denise felt her world collapse, but outwardly remained unaffected by the news except as that of an officer inconvenienced and insulted. She raised her finger, shaking with fury. "You will pay for this idiocy, Streicher! I will see to it you are sent to the Russian Front for this gross misconduct!"

Streicher's eyes narrowed.

"Just because you outrank me, *Sturmbannführer*, do not think that I am without friends in high places. Perhaps we should call Kaltenbrunner's office and see if he can clarify our positions in this matter?"

Denise watched with mounting horror when he went to the receptionist's phone and picked it up. Perhaps Streicher knew the man.

"*Ja.* Please connect me with Department IV."

He turned and gave Denise a smug smile that turned her fear into fury. But she had no time to waste; in moments her cover would be blown. Turning slowly, she looked around, her eyes snapping from place to place, trying to find an area she could run to. It would only take her seconds to transport. Then her eye fell on a SS guard as he walked into the lobby. He stared right at her, his expression one of mute surprise. Then it all clicked.

Jack!

Resisting the urge to fly into his arms, she saw him shake his head and then indicate the door leading to the street. He would meet her outside. She watched with growing apprehension when he walked to the door and disappeared through it. She turned and saw Streicher put down the phone, a look of triumph on his face.

"It would seem our dear friend Ernst has never heard of you. Is that not strange?" he asked, gripping her arm. His fingers dug into her bicep, making her wince. A second later a Luger appeared in his hands.

"You are under arrest in the name of the *Führer.*"

In that moment of blind panic, Denise's terrorist training took over. With a movement too quick for the eye to follow, she disarmed Streicher and punched him in the temple, stunning him. The panicked receptionist reached for his own gun and got off a shot that went wild before Denise struck him in the throat with her fist. He gagged, turned blue, and collapsed behind the desk, his gun clattering to the floor at her feet.

Streicher began to recover, prompting Denise to pistol-whip him into unconsciousness. She gathered up the weapons and dragged the *Haupsturmführer's* inert form behind the massive desk and laid him next to the unconscious receptionist.

She was angry about the gun going off. She'd wanted it clean and quiet. Luckily, no one had seen her dispatch the two men, but the shot had alerted others, who could be heard clattering down the hall to the lobby.

No time to run.

A moment later, a squad of guards led by a frantic *Untersturmführer* dashed into the lobby, their guns poised.

"A prisoner has escaped!" Denise screamed, pointing to the street.

"*RAUS!*" the *Untersturmführer* yelled and ran toward the door, followed by his men. Denise fell in behind them and pushed out into the street. The squad had taken off and was halfway down the block.

"Pssst. Denise."

She whipped around and saw Jack standing in the shadows of the building, smiling broadly. With everything else forgotten, she flew into his arms and crushed her lips to his.

"Oh God, Jack!" she said between kisses. "That son of a bitch said you were dead!"

His arms held her firmly, his hands urgently exploring her taut body. He breathed in the wonderful aroma of her hair and allowed himself a moment to feel her next to him. He pulled away and looked into her eyes and saw both love and fear reflected in them.

"I guess you missed me, huh?"

"Oh, shut up, Dunham. You almost got me killed!" she said, hitting him about the head."

"Me!"

"Yeah, you. Now, let's get out of here before your friend Streicher regains consciousness."

"Wait a minute. What did you do?"

She shrugged. "Just a love tap."

"Yeah, right."

He took her hand and they both took off at a leisurely jog. Turning the corner, they ducked down an alley and huddled against the wall. Moments later, more troops ran by, their officers screaming orders.

"Where are we going? Back to London?" Jack asked.

"Can't. We've still got Kruger to deal with."

Jack smiled. "Maybe not."

He told her about the drug-assisted interrogation and what he "revealed" to Streicher. "So, you see, I've just reinforced everything Hitler already believes. Even his astrologer thinks the invasion's coming at Calais. By now that information is on Hitler's desk."

Denise shook her head. "Streicher's nothing but an opportunist who thinks he's got high-placed friends. It won't stop Kruger from getting in to see Hitler."

"Maybe he won't get in to see him. Bormann was no pushover. He insulated the bastard until he was so out of touch with his people and the war that it all came crashing down."

"Do you really believe that?"

Jack felt the elation from his small victory over Streicher leeching from his body like air from a balloon.

"No," he said, shaking his head. "I guess the pentothal went to my head in more ways than one."

"It's okay, Jack. You tried. And maybe it will make it just a little more difficult for the prick."

Jack laughed. "All right, then. Where to?"

Denise frowned, trying to remember something.

"Kruger's first stop will be to see Field Marshal von Bock, right?"

"Right."

"Then that's where we go."

"But *where?* It's not like we can go and look him up in the phone book!"

"Why not?"

Jack began to speak, stopping suddenly. Denise laughed at the silly picture he made with his mouth hanging open.

He shrugged and smiled. "Why the hell not? Stranger things have happened. Why don't you zap us crosstown? I don't feel like walking out onto the street just now."

"Now you're using your bean, Dunham."

She grasped his hand, and seconds later they appeared inside another building.

"Where are we?" Jack said.

"*Tempelhofer* Field."

"The airport? Why?"

"Seemed like as good a place as any. Besides, it was the only place I could think of."

"It'll also be one of the places Streicher will look for us."

"You're forgetting something else," she said coyly.

"What?"

"Airports have phone booths."

Just as they pushed open the door, an elderly gentleman dressed in wing collar and a homburg hat strolled in. He glanced at Denise, looked at the sign on the door that read *HERREN*, and turned back to them, a haughty glare in his eye. He appeared not the least intimidated by their uniforms. He pushed by in a huff and disappeared into one of the stalls.

"Guess he had to go," Jack said.

"So do we," Denise said, pointing down the hall into the main terminal. He could see a group off SS soldiers rousting people for their papers.

"Do you think they're looking for us?"

"Maybe not," she said, looking past the group of SS men to the bank of phone booths against the far wall. "They don't look anxious enough. Don't forget, I'm just an impostor who slugged a fellow officer. They might not know you've escaped yet."

"Somehow that doesn't comfort me."

"Too bad, Dunham. Let's go."

Careful to look as if they belonged, they marched down the hall and into the crowded terminal, even going so far as to check the papers of a few citizens. They made the requisite noises and let their expressions of grave concern strike the proper amount of terror into the already-fearful travelers, then moved on. The other contingent of soldiers ignored them, thinking they were involved in other business.

Snaking through the crowd, they found all of the phone booths occupied. Soon a meek-looking man in round, horn-rimmed glasses turned and saw them staring at him. He quickly mumbled something into the phone and bolted from the booth.

Denise went inside while Jack stood guard, trying his best to look menacing. The MP40 submachine gun made the job a lot easier.

"Shit," Denise said under her breath.

Jack kept his eyes on the people in the terminal but inclined his head back toward the booth.

"What?"

"There are about twenty von Bocks in the Berlin area."

"The man's name is Fedor. F-E-D—"

"I know how to spell, for cryin' out loud. There are three of those."

"Three? Where are they?"

"Two are in the Tempelhof District and one is in Dahlem."

"That's the one."

"How do you know?"

"If you were a field marshal in the *Wehrmacht*, would you be living near a noisy airport?"

"You got a point."

He heard the page ripping and a second later he felt her standing next to him. "Back to the men's room?" he asked.

"No, this time let's go to my place."

❋ ❋ ❋

The car they'd chosen, a timeworn BMW from the pre-war years, backfired constantly. Its gears refused to mesh smoothly, causing an annoying screeching sound every time he shifted. Denise cursed Hitler, Kruger, BMW, and her own lousy luck with cars.

"Couldn't we have just popped in?" Jack asked, exasperated. "Do you find joy in hot-wiring cars?"

Denise held the map in her hand, keeping one eye on the road and trying to steer with the other. It made shifting gears even more impossible. "Just because I know the address doesn't mean we'll pop in at the right place. Besides, look for yourself. Anyone walking in this neighborhood would stick out like a sore thumb."

She was right. The houses stood far back from the road behind tall fences or hedges, remote and forbidding. The neighborhood never would feel homey and inviting; the very air said: "Keep your distance. Better yet, Keep Out."

"And that's another thing. What keeps us from materializing inside a wall or something?"

Denise frowned, flipped the map over, and cursed.

"Here," she said, thrusting the map in his face. "Take this and make yourself useful."

"How about answering my question?"

"I don't know, Jack! Maybe it has something to do with animate matter and inanimate matter repelling each other as in like-poled magnets. Shit, I'm not Chessman. I didn't discover Spatial-Temporal Teleportation—I just do it. Now will you shut up and find out where the hell we are, or have you got any other intellectual inquiries?"

"Take a left here," he said.

Denise spun the wheel and the old BMW groaned as it turned onto Hüttenweg.

"Take the next left onto Gelfertstrasse. It should be three houses down on the right."

Denise took the next corner slower, keeping her foot on the gas so as not to backfire. The street, though foreign-looking in some respects, reminded Jack of several tree-lined roads in Connecticut. The majestic-looking elms stretched their boughs across the road, forming a living arch through which the sun dappled their faces. With a shiver, Jack realized the area reminded him of another, more familiar place. The road leading to the Normandy Club. A moment later, he forgot his uneasiness when von Bock's house came into view.

Jack pointed. "That's it."

Denise eased up on the gas and pulled over. Staring through the wrought-iron gate, she examined the house, taking in the ornate details of its architecture while studying it for ways to gain entry.

"Chances are he's got nothing in the way of security," Denise said. "He either has dogs or thinks himself safe enough to do without anything. After all, who would take the time to kill a general without a command?"

Jack looked at her with undisguised annoyance.

"You don't mean we're going to break in?"

"You got any better ideas?"

"Yeah. Let's wait for him to come out."

"What if he's already gone with Kruger?"

"Then what good will breaking in do?" Jack asked, smiling triumphantly.

"You really are an asshole, aren't you?"

She slammed her hand against the steering wheel and bit her lip, her eyes focused on some point a million miles away. Jack touched her shoulder and she flinched, shaking him off.

"What is with you, anyway? Ever since we got out of Gestapo Headquarters, you've been acting weird. I thought you were happy to see me."

She turned to him, a tear rolling out of her eye.

"I was—I am." She sighed, shook her head, and continued. "When Streicher said you'd been executed, my whole world fell apart right then. I thought I'd lost you. I thought I'd be alone..."

"But I'm okay."

She fell silent.

"Come on, what is it? Tell me."

She shook her head, wiped away her tears, and looked at him long and hard. Jack thought he would scream.

"I'm pregnant, Jack. Until I see a doctor, I won't know for sure, but I feel it—I know it."

For a moment Jack felt like someone had pulled the rug out from under him. He sat there, stunned.

"Well, say something."

"ALL RIGHT!" he screamed. He took her in his arms and hugged her. Denise pushed him away, her tears flowing fully.

"Damn it, Jack! Listen to me!"

"Now what?"

She hesitated again. Jack felt a sickening dread.

"You're not going to tell me it's—"

"No, there's no one else," she said, waving the thought away.

"Then what? What?"

"There's a good chance that any child I have will... not be right. Spina Bifida runs in my family. My sister died from it. God, Jack! I couldn't live if that happened to my— Why the hell do you think I told you I wouldn't marry you?"

"Because you like to swing both ways. At least, that's what you said."

"Yes, I said that, but—"

Jack took her face in his hands and kissed away the tears. "But nothing. If we get out of this mess alive, I'll support whatever decision you want to make. Have it, not have it... whatever. Okay?"

She smiled back at him, her eyes shining.

"Okay."

The sound of a car's engine startled them both. Looking out the windshield, they saw a sleek Mercedes limousine glide through the gates of von Bock's estate. It turned left and passed them, picking up speed.

"It's them!" Jack said.

Before the field marshal's car had traveled more than half a block, Denise had slammed the car into gear, made a U-turn, and followed a discreet five car-lengths behind.

"I'll bet you Rubles to *Reichsmarks* they're headed for the Chancellery," Denise said.

"No takers on that one."

They fell silent keeping pace with the Mercedes. Whoever drove the field marshal's car evidently felt there was no need to follow speed limits. He treated the city streets as if they were on the newly completed *Autobahn*.

"Christ. If this guy doesn't ease up, he's either going to wrap us around a pole or get us pulled over."

The suburban atmosphere quickly gave way to a more urban feel, forcing both cars to slow to a tedious crawl. They were into the height of Berlin's morning rush. Even still, that had not slowed them. Everywhere they looked, rubble littered the streets. Old women and men, along with very young children, trudged along, sometimes cutting in front of them. All of them had a haunted, hungry look, their clothes torn and patched.

"Look at that!" Jack said.

Two policemen ran after a horse as it darted through the traffic. One of them halted, raised a P38 pistol, and fired. The horse dropped to its knees then fell over dead. Instantly, several of the civilians set upon the corpse and began butchering it, ripping pieces of the steaming flesh away and running off.

"Oh God. How awful," Denise said.

"Some people would think it's what they deserve."

"Not the people, Jack. It's monsters like Kruger and Hitler who deserve it."

Passing by the impromptu slaughter, they turned onto the *Potsdammerstrasse*. In the distance, Jack spotted the Chancellery smack in the middle of the *Potsdammer Platz*. Even from this far vantage point, it sent a chill up his spine. In both timelines it had existed as the cornerstone of Adolf Hitler's grandiose plan to rebuild the center of the city. His head throbbed as two versions of history clashed in his mind. In one, the Chancellery lay in ruins, the large *Reichsadler* on its roof dynamited by Russian troops. In the other, dozens of towering edifices, like the thousand-foot-high dome of the new *Reichstag* and the four-hundred-foot-high Arch of Triumph, dwarfed it. Still, it assaulted the senses in all of its pompous splendor.

The traffic thinned, allowing them to catch up to von Bock's Mercedes. The Chancellery took up an entire city block, and since underground parking did not yet exist, they had to drive more than half a mile before they found a place to park clear of bomb debris. It really didn't matter where they parked, for they had no intention of coming back to the car.

"All right," Denise said. "Chances are really good that the word is out on us, so I don't think we should walk the streets."

"Fine, let's go," he said, grabbing her hand.

"Hold on. Not so fast. Where would Hitler receive them?"

Jack tried to remember what he'd read and what he knew from his work in the Propaganda Ministry. The Chancellery existed in the 1990s much as it did now, kept as a shrine to Hitler.

"In my timeline, Hitler didn't hit the Bunker until January nineteen forty-five. He'll receive them in his private office."

"The one off that huge conference room?"

"That's the one. Between the two is Bormann's office. He's the one they've got to get beyond."

"If they're here, they already have. Ready?"

Jack nodded, and Denise closed her eyes. The familiar tingling washed over him. He blinked and discovered they stood behind a huge, fluted column nestled in the corner of the gigantic lobby. Footsteps echoed around them; workers and bureaucrats scuttled back and forth across the marble expanse, intent on urgent errands. The air smelled faintly of ammonia, as if someone had mopped the floor recently.

"You okay?" Denise whispered. She crushed up against him, trying to stay in the shadows.

"Yeah. I'm going to take a look."

Keeping his body as flat against the huge column as he could, Jack crept around it until he could see the front entrance. Dozens, maybe tens of dozens of people in every uniform imaginable dashed every which way. He didn't see how he would pick out Kruger in all of this. Maybe they'd already passed this location and he and Denise waited in vain, missing their one and only opportunity. Jack ducked back around, frustrated and annoyed.

"Too many people. I couldn't see them if I wanted to."

Denise took it in stride. "All right. Then let's go upstairs." She grabbed his hand and they both disappeared.

※　※　※

The driver held open the door for von Bock and then Kruger. Feeling the occasion warranted it, von Bock had dressed in his best uniform, every crease perfect—the gold trim gleaming. Kruger now wore the SS *Feldgrau* he had stolen from the dead guard at Gestapo headquarters. Bock had bristled upon seeing him in it but kept quiet. The gravity and urgency of the current situation mitigated any disapproval.

"Wait here for us," von Bock told the driver.

The man nodded curtly and turned off the motor.

Kruger's pulse quickened when they mounted the wide stone steps. He craned his neck and followed the lines of the building to their apex, where the *Reichsadler* sat perched, overlooking all with its fierce stone eyes. In front of them were the massive bronze doors, guarded by two spit-and-polished guards from the *Leibstandarte*-Adolf Hitler.

I am finally here, he thought. Finally able to make history in the fashion he believed his destiny entitled him. Checking his watch, he saw that it was just past 0900. The Führer expected promptness, and Kruger intended to be there precisely at the appointed time. No doubt the man would keep them waiting. That was his way, the way of all-powerful men who used power to intimidate. But Kruger had time on his side, all the time that could be counted. He would wait as long as needed, cool as ice.

THE NORMANDY CLUB

They crossed the lobby and took the stairs to the second floor. Though the outside of the building measured over four stories, the interior held only two. This gave every room the grand dimensions and aura Hitler demanded. Speer had given it to him in spades.

Kruger studied the field marshal as they marched down the long corridor to the rear of the building. The old man looked steely-eyed, vital—ready for action. He no doubt saw this as an opportunity for reinstatement, possibly as a replacement for Rommel.

After walking for what felt like days, they approached two huge doors that stretched nearly to the ceiling, a dizzying two stories. Covered in a vibrant crimson leather, each door had a gilded *Reichsadler* set in it at eye level. Two more black-uniformed guards of the *Leibstandarte*-Adolf Hitler Regiment stood by, their Mauser 98k rifles at parade rest. At Kruger's and von Bock's approach, the guards each reached for one of the doors and pulled it open. Kruger marveled at the engineering required to let one man open a door that must weigh at least a ton. Looking beyond the doorway, Kruger saw the anteroom to Hitler's inner sanctum, a large room that ended at the desk of Martin Bormann.

Bormann did not look up from his work when they approached, waiting until the last possible moment before acknowledging anyone. It was a behavior calculated to annoy, and it succeeded. Kruger saw von Bock's temper flare as Bormann turned the page of a lengthy report. Kruger used the moment to study the man. Stocky and of medium build, Bormann's head was broad and flat, making his face resemble that of an experienced pugilist. The scar on his cheek and his cold, beady eyes completed the picture of a street thug who'd made good. But the physical man belied the fierce intelligence within.

"You are early," Bormann said, still poring over the report.

Kruger flicked his gaze to von Bock, whom he saw had turned a pale shade of pink.

"*Jawohl*," he said, the word slicing the air like a knife.

"Well, the *Führer* is in conference. You may wait over there." He pointed past them to two chairs at the opposite wall, over forty feet away. Von Bock bristled, fighting for control.

"*Danke, Reichsleiter.*"

He fired a piercing look at Kruger, turned on his heels, and marched over to the two chairs. Kruger followed, his feelings decidedly mixed. Though Bormann was an egomaniac, he was no fool. He knew very well why they were here, and still chose to treat them with undisguised rudeness. Either the man could not help it, or he was maneuvering, waiting to see how the chips would fall and then swoop in to take advantage of the moment.

Kruger joined von Bock, who sat stiffly on the small chair, his field marshal's baton across his lap. Even through the black leather gloves, Kruger could see the man clenching his knuckles. Kruger sat down and marveled at how uncomfortable the chairs were. A sort of Teutonic Louis XVI, the upholstered seat and back remained unmoved by their weight. He felt like some blithering idiot perched on a dunce stool.

Kruger stared at Bormann, watching his every move, a sly smile playing across his face. He knew this bastard's game and enjoyed throwing a wrench into it by not showing the slightest discomfort. The man glanced their way for a fleeting moment and caught him staring. Kruger didn't move a muscle.

The intercom buzzed.

"*Jawohl, mein Führer?*"

"Send them in, Bormann," the voice said.

Even through the tinny-sounding speaker, Hitler's hoarse and gravelly voice commanded respect. It sent an electric jolt up Kruger's spine.

"Immediately, *mein Führer.*"

Kruger and von Bock stood as Bormann directed them through another magnificent set of doors. Von Bock swept past Bormann, his head held high.

"Thank you for your gracious welcome, *Herr Reichsleiter*," he said.

Kruger caught the subtle dig, saw Bormann frown, and thought, *von Bock has just made a dangerous enemy.* A moment later they stood in Hitler's office. The floor was covered by an immense carpet of red and gold, the ubiquitous Eagle and Swastika embroidered in heavy gold wire in the center. The windows, a full story-and-a-half tall, had the red and gold velvet drapes drawn. The room lay swathed in a Gothic gloom, the only light emanating from a single lamp on the *Führer's* massive desk. It sat nearly fifty feet from where they stood. Hitler, like Bormann, appeared preoccupied with reams of paperwork. He held a sheet of vellum at arm's length while studying it with spectacles. It was the first time Kruger could ever remember seeing the *Führer* wearing glasses. Grunting at something, Hitler tore the paper in half and tossed it in a wastebasket. He then looked up.

"Ahh, von Bock. It has been too long. Come here."

For a man facing the largest invasion in history, he appeared uncharacteristically jovial, especially to a general he'd removed from command. Von Bock moved and Kruger kept a respectable two paces behind. Hitler stood up and came around the desk, his hand outstretched.

"We are on the threshold of greatness, von Bock, the very threshold. Can you not feel it in the air?"

"Yes, *Mein Führer*. It is always the case when I am in your presence."

Hitler shook his hand warmly then turned his gaze to Kruger. Kruger now knew what others meant about Hitler's magnetic personality. It radiated from him in waves.

"And who is this you have brought me?" he said, his eyes narrowing appraisingly.

"May I present Werner Kruger, *Mein Führer*. He is the young man I told you about."

Kruger stepped forward, snapping his heels together and throwing out his arm. "*Heil Hitler.*"

Hitler smiled and returned the salute in his characteristically casual manner. "So, what can you tell me, *Herr* Kruger, that I don't already know?"

Kruger felt his heart accelerate. "I believe what I have to say will make all the difference in the world, *Mein Führer*."

28

Berlin, Germany
17 May 1944

The heavy, velvet drapes masked the light of their arrival. They were perched on the sill of a colossal window that must have measured over one story in height. The sun poured in through the glass panes behind them, making Denise feel like she was standing in a greenhouse. Looking out, she saw they were only one story up, but not easily visible from the street. But *where* were they? Had they made it into Hitler's study, or were they somewhere else?

Did she dare to look through the drapes to find out?

"Where are we?" Jack whispered.

Denise punched him in the arm and glared at him.

"Quiet," she mouthed silently.

Jack blanched as the sound of muffled voices carried through the heavy drapes. Denise smiled, squeezed his hand, then put her eye up to the crack in the drapes. The light behind her and the darkness inside the huge room made it difficult to see anything at first. Gradually, her eye adjusted and revealed the magnificent interior. From her vantage point, she could see they occupied a window toward one end of the room. Directly in front of her, about twenty feet away, sat

Hitler's desk, a grotesque monstrosity that held the only illumination in the vast room. Her breath caught when she spied Hitler and Kruger sitting opposite one another, appearing like two fighters about to spar with one another. The third man in the uniform could only be von Bock. The field marshal looked exceedingly nervous. Although the drapes hid her and Jack from view, she could hear them clearly.

Kruger sat forward in his chair and began.

"*Mein Führer*, I have come to you as a loyal citizen and because I have vital knowledge concerning the coming invasion—knowledge that *will* change the course of the war and bring us total and glorious victory..."

Hitler sat watching Kruger intently, his face a mask of stone. Kruger continued.

"Eisenhower and Montgomery will be launching the invasion on June sixth, and it will come ashore at Normandy. Rommel is correct in his assertions. I regret that I cannot offer further proof other than my word as a loyal German.

"Materials I had in my possession were destroyed, pictures of phony armies under Patton's command designed to fool us into thinking that Norway would be invaded, and that the main thrust will be at Calais. You must not be taken in, *Mein Führer*, you must move the Fifteenth Army to Normandy no later than June first."

Kruger sat back and waited. Hitler continued staring, his light-blue eyes unwavering.

Denise reached for the small air pistol in her tunic pocket. Its sleek, streamlined frame felt cold and heavy in her hands. Now was the moment. She was within range; she could take out any of them easily. But which one? Kill Kruger and the threat ended; kill Hitler and *all* of history would alter—for the better. Sweat poured down from her scalp, stinging her eyes.

Which one—damn it!

She felt Jack grip her shoulder and she turned to face him. He smiled and nodded.

He understood.

Denise smiled back, returning her gaze to the drama unfolding inside the room.

Hitler sat in his leather chair, his arms folded, his visage dark and troubled. Suddenly, he turned and glared at von Bock.

"What have you to say, *Field Marshal*?" he said, the sarcasm implicit in the way he pronounced von Bock's title, as if its very existence hung in the balance.

Von Bock straightened in his chair and looked his leader right in the eye. "Herr Kruger has shown me events that leave me no doubts, *Mein Führer*."

"No doubts, von Bock? No doubts at all?"

"*Nein.*"

"Then do enlighten me. What events are these that have you so convinced?"

Von Bock looked stricken. He turned to Kruger, who nodded.

"This man has a power I cannot explain. He somehow moved us both forward in time to nineteen forty-six! *Mein Führer*, I saw the war over, our dreams shattered, men on trial simply for losing that war. Göring, Kaltenbrunner, Jodl, all of them sentenced to death. It was terrible. I believe that all this can be avoided if we do as *Herr* Kruger asks."

Hitler smiled, the expression a dry and bitter one. "And what of me? Was I on trial too, von Bock?"

The field marshal swallowed, his face ashen.

"No, *Mein Führer*," he said, swallowing. "You... had not survived."

"Oh? How interesting. And what is my fate?"

"Suicide," Kruger interjected, his voice harsh and filled with emotion. "On April thirtieth, nineteen forty-five, while the Soviet Army encircles Berlin, you will put a Walther pistol into your mouth and pull the trigger. Your body will be taken out into the Chancellery courtyard, doused with gasoline, and set aflame along with the body of your bride, Eva Braun."

Hitler's eyes bulged and his face turned a dark, mottled red. He bolted to his feet, bellowing.

"Traitors! Fools! Filthy swine! You think your Führer would cower like a dog! That he would take the coward's way out? You have been taken in, von Bock! This man has hypnotized you with his defeatist propaganda! How can you, a man of intelligence, possibly believe such fantasy!"

"But *Mein Führer*, it is *true*! I saw it with my own eyes!" Von Bock said.

"Then you are blind and not worthy to wear the uniform of the *Wehrmacht*!"

Kruger stood at that moment and approached Hitler, his hand outstretched. "Let me show you, *Mein Führer*, let me show you the future as it will be if you do not act."

Hitler's eyes widened and he shrank from Kruger's hand as if it were a poisonous snake and began screaming at the top of his lungs.

"GUARDS! *Kommen Sie, SCHNELL!* Guards!"

Within seconds, the door burst open and a contingent of *Leibstandarte* troops dashed in, their rifles poised, their eyes wide with fear.

"Arrest these traitors!" Hitler screamed. "The field marshal will remain in his home, under house arrest until I decide what to do with him."

THE NORMANDY CLUB

Hitler walked over to Kruger, careful to stay out of reach. "This one... take this one into the courtyard and shoot him. AT ONCE!"

Stunned, von Bock began to sputter in protest as two guards grabbed him and frog-marched him from the room. Oddly, Kruger went with the other guards quietly, a wry smile on his face.

Denise watched with mounting horror

"Oh no," Denise said.

"What? What's wrong?" Jack said.

"No time. Hold on."

Denise grabbed his hand and they snapped out, reappearing back behind the pillar in the Chancellery lobby.

"Hurry," she said, pulling him along. Denise began to run, dodging past the people moving further into the building.

"Malloy! What the hell is going on?"

Denise ran faster, dashing past startled bureaucrats and soldiers. Jack kept up, increasingly alarmed when they ran deeper into the recesses of the Nazi government. Reaching a doorway, Denise burst through it and into the courtyard. There, encircled on three sides, sat the upper reaches of the bunker, a hulking concrete structure that only hinted at the vast complex far below the surface. Jack caught up with her and spun her around.

"Hold it!" he said, breathing heavily. "Will you tell me what just happened back there?"

"Come here," she said, pulling him around a nearby corner. "Watch."

Totally confused, Jack stared into the courtyard as Kruger and a contingent of SS guards emerged from a different exit. They marched in formation, the commander calling the count. Kruger matched their pace with a calm assurance that belied the tense situation.

"HALT!" the commander called out.

371

The commander, a *Hauptsturmführer*, ordered his men to line up and escorted Kruger to the wall.

Fascinated, and a little horrified, Jack and Denise watched as the firing squad assembled. The commander of the squad offered a blindfold, which Kruger declined. Nodding, the commander stepped back to his men.

"Ready!" he shouted.

The soldiers raised their rifles.

"Aim!"

The rifles zeroed in.

"You are all fools!" Kruger said, and began to laugh a loud, maniacal laugh.

"Fire!"

In the split second between the command and the explosion of shots, the air became oppressive, smelling of ozone. Kruger glowed bright blue and a sound like ripping paper rent the air. The soldiers began muttering, their voices turning to alarm when Kruger snapped out of existence right before their eyes.

Denise turned to Jack, her eyes filled with fright.

"We have to go back, don't we?" Jack said.

She nodded.

"Yes."

"But I don't understand. Why didn't he do that when Hitler was watching?"

"Because he remembered one simple fact. Hitler was mad. When Kruger told him how he would die, it went against all of Hitler's cherished beliefs in his own invincibility. Even if Kruger had popped out right then, Hitler wouldn't have believed it. Would have put it down to 'mass hypnosis.' Kruger knew he had failed. But he also knew something else..."

THE NORMANDY CLUB

Jack felt a chill run up his spine as a horrible thought crept into his mind.

"That he's got time on his side. He's going back to try it again, isn't he?" Jack said, already knowing the answer.

Denise nodded, her face grim. "And this time he'll bring undisputable proof. He'll be waiting for us every step of the way. He might even go back further and try to eliminate us *before* we became involved. We're sitting ducks. We have to go back."

"But when? If we go back, which timeline will we appear in?"

Denise frowned as she tried sorting out the Gordian knot of paradoxes. Suddenly she smiled.

"When did everything change, Jack?"

"What?"

"When did you wake up and realize everything had changed?"

"Hell, I don't remember."

"Come on, Dunham. Think! There has to be a moment, a date that the two timelines converge. You've got them both in your head."

Jack hated to think under pressure, had never done well with it. Now here, in the courtyard of the *Reichschancellory*, in the heart of Hitler's madness with soldiers all around them, he had to try and remember the most important moment in his life. And he couldn't.

"Halt!"

Jack looked up and saw an SS guard pointing a rifle at them.

"Get us out of here, Malloy!"

The soldier ran toward them, joined by others, their faces intent, their weapons raised and ready.

"WHEN, JACK?"

Then it came to him.

"August fifth, nineteen ninety-three!"

"Hold on!"

BILL WALKER

Denise grabbed his hand and squeezed her eyes shut. Jack felt the familiar electric feeling and saw the world turn white. He did not see the fusillade of bullets smash into the wall where they'd been standing only microseconds before.

29

They appeared just behind the pro-shop, the preternatural light of their arrival masked by a small copse of apple trees, their leafy branches heavy with fruit. The golf course, unlike the clubhouse, stood swathed in pitch-blackness. The air felt sultry and oppressive, hanging over them like a damp dishrag, smelling of the algae that proliferated in the stagnant water traps. Jack immediately broke out in a sticky sweat, born out of nerves as much as the humidity. All around them, crickets chirped ceaselessly. Jack leaned against a small sapling, rubbing his head. It throbbed above his right eye in sharp, stabbing pains. It was taking him longer than usual to gain his bearings, with a time shift as well as a spatial one.

"How'd I do?" Denise asked.

Jack squinted, scanned the area, and tried to make his dazzled eyes adjust to the gloom. Everything appeared as he remembered it.

"You look terrible. Are you okay?" she asked, coming to him.

"Yeah, I think so. God, that one really knocked me for a loop."

"Did we make it? Is this the right place?"

Jack nodded. "Yeah. The club doesn't exist in the other time-line."

"What now?"

Jack stared off toward the seventh hole and frowned. "The main building's just over that rise. The Nine Old Men will be up in their room. Kruger will be there too. Our best bet is to go right in."

"You like living dangerously," Denise said, smiling.

"I learned it from you," he said, returning her smile. "Besides, there's only one way in."

"Any security guards?"

"Just an old man who sleeps more than he patrols."

Denise nodded. "Okay, let's take a look."

Leading the way, Jack pushed through the trees and walked out onto one of the fairways. The ground squished under their feet, wet from the sprinklers. He slipped twice on the slick greensward, cursing under his breath at his clumsiness. He couldn't shake the eerie feeling that someone watched them. He could actually pinpoint a spot in the middle of his back that tingled as if someone were aiming a laser sight on it. He felt terribly exposed out there in the middle of the moon-drenched fairway, but it couldn't be avoided; there was no other way to approach the clubhouse. Besides, he reasoned, no one else in their right minds would be out here at this time of night, save for teenagers bent on mischief or lovers looking for a secluded rendezvous.

When they reached the crest of the small rise, Jack held up his hand, signaling for Denise to stop.

"That's it," he said, pointing to what was once the Anderson home.

"Looks like something out of a bad horror movie."

Jack scanned the parking lot and saw the limousines, their drivers huddled in conversation. Their raucous laughter and crude jokes drifted over the rolling landscape, a sharp contrast to the utter quiet.

"They're here," he said.

"Not all of them."

Jack turned and saw a lone car driving through the front gate.

"I've got an idea who that might be," Denise said, cracking a smile.

"Oh, no, you're not!"

Before he could protest further, Denise grabbed his hand and they disappeared.

❊　❊　❊

Dr. Morris Chessman turned into the cobbled drive of The Normandy Club feeling on top of the world. Tonight, all of his theories would be vindicated, his life's work proven beyond a shadow of a doubt. Aside from Armand Bock's little drama this morning and the abrupt change in the schedule, he felt ready. Kruger had mastered the abilities and, though Chessman detested the man intensely, he knew that the mission they shared would benefit them all. Passing the clubhouse, he rounded the building and pulled into the parking lot. He saw, with satisfaction, that all the "Waxworks" had arrived, and no doubt waited impatiently for him in their third-floor redoubt.

In spite of their dour natures, he had to laugh at their obsession with all things military. Every wall in the room held weaponry ranging from medieval to modern state-of-the-art, some of it quite illegal. For a fleeting moment he wondered if they would proceed without him. After all, they had no real need of him now that Kruger was fully trained. It would be just like their treacherous natures to cut him out of the deal. But Chessman pushed that unpleasant thought from his mind. They would not dare deprive him of his triumph.

Slowing down, he pulled his dilapidated Saab next to one of the sleek limos that choked the small lot. After Kruger left, and when he regained his memory of this timeline, Chessman intended to go out and splurge on the most expensive car he could find, one appropriate to his new exalted station. Yes, maybe a Mercedes or a BMW. Then again, the brave new world of the altered present might offer other, even more alluring choices. Chessman inhaled sharply and he felt one of his migraines coming on, very like the ones he got whenever he experienced an abrupt change in atmospheric pressure. But this time he was not in an airplane. He became alarmed when the interior began to smell of ozone. It could mean only one thing.

"Oh my G—"

Before he could finish, the car filled with a searing, azure light that snapped out, leaving his mind dazed and his vision swimming with spots. Blinking rapidly, he turned in his seat and paled.

"Dr. Chessman, I presume," Denise said, a wide smirk plastered on her face.

His eyes widened and his mouth flapped open in speechless terror.

"I wouldn't cry out, Doctor, or I may be forced to rain on your parade."

Chessman flicked his eyes to her hand and saw the strange-looking pistol pointed at him.

"What— Who are you?"

"Students of your theories. As you can see, they work."

"W-What do you want with me?"

"We want to join the little party upstairs, and you're going to get us in."

"No! You cannot!"

"'No' is not in my vocabulary tonight, Doc," Jack said, his voice a harsh whisper. "Now get out of the car slowly. No sudden moves and no crying out. The pistol my lady friend is holding carries a particularly deadly toxin. You try anything, you'll be dead before you hit the ground. Trust me."

Chessman continued to stare at them, open-mouthed.

"Doctor? Didn't your mother ever teach you not to hang your mouth open?"

The doctor snapped his mouth closed, an indignant look on his face.

"Very good. Oh, he's very good, Jack," Denise said facetiously.

"A prince among men."

"Let's go, Doc. Out."

Chessman opened the door and climbed out. Denise followed, keeping the gun jammed into the scientist's back. She could feel him trembling through his jacket.

"All right... move forward and act like we're old friends. You might not believe it, but we really are."

"'Old friends' do not hold their friends hostage," he said.

"Sorry, Doc. We haven't got time to explain."

Prodding him forward, they rounded the building and walked up the front steps, through the carved mahogany door and on into the foyer. The elevator stood open, beckoning. Jack saw the video camera nestled in the corner of the foyer and repeated his warning to Chessman to keep cool. Denise even went so far as to put her arm around the scientist and kiss him. He blushed a bright crimson in spite of the pistol digging into his ribs. Jack pushed the button for the third floor and watched as the door slid shut with a quiet hiss. No turning back now. The elevator "beeped" when it passed the second floor and slowed as it reached the third. Jack tensed as the door slid open, revealing the darkened hallway. The brass sconces along the walls were turned down. They emitted a sickly, yellow light that enhanced the dark and somber mood. The steel door at the end of the hall stood wide open, the light within spilling outward.

"Nice and easy, Doctor. You'll tell Armand and his buddies that you invited us along," Jack said.

Chessman glared at him like he was some pathetic cretin.

"*Herr* Bock will not care. He will consider this a breach of trust—he will kill you *and* me!"

Denise brought the pistol back into view. "We'll kill you if you don't fucking move," she hissed.

Intelligent enough to see the futility of resisting, Chessman marched forward, his face set in a grim mask. Jack and Denise followed. When they walked into the Nine Old Men's room, Jack had a curious sense of déjà vu, remembering Wiley's vivid descriptions from the night of his burglary. Sadness rose up in his mind when he thought of his dead friend. That feeling turned to a white-hot anger when he laid eyes on the infamous Armand Bock and the rest of the Nine Old Men. They sat around their table, their faces devoid of emotion—cold, dark, inhuman.

Only Bock reacted. Surprisingly, he rose from his chair, the picture of cordiality.

"Welcome, my friends. You have arrived at a propitious moment." He turned to the others. "Gentlemen, may I present Jack Dunham and his lovely partner, Denise Malloy."

He waved his hand with a flourish, as if expecting the two of them to bow. Jack could only stare, paralyzed by shock. Denise raised the air pistol and aimed it at Bock.

"How did you know us?" she said, her voice flat and deadly.

Bock smiled, revealing teeth yellowed and crooked. They gleamed like fangs in the soft light. "We have a mutual friend... or should I say *friends*?"

He turned and looked toward a door leading to a small ante-room. Jack watched in horror as Kruger emerged, resplendent in the SS uniform they'd last seen him in.

"Goddammit!" Jack said. "You were right, Malloy, he came ba..."

Jack's voice died in his throat when another man stepped out of the room dressed in a RAF uniform.

It was Werner Kruger!

A *second* Werner Kruger!

Denise gasped and lowered the weapon giving SS Kruger the opportunity he'd been waiting for. Before she could react, SS Kruger snatched it out of her grasp and pointed it at her. The other Kruger produced a Luger pistol and held it on them, an evil smile on his lips.

"You see," Bock began, "we were about to begin our little ex-periment when quite unexpectedly, Werner popped in. I must tell you, it—how do you Americans say it—'threw us for a loop.'"

Chessman started forward, a look of alarm on his face. RAF Kru-ger pointed the Luger at him, halting him in his tracks.

"Wait! You cannot allow this!" Chessman shouted.

"What is it now, Doctor?" Bock said, annoyed.

"This cannot be allowed to continue. This is a paradox of the highest order. You cannot have two selves in the same timeline. It could be disastrous!"

Bock appeared amused by the scientist's concern.

"Why is that, *Herr Doktor*? Do enlighten us."

"If they come into physical contact with one another, it will cause a chain reaction that could cause irreparable damage to the space-time continuum."

"My dear Doctor Chessman. You have been watching too many bad movies."

Chessman turned a bright pink and stepped forward.

"I have had enough of your condescension, *Herr* Bock! You do not know what you are trifling with!"

Bock's face darkened. He glanced at SS Kruger, a look of understanding passing between them.

"Perhaps I do not, Doctor, but at least I do not have to *trifle* with you any longer."

On cue, the SS Kruger raised the air pistol and fired.

Pfffuuhht!

The small pistol coughed, and Chessman staggered. Jack watched, horrified, as the scientist's face turned bright purple and his eyes blistered and cracked open, the jelly- like fluid coursed down his distended cheeks. A bilious foam gushed from his mouth and the skin of his face swelled outwards, threatening to burst. It made his head look like a giant grape. With a strangled cry, Chessman crashed to the floor, instantly still. The SS Kruger turned the gun on Jack and Denise.

One of Bock's eyebrows arched in amusement. "How baroque. I shall have to examine this weapon more thoroughly."

"Now, for the two of you. Please, sit over there," Bock said, indicating two chairs against one wall.

Denise looked sick. "I'm sorry, Jack. I should have known better. I led us right to them."

Jack shook his head. "It's okay, we had no choice. It all started here."

"Quite correct, my dear Mr. Dunham. All timelines lead to The Normandy Club, so to speak. In order to stop the cycle from repeating, you had to come here. Regretfully, we shall have to end our little game soon. However, I am not without some compassion. I will allow you to watch Werner's departure and then you will die."

About to protest, Jack relaxed. Bock was forgetting a simple fact. When Kruger transported, everything would change. Bock wouldn't have the chance to kill them because, for everyone, the clock would be reset, everything returned to that nightmarish future.

And therein lay the rub.

He and Denise would survive, but they would have to *relive* all of this again, the main difference being the additional memories of this cycle. Jack's heart sank. He imagined having to live all the danger and all the horror all over again. Would it stop then, or were they even now caught in a never-ending loop, destined forever to recycle through time like some eternally broken record?

Resigned, Jack sat on his chair and motioned for Denise to take hers. She scowled and plopped into the chair, taking Jack's hand in her own. SS Kruger kept the air pistol trained on them while RAF Kruger turned to his equipment and began preparing for his journey.

Denise leaned over to him and whispered, "When I give you the signal, go for RAF Kruger."

Jack kept his face expressionless as he spoke to her out of the side of his mouth. "Are you nuts?"

"Jack, the air pistol only had one shot. It's empty!"

Jack snapped his eyes to SS Kruger. The man watched them, his eyes shining with undisguised yearning. He couldn't wait to pull that trigger. Jack wanted to laugh, but instead turned his gaze to the other Kruger. He noted that the man's attention was totally absorbed in checking out his gear.

A moment later, Jack felt Denise squeeze something into his hand. He looked and saw that it was a one-shilling coin, dated 1942. Turning to her, he saw her nod toward RAF Kruger.

"Gentlemen, we are ready," Bock intoned as RAF Kruger sat down on the chair in the middle of the room.

Jack watched SS Kruger, waiting for him to move. *Come on, damn it! Turn!*

Almost as if the man had heard him, SS Kruger turned toward his temporal counterpart, giving Jack his window of opportunity. With speed and accuracy that surprised even him, Jack hurled the heavy coin right at RAF Kruger, catching him directly in the left eye.

RAF Kruger screamed and clutched his eye, distracting SS Kruger for the split second they needed. Jack and Denise bolted from the chairs and leapt onto the two Krugers, knocking them to the floor. Both pistols went flying, and in moments the room became a shambles: furniture smashed, militaria displays overturned and trampled, priceless art destroyed.

"STOP THIS, NOW!" Bock screamed.

They ignored him and the fight escalated. Denise utilized the martial arts training gleaned from her years in the Lambda Army, delivering crushing blows to SS Kruger's head and chest in a series of lightning-fast punches and kicks. Jack barely held on as he continued rolling around on the floor, trying to pin RAF Kruger.

Swinging around on the ball of her left foot, Denise kicked SS Kruger in the head, knocking him across the long conference table. The Nine Old Men scrambled from their chairs and cowered at the opposite end of the room.

Armand Bock raced to a display of weapons inside a glass case, grabbed a chair, swung it over his head, and brought it down onto the display case. Shattered glass sprayed in all directions. Reaching inside, Bock pulled out a vintage MP40, cocked it, and fired. Bullets slammed into the walls inches from Jack's head.

"JACK!" Denise yelled.

She rammed her fist into SS Kruger's face, knocking him out, and scuttled across the floor, careful to keep the huge table between her and Bock, who continued to fire. A second later the gun ran out of ammunition.

Bock pulled out the magazine and reached inside the shattered display case for another. Not seeing one, he threw the old weapon aside and grabbed for a newer, and more deadly, Micro-Uzi and two magazines.

Denise reached Jack, grabbed his hand, and they disappeared in a flash of light.

Bock ran to SS Kruger, who groaned and began to regain consciousness. RAF Kruger came up behind them.

"They are still here. I can feel them," he said.

Bock's jaw tightened. "Find them and kill them. I will not have them destroying all we have worked for."

RAF Kruger nodded and ran from the room. A moment later, SS Kruger sat up, shaking the grogginess from his mind. Bock handed him the Uzi and the two magazines and ordered him to join the search. SS Kruger sneered and followed after his counterpart.

Straightening up, Bock walked back to the ruined display case and pulled out a Hechler-Koch MP5, slammed a magazine home, and pulled back on the bolt. It snapped back with a satisfying clack.

He turned to the Waxworks and smiled.

"Gentlemen. I regret that the situation has changed. I can no longer afford partners."

The Old Men gaped in abject terror as Bock raised the machine pistol and fired. A hail of bullets raked across their chests, ripping through skin and bones and raising tiny plumes of crimson gore. Dead on their feet, they danced in place, collapsing only when the magazine ran out mere seconds later.

Slinging the MP5 over his shoulder, Bock ran over to the haversack left by RAF Kruger and ripped it open. He rooted inside and pulled out the Semtex, the detonators, and the digital timer. Working quickly, he divided the brick of plastic explosive into three separate charges and set them about the room in strategic places. Connecting the wires, he placed the timer behind the private bar at the far end of the room, set the timer for ten minutes, and pressed the starter button.

BEEEP!

09:59... 09:58... 09:57...

Satisfied, Bock unshouldered his machine pistol and ran after the two Krugers.

※　※　※

Appearing inside the deserted barroom, Jack and Denise hunkered down behind the mahogany bar, their breathing ragged and their hearts racing. Jack squeezed his eyes shut and rubbed his throbbing head, trying to figure a way out. He saw nothing but bad choices. Everything had turned to shit, and every alternative smelled just as bad. If they ran, Bock and Kruger would succeed. If they stayed, without weapons of any kind, they were dead for sure.

"What'll we do?" he asked, an edge of panic in his voice.

Denise clamped her hand over his mouth and raised her finger to hers. Jack heard the whirring and clanking of the elevator as it descended.

They were coming.

Denise let go of Jack and turned to the cabinet behind her. Sliding it open, she pulled out several bottles of Bacardi 151-proof rum. Jack smiled knowingly, remembering many hazy nights at Mike Gordon's bar. Long renowned for its flammability, 151 made excellent Molotov cocktails. Jack reached for dry bar towels and began tearing them up for wicks. Denise handed him four bottles and he stuffed the strips in, making sure that each one was fully saturated with the potent rum.

"You keep them busy," she whispered, handing him matches. "I'm going back up for weapons."

"What about the Nine Old Men?"

"You hear that shooting?"

Jack nodded, understanding.

"All right," he said, kissing her, "be careful."

She smiled, closed her eyes, and disappeared.

Jack held his breath when the elevator stopped. The door hissed open. He heard their determined footsteps as they strode directly toward where he sat. He gripped one of the Molotov cocktails, knowing he had one good shot before they cut him down. Maybe, just maybe, he could take one of them with him.

"It is no use, Dunham," Bock said. "We know you are here. It will not matter if you and your lady run to the ends of the earth or the end of time. We will find you wherever you go. We will not rest until you are dead! Do you hear me, Dunham?"

Jack knew Bock spoke the truth and hated him for it. He then heard one of the Krugers speak. He sounded far too close.

"It ends here, Dunham. No matter what. It ends here."

Jack crawled down the length of the bar, two Molotov cocktails clutched in his hands, the matches gripped between his lips. Reaching the end of the bar, he peered around and saw SS Kruger standing silhouetted in the entryway, an Uzi clenched in his hand. Jack retreated behind the bar, took the matches out of his mouth, and lit one. Touching it to the wick of the cocktail, he watched it sputter, then flare. Unlike gasoline, the flame burned a faint blue, barely visible. Counting to three, he jumped up and hurled it toward the shadowy figure.

※　※　※

Denise appeared amidst the carnage on the third floor and reared back, horrified by the slaughter. Aside from the horribly contorted bodies, the room looked as if a hurricane had ripped through it, tossing everything every which way like so much flotsam. She wrinkled her nose at the coppery odor of blood and suppressed the urge to retch.

The guns.

She had to get the guns.

Turning, she saw the destroyed display case and the empty spaces once occupied by various weapons. Bock was not among the dead. This meant that *three* of them now stalked her and Jack. She whipped around as if expecting the old creep to come jumping out of the shadows, gun blazing. Shaking off her fear, she grabbed an MP5, an Uzi, the requisite magazines, and made ready to rejoin Jack.

"Oh God!" she said, spying the Semtex and the wires extending behind the bar. "Not again."

She ran over and looked at the descending numbers.

05:49... 05:48... 05:47...

"Shit!"

She avoided the timer this time and ran to pull the detonators out. Her hand hovered over the first charge, reluctant to touch it. *Let it end here*, she thought. Then, as if drawn by a magnet, her eyes found the bottles of vodka, gin, and whiskey lining the shelves. Once again, she felt that inhuman craving gnawing at her guts. She reached for a bottle, her fingers trembling.

NO!

Rearing back, she swept the bottles off the bar and watched them shatter on the floor. Her nostrils were immediately assailed by the complex odors of mixing spirits. *Let it all end here*.

Retreating, she closed her eyes and disappeared.

❋ ❋ ❋

The Molotov cocktail crashed against the molding two feet from SS Kruger and burst into flame. The liquid fire ran up the wall and across the forest-green carpet. SS Kruger whirled and let loose with a burst from his Uzi that exploded the glassware and bottles across the back of the bar. Jack curled into a ball, his arms over his head, as the glass rained down on him.

"*Verdammt*!" SS Kruger said, cursing his poor aim.

The room filled with smoke as Denise reappeared beside him.

"We've got a little problem," she said.

"Little?"

"Bock's wired the Semtex. This place is going in about five minutes."

Jack nodded and lit another Molotov cocktail. He hurled it over the bar, hand grenade-style. He heard the crash and the whoosh of flame. It was answered by another burst from SS Kruger's machine pistol. Denise cocked the Uzi and threw it to Jack, jumped up and sprayed the interior of the bar, now obscured by a fog of noxious smoke. She ducked down as more rounds from SS Kruger's Uzi slapped into the bar. The chatter of the Uzi was joined by the report of RAF Kruger's Luger and sputter of Bock's MP5. Splinters flew from the inside of the bar when bullets punched through and pocked into the opposite wall. Jack rubbed his cheek, and his hand came away covered with blood.

❋ ❋ ❋

03:28... 03:27... 03:26...

❋ ❋ ❋

"It is no use, Dunham! We are holding all of the cards! Why not join us? There is more than enough to go around!" Bock yelled.

Jack had had enough. "Just like your partners upstairs? I don't think so!"

"They were weak, old, and in the way. They had no vision, *Herr* Dunham. You have more than proved to be a formidable adversary."

Denise grabbed Jack and glared at him. "Shut up! As long as you don't talk, they can't get a fix on you through the smoke."

Jack nodded and gripped his weapon harder.

"What about it, *Herr* Dunham? Will you join with us?"

✖ ✖ ✖

02:48... 02:47... 02:46...

✖ ✖ ✖

"Stick it, Bock!" Denise screamed, and held her weapon over the bar and fired off a burst, ducked back down, and leaned over to Jack. "You keep them busy," she whispered. "I'll pop up behind them."

Jack smiled and coughed. The smoke had gotten a lot thicker. If they didn't do something soon, they would die of smoke inhalation. Bock would win by default.

"Do it."

"On three," Denise said. "...One... two... THREE!"

Jack popped over the bar and spotted Bock carelessly exposed. He fired, striking the old man in the shoulder. Bock cried out and collapsed. Through the haze, he saw both Krugers turn to fire. Jack raised his weapon, aimed at SS Kruger, and pulled the trigger.

Click.

Empty.

Even through the smoke, Jack could see SS Kruger's wicked smile. Suddenly, Denise snapped in behind him, raised her weapon, and whipped it across the back of SS Kruger's head. In one fluid motion that reminded Jack of a balletic pirouette, Denise spun around and fired her machine pistol at RAF Kruger. It caught him square in the gut. Clutching his bleeding midsection, RAF Kruger moaned and collapsed.

❋ ❋ ❋

01:05... 01:04... 01:03...

❋ ❋ ❋

"JACK! It's clear! Let's get outta here, now!"

Jack dropped his Uzi and ran from behind the bar and joined Denise.

"Dunham!"

Jack and Denise turned and saw Bock leaning against a wall, his shoulder oozing blood.

"We can't leave him," Jack said.

"The hell we can't! All this is his fault. He deserves to die!"

Jack stared at her. "I can't believe you'd do that."

❋ ❋ ❋

00:59... 00:58... 00:57...

❋ ❋ ❋

Kruger regained consciousness and saw his counterpart crumpled on the floor, no more than ten feet away. Slowly, he began to crawl towards him. If he was to perish, then he would take them all to hell with him. Dunham, his bitch, and Bock—especially Bock. Kruger realized that one side of his body felt numb. The blow to his head must have caused serious damage, a stroke perhaps. But it didn't matter anymore. None of it would. Pain shot through his head, accompanied by a loud, ripping sound.

Another stroke!

He crawled onward, aware that the pain increased with every movement of his body. Only a little farther, now... then... peace.

❋ ❋ ❋

00:35... 00:34... 00:33...

❋ ❋ ❋

"I'll take care of this, Jack. Get out, now!"

"No!"

"We don't have *time* for this, Dunham."

"I'm not leaving this man to die," Jack said.

One entire wall of the bar now stood engulfed in flames.

CRACK!

One of the overhead beams broke in two and crashed onto the bar behind them.

Both of them turned and saw SS Kruger crawling towards his temporal counterpart.

"Oh God, NO!" Denise yelled.

She raised her weapon and fired, stitching a line across SS Kruger's back. He screamed, the blood flowing from his mouth. RAF Kruger looked to him, his own wounds equally mortal, and reached out his hand.

❊ ❊ ❊

00:05... 00:04... 00:03...

❊ ❊ ❊

RAF Kruger's hands stretched farther, a hairsbreadth from his dying counterpart's.

Whirling, Denise looked into Jack's eyes, love radiating from them like bright beacons. "I'm sorry, Jack," she said, and closed her eyes. Jack felt the familiar electric feeling and braced for the transport. Jolted by the force of her mind, Jack saw the world flash white, and a microsecond later he was back on the shallow rise overlooking the Normandy Club.

Alone.

"DENISE!" Jack screamed.

He started to run toward the building, his heart jackhammering in his chest. The night flashed incredibly bright as the Semtex detonated. The roof lifted off and the walls blew out in a gargantuan, roiling fireball. Black smoke plumed skyward, blotting out the moon. Jack heard the debris smacking against the asphalt of the parking lot as it rained down around him. The limousines closest to the building exploded, their gas tanks igniting with a soft *carumph*.

"NOOOOOOOO!" Jack screamed.

He watched with tear-stained eyes as all he knew and cared for was destroyed.

Then everything changed.

The ground shook, knocking Jack off his feet. An incredibly bright pinpoint of light appeared in the center of the clubhouse and exploded outward, dazzling in its beauty, a kind of earthbound supernova. Then it collapsed in on itself, taking the Normandy Club with it into the void. The air whooshed past him to fill the vacuum and the sky boiled with evil-looking clouds that flashed with electrical energy. Everything reeked of ozone.

Jack staggered to his feet and gaped at the crater left behind. It measured a full hundred yards across, and in the dim light, appeared bottomless. Sobbing, Jack fell to his knees and covered his face.

"Why, Denise? Why? Why didn't you come with me?"

Exhausted and with nowhere else to go, Jack sat and stared into the crater and waited for the authorities to arrive. They came screaming onto the grounds, the fire engines, the ambulances, the local and state police cruisers, several nondescript cars marked U.S. Government Motor Pool, and inevitably, the media.

"What happened here?"

"What's going on?"

"Do you have any comments?"

"At what time did the phenomenon occur?"

"Are you a member of the club?"

"We are going to have to ask you some questions, sir."

"Can you tell us if anyone else survived?"

The questions and faces blended together into a collage of meaningless sights and sounds. He pushed through the crowd and left them gaping in wonder at the deep hole no one could explain.

As more cars turned into the grounds, Jack passed by them and trudged down Ridgefield Road toward town. To the east, the sky had turned gray, signaling dawn's imminent arrival. In his heart he knew that his life had both ended and begun on this day. He would have to pick up the pieces and go on. He would have to somehow make it all work. Denise would have wanted it that way.

❋ ❋ ❋

"Excuse me, sir, can I get you a cocktail?"

Jack started from his reverie, looking up into a familiar set of electric-blue eyes.

"What? I'm sorry, I didn't hear you."

Terry Blaine smiled. "Would you like something to drink?"

Jack looked at her and found his eyes filling with tears. "Uhh... no thanks."

Sensing his discomfort, she nodded and made her way back to the galley, turning once to fix him with a look of wistful curiosity.

Jack reached up and turned off the overhead light, plunging his seating area into darkness. Despite all the thoughts that roiled in his brain, the bone-deep weariness in his body took over. Within minutes, he fell into a deep and thankfully dreamless sleep, lulled by the incessant thrum of the plane's powerful engines.

❋ ❋ ❋

Jack pulled into his regular parking space, taking small pleasure from riding in his blood-red Alfa Romeo once again. To him, it felt like a lifetime had passed since he'd felt the snug fit of the bucket seats and smelled the crisp, tannic odor of its leather interior. He thanked

God for small pleasures such as these, for they almost succeeded in allowing him a few moments' respite from the pain he felt. For a brief time, while speeding down Biscayne Boulevard, he was almost able to put Denise from his mind.

But pulling into his regular spot and seeing his name emblazoned on the sign bolted to the concrete wall brought it all back. It may have felt like a lifetime, but in fact, it had only been two days...

The elevator opened onto the fifth floor and Jack stepped out, marching down the corridor to his corner office.

"Hi, Mr. Dunham, we've sure missed having you around..."

"Hey, Jack! How are ya? Where ya been?"

"Good morning, Mr. Dunham. Mr. Bennings is quite anxious to see you..."

Jack nodded, keeping an insipid grin on his face. He'd forgotten how to smile and didn't care if he ever remembered. But what had gotten into everybody? You'd think he'd been gone for six months the way everyone acted. Shaking his head, he put it all down to the incredible experience he'd lived. If they only knew, what he'd done for them, how different all their lives would be. Thank God they would never have to find out.

He stopped in front of the door to his office, noting it stood ajar. What was this? He *never* left it open and hated it when someone else did. He turned to his secretary, Jenny, his mood suddenly dark and ugly. She wore an expression of helpless distress. "I'm sorry, Mr. Dunham. He insisted on waiting."

"Who?" he said, growing annoyed.

"He wouldn't say."

Jack frowned, pushed open the door, and barged in, ready for blood. "I'm sorry, but you will have to make an—"

Jack stopped in mid-sentence, his mouth hanging open in shock. "Hey, shithead! How the hell are you?"

There, sitting on Jack's leather couch, with his feet up on the glass coffee table, sat Wiley Carpenter, as big as life.

"WILEY!"

Jack tossed his briefcase aside, ran to his friend, and lifted him off the ground in an affectionate bear hug.

"Whoa! Hold it! Hold on a minute! This the way you usually act when you stand up your friends?"

"You're alive! GODDAMNIT! You're alive!"

Wiley held his friend at arm's length, looking at him with genuine concern.

"What's the matter with you? Of course I'm alive. But I should kill you, you knucklehead!"

Jack's expression turned quizzical. "What are you talking about?"

"You must be getting Old Timer's Disease, Jack. I called you two nights ago and told you to meet me at Mike's. You didn't show up. I called your house, I called Leslie, I even called your mother on the outside chance you were back in Connecticut somehow. Yesterday I called here, and *no one* knew where you were. And now you show up acting like nothing's wrong."

Jack sat down on the couch, let out a sigh, and rubbed his temples. He felt a dull throbbing over his right eye that promised to become a whopper of a migraine.

"Wiley, I'm sorry."

"Sorry? Is that all you've got to say after driving us all crazy with worry?"

Wiley appeared genuinely annoyed at that moment. His hair, never well-groomed to begin with, stood askew, looking like he'd slept on the couch. For that matter, his clothes had the same rumpled appearance.

"Look, I know all about why you wanted to see me."

"Oh, really?"

"Yeah. I know all about the Nine Old Men and their cockamamie plan. And take my word for it, it'll never work."

"Well, it's too late, Jack, you missed the vote."

"Vote? What vote? What are you talking about?"

"The Nine Old Men want to change the name of the club to—"

"—I know, I know. The Normandy Club, right?"

"Hell no. Can you imagine those old farts wanting to change the name of The Anderson Club to The Ridgefield-Danbury Golf & Racket Club after fifty years? Have you ever heard of anything so unwieldy, so stupid?"

Jack felt a chill run up his spine.

"You haven't heard, have you?" Jack said.

"Heard what?"

"The club's been destroyed—a huge fire."

Now Wiley really looked concerned, but not, as it turned out, for what Jack thought.

"What? Are you nuts? I just spoke with the board this morning. Their stupid plan was defeated by a margin of two to one."

Now it was Jack's turn to look stupefied. "What? This morning?"

He shook his head, wondering if he was losing his mind or whether everything he'd lived through these past weeks had been a fevered dream in the night. But then he ran his finger over the scab on his cheek and knew that something else, something unforeseen, had occurred.

"What about Bock? How did he vote?"

"Who?"

"Bock! Armand Bock!" Jack said, feeling ever more disoriented. "Don't tell me that name means nothing to you."

Wiley shrugged. "No, it doesn't."

Jack got up and moved closer to his friend.

"Listen. I don't know what the hell is going on, but none of this is making any sense. How can—"

"Hey, Dunham! You still in the market for a crazy redhead?"

Jack's breath caught in his throat. That honey-coated voice. A voice he never expected to hear again. He whirled, expecting to see a mirage, a phantom disappearing before his haunted eyes. But there, in front of him, dressed in the most exquisitely chic, emerald-green suit he'd ever laid eyes on, stood Denise Malloy, her hazel eyes shining with love and ill-concealed desire. Her smile widened as her eyes connected with his.

"Oh God," he said, flying into her arms. "I thought you were—"

"Dead? You oughta know me better than that, Jack."

"But how—"

"I transported about a nanosecond before the two Krugers made contact."

"But where did you go?"

"Frankfurt, nineteen twenty-eight."

This took Jack by surprise. He shook his head, trying to clear out the conflicting thoughts.

"Nineteen twenty-eight? Why?"

Denise leaned forward and kissed him on the ear and delicately bit the lobe. It sent an electric thrill through Jack. "Let's just say I paid a visit to Bock on his birthday," she whispered.

Jack pulled back and looked into her hazel eyes.

"You mean, you..."

She nodded. "Armand Bock won't be a problem anymore."

"AHEM!"

Both of them turned to face Wiley, who stood with his arms crossed, looking both bewildered and annoyed.

"I'm sorry to interrupt your little rendezvous here, but would somebody mind telling me just what the *hell* is going on?"

Both Jack and Denise burst out laughing.

"Oh, good. Now I'm an idiot too."

This made Jack and Denise laugh even harder. A few moments later, they calmed down enough to explain.

"I'm sorry, Wiley, this is Denise Malloy, my..."

He stopped, not quite sure what to say. Denise stepped forward, her hand extended. "I'm Jack's fiancée. I hope you can make the wedding next month. I know it's short notice."

Jack's eyes bulged in surprise and Wiley whooped with joy.

"ALL RIGHT! This is great! Congratulations!" he said, clapping his hands together and laughing. "Any woman who could land Jack Dunham has got to be something special."

Jack had recovered enough to smile. "That's an understatement."

He turned to Denise, his eyebrows arched questioningly. "I thought you didn't want to marry me because of your other *commitments*."

She shrugged and gazed at him, her eyes filled with love. "They're not as important to me as you are. Besides, someone's got to keep an eye on you."

Jack hugged her and Wiley slapped him on the back.

"Now, will someone *please* tell me where Jack has been for the last *two* days?"

Jack turned to his friend, his arm around Denise.

"Wiley, I think you'd better sit down. I've got a *long* story to tell you. Take my word, it'll curl your toes and put hair on your chest..."

AUTHOR'S NOTE

In researching and writing *The Normandy Club*, there were times when reality had to bow to the whims of plot. It is common knowledge to those living in Miami that nearly all homes there lack basements because of the extremely high water table. However, I wanted the Lambda Army to have a true "underground lair," so to speak, and to make Denise and Jack's escape from the clutches of the SS that much more exciting. By the same token, most commercial buildings, especially those on Biscayne Boulevard, do not have any sub-levels, much less the *ten* I gave the *Joseph Goebbels Ministry of Advertising and Propaganda*. But again, this was a building built by a totalitarian regime whose money is limitless and tenacity unbounded. In the nightmarish world I created, the water table has been conquered, as well.

As for what a Nazi America would be like, it is highly probable that upon conquering the United States, Hitler would have changed the country's name to further obliterate the past and to better consolidate his power over the populace. Various historians and war buffs have speculated as to what that name might have been: *Vinland*, taken from the original name bestowed by the Vikings, was one suggestion. *New Thule* was another. By far the most fanciful, and the one used in this book, is *Avalon*. Taken from the Arthurian Mythos

400

and referred to by Richard Wagner in his grand opera, *Parsifal*, Avalon is known as a mystical land to the west. I think this reference would have appealed to Hitler's warped sense of history. At least it does in my story.

As for the individual states themselves, I have retained their original names and identities so that you, the reader, could better follow along as Denise and Jack made their way to Canada.

And you also may have noticed that the characters in Nazi-occupied Avalon speak a patois sprinkled with German words and phrases, a lot of them derogatory. It is only natural to assume that a people conquered by a strong culture will eventually incorporate phrases from the conqueror's language into their own.

In the 1944 section of the book, I endeavored to be as historically accurate as possible, but again made some concessions to the muse. It is well known that by spring of 1944, Adolf Hitler spent most of his time at *Berchtesgaden* within the safe walls of the *Berghof*, his retreat high in the Bavarian Alps. But, for the sake of the story, I wanted him in Berlin, so that is where we, and Werner Kruger, find him.

As for Field Marshal Fedor von Bock, he was, in fact, a real person. A field officer renowned for his early successes commanding divisions in *Operation Barbarossa*—Germany's attack on Russia—he found himself in a military quandary when Hitler refused to listen to his entreaties to push on to Moscow. When the tide turned, as it inevitably did, von Bock was relieved of his command. Though he lived in Prussia, I gave him an estate in Dahlem, an exceedingly affluent section of Berlin at that time. Von Bock ended his life ignominiously, killed in an air raid at Kiel, May 1945.

Churchill's bunker, and the "War Room" within it, does indeed exist where I have placed it and has been preserved as a museum by

BILL WALKER

the British government. As for Sir Winston's taste in brandy and his eye for the ladies, I have again taken liberties for the story's sake.

In any event, I hope you enjoyed reading *The Normandy Club* as much as I enjoyed writing it.

Bill Walker
Los Angeles, California

Other Books by Bill Walker

Titanic 2012

A Note from an Old Acquaintance

Abe Lincoln: Public Enemy No. 1

Abe Lincoln On Acid

STALAG

D-NOTICE

Starring... John Dillinger

ABOUT THE AUTHOR

Bill Walker is a graphic designer specializing in book and dust jacket design who has worked on projects by Ray Bradbury, Richard Matheson, Dean Koontz and Stephen King. Between his design work and his writing, he spends his spare time reading voraciously and playing very loud guitar, much to the chagrin of his lovely wife and two sons. Bill makes his home in Los Angeles.